HATE YOU NOT

AN ENEMIES TO LOVERS ROMANCE

ELLA JAMES

CHAPTER ONE

JUNE

What do they say about kids and candy? No candy because it makes them wild...or is it *all the candy* because of the blood sugar crash afterward? Lots of sugar makes you crash, right? When I get those iced shortbread cookies from Miss Dora's Bakery, I'm falling asleep after.

Is it good for them to sleep right now? Or should they stay awake so they can process? Do they seem more sleepy or more hyper?

I glance into the back of the truck's cab just in time to see my niece and nephew click their giant lollipops together in a refined sugar high-five.

Someone giggles—Oliver or Margot?

"What are you kids doing back there?" I ask in my best teacher voice.

There's that giggle. "Margot? Is it you that giggles like a little church mouse?"

She does it again.

"That's adorable, darlin'."

"Darlin'!" Oliver's laugh is more snorty. "You're such a darlin'," he caws at his sister.

Give it time and you'll be drawlin' just like me. I want to say that—but it doesn't seem wise. Now is not the time to draw attention to the cultural shift my sister's kids are about to undergo. Are undergoing already...from the time they stepped off the airplane in Atlanta five and a half hours ago; Oliver wrinkled his little freckled nose and said, "The air is...sticky. Sticky icky wicky!"

Just you wait till summertime.

We made our way across the airport to my truck, hauling ninety-seven bags and both of their booster seats. It took for-freaking-ever to get out of city traffic. They were needing dinner, so I took them by the Steak 'n Shake for shakes and burgers—I don't care what vile lies my sister told her rich-boy husband, she got burgers for them last time they were home, two years ago—and that's when Margot asked for candy.

"What were you hoping for?" I asked with caution.

"Maybe...a giant lollipop?"

So of course I found a place—a very overpriced place off the interstate—and when Margot pointed to a sucker bigger than her little pig-tailed head, I got it. Got them both one. Eight bucks each. Say what you will about a bunch of sugar, but it always makes me feel better.

"How's those lollipops coming?" I ask, trying to emphasize the "g."

"Mine's comin' real well." Oliver pops his lips together.

"Make that 'real good' and you got yourself a deal."

He laughs, and Margot pops her lips together, too. "I love candy."

She sounds so much like Sutton just then. That weird feeling presses on my chest—the lead-heavy, maybe-I'm-about-to-wake-up, nope-I'm-not-and-I'm-all-filled-with-existential-dread feeling. I have to breathe out of my open mouth to make it ease up.

"What's your house like?" Oliver asks.

I glance in the rear-view. Mostly dark, so all I see is trees on each side of the interstate and a bunch of head and tail lights behind us.

"I thought you remembered."

"Well I don't." His voice is petulant, and I've spent enough time with them by now to know he might break out in tears at any second.

I shift into Fun Farm Aunt mode. "There are chickens. Roosters, chickens, all of them. All cock-a-doodling and strutting around."

"Struttin'," he mimics, and I hear the smile in his little voice.

"Well that's what they're doing. Standing out there in the mud, picking at grass." I try again to add the "g" onto the end of "picking," but I guess I don't do it all the way because Margot giggles.

"Pickin'," she echoes.

"There's some cows. A couple of big, fat milk cows. They lie down when the rain comes...sometimes, anyway."

"Do they stick their feet up in the air like this?" I see Margot's feet stick up behind the truck's front seat.

"Nope. They just sort of curl up so the lightning doesn't strike them."

"What else?" Oliver asks.

"Well, I have a horse, remember?"

"Can he be mine?" Margot asks, and I smirk.

"He's a she. And you already have a horse that's coming to live here."

"Oh yeah!"

"I want to ride your horse when we get there, Aunt June." Oliver yawns after he says it.

"I think it might be too late at night for that."

"It won't be!"

"I think he'll be sleeping."

"Will you put my Batman covers on my bed?" he asks.

"They won't be washed yet, but—"

"That doesn't bother me!"

"So then...yeah." I nod slowly. *Pushover.* "I'll put it on, and Mar, your *Frozen* stuff, too."

"No one ever calls me Mar."

Well, shit. "Margot." Pronounced Mar-goh. Surefire way to confuse every teacher from Heat Springs Primary all the way on up through the tiny local high school. "My bad, little lady."

She giggles. "No one ever calls me *little lady* either."

"I want to hear that music again," Oliver says.

I turn up the country. We're winning with some vintage Garth Brooks. As he drawls about having friends in low places, I can sort of sense them lying down. When I stop for a gas refill outside Albany, I find them slumped in their seats, their poor little heads hanging, begging for some neck pillows. I make a mental note to try to find some —somewhere cheap. Maybe the dollar store.

In the bright light of the gas station, I check the latch on my tool box, where all their luggage is. Then I shut the little gas tank door, climb quietly back into the truck, and straighten the slouched unicorn that's riding in the passenger's seat beside me. I think of snuggling him up beside Margot but figure that might wake her.

Maybe they should be processing, but they're so tired. It's near ten o'clock here, which is eight their native San Francisco time. Saying bye to their house...driving by their school again, and then the stables where their horses board—it was a long morning, and that was before we caught our plane.

I hang a left at the last light in Albany and watch the city's lights fade in my rear view. Maybe I can take them back up this way sometime soon, just so they can spend an hour in a city.

We start on a winding highway down toward Heat Springs, tall pines lording over the two-lane road. I feel a little like a kidnapper as pink clouds drift over the moon. Fields punch their way between tufts of forest, stretching on in fanning rows of cotton, peanuts, and corn. I swerve a little bit to keep from hitting a raccoon.

We pass the McKesson's vast farm, then the old, abandoned highway patrol post, overrun with kudzu. The speed limit drops. The forest thickens, and the moon peeks out. My thoughts wander—way down into high school, past my best friend Leah and I, to when Oliver was born. Sutton brought him home, and we fussed over who would hold him first. I think of Sutton herself, platinum blonde in her Heat Springs High cheer uniform, always so long-legged and muscular and pretty, like Athletic Barbie. It never even dawned on me that she—or anybody from my family—might move far away. I think of Mama getting sick right after Sutton moved off. Those care packages Sutt used to send, with all the Lush bath bombs and fancy facemasks and these trinkets she had found in San Francisco. Life is a strange thing. So taken for granted. Sometimes it feels like nothing ever happens, that every day is the same...and then everything you know is just *gone*.

There's a hard knot in my stomach all the time now. I can't even imagine how Margot and Oliver feel. And then I shake my head, because maybe I can just a little. I wasn't little bitty when I lost my mama, but I wasn't quite 18.

The open sign for Heidi's Place, a little restaurant and bar on the outskirts of town, flashes over on my left. That place is a mess, but I love going there. Jolene—she's the daughter of Heidi, who's retired now —was one of the ones who used to come by every Saturday and pray with Mama near the end. I won't ever forget that.

About a half mile after Heidi's, everything pops up all at once: buildings and mossy oaks and street lamps wreathed in gold light. The library sits, squat and dark and quiet, over on my right. Sidewalk starts

4

to run along both sides of the street. Three churches wait behind it on my right, while on the left, there's a line of storefront. Half the stores in Heat Springs—all right here.

I think of taking Oliver and Margot into Hester's Rare Birds, an antique shop, and Shirley's, the shoe store. There's a sewing shop, and an ice cream parlor that I know they'll love. Insurance place, two clothes stores—one's got kid stuff—and then the pharmacy. They can get slushes and taffy there, so that should be a winner. Dollar General... the Goodwill. What would they make of a Goodwill? Again, that imposter feeling... What would Sutton think if she knew?

Well, she'd be pleased as punch, you eejit. You were her choice.

Something about that thought makes my eyes tear up. I wipe them and brake for the stop sign by Pine Park. We'll be going there a lot now. They've got that rocking bumblebee thing—sort of like a one-kid seesaw. Plus the swings. Oh, and duh—the Floatin' Bean is right there by it. The kids would love to have a Heat Springs Float.

So weird to see this whole town from a parent sort of angle. Even though I'm *not* their parent. Kinda thought I'd never be a parent, at the rate things are going. Which is to say...*not* going.

I hang a right down what we call Hamburger Highway. Hardee's, Wendy's, McDonald's, Sonic, and Taco Bell. The Taco Bell is brand new. Wonder if it's really emu meat. Surely it's not. The kids could eat it if I cook at home most other times—and I will. I brought Sutton's recipe book for vegans, just to make them feel at home. Let's hope I can figure that out.

You and your fancy life, big sister. How am I supposed to reproduce that?

Neighborhoods branch off Hamburger Highway. We pass Willow Oaks, a little neighborhood where Dad lives now. Since Mama passed, he's been there. He walked out the door the day she died and never went back to our childhood home again.

Right after her death was when the bank came calling. Daddy couldn't face it, Mary Helen was panicking, and Sutt wasn't around. So it was up to Shawn and me to work out a deal. My big brother put up two of his eighteen wheelers for collateral—mostly because Mama's grave is on our land, behind a little church where all the Hinsons have been buried for a hundred years under the shady oaks.

It's called Lawler Farm now—starting when my parents married, out of deference to Daddy, who was farming the land—but it's not *really*. It's

Hinson land, going back generations. I'm a Lawler, but I'm Hinson, too, and I'm not letting the bank have our farm. So far, they haven't gotten it.

I think of all the money in my bank account right now, what I could do with it. But I push those thoughts away. I'll get the kids what they need, but I don't think it's right to use the money Sutt and Asher left their babies to bring the farm back steady into the black. Not even if it will be the kids' new home. I'll just have to keep on trying. Try harder. So I can keep them stable and secure.

I pass Shawn's acreage on the right—and then the double wide that serves as home base for his trucking company. He's got nine trucks now, doing real well. Our sister Mary Helen lives out near the Taylors' pond, a few miles east. She and her kids might come over tomorrow morning. That'll be good. Maybe.

I take a right onto my county road. It's not mine, but it feels like it. Only thing but our farm that's out this way is the old Helms place. Well, that and the water treatment plant. And hunting land. A lot of hunting land that's leased to big-league city slickers from Atlanta and a few I know from Albany.

After two point five miles driving between the tall pines, my dirt road comes into view. It's framed by fields where nothing's growing at this moment. Woods rise up around the fields—still thick and lush, despite our hard times. I hang a right, and my truck's tires bump over the old, familiar grooves. Pretty soon, it will be time to ask the Helms' boy to smooth it out for me. Daddy could, of course, but he won't touch the farm equipment. None of it. Feels like a failure, won't move past his pride. The Lawlers have a lot of pride. I know that, don't I?

This road always makes me feel good. I veer left at the fork, away from the path that goes out to the pastures and down to the low ponds. I'm driving in a thick wood. Mary Helen tells me anybody with some sense would be afraid to live out here alone, but I disagree. I've got Petey and Tink, my German Shepherds. I forgot to mention them to Margot and Oliver before they nodded off. I did talk about them yesterday, and Margot promised that she won't be scared.

Beyond the darkness of the woods, up on my right, I see a moonlit clearing. It's about twenty acres of bare fields where I can't afford to plant crops—yet. I turn right at a red dirt path marked by a mailbox, and my humble home glows in the moonlight. It's whitewashed wood, with a screened-in front porch where there's a porch swing and a braided oval rug and two tables I set up with books and candles. Long ago, my grandmama's spinster sister lived here. After we shut up my family's house, which is just a little ways down the road, it made sense for me to come here.

I've made it mine. As soon as I near my normal parking spot, under a giant pecan tree, all the barking starts, as if in testament to that.

Tink and Petey burst out the unlocked screen porch door like the wildlings they are. The kids rouse, but only a little. There's a moment where I panic over which limp kid to haul in first, but then Oliver sits up and frowns out the window and says, in his little city boy voice, "Oh. I hear your dogs."

"They're your dogs, too." I smile back at him. "If you want them to be."

I help him out of the truck, and he stands stoically in the pearly light as Petey and Tink whack him with their wagging tails and lick his face. And then he giggles.

"What do you think?" I murmur.

He looks at the house and fields and woods and then the dogs again, and me. And he says, "I think I can be a brave farm boy."

I think Sutton would be proud, despite her choosing city life. It's not like they really had a choice, with Asher taking over his father's real estate empire. The Masterson family has been in San Francisco for a century. They had power and money. No way Sutt was coming back to Heat Springs. But there's nothing wrong with here, I tell myself again.

My house is old and worn, but cozy. I haul Margot inside, carrying her lamb style, and Oliver walks in front of us. I make Tink and Petey wait on the porch so they won't overwhelm Oliver as he blinks around the comfy living room then joins me in the short hallway. There are two bedrooms, over on the left of the small house. While we were away, I had Shawn and Mary Helen swap them around, so that the larger one, which had been mine, became the kids', and I'm now in the smaller room without the en suite bathroom.

My throat aches when I see what they did. The little twin beds Mary Helen found somewhere and painted white and put white bedding on. The bookshelves stacked with kids' books. Nightstands I can see Shawn built himself, with matching powder blue lamps.

There's a Batman poster over Oliver's bed and a Frozen one by Margot's.

I smile down at Oliver. He beams back at me and leaps onto his bed. I lay Margot out on hers and fold the blankets over her. She doesn't stir.

Oliver takes my hand as I show him to the bathroom. He brushes his teeth with a new toothbrush and Sparkle Fun Crest paste like we used as kids, and then lies on his back on his new bed. He's asleep by the time I come back with their bags.

I crouch in the hallway so the noise of me removing their bedspreads from zipped bags doesn't wake them. Then I sneak into their room and drape one over each kid.

I can't fall asleep in my new/old room for a long time. I'm so exhausted, everything is spinning slightly. I keep seeing Sutton dancing in and out of my head, looking how she did in their last Christmas card. The long, thick hair...the pretty beaded necklace.

As soon as my eyes drift shut, someone whispers, "Aunt June?"

I jolt straight up in bed and find Margot on my rug with big eyes. Big, crying eyes.

"Aunt June..." She does something to her hair. I can't see. I fumble for my lamp.

"Ohh." It's the lollipop. The damn thing's tangled in her long, blonde hair. "Oh no, sweetheart."

She gives a whimper.

"We can fix this." I slide off the bed, trying to sound cheery as I wave toward the hallway. "Come on. Let's go to the bath tub."

I jabber as I lead her to the bathroom in the hall. "So you haven't seen this place yet, huh? You fell asleep in the car. Does it smell like cinnamon in here?"

With her little hand raised so she can hold the stick of the giant lollipop that's pulling at her hair, she gives the air a few sniffs. Then she nods, still solemn-faced.

"What do you think about the smell of cinnamon? Does it smell warm and homey or do you think it's stinky?"

I open the bathroom door and flip the light switch, revealing a claw-footed tub, a porcelain trough sink, a fluffy rainbow rug, and old-school tile walls done in an assortment of colors. Back when we renovated this place for my great aunt, around three years before Mama got cancer,

Mom went to the hardware store and brought home a few boxes of whatever they had. I smile at the memory.

"Toothpaste," Margot whispers.

I smile. "I like cinnamon toothpaste."

She says, "Me too," with her brown eyes on her little bare legs.

"Have you ever seen a tub like this?" I ask. "With feet?"

I point to the claw feet, and her eyes widen slightly. She shakes her head.

"Do you like your water cold, medium, or hot?"

She frowns at the tub.

"What about just a surprise? And how about bubbles?"

She smiles slightly, nods.

"I'll run the bath for you, and you can take your clothes off."

"No," she whispers.

"Not a go?"

"You take off. I hold lollipop."

I push the rubber plug into the drain, sprinkle some bubble bath salt in, and help her undress. Then I lift her into the enormous tub. She looks up at the silky purple curtain, streaming down from the ceiling. Then she looks at me.

"Did my mommy get in this bath?" Her little voice is soft and hoarse.

I swallow so mine won't be. "Yes. She did." This bath tub came from Mama and Daddy's house, so it's the truth. "We used to sit in here together sometimes. Your mama would tell me stories. She was my big sister."

As so often happens since I arrived in California eleven days ago—the first to get the kids from foster care after my sister and her husband died in a bad wreck—my heart freezes mid-rhythm, waiting to see how she reacts. But Margot's small, pale face remains placid. Her eyes hold to mine. "You were the little one? Like me?"

I nod. "I was the youngest one. Just like you."

That satisfies her. I can tell because her lips twitch just slightly before smoothing back into their straight line. Her hands arrange the bubbles in a small pile while I wash the lollipop out of her hair. As soon as it's freed, she reaches for my arm. She gets her fingers around the stick, runs the lollipop under the faucet, and sticks it back into her mouth.

"Aunt June." She smiles. "I like your house."

She sits there in the tub licking the obscene sugar disc for almost half an hour, asking every so often about the house.

"Do you want to see the rest of the place?" I ask when she's wrapped in a towel.

"Not tonight." She shuts her eyes and says, "Just take me to my bed. And lie down with me."

I do just that. My sister's daughter snuggles in beside me, wraps her arm around me, lets a quiet breath out. I watch the ceiling until my eyes blur…then slowly drift shut.

CHAPTER 2

BURKE

I cup my hand over my pants pocket as I stand in the elevator. From the parking deck up to the sixth floor. Always that moment of vertigo. I shut my eyes and lean the back of my head against the steel wall.

Smells like cake in here. Like fucking birthday cake. I open my eyes and blink at my reflection, bent like in a funhouse mirror. There better not be a party in the office today—or even worse, some kind of *in memoriam*. Surely they wouldn't.

A couple seconds later, the elevator doors limp open and I step out onto the marble floor. **Aesculapius**, the small, stone sign says, with an arrow pointing down our hall.

The app is being pitched to investors as just Aes—and it might later be re-named—but regardless, it's better to keep our identity and location under the radar. I learned that with my last two startups. No one's ever heard of Aesculapius—at least not outside Roman history.

I pat my pocket as I walk toward the door to the admin suite. Probably everybody's heard about what happened. Or maybe not. I bet so, though. Asher had an endless list of friends. He always did. But since he started working with our bastard of a father, he really knew the whole damn city. I bet his obituary was featured prominently in every Bay area magazine and paper.

Not that I would know. I wasn't here.

I stop and try to school my face into a "normal" look. Then, after a fortifying breath, I push the door open and step into what I think of as the waiting room. It's just a desk, a couch, a few chairs, and a coffee table—a place for people to wait.

Helena looks up from where she's seated behind the desk, balancing the phone between her ear and shoulder. She murmurs something in Spanish and hangs the phone up, and my heart thumps a little faster.

"Burke, hello." She stands up and steps around her desk, but doesn't move toward me. Smart. "I'm so sorry for your loss," she says, making a sad face.

"Thanks, Helena." I look her up and down, keeping my eyes and face neutral, then look around the small space like she just mentioned the weather. "How have things been?"

"The usual," she says after a moment. "How are you?"

I don't fucking know. My little brother died while I was on a Himalayan mountain with an investor who still hasn't invested and a satellite phone that didn't work. How do you fucking think?

I give her a bland smile. "Good trip."

"Someone shared one of the pictures you sent. The mountains were beautiful." Her voice sounds chirpish. Awkward.

"Very much so," I say—just as awkwardly.

"We're so glad to have you back."

I arch my brows. "Thanks."

I give her a strained smile before starting down the hall toward my office. But I only get a few yards before I hear, "Hey, man!"

I clench my jaw. Fucking Gabe has got his door cracked. I peer through to find him rising from behind his desk and striding toward me. I escaped a hug from Helena because she's older than us, plus she's kind of new. Gabe is a goddamn hugger, though. He goddamn hugs me with one arm and says, "So sorry, man."

"A heartfelt sorry always helps."

"Don't be a dick, dude."

"Don't wear some much product." I pat his blond head, which doesn't really have that much product.

"Jeezus."

"Don't take our Lord's name in vain."

"I'm Jewish," he says.

"So?"

Gabe rolls his eyes. I roll mine.

"Fuck you too, dude," he says. "I was just trying to offer my condolences."

I fix him with a death stare, and he walks back to his desk with his shoulders slumping. Guilt spills through me, hot and prickling.

"Sorry, man. I'm really low on sleep."

"Same here." His voice has got an edge now. "Three nights working on this fucking crash shit."

"Damn." I don't know a lot about what happened—presumably no one wanted to bother me with the details when they assumed I'd be taking time off work to mourn—so I ask, and he explains what happened with a facet of the beta app.

"I know how to fix it, but I haven't slept in three nights." He sighs. "Cara and the baby will be back this afternoon from her mom's."

Now that I look at him, Gabe does look like shit. The "baby" is turning one next month, but the little fucker doesn't like to sleep, and Gabe's a decent guy who takes turns doing bottle feeds at night. I turn toward the door so I can't see his face when I say, "Get a nap, man. I'll work on it for a while. Screen share it."

I shut his door behind me and pass the next three—all closed, thankfully—with no encounters. My door is on the back right. It leads into a space where Molly, my assistant, has a desk beside a giant potted tree with weird, wide, oval leaves. There's a wall of windows in front of her desk, so investors dropping by to chat with me can see the San Francisco Bay.

Molly is okay, but I don't want to do the awkward shit, so I lift my phone to my ear and walk through the door to our shared space with a look that's supposed to say "annoyed and distracted." I hold up my free hand in a half-assed sort of a wave, and then I step into my office.

Whew.

I shut my eyes, and when I open them, I stare at my desk for a long moment. There's a picture of *us* in a small, round frame. When Asher came by one time, he noticed the place was empty, so he mailed one to me. I swallow, thinking of how he had to mail it to me. I was always so damn busy.

I step over to the desk and put the frame in a drawer. Then I fire up my computer. I close my eyes again and inhale. This place always smells like hot computer parts and new carpet. I touch my wireless mouse and lean back in my old, familiar leather office chair.

When the computer powers on, I find the screen is all clear.

I jab Gabe's extension. "Seriously, man. Share the fucking screen and go to sleep."

"You're such a dick." But I can hear him chuckle.

My screen is filled with his work just a second later.

"Get some sleep, pal."

He hangs up on me.

Two hours later, and I'm relieved no one's knocked on my door. I think Zephyr's out. It's Wednesday morning, when the fucker goes for breakfast with his mother. I shut off Gabe's stuff—figured it out in forty minutes; he'd done almost all the work already—and stand up. I stretch, wipe some dust off the potted plant behind my desk, and rub my temples.

Better get it over with. I unlock my door, crack it open, and step slowly out into Molly's space.

She looks up from her desk with a smile. "Hi, Burke."

I nod. "Molly."

"It's so nice to have you back."

I snort. "Oh yeah?"

She nods, sincere as always. "It was quiet without you."

Molly's young, and here on a worker's visa from China. Sometimes when I rag on her, it makes her face turn red—and anyway, I don't feel like teasing her today. So I just say, "Yeah."

"I wanted to offer my condolences."

I tip my head a little, try to keep my mouth from tugging downward. "Thank you."

"Also, I should let you know...you got a call from Mr. Gurung," she adds.

"Did I?"

She nods, her short black hair bobbing around her chin. "It was very early this morning."

Well, shit. Maybe now that our mountain adventure is over, fucker finally decided to invest. "What did he say?"

"He asked that you return his phone call."

The dull throb at my temples flares. "Okay. Thanks."

"Of course."

"Oh—Molly?" I step closer to her desk and reach into my pocket. "Before I go—"

Her eyebrows arch.

"If I pay you some extra…" I hold out the five hundred-dollar bills to show her what I mean. "Can you take on a side project?"

She blinks discreetly at the money and then meets my eyes. "Of course. What do you need?"

I hand her the cash. "I need you to research someone. Do a background check. Find whatever you can."

"Okay." She nods.

"We'll start the mentorship stuff back tomorrow—you can shadow me the first two hours, like we had been doing—but you could work on this in any spare time you have in the next few days. You can have up to a week to gather information. But anyway. Look up June Francis Lawler. Lives in Heat Springs, Georgia. Parents Hubert and Patti. Also look up Lawler Farms. Find out everything you can about it, them, and her."

She nods, her features slightly drawn.

"The good and bad things. *Everything*."

She nods again. "I am on it."

I can't help a small smile. "Thank you."

I nod one more time and retreat to my office.

❦

JUNE

Charleigh, Rachel, and Jack—my sister Mary Helen's kids—tumble out of MH's van and stop dead in their tracks. Charleigh is 6 like Margot, Rachel is 7, and Jack is 9 like Oliver. Honestly, they're sort of jerk kids, but they're family, so they're *our* jerks.

They're jerks mostly because MH isn't assertive enough. And because MH isn't assertive, when they stop there in the dirt, gaping at their orphaned cousins through the porch's screen, MH just stands there looking awkward.

I reach over Margot's head and push open the porch door. "Hey, guys! Come on in."

Oliver and Margot are dressed in the nicest of their pricey, hipster clothes. For Oliver, that's black skinny jeans, Converse All-Stars, and a plain white, long-sleeved T-shirt. For Margot, it's magenta sequined sneakers, cream leggings, and a long-sleeved pink sweat shirt with fluffy polka dots.

Charleigh, Rachel, and Jack look like they're dressed for church, decked out in the deep South way, with dresses, hair bows as wide as their heads, and mary janes for the girls, and khakis and a plaid button-up for little Jack.

I wave the three onto my screened porch, and they stand gaping at their cousins.

"Say hello," I prompt them. *Rude asses.*

"Hey cousins," Rachel says.

"It's nice to meet you," Charleigh says.

"We met before," Oliver informs them.

Charleigh frowns as Mary Helen makes it up the porch steps with an armful of bags.

"You were little," Jack tells Charleigh. "But I remember."

"Me too," says Rachel. "Do y'all live here now?" She asks with some skepticism, and then looks up at the porch's ceiling with wide eyes, as if maybe they live up there with the porch fan.

Mary Helen's face bends in a look of caution. "Remember, honey? How I told you Oliver and Margot got new bedspreads and a brand new room?"

"I want to see the Batman bedspread," Jack says. "Mom won't let me get rid of my fish one." He rolls his eyes.

The kids stampede through the front door, no doubt headed for the bedroom. The farm house is so old that the hardwood floor shakes under the weight of their steps.

Mary Helen shakes her head. "Better stay right on them. No telling what Jack will say."

"Or Rachel," I smile.

"How are they today?" she murmurs. We step into the living room, and she takes off her sweater, hangs it on the coat rack.

"Margot has been pretty steady. Lots of big-eyed looks and not too much talking except to ask me questions about when we were all kids. I think Oliver is struggling more. He's said a few things about how *he's* from San Francisco. I'm pretty sure I overheard him telling Margot that California is their real home," I say quietly, glancing toward the hall, "like they're just here for a visit."

Mary Helen's lips purse in concern.

"The fact is, there was no way for them to stay. I just can't live in San Francisco. The money that's in their fund now seems like a lot until you really think about how much it costs to raise two kids."

"Oh yeah," she says. "It costs a shit ton."

"And college. You know Sutton would want Ivy Leagues for both of them."

Mary Helen smirks a little. She knows.

"I don't know what she would have wanted me to do *exactly*, since she never told me I was listed as their guardian."

"I think she would want us to do this," MH says in a soothing tone. "You're doing everything right."

I heave a silent sigh. "Thanks."

We head into the bedroom, where the girls are piled on Margot's bed and Jack and Oliver are bouncing on his.

"Hey, no jumping. We don't want to break the bed's boards. Then it'll collapse." I mime a collapse with my hand, and Oliver's eyes widen.

For the next half hour, all five kids play as Mary Helen and I unload the toys she brought from her and her husband Tom's house. Margot and Oliver have plenty, but it's going to be weeks before their belongings arrive—they've been shipped as freight—and they need something in the meantime.

Margot goes bananas over four wonked-out, barely-clad Barbies and a small, pink Barbie house.

"This one got a haircut," Rachel explains, touching a blonde Barbie's hacked-off bob. Mary Helen makes a face behind her raised palm.

"I've never had a Barbie," Margot says.

"What?" It's echoed by all of us.

She nods. "Mommy let me play with Calico Critters. But not little people dolls."

Mary Helen shoots me a what-the-hell look, again behind her hand. She and I drift to the other side of the room.

"Because of the image of Barbie, Mary Helen," I say.

"What image is that?"

"You know. She's long and skinny, like some alien or something. Real women aren't proportioned like that."

"They make curvy Barbie," MH hisses.

I shrug. "I didn't even think about it, but it's true—I didn't notice any Barbies when we packed their house up."

She widens her eyes and looks up at the ceiling, like she's asking Sutton *why*. Then she waves me toward the hallway. "Let's go get the rest."

We unload a plastic seesaw, a toy kitchen MH found at the Goodwill, and a basket of superhero figurines. Then we hear the screaming.

I rush off first and nearly collide with Margot as she bursts into the living room—in tears.

"Oh no, honey." I clutch her shoulders. "What's the matter?"

"Jack!" She wails. "He says my mommy is a zombie!"

"What the hellfire?" I crouch down beside her as the other kids spill into the room. "Your parents are *angels*, Margot. In heaven with *God*."

"Heaven isn't real." I look up. Oliver.

"Heaven *is* real," I say. "We will talk about that. Jack—"

MH strides over to him and snatches him into the kitchen. *Good riddance.*

"Jack asked if we saw our Mom and Dad...and if they looked like zombies." His voice cracks on the word.

My blood pressure shoots up. "Of *course* they didn't. They are angels, watching over you two."

"I want my mommy and daddy to come back from heaven!" Margot shoots off toward her bedroom. Oliver follows.

Jack loses his Nintendo Switch gaming system for the week—apparently he forewarned his mom that he might ask about the zombies, and she pre-threatened him—so MH and her kids run to their house to get it; Margot and Oliver will borrow it as part of Jack's apology.

I tell Margot and Oliver that sometimes life includes some really awful things along with really great things, and assure them the great things will come. And that their parents will be watching them forever, waiting for them when they die—which I remind them involves superpowers and being happy forever. (Fingers crossed.)

It's going okay until the conversation's almost over and Oliver says, "I'm ready to die now. Georgia is boring."

Margot says, "I want more Barbies."

I'm wearing my pearl necklace. I clutch it. Does that really help?

What helps is wine. Box wine, at 9:00 PM, after I get my two sad sacks to sleep. My bestie Leah brings it over, along with a giant bath bomb

—"from Lush at the Perimeter Mall; there's some kind of fancy jewel inside."

I take the thing from her. "I hope it's the swallowable, pharmaceutical kind."

She arches her perfect eyebrows. "That bad?"

"Oliver wants to die like mom and dad because Georgia is boring. Margot wants her Mommy's smell back. Then she got the idea that maybe *I* could smell like Sutton, and—hear this shit—you know what Sutt's perfume was?"

I cackle maniacally, and Leah widens her eyes.

"That Joy stuff!"

"What?" Leah tilts her head, not understanding.

"It's called Joy by Jean Patou, and it's made of—I don't know, like a whole bouquet of roses or something. Anyway, I can't smell like their mom because their mommy smelled like *money*. That stuff costs a thousand dollars."

Leah whips out her phone to search it, and her eyes widen anew. "Oh. Yikes. Yeah, it's six hundred. Who even was your sister?"

"Right?"

"Use the life insurance money, Juney."

"How do I know when to use it? What will actually improve their lives? Margot doesn't really want me to smell like her mom. Even if I did, I still won't be Sutt. No one ever will be." My eyes fill with tears that fall down my cheeks. I wipe at them.

"Shit, June. I'm so sorry."

Leah hugs me, and I hug her. "I'm not good at this."

"Yes you are."

"I'm going to mess them up, I know it."

"How so?"

"I don't know. I already un-vegan-ized them at the Steak 'n Shake."

She laughs. "Good. Didn't you go there with Sutton last time she came home? Because *she* wanted it?"

"Yeah, but still. Her husband was a devout vegan."

"California people." I can hear her eye roll even though I can't see it; we're still hugging.

"They were weird," I admit. "His whole family. Sutt said they were real cold fish, especially the dad. Not Asher—okay, *maybe* Asher; I barely knew the guy—but I'm meaning Asher's dad. Their mom was dead for a long time, and his brother—Burke? Icy cold stunner. That guy didn't even show up for the funerals."

"Geez. That's harsh."

"Oh, and by the way. Jack the Brat told Margot today that her mother is a zombie now."

Leah howls. "Oh dear baby Jesus in the manger! Are you shitting me?"

I fumble with the wine box spout in reply. When I get it open, it sprays on the floor, and I lean under it with my mouth open—mostly to offer amusement to Leah. I start choking, and she grabs the box and flips it on its back.

"You'll go zombie, too, if you're not careful, you goose."

I hear a gasp, followed by a yelped, "No!"

Then Margot is streaking through the living room. From behind the couch. Where she's been listening to every word.

CHAPTER 3

BURKE

Three Weeks Later

I look up from the gas pump, running my hand into my hair as a warm breeze tries to toss it around. As I do, a man across the way, filling a huge black truck, gives me a nod, as if he's...saying hi?

I can't bring myself to nod back, so I return my gaze to the pump. Gasoline is so damn cheap here. The pump clicks, signaling the tank of my rented Porsche is full, and I'm charged only $38.03.

Albany, Georgia—Where Everything Has Less Value. They should put it on the welcome sign at the city limits. It's the nearest pseudo-metropolitan area to Heat Springs, my ultimate destination, and the place does not impress, I'm sorry to say.

I feel like I stepped back into 1994. The number of the strip malls, run-down fast food joints, pickup truck dealerships, and Walmarts is off-putting. When I first stepped out of the Porsche at the gas station just now, I swear I could smell cow shit in the humid breeze.

Yeah, it's humid here. In February.

I don't know what I'll find when I get to Heat Springs—Molly only dug up one photo of June, my 26-year-old, GED-toting, food-assistance-getting, bank-loan-defaulting nemesis, and in that photo, she was twelve—but I know I can't let Oliver and Margot grow up here with her.

It's not about the sour grapes. Although...did Asher and Sutton *really* choose *this* over my place? Sure, I'm not the poster boy for guided meditation, karmic healing, and talk therapy like my brother was. I'm not taking apart my inner feelings and analyzing my true self and all that other intangible shit. I'm the type that puts everything into my job. But I'm an adult, and my home base is San Francisco.

This is about quality of life, and quality of education. Hell, even quality of food. I haven't seen a Whole Foods, Trader Joe's, or even a Natural Grocers since I stepped off the plane in Georgia.

There's no private school in Heat Springs, so June Lawler either plans to send them to the Heat Springs public school or, more likely, I guess, drive or bus them here to Albany to go to one of these private schools. Molly checked them all out, and they're shitty. There's nothing this far from Atlanta that would ever prepare them for a quality college. Assuming she plans for them to go to college.

Asher had specific college funds for both of them, so surely she does. It doesn't matter, though. I'll be there by nightfall, and I'm not leaving unless they're with me. I touch my wallet, resting in the passenger seat, and give myself a fake grin in the rear view.

Everybody can be bought for the right price, and thanks to Molly's research, I know June's. The girl is irrationally devoted to her family's sad husk of a farm. It's only eighty acres now—in the last ten years, they sold a lot of acreage to the neighbors—and if the paperwork is any indication, the land isn't fertile. Every year for the last five, June has operated at a loss. Somehow Molly even found a PDF file showing crops June planted versus what she harvested. I don't know anything about farming, but the numbers looked like shit.

Unless the paperwork is way off, it looks like she's only got nine cows and one horse. She's selling crop-planting and harvesting equip-ment for way less than it's worth on two farm websites, and she's taken out two new small business loans in the last year—both at near-preda-tory interest rates. The farm itself is financed through her brother's trucking company, which is probably struggling like a lot of trucking companies are right now.

This is why she took my brother's kids. She wants them for the life insurance money. Move them to the farm, then use the money intended to pay for private school, French tutors, and riding lessons to float her crappy family farm.

I went against my MO with my piece of shit father and contacted him to give him hell for letting Asher's kids get taken. The mother-fucker actually laughed. I shouldn't have been surprised. He put on a good front for Ash over the years because he wanted an heir to his empire, but my father is poison. Just because I'm the only person alive who knows it doesn't make it untrue.

I blow out a breath and turn onto a skinny, asphalt-cracked highway.

The trees around here are unnerving. They're too tall, too thick. I feel like I've been sucked into some other dimension—one where maybe it's fifty years in the past. Fields fan out around the narrow road, spreading in between dark swaths of Southern pine forest. I tap the steering wheel and check my cell phone. No service—not a surprise.

Finally I reach the city limits, marked with a small plastic sign that looks like someone made it in their basement. This is even worse than I feared; Heat Springs is barely a shit smudge on the map. I check the paper maps I printed off, but some of the roads I'm seeing through the windshield aren't on paper. A minute later, I pull over at a diner sort of place. It's got a brick façade, but there's a front porch with wooden rocking chairs.

I look down at my most casual pair of Salvatore Ferragamos—some black leather drivers I've got on with black jeans I thought might be appropriate for a rural area—and feel awkward as I pull the creaky wooden door open.

Country Western music fills my ears, and my eyes fix on a tall woman standing behind what looks like a podium. She's got a maroon apron on. Her white-blonde hair is in a net, and she's wearing a lot of very red lipstick. When she sees me, she leans forward with a confused expression on her wrinkled face, like she dropped her glasses and can't see me properly. She continues looking at me that way until I'm right beside the podium—which I can tell is an actual podium because there's a hole on the front for electrical cords.

Then she says, loudly, as if she means to alert someone through the kitchen doors behind her with her tone, "Can I help you, darlin'?"

It takes some restraint not to laugh at her slow, stretched-out vowels. Not out of meanness. I just haven't ever heard that sort of accent outside parody. I bite on the inside of my cheek and try to look like this is business as usual.

"Yes." I nod once. "I'm looking for June Lawler."

"JOLENE!" My gaze moves to the hallway to the right of the kitchen doors, where I think the shout came from. I hear a crashing sound, and then a woman says, "Goddamn it!"

The woman before me—Jolene?—turns around, and I spot her bra straps sticking out above the collar of her floral blouse. For some reason, the straps are held together by...a bread tie?

"If you're looking for that other pan, it's in the washer! Like I told you!"

She turns back to me and rolls her pale blue eyes, a look of disgust twisting her red lips. "Doesn't know how to find a damn thing, that one." She pronounces *doesn't* like dut-uhn.

I nod, for a second not sure what I'm even nodding at.

"You said—"

"It's not in there!"

Jolene's eyes pop open wide, like someone just grabbed her ass. "What the Sam Hill!" She storms off, leaving me to look around the little entry space. I turn back toward the door and spot a deer head.

Is that a deer? It's not a moose. So it's a deer. A deer's head. It's got horns, only I think on deer, they're called "antlers." I count them. Twelve. Seems like a lot to me.

"Yes, sir." I turn back toward the podium. It's her again. What was her name? *Jolene.* "What can I help you with?" she sighs. "You selling somethin'?"

"I just need to find June Lawler. Had some issues with my GPS."

She dabs her sweating forehead with a napkin. "Who?"

"I'm looking for the Lawler Farm. June Lawler."

"Oh, you mean the Hinson place. Ain't never been Lawler." She says it with disdain that I don't understand—or maybe she's just bitchy because of the woman who's yelling at her down the hall.

I nod. "Her mother's maiden name was Hinson. Do you know June?"

"June Bug?" She gives me a no-shit look. "Everybody 'round here knows June Bug. Got herself a niece and nephew from out in Californ-i-aye. Sutton's babies. I heard the little girl's real pretty." She says that gently, like it's a consolation prize for losing both of one's parents. But that's not what bothers me the most.

"Did you say June...*bug*?"

"Born early, with them big ole eyes. You know how them preemies look, a little alien." She widens her eyes, and I nod like I've seen a hundred preemies.

"I need directions to the farm. Please."

She frowns, giving me an exaggerated-looking suspicious frown. "Who're you again?"

I'm wearing a white button-up and a gray wool vest, like I might if I was meeting with investors. It's important that June see me as her ticket to a nice payday—which I intend to give her.

"I'm an old friend. From college." *Shit.* "When I went to college, I knew her," I clarify.

"Smart enough to run that college, June is. Didn't go, though." She frowns, and I can see a cartoon thought bubble over her head. "Too much going on out at the farm...and with her mama. You know that."

The woman draws directions for me on a napkin. "Before you get back moving, let me get you an iced tea. We've got cornbread, too. Why don't you take June Bug some cornbread for them sweet kids? The little Yankees need to get acquainted with the finer things."

I open my mouth to say "I don't think so," but what comes out instead is, "Sure."

I climb back into the Porsche with a to-go box of what I'm told is cornbread—it looks like a soft, yellow brick of cake and smells like butter—and a large iced tea in a Styrofoam cup. I ran out of water in my bottle a few miles ago, and I'm fucking thirsty. I bring the straw to my face and sniff...then take a small test sip.

Damn. It's not bad. Very sweet. I take another sip...and then another as I roll down the quaint Main Street. It looks like something out of a movie. Lots of brick, a bunch of striped awnings, even a little fountain at an intersection. The place has an abandoned feel, like small towns often do, but I see a few people. A woman pushing a kid in a stroller. A tall guy wearing a ball cap, overalls, and boots. There's a hardware store, a tiny library, a women's clothing store called The Southern Belle. I'm surprised they're still embracing all that Old South stuff. Better to re-brand, I would think.

On one corner, there's a vacuum cleaner repair store—*really?*— with a handwritten cardboard sign in the window that says "Fix Your Stuff!!" I count three antique stores, and I bet they've got the goods. There's a bakery. I wouldn't try their stuff. No self-respecting pastry chef would make their home here.

I inhale the butter smell that's filled the car now. Maybe I should try that bread the woman gave me. Shit, I should have paid her for it. I didn't think about it, but that was stupid. Maybe the stuff's poison. Why else would she give it to me without running my card?

I'm through the little downtown in no time. The napkin map and my GPS agree: I should veer right at the next light. I pass a leafy playground, an insurance agency, a big—I mean *really* big—tree with moss dangling from its branches. Then a shady cemetery framed in by a tall, iron fence. There's a Confederate flag emblem stamped into the iron gate, meaning that it's old as hell.

Another block, and things feel more industrial. I pass a dry cleaners, a Dollar Tree, a DVD rental place—didn't know those guys were still in business—and a secondhand electronics store. Then fast food. There are several fast food joints here, including one I've never seen called Hardee's. There's a burger on the sign that looks like a cardiologist's wet dream.

Past the Taco Bell, there's a bank and then a Walmart—I guess every little country town has gotta have a Walmart—and something called Piggly Wiggly that looks like a grocery store. Just beyond the store, right there on the main drag, is a brick sign that says PINE HILLS in a cursive script. I frown at it. Half a second later, houses start to line the roadside. A few big, columned homes with porches that I figure have got to be pre-war, or from around that era. Then some little brick ones.

Finally, there's nothing more for me to gawk at except two gas stations and a tire shop, and then a car dealer. Then just forest. The sun is going down, and I can't see it for the treetops. The pines are tall and thin, their tips swaying gently in a breeze I couldn't feel when I stepped out into the humidity back at the restaurant.

I follow the highway down past a shack that's got a neon BBQ sign. Then I hang a right onto a smaller road and start into the sticks. Ponds and fields, sometimes barbed wire fences wrapped around ordinary-looking woods, with "No Trespassing" signs mounted to trees as if someone would want to trespass in that patch of forest. Maybe hunters. I wonder what they hunt here. There's no big game—at least I don't think so. Maybe wild boars? I wouldn't want to face off with a boar, that's for damn sure. I read once that they can eat an entire human body, bones and all.

As I drive, I picture June Bug, smirking at her name. At least I won't be thrown off by her looks. That picture Molly dug up showed a girl with a tight ponytail, braces, and glasses, plus big chipmunk cheeks. It was black and white—maybe a yearbook photo—so I couldn't tell. Her eyes were probably bug-like, but the glasses would obscure that.

Molly's research didn't show what kind of dwelling hers is, and the Google satellite photo wasn't clear because the house is shielded from the sun by a bunch of tall trees, but I wonder if it's a trailer. I picture June Bug wearing overalls, barefoot in a patch of red dirt outside the front door, one arm around each kid. Maybe the kids are eating fried chicken.

Hell of a time to break down and go for the bumpkin fare, but my stomach's growling, and I need to have my game face on when I get to her place. My GPS—if it's right—thinks I'm six minutes away. So far, it matches the napkin, so it's probably right.

I cup my hand around the bread and pull off a chunk. It's so soft it crumples in my lap.

"Fuck."

I brush the yellow crumbs into the floorboard. Who cares if I have a grease stain? I'm sure she won't notice. I cram the cornbread into my mouth, trying not to spill more. *Whoa.* It's so good, I'm going in for seconds, clothes be damned. This is some delicious shit. Warm and buttery, and a little sweet. Guess I know why people go to Southern food joints. I was never really one for barbeque or beans or any of that, but this bread...I could eat it all day.

In fact, I eat the whole box full. By the time my GPS tells me to turn right onto a dirt road, I have to hit the brakes hard. My fingers have left grease stains on the wheel.

"Fuck." I pull to the roadside, sweep the crumbs off my lap, and stash the box in the trunk for good measure. Don't want the kids to think I didn't save them any. I guzzle some of the tea—okay, almost all of it. Then I pour it in the dirt—red dirt, I notice with satisfaction—and stash the cup. No reason for anyone to know I made a pit stop at the local honky-tonk.

I run my hand over my shadow—I can grow a beard in like six hours, so it's scruffy already—and check my teeth in the mirror. Wonder what her teeth are like. I'm guessing that's a stereotype. I make a mental note to dial back the assumptions.

I'm driving along, checking out some empty fields and the thick trees that tower over them, when I realize I've been bumping over this road for a while. I check the napkin.

Shit—I went too far.

I turn back around, the car's tires kicking up a cloud of reddish dust as I press the pedal and head back in the direction I came from. I notice little things in the amber light of almost-sunset: a sliver of busted tire in the little ditch that runs along the left side of the dirt road...a little outhouse-looking wood shack with a tin roof off to the right, just behind a rickety metal gate. There's barbed wire fence on each side of the road, framing barren fields and, in one case, a grove of trees. Not sure what kind. They're tall, with regular leaves, so I can tell they aren't pines.

There's a barn out on the left. Looks like it's a hundred years old. Dark wood, two stories. Kind of pretty if it wasn't caving in. I think that's a grain silo beside it. Tall, cylindrical, metal sort of thing with vines around the base of it. Same vines growing up the barn, too. Kudzu. Is that what it's called?

I hit the brakes. There's a driveway on the left, a little ribbon of dirt. My gaze darts down it, then snaps onto a house. It's got to be hers. It's a small, rundown farmhouse. White, two stories, with what looks like a screened porch on the front, a few trees around the front walk. It reminds me of Dorothy's house in *The Wizard of Oz*.

Margot and Oliver are in there. My throat tightens thinking about them. It's such bullshit, what happened. The last thing a kid needs after losing their parents is to have everything else they hold dear snatched away from them. I wonder how they're holding up.

I get a deep breath and start down the driveway at a crawl. It's got a ton of bumps. Someone needs to smooth it out. Tractors can do that, I bet. She's selling a tractor. She should fire it up and fix this pitted driveway. My rented wheels bounce over it. Once, the underside of the car scrapes as I bounce over a dirt hill.

June Bug, sweetheart, payday's coming...

I park under one of the trees and slide my wallet into my back pocket. Then I walk to the screen porch door, open it slowly, and step inside. The porch is surprisingly cozy, with a white porch swing, a colorful rug, and a small bookshelf beside the front door. I look down at the welcome mat. It's a smiling pineapple. Strange.

I take another deep breath and knock twice, and hope to hell the kids are happy to see me. I hear footsteps. Oliver, maybe, because they're heavy. Instead, the door opens and— *Who the hell is this babe?*

My first thought is that June left Oliver and Margot with a babysitter. I give the girl a quick glance, my gaze moving from her high, blonde-brown ponytail to her delicate face. I don't know who she is, but this girl is big-screen beautiful.

Her eyes are gold-brown and her skin is creamy. She's got soft, pink lips that part as I stare at them. Her eyes widen—she could be posing for a contact lens commercial—and my gaze darts down her body. Small. Soft. Nineteen at most. She's got on a long, gray shirt that clings to her breasts, a strange owl necklace, and black leggings. Definitely the babysitter.

"Hi." I flash her a charming smile. "I'm here to see my niece and nephew—Oliver and Margot."

Her eyes widen wider. "I'm sorry, who are you?" Her voice is softer than her curves. Melodious.

I hold my hand out. "I'm their paternal uncle." I look her over again, trying not to let her see how fucking hot I think she is. "Your name?"

"Who do you think?" She twists her lips—part smile, part scoff.

"Should I know?"

"I don't know, *should* you? You made it to my house, after all."

My eyes dart around, taking in the swatch of living room I see behind her. "Your house? Are—You can't be…"

Her face hardens.

"Are you *June?*"

She blinks twice. It's condemning. "I am June. Are you *Burke?*"

"Yeah." I take a small step back, then try to peek into the house behind her. "Where are Oliver and Margot?"

"I'm sorry," she drawls. "I had them dressed in Sunday best for you, but…" She turns around to look behind her, and her tone is so deadpan that I think she's serious and wonder if the tea and cornbread lady called her. Then she swivels to face me. Her eyes narrow. "I'm not super sure that's really your business. You…were out of town for a while? Traveling for work, is that right?"

Anger and shame make my face hot. "Yes. I have a job. It takes me out of the country at times, sometimes for a few weeks."

"Okay." Her eyes fall to her feet before returning to mine. Jesus Christ, she's gorgeous. Her sister and my brother had a spur-of-the-moment, destination wedding, so I never got to meet her, but still—how did I not know this?

"Let me cut to the chase, June." I fumble for a second—probably because she's looking into my eyes now like she can see my fucking secrets. "June, I—" Fuck, she's gorgeous. It's unnatural. "I came here because I want to bring the kids back home," I manage.

Her eyebrows pinch; they're dark and delicate...and angry.

"Home to San Francisco," I add. "You know, they grew up there. It's their home. My brother's house hasn't been sold yet. I could move them back into it. Re-enroll them in their school, where they've been going for...a lot of years."

"How many years, would you say?" She leans her shoulder on the door frame, folds her slender arms under her breasts. Whoa, they're nice and...ample.

I blink. She's giving me a death stare. "Sorry. I—what does it matter? How many years? I didn't do the math on that," I say, sounding a bit defensive. "They went to that school since they were little. Like, one year old."

"Try three and a half." She winks. "Before that, my sister was at home with them. After that, in fact, she was at home with them. Neither child went to 'that school'—which, by the way, is named Bay Area Friends—for the entire day until age five."

Okay. Clearly I've underestimated her. I straighten my shoulders, try to regroup. So she's attractive and passably articulate. So the fuck what?

"I don't know what your point is. *My* point is I can take them back to the place they know. To their house, where all their stuff is."

"Actually it's in crates, being shipped here. Where they live now." She arches an eyebrow.

"They don't *have* to live here. That's my point, June. You don't have to take them in. I want to do that. And listen, if you've factored in the insurance money..." I pull out my wallet. Give her my yessir-I'll-do-right-by-you look—the one I use on big investors. "I can give you that, too."

She throws her head back...*laughing?* Fuck, she is. She's fucking laughing at me.

She squeezes her eyes shut, gives a little shake of her head. Then she looks at me like she's trying to murder me with pupil lasers.

"Listen, buster. I don't know who you are or where you come from. I mean, I know, but I don't really *know*. And I don't want to." She twists her lips, like she just tasted something sour. "Sutton told me about

Asher's family." She sinks her teeth into her lower lip and shuts her eyes for just a second, clearly trying to muster up some resolve. Then she heaves a breath out, looks me level in the eye again with a gaze that's just a fraction warmer this time.

"I don't know you, okay, Burke? So I'm going to just *assume* that you have great intentions. Get them back into 'that school,' let them keep on living in that giant, empty house my sister had to have a fulltime housekeeper to take care of. Cooks in the kitchen. You can do that. And you want to. Because they're your niece and nephew. Okay. *Capiche.* That's great. But let me tell you something. I was in their will, listed as their guardian. *I* was. I, who work from home, at something stable. Sutton knew what they would need, and she knew I could give it to them here. Where she herself grew up. It's quiet, it's—" She shakes her head with a look of disgust. "I don't have to sell you on this. You don't have to understand. I get it, it's not San Francisco. Thank God."

She laughs, like she knows some kind of private joke, like the Bay is going to be leveled by an asteroid in an hour.

"You can visit them," she offers. "If you stay in your lane and out of mine. They'll be back later. They're at a...thing. You can visit any time you like if you can be polite and respect me. But otherwise?" She shakes her head, her slender jaw hard. "Get back in that fancy car of yours and go back where you're from. And take your judging with you."

I'm not letting this end here. "What am I judging, with an offer of helping you out?" I ask, being completely disingenuous.

"See!" She throws her arms up. "That's it. 'Helping me out.' I don't need your *help*. Why do you think I would?"

"Oh, I don't know?" I arch a brow. "Your recent acquisition of two young children?"

"Acquisition!" She laughs, but it's derisive. "Of course to *you* that's what it is."

"It's a word," I say sharply. "I used it correctly."

"Yeah, well, I'm great with kids. I'm a kid person. In fact, I always wanted children."

"Are you married?"

She pops her eyes like she's surprised I asked, then quickly says, "It doesn't matter."

"Do you have a boyfriend? Or a girlfriend?"

I can see surprise cross her face. "Not a girlfriend, no. A boyfriend

—" She shakes her head, one brow lifting as, again, she gives me a censuring look. "That's not any of your business."

"So you do." I smirk. "Is he good with children? It takes patience."

She laughs like she thinks I'm crazy. "I never said I have a boyfriend, first off. But if I did, it wouldn't matter. I'm their guardian, so they come first."

"And the farm?" I say it softly—playing a card.

"What about it?" She knows I know. I can tell she does, because her face takes on a look of bareness, that sweet, soft mouth of hers going softer.

"What if you don't make it?"

"Make what?" But she understands. Again, it's all there on her face, which has gone hard and cold.

"What if the bank gets the farm?"

Fury twists her pretty features. "Just who do you think you are? You don't know anything about my life. My family's farm. You don't know anything about us! You should leave now." She walks forward, which forces me to take a few steps back.

"It's a reasonable question," I say, now standing in the screen porch doorway. "Will you have to move them? Uproot them again?"

"That is *not* going to happen!" She folds her arms, her chest heaving. "This farm is just fine, thank you very much. It's a better life here than that cesspool you call home, with all the drugs and the garbage in the streets and the nobody giving a horse's rear end about what happens to any of it, least of all you! You didn't even come to their funeral! Who are you to come down here and tell me what for!"

"Tell you what for?" It's so damn funny, I'm near laughing.

She gives me a death glare. "Don't make fun of me because you're unimaginative and like to use foul language."

"Who said I like to use foul language?"

She shoots me a yeah-right kind of look. "I know your type the second that I seem them."

"Second that you see 'em, eh?"

She nods. "Condescending, rude, presumptive."

"I believe the word you're looking for is *presumptuous*."

"I believe the word I used is just fine."

"Say that again. Say 'fine.'" I drag the word out the way she does, with her twangy accent.

Her eyes glitter, and I think I see her swallow. "You're a bully."

"I want what's going to be best for my niece and nephew. Nothing more and nothing less."

Her jaw hardens. "I'm good with them—and for them. I'm like their mother. Their mother was my sister. I'm familiar, and I've got a good home for them here."

My pulse kicks up a notch. Now she's second-guessing herself, softening. Now's the time to go for the jugular.

"I see an untenable situation. Where's the crops here? Where's the cattle? What about school?"

"They're enrolled at school."

"What school?"

"The one their mama went to," she says in a hard tone.

I feign shock. "You don't mean the *local* school?"

"The local school, yes. It's a wonderful establishment."

"It's got subpar ratings. Something like a C- on those school rating sites. I looked."

"No it—"

"*Yes*. It does. They'll never get into college from there."

"They—"

"And who will study with them?" I ask.

"I will."

Her cheeks are red now, so I know she's good and pissed off.

"Did you go to college, June?"

"I don't think that's—"

"Any of my business? No, I'm sure you don't, because you didn't. What about high school?" Her face pales. "How can you educate them if you yourself aren't educated? That's a valid question."

"Oh, you know what is a valid question?" She steps closer, her face mannequin still. "I'll tell you a valid question."

She slaps me so hard and fast, I never see it coming. I'm holding my throbbing cheek right after, gaping at her through my fingers.

"The question is, who's gonna believe I slapped you? Eh?" She jabs my chest with one finger, and I step backward down the screened porch steps. June whirls on her heel and stalks into the house's door.

I laugh, a harsh, low sound. Then I turn toward my car. "I'm gonna make you pay for that, sweetheart."

CHAPTER 4

JUNE

He's an awful man. Just terrible.

He must have more money than God, because it's only two and a half hours later that the first of his *retaliations* shows up on my porch. Someone he paid. I know it must be, because the devil drove up in a fancy sports car, but the person who drops it off is in a truck.

By the time I reach one of the front windows, I see an F-250's taillights glowing in a dust cloud that's tinged orange like the sun-streaked sky. Whoever it was left a cardboard box. I hear it whining as I step outside.

"Oh no he didn't..."

But he did. That mothertrucker left a trucking puppy at my house—or, rather, he paid someone to. There's a note taped to the box.

Oliver and Margot, I came for a visit. You weren't here, but that's okay. I'll come see you tomorrow. I'll bring a surprise. This is my surprise for tonight. They are AKC registered German Shepherd puppies. What are you going to name them? One girl, one boy—just like you.

Love, Uncle Burke

What the mothertrucking truckness is this?

I open the box with my jaw on the floor, and there they are. I pick one up, and then the other.

"Oh my gosh, you're butterballs, aren't you? Barely old enough to leave your mama. Who is mama? Who around here has a litter of pups?"

Oh, they're so sweet. I lift one up to my face and sniff the puppy scent.

"You have two big doggo siblings. And a human brother and sister. Who will be so excited...if I keep you. Should I keep you, though?"

I set the pups back in the box and drag it over by the door that leads into the living room. Then I go in, shut my big dogs in the laundry room with treats, and bring the pups into my living room.

"I'm gonna kill him. Yes I am," I puppy talk them. "It'll be murder."

They're so precious. Their little ears are sort of soft and floppy. Their sweet noses are all warm and damp. I set them on the rug before I think about it, and they bound around the living room.

"Dangit! Don't pee!" Just as I catch one of them and lift the puppy to my chest, he or she does just that—pees all over me. I look at my phone, over on an end table. I don't have his number, do I?

I text Leah instead.

LEAH. Come now!! I need you!!! (If you can't, it's okay, it's just a puppy crisis).

PUPPY?!?

Come, I tell her.

I take the puppies out to potty. So nice of Dickwad to buy supplies for them. The pups bound down the steps, and that's when I spot their stuff in the yard. Crates, collars...all of it.

So what?

He's still a dickwad.

I get them collared and leashed, and by some miracle, they seem to know it's time to potty. When they're finished, I grab a pack of pee pads from the pile of supplies and spread one in the screened-in porch. If I don't want to keep the pups, I'll need to send them off with Leah before the kids get home from community center art class at 6:45 PM.

If I send them off, he might tell the kids I did. He wouldn't do that, though, would he? I don't know him.

I check my phone for a text from Leah. Instead, there's one from an unknown number.

What do you think, Mama? You can handle four, so what's two more?

He knows about my other dogs? How creepy.

You have problems, I say.

Only one, he replies.

I hate you.

I can be gone tomorrow. All I need is two small humans.

Dream on. I do have two small doggos you can take, though. Two doggos for one son of a bitch.

I'll give you two mil.

My stomach rolls. *You're really trying to buy the kids? That's disgusting.*

Puppy piss on your clothes is disgusting.

I suck a breath in, then look through the screens out at the night. *Are you watching me right now?*

Bwahaha. Just a lucky guess. Did one of them really get you?

Should I be scared of him? *Is* he watching right now? Maybe he's unstable. He must be reading my mind because he texts, *If you really did get pissed on, don't be freaked out. I didn't know that. I'm in Albany right now.*

He shares his location with me, and I feel a tinge better.

Drive right on back up to Atlanta and get on your plane, I tell him.

I'll see you tomorrow, June Bug.

I'll be sure to take them fishing. All day.

🐾

BURKE

It's true that I'm in Albany, but not to stay the night, as I'm sure she assumes. Heat Springs has the shittiest 4G anywhere I've been inside the continental U.S.

I've got a mountain of work to do, and I can't do it via ESP. So here I am—in Mama G's Coffee & Biscuits, a freakishly quiet little place on Albany's Main Street. There's an apron-clad high school guy behind the counter and a bunch of little orange booths with no one in them. Except me.

The internet here isn't great either. Gabe is having a coding issue, and he and I are working on it in tandem, so I need a healthy internet connection. I've just gotten into a flow with the work when a bell dings. I lift my head and look around.

The high school guy with the floppy black hair nods my way. "Sir, we're closing."

"What?"

He points to something I can't see from where I'm seated—presumably the hours posted on the door. "We close at nine."

"Dammit," I mutter. *Seriously?*

I scoop my laptop up and rise from the booth. "Where else in this town has reliable internet?"

"There's a bookstore that has coffee, too, out on the main drag. It's called Pages. They're open until 9:30 or 10. I think it's 10."

I get in my car, order a satellite modem like the one I took to India, and pay over the phone and through the nose to have it delivered to Pages. The courier will have to drive down from a southern suburb of Atlanta.

When the modem arrives an hour and a half later, I get in the car and drive back to the one-room cabin I rented on some wooded acreage just outside of Heat Springs.

As soon as Gabe and I think we've got the mess untangled and I hop into the shower, he calls to tell me the voice recognition company that's working on the voluntary monitoring part of the app has run into a problem that's ultimately on our end. By the time Gabe and I have got it figured out, the sun is coming up.

I make some coffee with a hunter green Keurig on the counter and step outside onto the back porch—made from the same dark-stained wood as the cabin's exterior walls. A stiff breeze ruffles the needles on the tall pines. I watch a black bird fly from tree to tree. A raven? I don't know what birds are what. I sort of wish I did, but that's a little pointless. When would I ever need to know?

I step back inside and check on Gabe's screen. Everything still looks good. I can see him scrolling through the work we did. Work I hope will translate into lives saved one day. I don't care how hard I have to push to get this app on people's phones or how much money it takes. To me, it's worth it.

I take a few deep breaths and then remember my suitcase is in the car's trunk. I haul it inside, set it on the twin bed opposite my own, and pull some clothes out. I packed like I was headed to the east coast, not the South. It seems the clothes I have are quite a bit too warm for Georgia, even in the winter season.

I slough off the dress pants I pulled on commando after showering earlier and pull on clean boxer-briefs and a different pair of black jeans. I've never worn them, didn't even buy them—I pay Molly to do my shopping—but they're my normal brand; they fit fine, maybe a little loose, although they're my size.

I pull a thin gray sweater over my head and pluck it off my abs. Fuck, this thing is tight. I move the shirt around and check the tag. It's a medium. I check my bag. Did she order all these new shirts in size medium?

Yep.

Nice.

I'm six-foot-one and fairly lean, but I've got big bones. I smirk in the mirror and shake my head. I look like a fucking yuppie in this tight-ass, thin wool sweater.

Well, you are a fucking yuppie.

I'm sure June will think so. Not that she looked the part of a "farm girl" either. She looked like any girl. Correction: any hot girl. She's not really a girl, I guess, though, is she? I think of what I know about her, from the dead mom to her lack of high school diploma.

"You don't know anything about my life. My family's farm. You don't know anything about us!"

Doesn't fucking matter. I don't need to.

I text Gabe and check in with Molly and call Richard, who functions a little like a chief operating officer when I'm away.

"What's it like down there?" he asks. "The land?"

Oh, right. I told him I was here to look at land—for an investment.

"Looks good," I lie. "Dirt cheap."

"Far from Atlanta?"

"Nah, not very."

"When're you going to get down there to do the hunting?"

Hunting? Oh—I guess he thinks that's why I want the land.

"I'll take off time when the app is functioning cohesively."

He laughs. "That'll be at least two years, with all the moving parts we've got. Too bad fucking Gurung won't buy in. He's got some of that infrastructure that could really expedite this."

"No shit."

I ask the questions I called to ask Aes' very own Captain Obvious and smirk to myself as I make one final phone call, letting the company I booked with know that I still need their services this morning.

"What time would you like it set up?"

"Hmm, let's say in about an hour?"

"At the address we have on file?" the woman asks.

"Yep."

"Thank you, sir," she says. "You have yourself a nice mornin' and we'll see you then."

"Perfect."

I grin, then give a low laugh, feeling pleased with myself. I can't wait to see June's face when she gets her eyes on this.

The dirt road from my rented cabin to the nearby county road is fucking jarring on the car. Rocks pop up against its underbelly and a hazy dust cloud rises up around it. I grip the wheel and turn the radio down, stealing glances at the woods around me. These tall, skinny pine trees aren't as picturesque as the east coast with a coat of autumn or the snow-slung evergreens out west, but there's a kind of magic to them. Understated, maybe you would call it. Doesn't feel like anywhere special, I decide as I turn left onto the narrow, paved road; its faded asphalt is veined by cracks.

You could see a murder happening out here. I glance up at the blue sky, pale with white clouds peeking in between the walls of pines on both sides of the little road.

Maybe crazy shit happens in a place like this, but you can kind of see things going the other way, too. Maybe this place *is* a place that people love, despite its lack of everything.

Maybe all the things it doesn't have are things nobody really needs. I wonder if Heat Springs has things like food delivery and laundry service. I try to imagine going to some job here—the farm supply store or the police station. Or maybe doing carpentry. I bet they always have a need for that in parts like these. And what about June? What the hell is her day-to-day like? By herself out in that little farmhouse. Does that make her happy?

I remind myself that I don't care. June is no one to me. After I take Margot and Oliver back home, she'll be someone I see once or twice a year at most. And I *will* take them back with me.

I know I can make her see things my way. I just have to get her past that bite of horror she felt when I mentioned giving her money in exchange for guardian rights. To someone like her, it probably sounds sinful. Maybe even like a lie. But I'll show her that it isn't. I'm going to show her today that I'm a cool dude, that Oliver and Margot know me—

probably better than they know her—and I have all the money needed to make them happy. Plus some for her.

There's nothing wrong with needing help, and I'm a helpful guy. She'll see. I turn onto the dirt road that leads toward her house, and there's a dust cloud right in front of me. I think the evidence of how fun I am is en route to her house, just like I am.

CHAPTER 5

JUNE

Should I go for the satisfaction of a hands-on killing—maybe good old-fashioned strangulation—or will this be a hit job for the sake of the kids? Either way, I'm going to have to kill him. Burke Masterson is going down town Charlie Brown—something that my mother used to say when we were kids, though I have no idea why. What was Charlie Brown going to do to us once we got downtown? Or were we going downtown *like* Charlie Brown? Did he go downtown a lot? I know surprisingly little about the famous comic strip star.

Whatever. It doesn't matter. What matters is that Burke *sucks*.

I narrow my eyes at the scene before me—a scene in which his suckage is at center stage. Burke is sitting on a mossy rock below a pecan tree in my front yard. Mario and Peach, the puppies, bound around his black-jean-clad legs and shiny new black leather boots, while Oliver and Margot the humans climb all over his broad back and shoulders, frolicking around him like sad orphans who just found the family member they like best. Which is exactly what they are—maybe.

I blow a breath out. Covertly, of course. I can't have Mr. Masterson glancing over here and seeing how annoyed I am. And conflicted. But mostly annoyed. You see, the frolicking is taking place about ten feet from the *monstrosity* Burke had set up on my lawn: a massive, Super Mario-themed bounce house, rented from a blow-up bounce house company in Atlanta.

He rented a bounce house for *my* lawn *two days ago* from his lair in

San Francisco. And unless I throw a giant shit fit, it's going to be here killing the grass for three more days. I would have never let the company set the damn thing up, but we weren't here when they arrived. The kids and I had driven to the fire station to grab some fresh fruit from the farmer's market.

When we spotted the thing—from way back at the end of the driveway—Oliver recognized it right away. Apparently it's a Bowser castle. Bowser is a villain, Oliver said, so at least Burke got that part right.

The worst part of all of this is that despite the bouncy house right there in plain sight, the kids have been glued to Burke since they leapt from the car and raced toward him. It's awkward, and it's worrying. What if they actually want to go home with him?

I've been staring at their frolic-fest for probably what feels like eternity, and I can't even hate him properly because he's so attractive. He looks like an Instagram model posing for a dad-themed photo shoot.

Not that I would ever follow male models on Instagram—especially not the gorgeous, statuesque foreign ones from far-flung places like Milan and Hamburg and Johannesburg. But if I *did* do that, I might think he looked just like one with those sleek black boots, his slightly snug black jeans, and an even more snug gray wool sweater.

It's not a regular sweater. It's thinner, more like a shirt, and I can tell from looking at it that it cost a lot. You can just tell when something's well-made—even when you don't know that the person in it is worth like nine gamillion dollars.

Yeah. So he *is* rich. I knew he was some kind of tech smarty, but I didn't know just how successful my new arch nemesis really is until I did some web browsing this morning. Apparently the villain Mr. Masterson has started and sold two startups already, and is working on a third one, financed mostly by him.

The tall, dark, slightly scruffy male-model knockoff occupying my mossy rock and wrestling with my charges is worth a screaming 120 million dollars.

So he's ridiculously wealthy, enviably smart, *and* he's clearly good with children. I was skeptical, based on his absence at the funeral and his absolute asshole act when he knocked on my door yesterday. But it seems crystal clear now that the kids adore him.

I chew the inside of my cheek—the cheek angled *away* from him.

He lifts his head, laughing at Margot's tickles—which I know from experience are a lot more like pinches, so he's probably impervious to pain like the super-villain he is—and his gaze catches mine. He looks radiant. Like he's waited his whole life for this one shining moment. Like Margot and Oliver are all he needs to live his best life. I lift a brow and try to smile when our eyes lock, but I'm ninety-nine percent sure it comes off as a grimace.

When we rolled up a few minutes ago and the kids first ran to tackle hug him, he smiled at me as he wrapped them in his muscled arms. It was a *gotcha* smile, an I-took-over-your-lawn smile. A this-is-what-my-money-can-buy, and-it-can-buy-you-too smile.

So yeah. When he looks at me again a second or two later, still wrestling with the kids, I give him the full scowl he deserves. I can be civil when the kids are looking, but right now they're climbing on him.

Burke winks at me.

The mothertrucker winks. As if he thinks I think he's charming or attractive.

I arch a brow. *Nope. I don't.*

He grins as he tickles Oliver, and it's a wicked, evil grin. *I know*, it says. *And I love it that you hate me. I'm a villain, so this is my version of fun.*

Fuck villains, I say with my face. *But not literally.*

He heard my freaking thought. He smirks as if he means to tell me, *yeah, I know you want it*, and he winks again. That freak!

I stand up...because I can't just sit here all day. I stride over to the bounce house, and the kids scamper over behind me.

"Look, you guys!" I wave at its arched entrance. "Uncle Burke and I rented this castle for you!"

Now it's my turn to flash a villain's smile his way.

"Are you our *uncle?*" Margot asks, frowning up at him.

Burke laughs, a husky sound. He swipes a hand back through his wavy, dark hair. "Of course I'm your uncle, silly."

"How come we don't call you uncle?" Oliver asks.

"I don't know." But I can tell from his face that he's lying. I smile down at Oliver.

"Sometimes, people don't like to be called uncle if it makes them feel *old.*"

A notch appears between Oliver's eyebrows. "'Burke' sounds like

maybe he could just be your buddy. Uncle means he's old enough to be
—" Your dad, I almost say, but stop myself. "Your uncle."

Margot smiles up at Burke. "You *are* old! You're as old as Santa." She
says it matter-of-fact like, with a cute little grin, then shrugs and disappears into the castle.

Oliver follows.

I stare at the air-inflated castle wall for half a second, then take a few
steps back so I can pretend to focus on the kids; I can see them jumping
through a mesh spot on the wall.

"Santa does bring all the toys, huh?" he says.

I lift a brow, not taking my eyes off the kids.

"I'm not sure if you're aware," I lower my voice. "But that's a myth.
For children?" I smirk his way. "It's actually the children's *guardian* who
does that."

He steps closer to me. "And you want that to be you, huh? You're
the new Santa?"

I nod, not looking at his devil face. "I'm the new Santa."

"I could buy them this, you know." He steps closer, so close I can
feel the heat of his big body. "I could put this in the backyard of their
old house. More than one of them."

"Because what children need is extravagant toys. That solves every
problem."

"It doesn't, but you know what does?" he asks me.

"Benjis and sports cars?"

"No," he deadpans. "Therapy. It's expensive, and it's hard to find a
good psychologist unless you're in a bigger city. I could do that,
though."

"Oh, yes, I have full confidence that you could pick a qualified therapist for children."

"I could read reviews, June."

It's the first time he's ever used my name. I swallow.

"They won't need a therapist if they have someone present for them.
Someone who spends time with them." I can't believe I'm doing this—
that I'm arguing about this with him. "I'll be here daily. I practically
never travel. If I do, it's to the beach with family. I'm a good cook, and
I'll offer them a stable home."

"If you let them come back with me, you could pay the bank loan
back on this place."

I blow out a breath and cover my face. "And just why would you do that, hmm?"

"I want them in San Francisco. I want them to have the life my brother would have wanted."

Anger tightens my throat. "What about the life my sister wanted?"

"She was raising them in California."

"Yes, because your brother had to move back there!"

Oliver's giggle interrupts us, and I realize he is hanging from the mesh wall, watching us. And listening, I realize when he shouts, "I don't have a brother, silly goose!"

My face heats up. "No, of course not. But *I* do! Your Uncle Shawn. Did you know you're going to meet him *tonight*?"

He frowns. "We have an Uncle Shawn?"

"Yep, just like Uncle Burke here. But Uncle Shawn has big trucks. Giant ones. Sometime soon, he'll let you get into one."

"I want to get in," Margot says. She's crouched beside her brother now, peeking at us through the mesh wall.

"Tonight, we're going to the rodeo. And Uncle Shawn will sit with you. He used to ride on bulls, but now he's retired, so he just sits in the stands."

"Where will you be?" Burke asks.

I smile. "On my horse."

CHAPTER 6

BURKE

She rides a horse? I guess should have known, but I'm surprised to hear her say it.

"Where's the horse?" I ask.

"In the barn."

"Where's the barn?"

She gives me a look that screams *city slicker*. "Behind the house."

"I want to meet him!" Margot bounces toward the castle's exit. A second later, she's pulling her shoes on, and Oliver is doing jumping jacks beside her.

"Can we see him now?"

"Sure," June says. She keeps her gaze away from my face, like she's trying to pretend I'm not here. "If you want to," she tells Oliver.

"Can I ride him?" Margot asks.

"I don't know." June looks thoughtful. "He has to race tonight, but maybe you could ride him around my little dirt track one time. Would y'all like to do that?"

Both kids answer with screams of glee. June turns to me with a wide-eyed, arched-brow look, as if she's trying to say, *Okay, time for you to go.*

I smile. "What's the horse's name? I want to meet him, too."

Her lips press into a thin, annoyed line.

"Hot Rocket," Ollie says, holding his arms out airplane-style and then pretending to take flight.

"Hot Rocket, huh?"

"I didn't name him," June mutters.

I turn to her, pleased that she's addressing me. "What would you have picked?"

She scrunches her nose and gives sort of a huff. "Anything but that."

Hot Rocket. And then it hits me. "That wasn't his *original* name, was it?"

Her face reddens as we start to walk after the kids, so I know I'm on the right track. "Was it...Crotch Rocket?" I murmur. "Hmm?"

She gives me a death glare. "Like those motorcycles," I say, grinning. That is so damn funny.

"Yes," she says dryly. "Some fool redneck named him Crotch Rocket."

"Hey, they're fast."

"He's fast," she affirms.

"Is he? He's a race horse?"

"He's a horse who races," she says, striding out ahead of me as the kids disappear around the side of the house.

"Same thing," I say.

"Not so much. He's not an income earner with me. I just ride for fun."

We jog after the kids for a moment, and I try not to look at her ass. It's an amazing ass. I focus instead on her ponytail. "Slow down now," she shouts at the kids. "We're old folks." She cuts her eyes at me. "One of us is."

"Hey, I'm still in my prime."

She snorts.

Oliver turns around to look at us, and he and Margot start to walk backward. "Are you riding in a rodeo tonight?" Oliver asks.

She gives him a small smile. "Something like that."

"What do you guys think?" I ask the kids. "I think we'll have to go and watch her."

"Yesss!" Margot says.

June shoots me a look of loathing.

"What? We want to cheer you on, Aunt June."

"I'm not your Aunt June." She gives me a baleful look. It makes me grin. "Okay, June. You know, I heard it's actually June *Bug.*"

"Doesn't have the ring that Burke Bug does," she claps back.

Again, I give a hoot of laughter. "I'm more of a stallion."

I'm going for ridiculous, but she won't even crack a small smile. June rolls her eyes, pulls her hair from its ponytail, and tosses the thick locks over her shoulder.

"Is that right?" she says, sounding dry and unimpressed.

"I can ride, too, you know."

"Oh, can you. You take some fancy lessons?"

"Like the kids here."

"That's...so wonderful," she says, her tone syrupy as we continue walking after the kids.

"We ride horses out in California, too."

She looks at me, and I can't read her face. "You want to ride Hot Rocket?"

"Sure."

She strides ahead of me as the kids crest a little hill, approaching a big, red barn. "Sounds like a plan."

From the outside, the barn looks about the size of your average roller skating rink. It's got a gray tin roof, the classic-looking double doors on one side, and a little round hole by the doors. The round hole, near the bottom of the barn's external wall, and some of the lawn around it are surrounded by wire fencing.

June stops by the fencing, makes a clucking sound, and chickens start to march out. They gather along the fence, and I watch June's face spread into a big grin.

"Hi there! Cinderella...Snow White...Ariel...Moana...Sleeping Beauty...Elsa...Anna...Rapunzel." She holds her hand open, facing the kids. "Hold your hands out and I'll give you some feed to sprinkle in there with them."

Margot squeals. "They like me!" The birds squawk and scatter at her delight.

"You scared the chickens," Oliver says, giving her a glare.

"It's okay. Just throw this in. There are some roosters, too." They come out on cue. "That's Aladdin and Peter Pan," she tells them, pointing out each rooster.

For the next few minutes, I watch as she explains the birds' quirks to Oliver and Margot.

"This one here, Elsa—she likes to be held. Do you want to see me hold her?"

It's a fucking treat to watch June scoop the little chicken up. She holds her hands out, palms spread, like she's miming a bird, and Elsa the mostly white chicken scrambles over. June seals her hands around Elsa and then quickly brings the bird against her chest.

"Do you want to know why she likes this? Because Elsa is a rescued chicken. She was my first chicken. She was raised since she was tiny by an older woman nearby who really liked to hold her. So when that woman...couldn't care for her any more, I took her."

I'd be willing to bet the woman died, based on June's face when she said it. But the kids don't bat an eye. Eventually, they both hold Elsa. Then June leads us inside, to a stable that has eight stalls.

"At certain times, we've had more horses. My grandmother's sister, who's in heaven now, had this place built. She loved to breed race horses. That was a long time ago," she adds with a small frown, which she quickly covers with a smile. "Hot Rocket is down here..."

And like his owner, the old boy is damned beautiful. He's black-brown, with healthy muscle and a shiny coat. Looks like he's maybe a quarter horse.

As soon as we get within his range of vision, he steps over to the rail, and June feeds him something from her pocket.

"What was that?" Margot asks.

June grins. "He likes raisins." From this angle, I can see she has a little dimple on her left cheek. She swipes her hair back from her face and pulls it up into a hair band she's been wearing around her wrist. Then she digs more raisins from her pocket.

"He really likes those?" Oliver asks, wrinkling his little freckled nose.

"Oh yes. He would eat them all day, wouldn't you, Hottie?"

The kids pet him and June shows them how to feed him raisins from an upturned palm. I watch from behind them, thinking she looks more content than she has since I met her. After that, she sends us out to walk around the track while she fusses over the stallion and saddles him up. When she and Hot Rocket stroll out, Margot and Oliver flip a coin, and Margot gets to go first.

June grins as she leads our niece around the track. *Our* niece. That's weird. But accurate. The weirder thing is me trying not to look at Auntie June's ass in those leggings she's got on today. I'm finding that it tends to be her ass I get hung up on—that or her smile. Woman's nothing like I expected.

In a few minutes, she, Margot, and Hot Rocket are back beside me. June helps a beaming Margot down and waves Oliver over.

"I got it." I grab him by the hips and lift him up into the saddle, and Oliver tips a pretend hat at me. "Thank yeh suuuur."

"Yes, sir, my pleasure."

June rolls her eyes. Then she pulls the elastic band out of her hair, puts it between her teeth, and starts to fuck with it. Even her hair's abnormally pretty—sort of golden. With her smooth, tanned skin and those brown eyes with little gold specs—

I divert my eyes down to my boots.

When I look up, she's still at it. I frown.

"Braiding," she says. "Have you heard of braids, Burke Bug?"

The kids giggle at that. I roll my eyes at her like she just did at me.

"Maybe on"—I wave my hand, searching for the word— "on little dolls. Are you a doll, June?"

I add some innuendo just to irritate her and am rewarded with a puritanical widening of her eyes.

"Not so much." She shifts her attention to Oliver. "I'm going to walk you around. This is just to get you used to his rhythm and pacing. We don't want to tire him out. Does that work for you?"

Does that work for you? I don't know a hell of a lot about kids, but I don't think you ask them if something works for them. My thoughts must be painted on my face, because she gives me a covert *"what?"* look.

I flash her a phony smile. *Go and start walking him around the track, sweetheart. Let me see the back of that fine braid there.*

I smirk as she passes.

She sighs like she can feel my eyes on her ass.

"Aunt June is silly when you're here. I like that." I look down at Margot. Her hair is in pigtailed braids, too, I realize. She's smiling up at me angelically.

"I forgot you were there, kid."

"I'm sneaky like that." Her smile widens. She looks so peaceful and content right now. It's almost impossible to believe she just lost both parents. Six is a better age than nine, though. Maybe she'll fare better than I did.

I give her cheek a soft pinch. "How ya doing, kiddo? What do you think of Aunt June's farm?"

"It's my farm now." She lifts her chin a little.

My stomach gets that topsy-turvy feeling. "Is it?"

"Yeah. I'm just gonna be a cowgirl." She shrugs, and I can't help laughing.

"Are you?"

She shields her eyes with one hand and looks out at the woods surrounding the field we're in. "It's a little hot here, but I like the big trees. And I like Aunt June, and her chickens. Do you?" She frowns up at me.

"Do I like the chickens?"

"Do you like Aunt June." She rolls her eyes.

"Yeah. Oh yeah. I like her."

"I don't know if she likes you. Maybe." She shrugs, looking contemplative.

Then she wraps an arm my leg, below the knee. I touch her hair and try to swallow, which is suddenly harder than normal.

"I miss Mommy," she whispers.

I suck a breath in.

"Why can't I see her?" Her voice cracks, and I bite the inside of my cheek and squeeze my eyes shut for a second. "I just want to see her one more time."

She sniffs, and my eyes throb as I grit my teeth. Then Hot Rocket is bounding toward us. Oliver is laughing, and June's running beside him.

I wrap an arm around Margot's back and hug her little body to me.

"I'm sorry," I manage. It's inadequate, I know, but I'm not sure what else to say. "Hey...you want to see some cool tricks?"

She looks up at me, wiping her eyes, and nods solemnly.

I give her a wink then stride over to lift Oliver off the horse.

"Nicely done, my little dude." I mount the horse and give June a grin when I'm up in the saddle. "What do you think? Trust me to give him a whirl without an escort?"

June's flawless face is wary, her eyes held wide in that irritated way.

"Stay on this track," she warns. "Don't try the jump course." She points to the course, which, like the barn, is up atop the little hill. It's closer to the woods, though, and I'm surprised to find that it looks pretty advanced. June must be an accomplished rider. "Hot Rocket is sort of a one-person horse," she warns me. "I know all his quirks, and I know how to manage him."

"Is the course safe?" I ask. "In good condition?"

"Well, yeah."

"Is he?"

She looks annoyed—a state I seem to bring out in her. "I said he's racing *tonight*, didn't I?"

"Good." I wink. "Then we'll manage."

I take off, trotting at first, sizing up the course that's separated from this dirt track by maybe twenty yards of dry grass. It's legit, but nothing I can't manage. I've been riding since I turned three.

I board my horses at some stables near Moss Beach. I don't get by there as much as I did before phase two of this app started kicking my ass, so the rest of the time, my mares participate in a program that helps disabled kids. Works out for everybody.

It's kind of dickish to take Hot Rocket through the jumps course without doing whatever warmup he's used to, but he seems pretty chill, and I want to amuse Margot. It's not like I'm going to fuck this up. I'll take it slow, and we'll both be fine.

I go extra easy the first time around. There are a couple doubles and triples, a ditch obstacle, a log fence, and a bunch of barrels toward the course's rear, which I avoid.

In my periphery, I can see June and the kids rushing over. I give the kids a hoot and a wave, and Hot Rocket and I start through the course a second time. I don't want to tire the guy out, so I tell myself we'll stick to three times around.

He's a talented dude. We get good clearance on the rails and sail over the log fence. He doesn't hesitate either time for the ditch, so by the time we come up on the barrels, I decide to go for it.

Barrel racing isn't something I've done much of, but I've done it on a few courses, mostly at summer camps. Right before we reach the first one, I nudge him with my heel.

Normally that gives a horse a little jolt of speed, but Hot Rocket takes it as a cue to blastoff. He lurches forward so fast my ass comes off the saddle. As he whips around the first barrel, I tighten up and move with him. We fly around the next two barrels, and there's two more. I get a hamstring cramp just in time for him to jerk left around one of them—*hard*.

I don't expect to fall. The only time I've ever toppled off a horse's back, I was fourteen and at camp and standing in the saddle like a jackass.

It happens so fast, I can't process. One minute, I'm cringing from the hammy cramp. The next, I'm eating dirt. I blow like a light bulb for a second, opening my eyes to the sensation that I can't breathe. Knocked the wind out of myself. I get a gasped breath just as my head starts going hazy. I push myself up on one arm.

Fuck. My shoulder zings when I move, and my head…really hurts. A wave of nausea prickles through me, so strong that I think I might get sick. Then there's Oliver and Margot. June is dropping down beside me.

Her eyes are huge, and the kids—behind her—look like they might cry. Somehow, I make it to my feet and spread my arms.

"So what'd you think?" I look at Margot.

She looks horror-stricken. I laugh—which makes my head throb. "Did you like my trick?"

The kids look at each other, skeptical and seeking clarity. June frowns deeply.

I grin, and she gives me a what-the-fuck look that's so damning, I can't help another laugh.

Shit. I wince, and she steps closer to me. Her hand reaches out, her soft fingers touching my forehead before I can jerk away. "You've got a shiner coming up there."

In a low hiss, she adds, "What were you thinking?"

I frown like I'm confused. "I don't know what you're talking about."

"I asked you not to ride him over here."

"Say that again."

Her eyes are warm on mine—too warm, so I give her a smirk. "Say what again?"

Oliver helps her out: *"Raaaaahde,"* he mimics with a delighted smile.

She rolls her eyes—at me, not him. "You're totally ridiculous." Her dark brows draw together. "Are you really okay? You look a little bit dazed."

I move my hand over my eyes, which are still throbbing and feel sore with sunlight in them.

"I'm fine. That was just the trick I promised Margot."

Behind June, my niece giggles.

"I think he *fell* off," Oliver says.

56

I lean around June so I can see him better. "What?" I act offended. "Me? Fall off a *horse?*"

While I'm not looking, June wraps her hand partway around my wrist and tries to tug my hand off my eyes. I grin when I realize that her little fingers won't fit around my arm.

She gives me a death glare. "What now?"

"What now?" I laugh—or start to, but I stop myself because I know it'll hurt. "Am I such a pain in your ass?" I say it quietly, so the kids won't hear the bad word.

She widens her eyes, clearly incredulous. "Is that even an actual question?"

I give her a for-shame frown. "You don't mean the gifts I've sent?"

"Oh yeah, the *gifts.*" She rolls her eyes again. "In fact." She looks over her shoulder. "I bet your *gifts* are peeing on my porch this very second."

She looks behind me, and I turn around, too. Hot Rocket is standing just a few feet away, looking at us with his somber eyes like he's sorry I fell.

"I get the rocket part," I mutter.

"You were riding like an idiot," June hisses.

"I was riding like someone who doesn't know they're on a barrel racer. That's what he is, isn't it?"

"I tried to tell you to be careful, that he was a one-woman horse. It's not my fault you're afflicted with Male Ego Syndrome."

The kids dash off, checking out the jump course, so I'm able to speak louder when I say, "Oh, c'mon, is that the best that you can do? Male ego?"

"If it walks like a duck, tries to mansplain like a duck, and falls on its ass like a duck, then maybe it's a man with a big, stupid man ego."

I let out a low whistle. "What chapped your ass—or *who?*"

She sniffs. "Nobody did. I stick in my little corner of the world and they all stick in theirs. I don't have time for bullshit."

"That sounds awfully bitter, Miss Lawler."

She steps away from me before I get the chance to ask who made her bitter. "Oliver and Margot?" she says into cupped hands. "Can y'all walk over to the house and let the puppies out to potty?"

Oliver nods.

Margot frowns. "Are you sure you're okay, Burke? You've got a bump on your head. It's a little purple." Little sounds like *wittle*.

"I'm all good, sweetheart." I wink, and she smiles like she knows it's bullshit. "Don't get back on him," she tells me sternly.

"Promise."

She nods like she's satisfied and follows her brother toward the house.

I arch a brow at June. "You think they're okay to go alone?"

"What? All of a hundred yards to the house? What do you think is gonna happen?"

"I don't know. Coyotes?"

"Yeah, they're sleeping. But I hear the snipes are movin' something fierce this time of day." She's smirking, making me want to run my finger over her lip.

"What's a snipe?" I ask.

"Just these wild and crazy critters. Thick hide, got a big snout." She pushes up on the tip of her nose, making a pig face. "Sometimes rise up on their hind legs." She holds her arms out, zombie-style.

I screw my face into a skeptical frown, which makes my damn head hurt. "You're making this shit up."

"Nah. There's snipes all around these parts. I think I'd know." She smirks again before taking the horse's reins and leading him back toward the barn.

Goddamn that ass of hers. It's nearly impossible not to stare. She's got a longer type of blouse on, but it hugs right to her. How the hell did Molly not discover how damn hot she is? I would have changed my plan. In fact...I still can.

"You want me to go to the house with them?" I call.

"I don't care what you do."

"Oh, c'mon. You mad I took a tumble off your barrel racer?"

"I'm annoyed that you were reckless," she shouts, turning partway around. "And a showoff."

"You think I did that shit on purpose?"

"I'm not sure it matters," she says pertly. "You don't think of anybody but yourself."

Even though it's bullshit, it still hits me right in the chest. "I guess you know me pretty well, huh?"

"I know guys like you."

I follow her into the barn and get some water from a sink that doesn't look especially dirty. She leads Hot Rocket back to his stall.

"I'm sorry I trusted you to obey my instructions." She leans down where I can't see her for the stall's wooden gate, probably undoing saddle buckles. "Does your head feel okay?"

"Spinning from those leggings you've got on." I snicker at myself, because—*fuck me*—I didn't mean to say that.

June gives me a withering glare. "Why don't you spin it back to California?"

"I'm not leaving yet."

"What are you waiting for?" She lifts the saddle off, so I can only see her head and shoulders for a moment.

"Those two tiny humans."

"You'll be waiting for a long damn time." I hear the creak of leather as she sets the saddle down. Then she straightens up and tosses me a brush so fast I barely catch it. "You can finish up with him and brush him down after you do."

My gaze clings to her as she saunters out of the stall. "Can this count for a sorry?" I ask.

"Not so much. But it'll pay your ticket to keep loitering around my farm."

I throw my head back on a low laugh and pay the price in pain that splinters through my skull. I grin so she won't notice. "Count your money, darlin'. I'll see you in just a little bit."

When I hear the barn door creak shut, I push my stiff dick down in my jeans and laugh. I've been playing this all wrong. June Bug is no country bumpkin spinster aunt. She's beautiful. Demanding. And discriminating. What I need to do is win her over.

CHAPTER 7

JUNE

He thinks he's funny. Charming. Slick. I bet Burke Masterson is a real lady magnet where he comes from—what with his big pile of money and the fancy cars and schmancy house I'm sure he's living in. No doubt those high-rolling California women love it.

I am not impressed.

I'll admit, I was surprised to find that he can manage my show course. He looked sexy as sin sailing over my rails, every muscle in his big, hard body moving with Hot Rocket's. Then Hottie threw a shoe—something I don't even think Burke realized—and the devil took a tumble.

Okay, being honest, I was even just a little bit impressed with that because of how he tucked and rolled. He still ate dirt, due to the angle of it, but it was an elegant sort of fall—a fall that just screams "I'm athletic."

Then that way he jumped up and tried to play it off? I have to give him credit, he was thinking of the kids, or seemed like he was. But he's a showboat. Clearly. All that arrogance he's shown me since he got here…

Just like almost every man I've ever known—except my Daddy. Mama got a good one in him, and look what happened to him since she passed? He's been damn near crazy, even if he never owns up to it.

So anyway, I know there's good ones, but who needs an arrogant son of a bitch? I don't know who, but it's not me. I don't have time for that stuff, or the energy. I did that once before—tried to be somebody's moon and sun and stars—and let's just say that everybody in the county still remembers how that ended.

I bet he's no different than Lambert was. Probably always wanting everyone to tell him how amazing he is. Mr. Startup...Mr. Richy Rich Guy. Grew up with a silver spoon. That's what I read on Google. More important than all that is what he said to me about the college degree.

Goading me about not finishing high school? That's a douchebag move. I don't make exceptions for a man under duress. I just lost my sister, same as he lost Asher. You don't see me acting like a dick. Okay...well, maybe at times I've been a little bit prickly, but he earned it. Even riding to the jump course when I asked him not to—that's a dick move.

I do hope his head's okay. Would be a shame to ruin something so pretty. But that's crazy talk. I laugh at myself as I pull the porch door open.

I find the kids in the kitchen, having taken the pups out, returned them to the laundry room, and served themselves popsicles.

"Making yourselves right at home the way I want you to." I kiss Oliver's head. "What do you think of those?" I ask, nodding at the Fla-Vor-Ice tubes in their hands.

"They're popsicles in a plastic bag," Margot says.

"Well that's true. All popsicles kind of are, though, aren't they?"

"Not if we make our own at home," she says, taking a bite of her blue popsicle. "That's better for nature."

"Oh, like the environment?"

She nods, and so does Oliver.

"Okay, well, let's do some of those then. I can buy the plastic molding for them next time we go to the Piggly Wiggly."

I get a popsicle for myself and peek out the curtain covering the door that leads onto the screened porch. No Burke in sight, so it's safe to ask them, "What do you think about your uncle showing up?"

"Burke?" Margot asks.

I laugh. "He really doesn't like to be called uncle, does he?"

Oliver shrugs. "He's not old like an uncle."

"Am I old like an aunt?"

The kids shake their heads. Smart kids.

There's a silence, and I feel like I can guess what they're thinking:

Neither of us are as old as their parents. Neither of us is a mama or a daddy for them.

I go stand behind Margot and wrap an arm around her. "You did good on Hottie." I hug Oliver. "So did you, cowboy."

He turns around and looks up at me. "I like that Burke is here. He's funny. Do you think he fell off the horse on purpose?"

I smile. "I think maybe not. But he played it off real well, huh?"

They nod.

"What does your uncle do in San Francisco?" I ask them, blatantly fishing.

"He just works a lot. My mom said like a thousand hours a day." Margot takes an icy bite of popsicle and looks down.

"He does startups, right?" I ask them.

"I don't know what that is," she answers. "He's just working all night and all day. Daddy said he's going to put himself into an early grave. Too much screen time isn't healthy."

I have to work to mask my reaction to that. *Damn, does he work that much?*

"Did he come over sometimes?" I wince as I ask, and wish I could stuff my foot into my mouth. It's not good to ask about their old life— or at least, it shouldn't be done unless the question is important.

"Sometimes," Oliver says. "Like maybe three times."

"When did you see him?"

"We keep our horses at the same place as him. He would take us riding sometimes on Sundays. But that was a long time ago."

"Oh, okay." I file away that nugget of information. "So he's real into horses?"

"*Real* into them," Oliver says with a mischievous grin.

"What do you propose I say other than 'real?'" I ask them, arching my brows.

"You could use the word very. V–E–R–Y." Margot finishes her ice pop and starts to fold the plastic wrapper accordion-style.

"Very?" I say the word as if it's all new to me. "Now that just doesn't feel right."

They both mimic me saying "doesn't," drawing it out so it sounds like *dut-uhn.*

"Thank you for the notice of my accent. I aim to amuse."

"Do you?"

I jump. Burke is standing in the doorway between the kitchen and the dining room.

"Where the Hello Kitty did you come from?"

He gives me an easy smile. "Front door was unlocked."

"I tend to keep it that way."

"Open invitation for those snipes you mentioned."

Both kids whirl around on their barstools with wide eyes. "Snipes?"

"What are snipes?" Oliver asks at the same time Margot says, "Are they bad guys?"

"They're crazy creatures," I tell them, "but they love kids." I toss a glance at Burke before stepping over to the refrigerator. "It's big bullies they come after."

"There's no bullies in here," Oliver says, relieved.

I cut my eyes toward Burke. "I hope not." I hold up an ice pop, then chuck it his way. There's something gratifying about watching him fumble for it. He chuckles, maybe just a little awkward, as he rips it open with his teeth.

"Never use your teeth as tools," I tell the kids, who are both watching.

"That's what Mommy..." Margot trails off. Burke steps up behind her. He drapes his big hand over her small head and ruffles her hair. "You missing your mommy?" he asks, and his low voice sounds so soft and kind.

Margot nods; her face looks like it does before she cries.

"Let me tell you something." He comes around beside her, propping his elbows on the counter's edge and leaning over, looking at both kids. For a second, something tightens his face. Then he locks his handsome features down on neutral.

"My mom went to heaven, too." His voice is steady, but he sucks a breath in after he says it; I can see his nostrils flare. "When I was as old as Oliver. Did you know that?" I see him swallow.

The kids nod, rapt now.

"Crying is okay to do if you get sad." Another covert inhalation; *is he struggling to say this?* "Big boys and girls can cry whenever they want. As long as they're not throwing a fit about something. Isn't that right, Aunt June?"

"Yeah, for sure. Crying is like a shower for your brain. It washes out all the old stuff and makes your brain chemistry all sparkly and new."

Burke nods, giving me an unreadable look over the kids' heads.

"When I was a kid, people didn't know crying is a good thing," he says, his face stoic. "But now they know."

"Did you cry when your Mommy died?" Oliver asks.

"Our Mommy didn't die," Margot snaps, whirling toward him with her lower lip out. "She's in heaven!"

Oliver's lips fold into a mean-looking smirk. "Mom and Dad are dead. There's no such thing as *heaven*. That's a *myth*."

He hops down off the bar stool and runs toward the bedroom. Burke gives me a brows-raised look and sets off after him.

I focus on Margot. "Your Mom and Daddy are in heaven. I think Oliver is just being a little bratty."

She nods, then sighs. "Yeah." She wipes her finger under her eyes, and I see they're filled with tears.

She looks up at me, her little lower lip quivering, and I wrap her in a big hug. "I want to see them up in heaven," she sobs.

I don't know what to say. I'm not sure words can even really help with something like this. I pick her up and haul her over to the couch, and she cries in my lap for what feels like a long time. When she's finished, sniffling and wiping her eyes but not sobbing anymore, she seems almost happy. She smiles and blinks around the room, her eyes fixing on a paper cutting that's framed and mounted on the wall that leads to the hallway.

"What is that?"

I drag a breath in through my nose, debating whether to tell her the truth.

"It's called a paper cutting."

"What's a paper cutting?"

"It's where somebody makes art by cutting patterns into a piece of paper."

"Who's in it?" she asks, and gets up, walking over to it.

I follow. "This one is a mother and a baby."

"Did you make it?"

"No," I tell her.

"Mommy did."

I smile slowly as chills run up my arms. "Yes. Your mommy made this when she was in college, and she gave it to *my* mom."

"Where is your mommy?" She frowns, like she truly doesn't know—even though it's something I've mentioned a time or two.

"She's in heaven, too. Our moms and your dad are all in heaven together."

"Do you miss her?" she asks softly.

"Every day."

She smiles like we have a secret. "Me too," she says in her sweet, soft voice. I'm struck with devastating sadness for what my sister lost, and lit up with the weirdest giddy shock at what I gained.

We walk down the hall and to the kids' room, where we find Oliver reading a book and Burke lying on the bed, facing the wall. His knees are bent, his broad shoulders tucked in just a little. I frown down at him, and Oliver grins.

"We were talking, and he just stopped."

I watch his chest for a second before letting out a breath.

"Let's get out of here," I whisper, beckoning the kids.

I take them to jump in Bowser's Castle. They pull me inside, and we all jump, but I'm distracted by his presence in the house. What is he doing in there? Is he really that tired?

And then it hits me: he fell off of Hottie.

Shit!

I bet he has some kind of concussion. He's probably dead in there right now.

"Hey guys, I'm going to the potty. Be right back."

I bounce out of the Bowser Castle and sprint toward the screened-in porch like Mario running to save Peach. I'm intent on getting to him—on shaking his shoulders, making sure his devil ass will wake up. I throw the screened porch door open, zip across the rug, and slam right into him as he steps out through the living room door.

I feel the impact of his solid chest under my cheek and palms, and then I'm ass-planted on the porch floor, looking up at him, and I can see he isn't dead at all.

His rich brown hair is ruffled, sticking up in one spot, and his long-lashed eyes are sleepy. Also *blue*. He has blue eyes. I never noticed until right now, at this exact second. His lips curve, and *hot dang, he's gorgeous.*

He's grinning down at me like he's happy to see me.

He holds a hand out. "Need some help up?"

I huff, but take his hand and let him pull me to my feet. I roll my eyes, and he gives me a sexy little frown, his dark brows pulled together.

"Everything okay with you?" he asks.

"Yes. I just have to...do something." I walk around him. As I step into the den, he says, "Kids okay?"

"In the Bowser castle," I call. Then I make a beeline for the bathroom. Potty time for damn sure. I whip my phone out of my pocket and text Leah. *Holy fucknuts, this is not good.*

She replies immediately. *What's not?*

*The Evil Burkser is here and he brought a bounce house. Set it up on my lawn, killing all the grass. He's wearing jeans that are a *little* tight. He has the kind of ass that you could bounce a penny off of, and blue eyes. Also he took Hottie for a run around the show course, and Hottie threw a shoe and B fell. So now I hate him but I also am scared he might have a concussion & he's stopped being a dick & now he's being nicer? Help me. Come over...can you? I need backup.*

She replies a second later. *Aww, sweetie. I really wish I could but I'm covering my sister's shift at the Shake & Bake till 1.*

Maybe after?

You're desperate aren't u, she asks.

YES. I'm desperate!! Help me. Oh, hell, I forgot the puppies. Bet they've peed all in their new crate in the laundry room. G2G, please call at 1 when you get off. Help meeeeee!

Leah sends a winky kiss face. I heave a sigh and wash my hands and flush the empty toilet and check on the puppies, who in fact have not peed, so I haul their fuzzy little selves outside again and point them toward a rough patch in the grass.

Burke's peering into the castle's mesh window, but a second later, he and the kids stroll over.

"Margot and Oliver were just asking me about the rodeo," he says.

"Mmm?" I look at Oliver and Margot. "Whatcha wanna know, babes?"

"Will there be butter popcorn?" Oliver asks.

"There will be. Do you like butter?"

"It's better than ghee. Sometimes Mom would let us get it at the movies!"

"Is that right? So you want buttered popcorn tonight?" I grin.

They nod their little cute heads.

"Done," Burke says.

I arch my brows at him. Since they're both staring at us, I can't give him the glare I want to.

"My brother was planning to take them," I tell Burke pointedly. "He's got their tickets."

"That sounds good. We'll sit with him."

I bug out my eyes—is this guy freaking serious—and he smirks. "No?"

I bug them out again, then look down at the kids. Lord help me. I need some sort of palate cleanser or I'm gonna combust. "I feel like it's ice cream time, kidlets. What do you say? You want to get a Heat Springs Float?"

Oliver picks up Mario, and Burke scoops up Peach.

"I love ice cream," Margot sighs.

"I'll drive," Burke offers.

I almost say I've got the driving covered, but I realize if we roll up in my truck and he gets out alongside me, I'll be talked all over town. His car would be the smarter choice. Let them know he's just a visitor, come down to see the kids.

"Y'all want to ride in your uncle's snazzy sports car?"

Of course they do. I take Mario from Oliver and send the kids toward the potty.

Burke follows me into the laundry room.

He puts Peach into the crate the pups are sharing and then stands up and squints at what's on the wall beside the dryer.

"Is this a map?" he asks.

"It's a constellation map. Yes." I'm trying to look at his face but not stare. He's so freaking attractive it's just awful, really.

"Did you make it?" he asks.

"Yeah, you know. I'm mainly a farmer, but on the side I just make these maps."

I can tell from his face that he's not sure if I'm serious.

"Of course not." I give him an eye roll. "It came from Amazon."

"You guys get Amazon Prime here?"

"Honey, people get Amazon all over the world. Even us little country bumpkins down in Nowhereville."

I lift my brows, and he looks like he might be contrite. I notice a bruise on his forehead.

"I'm sorry about yesterday," he says quietly.

I brush by him into the kitchen, mostly so I don't have to worry that I'll accidentally stare too long at him.

"Thanks," I say, grabbing two bananas from the counter. I lift my purse off a kitchen chair and stash them inside.

"Can I get one of those?" he asks.

I glance at him. "A banana?"

"Anything, I guess. But a banana works."

"Didn't pack any of your special San Francisco snacks? No organic granola? This banana is organic. That should bring you peace."

He lets a breath out. "I'm sorry, June. I really am. What else can I say?"

"Oh, nothing." I shrug. "Never can be too sure that I would understand it anyway, what with my limited education and all."

The kids come bounding down the hall, and I walk toward the front door.

"Let's go eat some ice cream, kiddies."

CHAPTER 8

BURKE

She's right. I was a dick. During negotiations in my corner of the world, it's pretty normal to low-key shit-talk someone. Twist their arm a little using insults—especially if those insults focus on past failures. Everyone knows tech is mostly one big sausage fest, so I don't worry about being dickish to the other dicks.

Yesterday, I was in default dick mode. I didn't think about how she would feel. Mostly because I didn't give a shit.

Today, that's not as easy.

I'm driving us toward "town," where the bookstore/coffee place is— where they apparently they serve some kind of Coke float that the kids are squealing about. June is in the front seat beside me, her knees angled slightly toward the door. She's wearing pale blue-ish leggings and a big, thick, corded beige sweater, with her blonde hair in a top-of-the-head ponytail, Ariana Grande style. She's got on big, dark glasses like some kind of movie star, and every time her gaze is pulled in my direction—usually by something the kids are doing in the back seat— she makes an irritated face, which only makes her pretty mouth twist in a pretty pout.

I've got something I could put in that mouth.

I clamp my molars on the inside of my cheek and tell myself to get a fucking grip. I work so much, I'm hardly ever with a single woman for more than an hour or two—not unless you count the women that I work with, and I don't, because I'd never fuck someone from work.

Unfortunately for me, June is billboard beautiful, like one of the old-school cover girls I used to jerk off to when I was thirteen, and she also seems to hate me. Every time she rolls her eyes or sends a glare my way, it makes me want to carry her to bed and fuck a smile onto those soft lips.

At the very moment I think that, right as my dick is twitching like it's ready for a party, she flicks her eyes over at me and then digs something out of her purse. And that something is a little tub of lip stuff.

Fuck me. She rubs her finger in the pale pink stuff and starts to smear it on her lips, and I'm hard. Just like that. One pass of her finger over that full lower lip, and if she looks my way—if she looks down below the steering wheel—she'll see my dick outlined in black denim.

My dick that hasn't fucked in almost three months. My dick that could have gotten play at a fundraiser last week had I not been in a weird place because of Asher. My little brother. Who is dead.

Even saying those words in my head doesn't put my over-eager dick back in its place. I grit my teeth.

"I didn't see this place when I drove through before," I say as I turn onto the paved county road.

"Probably because you don't know where it is."

She pops her lips together just a little, and I grit my teeth.

"Yeah. I don't."

She does something new with her mouth. Is that a smirk? I can't tell without shifting my eyes from the road, but I think it is. A little fucking smirk. I let my breath out, trying to be quiet about it.

"You gonna tell me?" I ask.

"Unless you have mind-reading capabilities and plan to read it from my brain, I guess I'll have to, won't I?"

I have to press my lips together to keep from laughing. I guess I do a lousy job of keeping my amusement off my face, because she says, "What?"

I hold my hands up. "I didn't say anything."

"It would be ideal if you could hold onto the wheel."

"I had it with my knee." I put both hands around the wheel again, still trying to hide how damn much I'm enjoying this.

"Do you even drive?" I know the muttered question wasn't mean to be voiced, because her jaw drops in surprise just after she asks.

"Do *I* drive?" This time I can't help a laugh. "You mean at home?" I grin at her. "You think my driving skills are shit, huh?"

"I think what you mean is *crap*." She lifts an eyebrow, reminding me the kids are right behind us.

"Why wouldn't I drive?"

She lifts a shoulder, staring out the window with her jaw set like she's feeling stubborn.

"All that money," she drawls after a second.

"You think I use my money to pay someone else to drive me around?"

She makes a soft sound, maybe a snort, but I can't tell because I'm turning left, so I'm focused on the road. "People do it," she says.

"That's true." People I know do it. "But I don't."

"Don't what?" Oliver says. He leans up toward us, then looks out the window. "I just saw a cow!"

"I want to see a cow," Margot says.

"That money I offered you," I say quietly to June, "was because I care about this. Not because I have plenty to throw around."

She snorts loudly. "Oh, *puh-lease*. I know how to navigate to Wikipedia, believe it or not. And *Forbes*, and the *San Francisco Chronicle*. I even have a little bitty sort of photographic memory. So anyway, don't give me that baloney sandwich."

I chuckle at that. "Baloney is for people who can't afford *bologna*, you know."

She throws her head back, rolling her eyes. "They're the same thing, Burke Bug."

I wink, looking over at her as I roll up to a stop sign.

"Mama knows her Oscar Mayer." She smiles. Then, without looking at me, she turns around and talks to the kids between our seats until we're on that little strip with all the shops, and she turns back around and points. "Take a right there, into the playground parking lot."

I do, and I see it—a little shed-looking building with wooden walls and pale, worn shingles. It's about the size of your typical boardroom. Definitely no bigger.

"There's a playground!" Margot shouts.

June nods, looking smug. "I thought we could go there with our floats."

The kids squeal happily, and I help Margot out of the car on my side.

The inside of the Floatin' Bean looks like a barn, but with racks and shelves filled with strange things like cans of peanuts, dark brown walnuts in gift bags with silky red bows, a whole, big case of fudge, a jukebox with stickers slapped on every inch of it, and three mounted deer heads whose antlers are laced with blinking Christmas lights.

The jukebox is playing twangy country music, which doesn't surprise me. What does is the reaction of the cashier to June. When she first sees our party of four, her heavily-made-up eyes widen. Then she bolts around the counter, smushes boob-to-boob with June, and hugs her like they're long lost sisters. Then a second later, I hear a sound that can only mean that one of them is crying.

Shit. Should I distract the kids? I look around and realize they've gone over to the jukebox, so I join them there. I don't know how much time June needs, but I don't want to be around for that stuff.

Naturally, the moment I glance over my shoulder to see if they're still doing the waterworks, June is wiping her eyes. Her gaze fixes on my face. I try to smile, but I think it's a grimace. The woman beside her doesn't notice. She must be old enough to be June's mother, though I know she can't be. She wipes her eyes, too, smearing mascara all over her face, and then gives me a quivering, red-lipped smile and starts toward me.

Hell, no. I can feel it coming, can sense it in her long strides and that focused look on her face. *Yep*—she goes in for it: the hug.

I grit my teeth and try to stand still and just breathe. That's when I smell it. I haven't smelled it in so long, but there it is. It fills my nose and then my head, and then I have to get away from it. I have to get away from her, from how it feels to have her hugging me and smelling like...*that*.

I can't breathe, can't think, can only move. And then I'm outside, and it's windy and the air is too cold, and I'm fumbling for the car keys and I'm striding to the car. I'm getting in the car. I want to drive. I really want to drive away, but I can't, so I lay my chair back and put one shaking hand on my chest. I try to feel my diaphragm moving below my palm. Just feel it. And nothing else. There's nothing else.

My heart is racing, though. It's hard to breathe. I run through my mental checklist. What color is the car? The ceiling's black...maybe more charcoal. The dashboard is black. The seats are tan. I look at the buttons on the dashboard, and the text and numbers on them is white. I look at the miles-per-hour gauge. It goes to 160. That's higher than average but not so high for a car like this.

It's okay. If you start breathing too fast, just observe what's around you.

I remind myself that my reaction is just physical. I've never really talked to anyone about it, but I read all the books. It's all about breathing if this stuff happens.

I do that for a while, and then I sit back up and spot June and the kids at a picnic table under a big tree, right beside the playground. Thinking of walking up to them makes me feel so fucking cringey, but I have to do it.

I don't have a plan until I'm right there by the table. Then I give June a little nod and say, "Sorry, got a phone call."

"Did you?" She frowns down at her float.

The kids jump up right then and run off toward the playground.

"Yeah," I say sharply. "I did."

"Well that was rude." She looks up at me, and her face is guarded. "Sadie thought she scared you off or hurt your feelings."

"Hurt my feelings? How would she do that?" I ask in a tone that says the idea is ridiculous.

"Offended you, is what I mean."

"All she did was hug me."

"Maybe you don't like hugs. I think she thought it might be something like that. There's a little boy in Heat Springs who has autism. He doesn't like hugs. Overwhelms him."

"Yeah well, I'm not a little kid. And I don't have autism. I'll have to use that next time I'm somewhere and want to leave, though."

Disgust twists her face. "Yeah, Burke. You do that. Pretend that you have autism. That's real mature."

Then she stalks off toward the playground. She won't look at me for the rest of the outing, not even when I get up on the jungle gym and start playing Wild Attack Ape with the kids. Just as I'm feeling almost like myself again, she whistles between her fingers from where she's sitting on a wooden bench and the kids run to her.

"I think we've gotta be going. Burke will drop us off at home. You two can nap, and I'll have some June time, and then we'll get ready for the rodeo."

I smile down at her, because when she seems pissed at me, I think I find her even hotter than I usually do. "June time?"

"Yes." She looks at me with her mouth pinched, batting her lashes like a malfunctioning doll. "Time to center myself. Sometimes I do yoga."

"They do yoga down here?"

"I don't know who 'they' is, but I definitely do yoga. In fact, I teach a yoga class at the community center every Saturday. What about you, Uncle Burke?" She folds her arms. "Do you do yoga?"

"I can get down with the downward dogs."

I look down, mostly to look away from June, and I find tears on Margot's cheeks. "Oh no, buddy. Uh, buddy girl," I correct.

That makes her giggle.

"You're not buddy, are you?"

She shakes her head then wipes her eyes. "What are you, then?" I ask. "Little sistah?"

She gives me her kid version of a what-the-fuck look. Then she heaves a deep sigh. "You're so weird." She wipes her eyes again, and I ask, "What's the matter?"

Her lip trembles, and I pick her up. I don't know why. I used to carry her around more a few years back, before I got so busy with work. It feels natural, but she's heavier now.

I pretend I'm swaying. "*Whoooaaa!* When did you get so heavy?"

"I'm not heavy. Maybe you've lost...energy or something."

"What?" I feign shock.

"Superheroes can lose energy, you know."

"And I'm a superhero, right," I nod, "so that makes sense."

"You're not a superhero," Oliver says.

"Oh yeah I am. I'm Captain Burke."

I hear a snort, and I assume it came from June, who's slightly behind me as I sway like a tree in the wind under Margot's pretend weight.

"You are a superhero." Margot wraps her arms around my neck, and I start walking, stumbling zombie-style toward the rental car.

I wrap her closer to me with one arm and then dip down and give a low roar.

"It's the crazy ape again," Oliver cries.

I keep it up until the crazy ape has deposited both kids into the car's small back seat. June won't look at me as she buckles Margot. She slides into the passenger's seat and says, "Go straight to my house," as if there's grave danger I might go somewhere else.

"Damn," I murmur, snapping my fingers. "Wanted to go rob the bank."

"Team Greedy," she mutters dryly, sliding her shades off her face so she can rub her eyes.

"You got a headache?"

"Can't imagine why I would," she says drolly.

"I'm Team Minimize," I say as I turn up the radio and fade it to the back of the car. "Just for the record."

She snorts. "Oh yeah." She lets her gaze rake over me and pulls her ponytail out of her hair. I can't see what she's doing to it—my eyes are on the road—but I can sense her messing with it.

"I like your hair." I don't know why I say it. What is this, the fucking salon?

"I care a whole awful lot."

I swallow. Guess I asked for that. But I can turn the tides again. Fuck, I've gotta try a little harder, but I still think maybe I can charm her. "You a Seuss fan?"

"What?"

"Well you said the phrase 'a whole awful lot.'"

"Yes, as a descriptor of how much I care what you think about my hair. That was sarcasm, by the way. I don't even give one shit." She's whisper-hissing so the kids don't hear.

"What did I do to earn this kind of ire? I can't even compliment your hair?"

"Are you gay or a cosmetologist?" she chirps.

"Uh, no. Why?" Inwardly, I'm cringing, though. It really *was* a weird comment for me to make.

"If you're not, then that was a come-on. Even if it was reflexive. I don't want a come-on from you. Ever. I don't even want to ride in this car with you right now. I wish you would drop us off and not come to the rodeo. Just go back to where you came from. But you're not going to do that, are you?"

I swallow. "I'm not."

"So we're not friends. And I don't care if you think my hair is nice—which it is. When I was a kid, a model scout in the mall tried to get me to try out for a shampoo commercial."

Holy shit—I knew it! It's shampoo commercial hair. I smirk to myself at my prescience. Or postscience. Whatever that would be called.

"You think that's funny?" she demands. "That a farm girl like me—a farmer—could be scouted as a model?"

"No. Why would I think it's funny?"

"You were smirking."

"No I wasn't." I stop at a red light and give her a look that says "I'm innocent."

"You're so full of crud," she says.

"Full of crud?"

"I can tell you're lying or at least uncomfortable right now because your nostrils are flaring."

"What?" Oliver leans between our seats. "Did you say no drills? Do we have to see a dentist before we go to the rodeo?"

June laughs. "What? No, you silly goose." She ruffles his hair—dark like mine...and like my brother's. "No dentist. I said Burke had something in his *nostril*. A booger."

I make a *pshh* sound. "I did not. That's crazy talk."

"Sit back, Oliver sweetie. I don't want that booster seat sliding around or your buckle coming undone."

"Is that what happened to my Mom and Dad? Did they come out of their buckles?"

June leans into the back seat, and I'm amazed at how her bitchy tone gentles for the kids. "What do you mean, darlin'?"

"I heard someone at the visitation say they had a vibe on impact. What's a vibe?"

I swallow hard. I sense more than feel June's body tense beside me.

"Oh, a vibe? Um...like a feeling. So your parents were in the car when it happened," she babbles. "Something happened to the car."

"What happened?"

"Oliver, she said already," Margot snaps. "Mom and Daddy's car got broken. That's what hurt them."

"Did they have their seatbelts on?" Oliver asks in a small voice.

"I think they did, sweetheart."

"Why didn't they *work*?"

"The seat belts?" June says gently.

In the rear view, I can see him nodding. Poor kid.

"Well...sometimes something happens to the car that is a different kind of thing."

"Did it get crunched?"

June's shoulders rise and fall as she inhales and exhales. "It didn't get crunched."

"Can I see it?" Oliver asks after a minute.

"I'll see if I can get the pictures."

Damn. Now that's a bad fucking idea.

"It was their time to go to heaven, Oliver," Margot tells him.

"Shut up, Margot."

I turn onto the county road that points us toward the farm and then pull over. "I've got an idea. Why don't you guys help me drive?"

June sits back in her seat, her eyes nearly popping out of her head. "What?" she hisses.

"It's a rural road. We can poke along." I turn to look at the kids in the back seat; they both look hopeful and distracted, as intended. "You guys can sit in my lap. What do you think?"

If June had superpowers, the look she's giving me right now would definitely kill me.

"You *do* see the irony of this?" she murmurs. "And not in the funny, cool way."

"There's a funny, cool kind of irony?"

"I don't know that we should do that," she says, projecting her voice toward the back seat.

But the kids protest, and she gives in when Margot's lower lip trembles.

"We can do it on the dirt road," she snips. "Not the highway."

"This is hardly a highway. Isn't it a county road?"

She gives me another glare.

I need to talk to her about giving in when the kids protest. Not that it will matter since I'm taking them home.

When we reach the dirt road, June squeezes into the back seat and Oliver sits in my lap.

"I can really steer the wheel?" He looks so happy.

"For sure." I give him some instructions, put my foot on the pedal just a little, and he starts giggling.

That gets me laughing, too. I push the pedal more, and he screams—okay, really more a squeal.

"You're doing it! You're driving!"

I'm afraid one of the kids will ask which of their parents was driving at the time of the wreck, but thankfully neither of them does, and Margot is just as gleeful when it's her turn.

I let her help me steer down the driveway. By the time I park, both kids are in better spirits than I've seen them yet, I think, and June is clearly furious. She won't even lift her eyes in my direction.

She and the kids head toward the house; she's walking in short, angry strides. I don't know why I follow. I'm walking so slowly that by the time I get to the second porch door—the one that opens into the living room—June is heading back out to the yard with the puppies.

I'm directly in her path. She stops and blinks up at me. "Could you please *move?*" I do, and she steps around me. "And maybe could you *go* now?"

I follow her onto the lawn, where the puppies dance around her feet. I drop down, petting Peach's head.

"Don't bond with them," she snaps. "You're not getting them."

I look up and see she's folded her arms.

"No?"

"You should go home. The kids saw you. They had fun. Now you're interfering with their progress here."

I stand slowly. "Am I?"

"Yes. You are. And you're throwing me off, too."

It's such an easy in—I can't help myself. "What about me throws you off?"

I fold my arms like hers and tilt my head to one side. I know I'm not too tough on the eyes. Never had trouble getting girls or anything. I also know I'm good at being a prick—and I'm channeling that now.

I give her a grin, and she gives me a glare, and I can feel my cock twitch behind my fly.

"What?" I goad her. "Puppy got your tongue?"

"You're throwing me off because you're impulsive and you put the kids at risk, and you undermined me by saying they could do that without asking me first. Not to mention the fact that their parents just *died* in a *car wreck* so, you know…"

She swirls her finger around her ear, the way kids in middle school used to do to mime 'crazy.' "Also you're rude. You hurt my friend's feelings. And you're insensitive e.g. the autistic children."

I frown. "Did you just say 'e.g.' in a sentence?"

"Don't you dare insult my grammar right now. Don't you even think about it."

"Actually, I think you used it correctly. A lot of people say i.e., but e.g. is probably more appropriate in that sentence."

"I'm sorry, are you an English teacher?"

I run a hand through my hair. "English was one of my college majors."

"Oh, I fuckin' bet it was." She whirls on her heel and stalks inside. Even the puppies must be able to feel the rage that's rolling off her. They scamper after her, leaving me alone in the yard.

CHAPTER 9

JUNE

I hate him. More than tights under cutoff shorts and socks with sandals. More than bad highlights and bowl-cut bangs and people who use the word "moist" to describe…well, I guess anything. I hate him more than the line in that Justin Timberlake song where he asks, "how'd they get that pretty little head on that pretty little frame," like the woman he's singing about is nothing more than a doll. I hate him more than oatmeal and house flies you can't kill no matter how big a fly swatter you've got. I hate him more than being outside when it's more than a hundred degrees and so humid your contacts are shriveling off your eyeballs. I think I even hate him more than roaches, and I don't hate anything as much as those evil, hideous creatures; one fell from the ceiling down onto me once when I was peeing, and I've never been the same, nor have my lady parts.

He's a prick, and that's the beginning and the end of that sad tale. It's getting sadder, too, because he ain't leaving with my kids. *Isn't* leaving, I correct myself. Even in my head, I have to do that, because he thinks my way of speaking means I'm stupid—or he would, if he heard me get Southern. I've been trying not to around him.

I can't believe I let him spend even one minute with us today. That was my bad, my mistake. That was me being naive and weak, just trying to please everybody—mostly Oliver and Margot.

I sit on a bar stool in the kitchen and hold my head in my hands. It's aching. I've always had allergies at all times of the year. Winter is no exception. I get up and grab myself a Zyrtec. Then I check on the kids, who are in the bathtub with two blankets, pretending like they're Poke-mons or something.

"Do you want us to get out?" Margot asks me with wide eyes and a cautious face.

I almost smile, because I know her mama wouldn't let them play in a bathtub. My sister was a germophobe. She used to clean our bathroom twice a week sometimes when she was back in high school, especially if something else in life was making her nervous.

"Nah. You stay in there and play. That tub is clean enough. I'm going in the den to drink some tea and read a magazine."

I sound so much like my mom when I say that. Makes my throat lock up a little bit.

Instead of doing what Mama would do, I text Leah and Mary Helen —*Today sucked. If you see that prick tonight, AVOID.*

Then I give my big pups a bone each and spend some time on the laundry room floor playing with the newbies. It feels good to cuddle them. When I think that he only gave them to me so he could take them away—he was so confident two puppies would break me—fury fills my chest and tightens my throat.

After tonight, he will leave. Somehow, I'll make sure of it.

🐾

BURKE

One of my friends from MIT hailed from Dallas. One Christmas, he brought a couple of us home with him, and on Christmas Day there was a rodeo. It was nothing like this.

The people here are...rougher. Their accents are thicker, their skin more tanned, as if they spend all day outside plowing fields or some-thing. The women are dressed up in ruffled blouses, legging jeans, and expensive-looking leather boots. They're carrying designer purses and wearing their hair not just in the classic cowgirl braids—as one might expect—but also curled and in elaborate updos. Their lipstick is red, their fingernails are freshly manicured, and most of them have got on lots of eye makeup. As a group, they're curvy and vivacious, reminding me a little of the women in Brazil, where I spent a college summer helping install solar panels in an economically depressed neighborhood.

The men are dressed like they're going somewhere completely different. Ratty T-shirts, mud-stained jeans, and big work boots that are caked with red mud. One dude's got some vines around his ankle, like he just tromped through the kudzu on his way here. I know he didn't walk here, though, because no one seems to walk in Georgia. Most people rolled up tonight in big trucks with hulking off-road tires.

Including Shawn—June's brother—whom the kids and I encountered at the ticket stand.

Shawn is six-foot-five, with big bones and a beer belly, kind brown eyes, and a receding hairline he keeps covered by a Georgia Dawgs ball cap. He's wearing a white undershirt, dark, stiff-looking jeans, and what I think are work boots. When we first encounter him, he gets down on one knee and holds his arms open for the kids.

"Hey there, aces," he says as he hugs them.

"What's an ace?" Margot asks.

"You know, a flying ace!"

"What's a flying ace?" Oliver asks.

"A brave fighter pilot!"

"Who is he fighting?"

"It's a *she*," Margot says.

Shawn throws his head back and laughs like they're the funniest things he's ever seen. Then he stands up, holding his hand out for me. "Hey there. I'm the brother." He grins, and I notice he's got freckles on his face.

Turns out, Shawn got all the friendly genes that skipped June. The dude's just fun. He walks the kids and me all around the bleachers, which are cased in by white-washed concrete blocks and covered with a tin roof. He introduces us to what feels like must be everyone in Heat Springs. The men shake my hand or slap my back, and some of the women look me over when they think I'm not looking. Everyone is excessively friendly. It's a shock, after the reception I got from June. I remind myself that was my fault, though.

Since my new strategy involves winning her over, I play nice with everyone I meet. Thirty minutes in, we've played horseshoes plus that game where you swing a ball bat and bash a machine that lights up at the top if you hit it hard enough. I won a stuffed beaver, of all damn things, and Oliver and Margot are taking turns holding it.

We find a place to sit on the metal bleachers, and Shawn disappears and then returns holding a Miller Lite for me and two bags of what appear to be wet peanuts for the kids.

"Oh, and here." He pulls two juice boxes out of his pocket. "Got y'all some lemonade too."

The wet peanuts are, apparently, *boiled* peanuts. Shawn pushes me to try one, and to my shock, I like them. He's so entertained by my enthusiasm that he gets me my own bag.

"You're a great date, man."

He gives me a funny look for half a second before we're both laughing.

"I got a girlfriend," he says in his low drawl.

"Not into me?"

He gives me another wide-eyed look, and I snicker. "Too taboo to talk about that shit down here below the Mason-Dixon line?"

"Naw. I'm on board the love is love train." Margot drops the beaver while jamming the straw in her juice box, and he scoops it off the cement floor and holds it toward me with a shake. "I just want me one of these."

A crackling sound comes over the loudspeakers, but then the country music comes back. He shrugs. "It's pretty backwoods around here," he says. "Especially with tech shit." Of course, it sounds like he's saying 'round here. I try to keep the smile off my lips, and he elbows me like we're old friends.

"You laughin' at our accents, brother?"

"I'm not laughing."

"You appreciating them?"

"Oh yeah."

He snickers. "Sure you are."

"I am."

"You sound like a guy on...what's it?" he says, adjusting his cap. "Oh, the NPR."

I laugh. *The NPR.* "You think so?"

He takes a swig of his beer. "Oh yeah. Nice, clean accent."

"Is yours dirty?"

"You know it."

"So you're a trucker?"

"Naw, I own the trucks. I let other people drive them."

"What's that like?" I ask.

"I've got a few good ones. But some of them are pains in the ass." He glances down at the kids. "Pain in the rear end." He nods at Oliver, who looks confused.

"You have a pain in your rear end?" Margot asks loudly.

Everyone around us laughs, and Shawn covers his face with his cap.

As he's fitting it back atop his head, a tallish dark-haired woman and two well-dressed kids walk up. The woman sits beside me like we know each other, and for a second, I stare at her. There's something familiar about her, but I can't say what. Then she leans behind me to give Shawn a half-hug, and I realize she must be June's other sister, Mary Helen. What were her kids' names? Charlie and Jack?

I try to get a peek at them, but then the woman wraps her arm around me. "You must be the wicked interloper."

"Is that what you've heard about me?" I pretend to be offended.

"Well, Miss June's not happy."

"Miss June?"

"That's what our mama used to call her," she says, somewhat wistfully. "Miss June. She was that little girl who put on all of Mama's necklaces and painted her own fingernails when she was…well, about three. You should have seen those red hands. Looked like something from a horror movie." She smiles and nods at the small arena, where a man in jeans, boots, a white button-up, and a black cowboy hat walks almost to the middle and then gives a bow.

"Good evening, ladies and gentlemen. Welcome to the twenty-seventh annual HEAT. SPRINGS. WINTER. RODEO!"

The crowd cheers like he just announced the end of world hunger.

"We're so happy you came out," he drawls, "and we want you to know, ten percent of tonight's proceeds will go to the fundraiser for little Lacy Hammond and her family."

Another round of applause goes up.

"That's a little girl with cancer," Mary Helen murmurs behind her program, telling me as if she believes I need and want to know.

"The events will proceed according to the program, but first, we'll kick this off with a lovely rendition of 'God Bless America,' from our very own Bobbi Seymour."

"Oh Lord, she's awful," Mary Helen tells me. She leans back a little, and for the first time I get a good look at her face. She has different eyes than June's—gray-blue, and more cat-like, where June's are more round —but they share a similar bone structure and the same lips. She leans back a little, nodding at the kids beside her. "These are two of my three —Charleigh and Jack. Other one's home sick."

A few minutes after what is indeed a terrible rendition of "God Bless America," the rodeo events start with a few rounds of calf roping.

I finish my beer, and Shawn offers another one. I'm not sure if I have to drive the kids back to June's house, but I can tell you don't say "no" to Shawn Lawler when he offers you beer, so I take it and just hold it. All around me, everyone is talking, cheering for whoever's riding. Strangers keep stopping by to introduce themselves to the kids and me, as if they've been wanting to meet us—all of us, even me—for years.

During a brief break between the calf roping and whatever is next, I get up to get more peanuts—for the kids, of course—and look for promised popcorn. I'm in line behind two teenage girls. They both have braces on their teeth and something shiny that looks like Christmas tinsel braided into their hair. They're wearing jean skirts, fringed boots, and button-up plaid shirts, and the taller one is wearing a white cowgirl hat. The line is long, and like usual, my cell phone's service isn't good, so I listen to them to pass the time.

"You are so weird," one laughs, shaking her head.

"I'm telling you, the dark matter is something important. It's the way everything is tied together. Or it's God or something. I don't know. I have a sense about it, though," says the girl with the hat.

"Oh I believe you, chica. You're the one that's got the scholarship to Duke."

"And you're the one going to Georgia Southwestern. With my boyfriend." The girl wearing the hat sighs, and then they're up to order.

I look both of them over—discreetly, of course. To me, they look about twelve years old, but I guess they've got to be somewhat older.

Then the girl behind the counter says, "Junior punch card?"

They whip something out, and I realize that must mean they're in eleventh grade.

I chew on that as the kid behind the counter gets my order together. Both of those girls already have colleges picked out. They're planning to go.

"Here you are, sir."

I take my debit card back, and as I make my way back to my seat, I think of what went down between June and me when I picked the kids up. She said, "Don't go anywhere you shouldn't. Such as north and toward that airport. I've got all the paperwork, and you will not win."

I told her "Good luck," and she said, "Yeah, I bet you hope I break a leg or two."

She leaned against my rented car and kissed her finger, pressed her fingertip to the window by Margot, and then sashayed back inside.

"She looks beautiful," Oliver said to me as I started down the driveway. And she really had. She had on a white, flowing sort of shirt, suede-looking riding pants, and a pair of shiny, dark brown leather cowgirl boots. Her hair was curled in ringlets that flowed down past her shoulders.

When I get back from the concession stand and see Shawn standing at the rail in front of the bleachers with Margot and Oliver beside him, my stomach ties itself into a tight knot. Mary Helen stands up, too, and waves me over. "Look, that's June!" She points. "She's over on the dark horse."

"Oh yeah, I saw him today. Hot Rocket?"

She snickers. "Used to be Crotch Rocket. She bought him off the biggest pig of a man. Drunkard with no sense to his name. But he's a fast horse. Trained since he was young, and he's not old now. Only four and a half."

I laugh. "Do you know his birth month?"

She smiles. "Shawn here delivered him."

"Wow, does he work with a vet?"

"Hell no. Don't take a vet to deliver a foal. Shawn's sort of a horse whisperer."

Everyone's attention shifts to one end of the arena, and Mary Helen says, "She's gonna come out over there. Horse will race around the barrels in a pattern. It's a timed thing."

I knew that already, but I nod as if I'm grateful for the info.

June and Hot Rocket shoot out into the small arena with a decent bit of speed. I watch as she and "Hottie" whip around each barrel, noting that she's got a cowgirl hat on. She's fucking good—a better rider than me, and during Asher's cowboy phase, he and I trained at some of the best stables in the country.

June moves effortlessly with Hot Rocket—right until the moment that a firecracker pops, and the horse stumbles. It seems to happen in slow-motion. The big horse goes down. June flies almost over his thick neck, then slips off his side. My brain seems to speed up, surging out ahead of her. *She isn't moving.*

"OH MY GOD, HER FOOT!" Mary Helen wails.

There's a millisecond when it looks like June's leg might twist right off. Then she's on her back in the dirt, and the track is flooding with people. Oliver and Margot are crying. Mary Helen pulls them up against her, and Shawn grabs my arm.

"C'mon."

CHAPTER 10

BURKE

Shawn leads me onto the dirt floor of the arena. Why, I'm not quite sure, but the sea of people parts for him, and therefore for me.

June is lying on her back in the mud by the time we reach her, fat tears streaming down her cheeks as some older man holds her leg, rolling her foot at the ankle. A line of blood runs down her chin, and I realize in horror that the pain is making her bite through her lip. He lifts her foot a little, and she recoils, moaning.

"Fuck!" I wave at the moron. "Stop that!" Everyone quiets, looking at me. I sigh. "Who's got scissors?"

Shawn hands me a pocket multitool, and I use the little scissors to cut her leather boot a few inches. When I can tell the scissors aren't powerful enough for the job, I get her foot at an angle I don't think will hurt and use both hands to rip the leather open.

June gasps and starts panting. I can feel her body trembling, and I see why. Her ankle's so swollen and bruised, I'd be shocked if it's not broken.

I look around at all the faces—men and women looking pale and stunned. "Anybody here a doctor?"

A woman raises her hand. "Dental assistant." It takes some self-restraint to keep from groaning.

"Is there a local doctor?" I ask.

"We drive over to Dawson."

Okay—so that's another little town nearby. "Is there no ambulance here tonight?"

Shawn mutters something, and someone else says, "Probably up at the damn Sonic!"

There are other mutters, and I catch the word "hussy."

"You a doctor?" Someone asks me.

"No, but I'm a paramedic." Or I was in college. My mother was an orthopedist—the kind of doctor June needs to see—but that's nobody's business.

"I can carry her," Shawn says. "Where we taking her?" His eyes catch mine.

"The nearest hospital. Not a clinic, but a real ER. Is that in Albany?"

He nods, looking worried.

"Thirty minutes?" I ask.

"Yeah."

"We can get here there a little faster in my rental."

"Put me in the GD car," June hisses. "This isn't...the freaking water cooler."

It's a struggle not to laugh, but then her face tightens in pain, and I see sweat along her hairline, and that helps me focus.

"Shit. I'm sorry." I look up. "Does anybody have a pillow or a pile of blankets?"

"Blankets," someone says.

I look at Shawn. "Can you get a bunch of blankets and meet me at my rental car?"

"That silvery one?"

I nod.

"Yeah."

I get the key fob in my hand and then scoop June up. There's no way to grab her up out of the mud without jostling that leg around. She cries out in pain and curls herself against my chest. She's panting.

"I'm so sorry, baby."

"Not...your baby," she whimpers.

Then she presses her head against my chest and lets out a groan.

"I'm so fucking sorry."

"Watch your language," she moans. "Baptists...here."

I change my grip on her a little. Then I'm walking with her, and everyone in the little arena is clapping. We pass Mary Helen, and I look at Margot and Oliver.

"She's okay. She's only got a hurt foot, nothing major. We're just going to the doctor. Then I'll bring her back. I promise."

June lifts her head, and I angle her so they can see her. Both of them are crying.

"I'm okay. I'm not going to heaven. You're stuck with me."

Margot says, "Good!"

Oliver wipes his eyes and looks around to see if anybody saw him crying.

"Okay. It's okay," I murmur as we move toward the exit, cutting through the line at the concession stand. "You're going to shut that mouth and try to relax. Let me take care of you. I won't bite. Just let me be your friend for an hour or two."

"I would...rather die," she manages.

I stifle a laugh, so as not to jostle her around. "Oh, c'mon. I'm not that bad."

"You're the villain."

"Sometimes the villain turns out to be the prince."

"Or the other way around," she whispers.

"Oh," I grin, "so you think I look like the prince?"

I think her adrenaline rush is wearing off now, because she moans as we reach the car, and then she's just whimpering as I hold her against me and watch Shawn run across the parking lot with what looks like an armful of blankets.

He runs up, shaking his head. "Shit, my fuckin' pants are slidin' down." He tugs them up.

"Can you open up the door, man?" I ask. "Put some blankets in here behind the driver's seat to prop her foot on? And then hold one out so we can cover her up?"

I know June is in a lot of pain, because she's quiet and still except the panting and shaking she's doing. My stomach pulls into a knot as Shawn does what I ask.

"You trust me with your wheels?" he asks me. "I can get us there fast. I know the route."

"Yeah. I'm kind of a backseat driver, though, so nothing crazy." I start to lay June across the back seat, but as I do, I realize it makes more sense for me to stay back there with her.

"You care if I hold you? I can throw your legs over my elbow so your foot stays elevated."

She gives a shake of her head. I get us into the car, and I can feel her shoulders sort of curling in. One of her hands covers her face, and I can tell from how her torso shakes that she's crying.

"Dammit." My stomach tightens. "I'm so fucking sorry. Let me tell you something that I think will distract you." She shudders, and I shift so that I'm holding her a little closer. I lean down, so close that I can smell her shampoo—or perfume. It smells fruity, like peaches and vanilla.

"I'm gonna let you keep those puppies," I whisper. "And those kids. If you're sure you want to. We can talk about it more, but if you want to, I'll step back and try to help and let things lie."

She goes absolutely still for one long moment. Then she groans, "Why?"

I think of the girls talking about dark matter. And June's sister pulling the kids to her side when June and Hot Rocket fell. And I tell her the truth, surprising myself as much as I bet it surprises her.

"Because you're who they picked. You've got a bunch of family who can help if you need it. And even though this town is small, and I'm still worried about them having every opportunity, I can help with some of that. If you want to raise these kids—like if you *really* want it—who am I to stand in the way? You were right; I do work a lot more than most people. They would be raised by hired staff. Like I was." My throat feels stiff on those words, so I swallow hard, staring at the road as Shawn drives like NASCAR.

"You were?" she whispers.

"Yes." I tighten my grip around her.

"Did you like them?" she asks in a voice that trembles. Cold sweat moves through me; it's like a sympathetic sensation.

"Some of them were okay. Then at a certain point, it was me doing the watching. Asher was the younger one." I clench my jaw, unsure why I pointed that out.

She nods, and I hear her sniffle. "I'm sorry you lost him."

"I'm sorry for you too."

"Do you...really...mean it?"

"About what?" I murmur. "The kids?"

She nods. I smooth her hair back off her clammy forehead. "Yeah. It was the rodeo that helped me see it. Everybody is so damn nice around here. Friendly and involved in one another's lives. It's not like where I grew up. But I think it could work. Especially if you're being honest and you really want to take them on."

Her eyes squeeze shut. "I still think you're an ass."

"Don't you listen to her," Shawn calls from the front seat. "She's hurt, talking crazy."

"Traitor," she hisses.

He laughs. "She's got a mouth on her. Don't let anybody tell you she don't."

"Don't worry, no one has." I grin down at her, and June's biting her lip again. She starts to pant, and I can see the stark pain on her face.

"You hurting?"

She nods once. Her eyes squeeze shut. I think she's crying. Goddamn it.

"You feel sick?"

She nods once.

"Sort of a stomach ache?"

She gives another little nod.

"That's normal." I move my fingers through her hair, hoping to use one sensation to distract from another. "You feel dizzy?"

"Kind of."

"It's okay. That's normal too." Especially if the bone is broken, but I don't say that part out loud.

"Have you ever gotten hurt like this?" I ask.

She gives a little jerk of her chin, and Shawn says, "Fell out of a tree in our back yard when she was seven. Broke her arm near clean in half."

June groans at his words.

"That make it hurt worse?"

She nods, and tears start dripping down her cheeks. *Shit.* "I'm so sorry."

I'm holding her so I've got an arm around her upper back, and my other one under her knees; my left bicep is aching from the strain of holding her legs so that her ankle's elevated. But it's worth it. If I could do more for her, I would.

Shawn slows for a lone, country red-light, and her body quakes a little harder.

"Let's play question and answer. Focus on my words, okay?"

She sniffles.

I lean my head down, so my cheek is pressed to her hair, hoping that might make her feel a little like I've got her. "Let's start with something basic: Coke or Pepsi. I'm going to guess the answer's Coke, since it seems to be your state's official beverage."

She nods once.

"Yeah? I figured that. You drink the Zero kind, or regular, or diet?"

"Diet," she rasps.

"Better without sugar. I'm not a big fan of carbonated drinks, but if I have one, it's a Diet Pepsi."

She makes a small dissenting noise, and I try not to laugh; I don't want to jar her.

"I like that it's kind of spicy. You know what I mean?" I ask. "Sort of a pepper taste at the end?"

She makes the noise again—like she disagrees.

"I had Dr. Pepper—the sugar-free variety—a while back, and that was good too. Maybe that should be my new official restaurant beverage," I muse.

We must be going through a little town now, because there are street lights illuminating her face, showing me her damp cheeks and her bloody lower lip.

"This is Dawson," Shawn says.

I place it on my mental map. "Okay." I look back down at June. "Pancakes or waffles?"

"French toast," she croaks.

"A dissident."

"Better," she says, so softly.

"Yeah, it's better. I can get behind that." I wipe my thumb over her chin, but the blood's dried. Then I push my fingers gently against her throat, wanting to get a read on her pulse—something I should have done already.

It's fast, but I'm not surprised.

"You doing okay? Feel any more sick or any more dizzy?"

She shakes her head, burying her face against my chest, which makes my heart kick harder. "It hurts *so bad*."

"I'm so sorry." I hold her a little closer and tense my left arm more so her leg stays elevated.

Then I brush my lips over her forehead.

CHAPTER 11

JUNE

Surely I'm hallucinating. First the devil says he's gonna let us be. Then he's holding me against him like some sort of Disney hero. Now I'm pretty sure he might have kissed me on the head.

I *know* I'm hallucinating, because when his lips touch my skin I flush like a firecracker, from my forehead all the way down to my toes—which means the firework moves through my ankle. And that hurts like hellfire, so I moan, and I can feel his chest tense under my cheek.

"Sorry." It's a whisper.

"You're the devil," I say weakly.

That makes him laugh. His torso gives a small shake, and I grit my teeth because it hurts my ankle.

"Shit, that hurt? I'm really striking out here, aren't I?"

"Do you...*want* to hit it?" I manage. My head is spinning from how bad my ankle hurts.

"I'm not laughing at that question. But it's a tall order."

Against my will, I give a laugh then grit my teeth. "Why does it hurt so bad?" I press my forehead against his chest—anything to distract from how damn bad it hurts.

"You want an honest answer on that?" he asks quietly.

"Yes."

"Probably because it's broken."

"I know," I moan. "I heard it."

"Did it make a sound?"

His palm is cradling the back of my head, thick fingertips pushed into my hair. "Pull it," I whisper, instead of answering.

"Pull your hair?"

"Yeah."

He does, and it feels good. I can get a breath without my lungs constricting from the pain.

"You like that?" His voice is so gentle, it doesn't even sound like him.

"Yes," I breathe.

"Tell me if you change your mind."

I shake my head. His fingers tug my hair again, and my head spins.

"Are you hanging in there, little sister?" Shawn asks from the front.

I nod, and Burke says, "She said yeah. I checked her pulse a little while ago. She's doing okay. How much longer?"

I'm too lost to track Shawn's answer. Burke keeps pulling my hair, and I'm panting with relief each time. I can feel my heartbeats in my ankle. Then the car turns sharply. I feel either my leg or Burke's arm, where it's propped up, shaking. Then we bounce a little, and I groan. Shawn says, "Sorry, Buggie."

His phone rings? I don't know. It hurts so bad I'm just delirious. Burke and Shawn are talking, and I'm gritting my teeth. Burke is reassuring him. I don't know why.

"Are we here?" I'm pretty sure the car's stopped moving.

The door opens. I know because I feel a breeze. Someone touches my good leg. Must be Shawn, because he's by me as I hear him say, "Hey June Bug, listen. I've gotta go for just a little bit. Mary Helen called and said Hot Rocket's got an injury. She's tried to talk to Dr. Smithson, but you know how she is on shit like that. I want to check it out myself."

My heart stops. "What?"

"I don't know. She didn't tell me. Probably so I wouldn't tell you. I'll call, okay? In just a little bit."

"I've got you," Burke says in a low voice. "I can get you shuffled through the ER, help you get this foot fixed, get you back home."

"I'll be back soon," Shawn says. "MH has the kids and says they're doing just fine. Eating ice cream sundaes."

"Okay," I manage.

Then we're out of the car and Burke is carrying me. I'm crying because the lights are bright and Hottie is hurt, and I'm afraid I'm going to get sick.

The smell here reminds me of Mama's chemo appointments. All my senses blur together. Talking, beeping, other people speaking in tense tones, and then Burke leaning back, maybe against a wall, so I'm cradled more snugly up against him.

"It's okay, baby. Don't be mad at me for saying *baby*. You hurt yourself, someone should call you baby. That's the rule there."

I smile, somehow, and think: *bring back the real Burke*. But I'm too tired and cold to say it out loud. Sometime later, I hear: "LAWLER," and he's walking again. There's a woman talking to him.

"I'm just going to lay you down," he murmurs to me. Then he does, and the movement hurts so bad I see black spots swimming in front of a pale green curtain. I've never felt so bad as when the nurse is messing with me.

"Painkillers?" I manage.

"Just a minute, darlin'. We just need to check on one more thing."

Hands in my hair...gentle.

"I like when you pull it," my voice says without me. I feel like I'm floating.

"I can do that again. But I'd rather play with it."

"You're gonna feel a little jab," a woman's voice says—and I do. "There now. We'll get her back to X-ray pretty quickly at the look of this. This looks like a nasty one."

Then it all goes good and soft and warm.

***

It's such a weird dream. Burke is with me, and it's like we're friends... or lovers. He's feeding me little, round pieces of ice with a spoon, and I'm grinning, and he's grinning back. He rubs my hair, and my eyes close. I say, "I like that."

He smiles, and I think he looks sad. I don't know why. I smile to tell him it's okay, and someone pulls the curtains down.

· · ·

***

"C'mon, Sleeping Beauty." I lift my eyelids open and blink until the blurriness congeals into...the inside of a car?

"We've just got to get inside here. Then we can go home."

I shut my eyes, and warm hands squeeze my shoulders. "Can you open your eyes, June? Just for a second?"

Ugh. I do it, and he's right in front of me. *Burke.*

"What are you doing?" I ask—or I try to. Everything sounds like it's underwater.

"I'm going to drive you home. Do you remember where we are?"

I look around. "Outside," I whisper. Outside at night.

"They set your ankle. We're leaving the hospital now."

I look down at myself, at the boot on my foot. Then I shiver because...it's shivery out here.

"Okay. Here's what I think—I'm just gonna get you."

He pushes the wheelchair back, leans down near me, and then I'm being lifted in his arms. My foot gives a throb, and my stomach feels a little seasick. I smell something good and smile to myself.

His hand, on my shoulder. His eyes and his concerned face.

"You smell good," I whisper.

"You think so?"

"Yeah." I giggle. "Like a man. And Satan," I add, but he's not there anymore. He's climbing into the car. He's driving.

"I am fucked *up.*" I laugh because it's crazy what those ER folks will do for you.

Burke's voice comes, seeming disembodied because my eyes are too heavy to open. "When they were setting it, you weren't having an easy time. I made them keep trying stuff until you weren't feeling it so much."

"At the dentist office..." I want to explain how I'm such a light-weight that even basic Novocain keeps my mouth numb for like twelve hours. But I can't seem to form the right words. I laugh again and lean my head back, and he pushes something up against my cheek.

"This is just a shirt of mine. Thought you might want a pillow."

"I'm...high," I confess.

"Are you cold?"

"Yeah. Like a burrito." I laugh, and it's a crazy cackle. "I mean an *igloo*." It's so funny that I mixed those two words up. Cracking myself up here.

I feel him moving over me. I smell him. Something in my belly warms at the cologne smell. Then I feel a blanket settle over me.

"I can lay your seat back…"

I blink sometime later, and all I see is the car's ceiling. We're in motion; I'm not sure what's going on. I want to ask, but I'm so sleepy, I don't care.

Then I'm bouncing. My whole lower leg hurts like a bitch. I open my eyes, and there's a road that's lit by gold beams—*headlights*.

I look around. I'm in a car with someone. "Burke?" I don't know how I know it's him.

"Hey there, Juney."

I swallow, noting that my head hurts and my foot is throbbing. "Who is Juney?"

I can hear his smile although my eyes are closed. "That's you."

"No nicknames," I order.

"We're not tight enough for that?"

"At all." But my lips twitch, and then I'm smiling against my will.

"I can take you to your brother's house, or to your own house. Which one do you want?"

"Mine."

"Good, because we're almost here. Your brother said you'd want to come home. How ya doing?" he asks. "You in any pain?"

"You're not taking them?" My voice cracks as I think of my babes.

"No." He lets a breath out. "I'm not."

When I open my eyes again, I'm staring at the darkness, with an amber light on my right. It's the porch light. We're at my house.

His hand touches my arm. "Hey, June?"

I blink up at him. It takes some effort, but I hold my eyelids open and try to cling to his gaze.

"I'm sorry again. For how I acted. I might be a dick, but I know when to say I'm sorry. And I really am. I'm sorry for insulting your education and your ability to be a good guardian to them. And I'm sorry for judging…I don't even know what. I guess your culture? I'm going to confess something now."

My lips twitch. Even though my head feels sort of spinny, I'm sort of enjoying this. His earnest face... "So hit me with it."

"I've never really spent any time down here in the Southern United States before now. It's a lot different than where I'm from."

"I know," I slur. "Like...what is Safeway? We went to Trader Joe's—" When my family was out in California for the funeral. I smile at the memory of the good smells in there. "I like Trader Joe's."

He smiles like he's amused, and I know I'm still loopy. "Did you?"

"Good nuts." That makes me crack up laughing. "Did I say 'good nuts'?"

He chuckles. "I think you did."

Then he's scooping me up, shifting so my weight is leaned against his chest. He's carrying me up the stairs to the screened porch. I feel his arm flex, hear the dogs bark.

"Maybe you are the prince," I whisper.

"Your friend has the puppies," he says. "Just in case you think I've stolen them back."

Then we're in the living room. He starts down the hall with me, and as we near my room, he says, "June?"

"Mmmhm."

"I'm not the prince." So grave.

"Why not?"

My cheek is pressed to his chest, then it's not because he lays me on my bed and reaches over me, pulling the covers back.

"Just not the prince," he says.

"You're Slytherin, aren't you?" I lift my head a little—or try to. "Do you know what that means when I say that?"

He presses his lips together, the corners of his mouth twitching.

"You *do* know! Burke Bug is a Harry Potter nerd."

He fluffs my pillow, folds his muscled arms. "What one are you?" His face is neutral, like a poker face.

My mouth is dry. I lick my lips. "What do you think?" I rasp.

"Do you really want to know?"

I snort, then wince because my ankle hurts each time my muscles tense. "I *do* want to know. Let's hear your dumb assessment."

That makes him chuckle. It's a soft, rich sound. In the light of my bedside lamp, he looks painfully handsome, chestnut brown hair shining gold-red, framed by a faint amber halo, white teeth flashing as he tilts his head a little. His lips twitch. "I call Slytherin."

"Oh I just bet you do." I snort again, this time more careful not to move my sore leg. "Spoken like a Slytherin himself."

"Hey, there's nothing wrong with Slytherins," he says.

"I knew it!"

"Oh, c'mon. Do I seem like a Slytherin to you?" He arches one brow, and I guffaw.

"Hiss, hiss, baby." I smile. "No one is more Slytherin than you."

"And I do what for work?" he asks.

"I don't know? Start companies? Sounds hissy to me."

He chuckles at that. "Do you know where I went to college?"

"Oh, college! I don't know, the Golden School of Yuppie Asswipes?"

He lets out a guffaw. "What the fuck? You *are* high."

"It's your fault," I murmur. "You told them to drug me."

"Yes, so they could set your ankle."

"Did they set it up real good?" I croon.

He laughs again. "Oh yeah. *Real* good."

"Don't make fun of me." My voice sounds whiny.

He comes to stand beside me. "Look, I'm going to drag you up onto your pillow. Unless you need to—"

"To what?"

"Use the restroom."

"Oh you mean to take a pee." I smile up at him. "Kidding. Southern girls would never, ever say it like that."

"Why not?" He looks thoughtful.

"Classless. Tacky. Crass."

"Well, you are none of those things."

Then he's leaning down, wrapping one arm under my back, the other one under my knees. He scoots me up then settles my foot on some pillows.

"It does hurt like a bitch," I rasp.

"You might need more medicine. I got the prescription filled while you were sleeping at the hospital."

"What a...Ravenclaw." I cackle like a moron. "You're motherfrickin' *Ravenclaw*. Who went to *MIT*." I snap my fingers. "Real big *brains* you got there."

"Now who's making fun of whom?"

I roll my eyes.

"And you're Team Gryffindor," he says.

"The brave and noble sink with the ship folk," I manage.

"That's how you define yourself? Brave and noble?"

I open my mouth to retort that yes, I'm plenty brave. But he says, "I'm not surprised by that. At all, actually." He turns away from me. "I'm going to get some water and your bag out of the car."

How rude, I say to myself in my Stephanie Tanner voice. But it wasn't really. Just abrupt. As if he didn't know what more to say, he didn't want to look me in the eye or actually connect, so out he went.

CHAPTER 12

BURKE

The Golden School of Yuppie Asswipes. I chuckle at that as I hustle down the stairs and grab her stuff out of the car. It's a cool night, cloudless. There's a not-quite-full moon, and even with its brightness, I can see so many stars when I tilt my head back that it almost makes me dizzy.

What a place. I think back on the seven hours we spent at the hospital with something that's akin to wonder. The nurses and doctors moving in and out of our space—first the curtained area behind the doors of the ER and later on, an orthopedic room—were slow-moving, slow-speaking, and had an easy, not-so-urgent pace. Everyone had the same slow, twangy drawl and neighborly manner. Someone even brought me coffee while we waited to be discharged. Just so fucking *friendly*.

The nurse who pushed June's wheelchair outside to my car was asking me about my job, and I was telling her about my work right now. For some reason—I guess the strangeness of the location and my own anonymity—I found myself giving her details about the app's mission. She wrote the name "Aes" down in her phone so she could look it up later—when we've had success. As we were leaving, she said, "Good luck, honey. I hope it make you big ole piles of money."

I didn't see a reason to tell her I don't need the money. The startup's success is important to me for other reasons. That's why I'm going to keep on pushing with it, even if I have to keep working 90-hour weeks.

My brother had that wrong, I think—that life should be about balance. What does my health really matter? Who cares if I live until I'm ninety? And why would I even want to?

I couldn't help thinking about the app the whole time we were in the hospital. If everything goes right and I can get the app done before I run my own coffers too low, one day, everybody working here might know the name Aes.

For June's part, she was fucking furious most of the middle two hours. She bitched and cussed the doctor and the nurses—and me. Especially me. Then they got the painkillers right, and she was laughing and smiling, giving me these looks like she was checking me out. I know it was all just drugs, but it was nice to be on the receiving end of one of her smiles.

Back in the kitchen at her house, I get her some water and shake a pain pill out into my palm. But by the time I get back to her bedroom, she's asleep.

"Hey June..." I shake her shoulder just a little, then again. She lifts her eyelids, looking up at me with glassy eyes.

"I think you should take this." I hold the pill up for her. She opens her mouth and fixes her wide eyes on mine. I set the pill on her tongue. Then she tips her chin up, takes some water from the straw I'm holding out for her.

"Thanks, hiss," she murmurs. She sinks back down into sleep, and I'm alone in her room.

I've laughed at her antics all night, but I know I shouldn't. If she weren't drugged, I have no doubt June Lawler would hate everything about this situation.

I check my phone clock, find it's 3:40 AM, and text her brother.

She's sleeping in her bed. Do u think she has a baby monitor somewhere so I could watch her from another room?

When he doesn't answer, I lie on the other side of her queen-sized bed, on top of the covers. I curl over on my side and put a hand over my face, smelling the sanitizer residue that still lingers on my skin.

My chest tightens, like there's a black hole inside sucking everything else inward. My mind circles past my mother—as it does at odd times like this—and around to Ash. He hated to be called that when he was a teenager, but in the last few years, he signed all the cards he sent me that way.

Little Ash. A little boy—just five—on that Tuesday night when I was a stupid little fuck and changed the course of our lives.

My throat aches and my eyes sting as I think about the box of clothes I found when I was cleaning out my childhood home a few weeks back—shirts, jackets, and shoes from when Asher was in kindergarten. I squeeze my eyes shut, and I see the two of us on the back porch eating those popsicles, the triangle-shaped ones. Minute Maid, I think was the brand. He would always want the red. Everybody wants the red, but I would always take the orange or purple.

I think of Asher the man, the way he always looked when he was with Margot or Oliver—just total happiness...almost goofiness. I didn't go to their house much, even though he asked me often. It made me feel...different. Too different from him. Asher was living a real life, while mine was only a facade. It made sense, I guess. Ash had Sutton, and I think she lifted him up. Elevated him above the bullshit we grew up with. But more so than that...Ash was never fucked up like me.

My eyes ache as I think of what I told him in a fight we had before I left for India.

He asked me over for a cookout, and I said I couldn't—like I almost always did—but that day, he was less patient. He asked what was wrong with me. I told him "nothing" and he said, "you're lying to yourself." I didn't take that well and told him maybe he was too content.

He laughed his ass off at that. "Yeah, that's it. I'm too fucking content, Burke. You gonna shake things up for me by going to climb Everest and die in all the long lines?"

"You have to train for that, so no. No Everest."

"Okay. Well, too content. I'll keep that in mind in case I need to do some mental troubleshooting. What do you recommend the most, B? Chronic sleep deprivation or working every second of each day on crazy shit that might all be a gamble, hoping it might ease some of the guilt you're carrying that's not yours to begin with?"

"Nothing I have done has ever been a gamble. Especially not this venture right now. That's some special bullshit."

"I'm not 'too content.' You're *unhappy*. Everything inside you is still cracked in a million pieces, and you hate to see me because it makes you feel like a fish out of water."

"Fuck you, Ash. Take it to family therapy."

"I will, and you should come with. Thursday afternoons at 4:30. Might be the best thing you could ever do."

"Have fun, little brother."

"Think of what you're working for, and if nothing comes to mind to fill that spot, then maybe you've got everything bass ackwards."

"Always were the clever one, weren't you?"

We texted the next day, as I waited for my plane at SFO. We both said "sorry." But that's what I thought about the whole goddamn miserable trip. Asher and his smugness. Asher and his worry for me. Asher saying I was messed up. How ridiculous. I told myself that maybe it was jealousy. The bastard whose roof we grew up under has always prized money over everything else. Asher says—he said—that he was nothing like our old man, but he worked for the fucker day in and day out. So I told myself he envied my success.

I chew the inside of my cheek and trace the shadows on the wall with my gaze. I'm worth almost a hundred million dollars, and I can't get my niece and nephew back to where they're from. That's how little Asher and Sutton thought of me. They would rather have their kids grow up at rodeos and county schools than be shepherded through life by someone like me.

They didn't leave the kids to June by accident. The two of them *preferred* June. I rub my forehead, and I'm forced to admit I understand why.

Right before they set her ankle, June insisted on calling Mary Helen to talk to the kids. She told them two knock-knock jokes about breaking a leg—I later realized she was reading them from a laminated poster just over my shoulder—and was nodding at whatever they said in return as her eyes started to roll back from her latest infusion of pain meds.

After they had set her ankle, when she was high off her gorgeous ass, she started cackling about the weird-looking design on her gown. She did this epic, pig-snort laugh. She threw her head back against the pillow and said, "Don't you fuckin' push your finger to your nose. When I was a kid..." She shook her head. And then *she* did. She made a pig nose, and then laughed her ass off at that. "Pig laugh. Ever since first grade."

And I realized in that moment that June is not the problem. And she hasn't been. How I interacted with her was the problem. My presumptions and assumptions, and my judgments. Really makes me feel like fucking shit now.

The shit feeling fills my chest and head, and for the longest time, I just lie there on her bed—feeling heavy and cold. I half-dream about a stump that's looking up at tall pine trees around it. Everything is moving, but the stump is still and cold and hollow. Then it's cracking.

Then it's morning and the birds are chirping outside. It's morning and someone murmurs, "Burke."

The voice is soft and husky. It spins through my head like sugar tendrils into cotton candy, and I open my eyes and it's *her*. She looks a little pale, and she's got tired smudges under her eyes, but she's smiling, and it's so gentle and and sweet that for a moment I'm sure I'm still dreaming.

I smile up at her. "Did you just call me Burke and not the devil?"

She grins back, but then squeezes her eyes shut. "I think the pain pill wore off," she groans.

"Shit." That one's on me. I didn't think I'd sleep—it so rarely comes that easily—so I didn't set my phone's alarm. "I'm sorry," I say, getting off the bed. I stride toward the bedroom door. "Be right back."

My heart hammers as I walk through her empty house. I hear her dogs' nails clicking on the laundry room floor as I grab a pain pill and some water, and I make a mental note to let them out soon.

When I get back to her room—a girly space with lacy curtains, two paintings featuring a lot of abstract pink and sparkle, and an excess of what look like handmade patchwork quilts—I find her lying back against the pillows with her eyes closed.

I stand by her for a second, not knowing what I should do or say.

"Hi," I whisper finally, feeling awkward as fuck.

Her eyes peek open. Her mouth twitches up on one side. "Hey there. You got my fix?"

I hold the pill out. "Sorry that I didn't wake you to take it."

She opens her palm, takes it from me. I hand her a glass of water with the red straw I found in her cutlery drawer last night. I watch her slender throat move as she swallows the pill.

"Not your fault." She sets her drink on her nightstand and tilts her head back on the pillow, squeezing her eyes shut again. "Distract me, Sly."

"Hey, now—wait a second. Does that stand for Slytherin?"

She grins, maybe a little smug despite her tired face.

"You know, you don't strike me as an HP fan," I tell her.

Her face twists and her eyes peek open again, just so she can narrow them at me. "Who calls it HP?" she asks, heavy-lidded.

"I do."

She cracks one eyelid while the other stays shut, throwing me some hard shade. "When'd you read it?"

"The year it came out. Which, for you young'uns, was 1997."

"Really?" Her soft voice drips skepticism.

"Oh yeah." I fold my arms.

"How old were you?" she asks, arching a brow.

"I was fourteen."

"How'd you come across it?" She brings her palm to her face and presses it against her forehead. It catches my notice because it's something I do when I don't feel well.

"School library," I say.

"And you're how old now?"

"I'm turning thirty-six."

She shakes her head. "Old-school oldie from Oldsville. You know I'm ten years younger."

I roll my eyes. "I'm in my prime."

"Are you, though?" She takes a strand of her honey-colored hair between her fingers, playing with the ends as she looks up at me.

"Oh yeah."

She gives me a strained smile. "Can this be verified?"

I have to work hard to contain the answer that springs to mind—and twitches my cock. "No need for that." I arch my eyebrows. "It's obvious to everyone."

She laughs, then recoils. Pain drags at her features, and I feel a kick of guilt for not waking her up to take the pain med.

"Fuck. I'm sorry."

After a slow, careful exhalation, she opens her eyes again and looks up at me. "We must officially be friends now. That's a couple different sorries in the last twelve hours."

"Do you want to be friends?"

"I don't know." She tries to smirk, I think, but it looks like a wince. "What's in it for me?"

"Not very much," I tell her honestly. "Maybe some packages from overseas with weird candy."

"Weird candy? Like little gummy microphones from Tokyo, that sort of thing?" I nod, and she smiles. "Sold."

"Don't forget the five-star mattress-side service. Are you hungry?"

She makes a face, looking pale and weary. "I don't know."

"Eating is a good thing. Just tell me what to get you."

She runs a hand through her hair. "Toast?"

"What kind?"

"Umm, butter and jelly?"

"Butter first, then jelly?"

She nods, looking amused.

"Okay," I say. "I'm on it."

When I return with a plate containing one slightly toasted piece of bread that's topped by butter and a layer of homemade jelly, her eyes are closed.

"How are the kids?" she whispers without opening them.

"I don't know." My gaze jumps to the clock on her beside table, which says it's 9:05 AM. "I'll call if you want, though."

"It's okay," she murmurs, her eyes still shut. "I can, since you don't know her."

Fuck...her voice is quiet. And she's still. Jesus, she looks small under her blankets. She even looks small compared to her big, black boot. I hope the hard edge of her pain is blunted by the medicine I brought her.

"I do sort of know her," I say, of her sister Mary Helen. "We talked some during the rodeo."

Her eyes lift open, and even in her more sedated state, she gives me side eye. "Did you?"

"Yeah." I grin, feeling a flash of silly pride. "She liked me."

She snorts. "MH could talk the ears off of a chicken."

I narrow my eyes at her. "Do chickens have ears?"

Her lips curl in a slow smile. "Yes, you dumb-dumb." She shuts her eyes. "Lil' trivia. The eggs they lay..." She pulls her eyelids open again, and her gaze is less focused. "Same color eggs...as the color of their ears."

"That's just weird."

She yawns. "I'm a wellspring of knowledge. Whip your ass at trivia night," she murmurs.

"I'd like test that out sometime."

"You're on, Sly."

She rubs a hand over her face, and I step back, aware I'm staring at her with more than a little intensity while she's only partly awake.

"You want anything else, Gryffy? A big bag of ice to put over the boot or something?"

"No," she whispers. Her face tightens, like the mention of ice hurt her.

"You still hurting?"

She nods, just a little motion.

A flush of heat spreads down my cheeks and neck and settles in my chest. I look down at her. She's got her shoulders sort of curled in. Her eyebrows are rumpled, her smooth, pale face tense. I don't like it.

My gaze moves all up and down her a few times. I tell myself that I should step away, stop staring down at her like some weird stalker.

Instead, I reach down slowly, gather a handful of her blonde-brown hair in my hand, and rub my thumb down the smooth locks, until it's right there at the slightly prickly ends. Trying to remember how she did this to her own hair, I just sort of toy with them. I'm holding my breath, and then she groans softly and my heart starts to pound.

"Feels so good," she murmurs. Her lips twitch a little, so I keep sifting through her hair. And very soon, she's sleeping.

CHAPTER 13

JUNE

"Yes! *C'mon...*" Then there's a long, put-out sigh. "Don't close your eyes again, June. I've got needs!"

The words trail slowly through my brain, a distant comet I can't quite make out. And then I do. *Needs?*

I squint my eyes open and recoil at the face nearly mashed against my own. "Leah? What are you doing?"

She sighs again and stands to her full height—which is a good thing.

"Finally," she sighs. "I've been waiting for a half an hour."

I blink around my room, feeling so confused. "Waiting?"

"For you to wake up and explain that—" She nods toward the door, then waves both her hands in the air, as if we can talk via some drunken sign language.

"What is that?" I rasp, then swallow to steady my voice. "A mime of a dying bird?"

"Who is that schemxy thang out in your living room?" She bats her lashes.

"Are you having some kind of malfunction?" I squeeze my eyes shut, then attempt to shift my butt, which is asleep, but somehow still aching. "I think I've got bed sores."

"How are you? How is your foot, poor baby?"

I roll my eyes. "*Now* you ask."

She pulls the blankets down, revealing a plain white shirt and thin gray pants I must have gotten at the hospital—and my giant black boot.

Then her eyes fly back to mine. "I'm serious, Bug. Is that really Mr. Puppy Surprise?"

"Yes." If my voice is snippy, it's because I've been hit by a horrifying memory.

"What's the matter?" Leah frowns down at me.

"Nothing."

"You are acting so weird. Maybe it's the drugs. What are you taking?"

"I'm not acting weird," I lie. "But I do need to pee. Like immediately."

Leah rambles nonstop as she and one of my brand new crutches help me to the bathroom. Then it's time to sit down, and she's staring at me.

"Turn around, you Looky Lucy."

"How're you going to lower yourself down onto the—*Buggie!* Did he do that?"

"Do what?" My ankle is pounding.

"There are rails on your toilet! You've got those old people rails."

I look down—she's right; I do—then look back up at her. "Well, hot dog."

"He had to have done it. No one else has been at your house."

"What time is it? And turn around."

She turns around, revealing ombre hair that fades from dark brown then to medium and then to blonde down at the bottom.

"It's half past noon."

"Y'all left me out here by myself till noon?"

"He's your brother's best friend now, girl. Shawn has got a keg for tonight."

"*What?*"

Leah flashes a lipsticked smile over her shoulder. "Oh yeah. Shawn and Mary Helen are ready to marry you off to Mr. Moneybags. That or Shawn's gonna go gay for him. But if that doesn't work out, imma get my claws in him. You said you hate his blood and guts, right?"

I shut my eyes again and finish doing my business. Then I stand up, using the rails.

"Are you *sure* you didn't bring these?" I ask.

"Sure as shit, babe." She steps closer, frowning at the rails attached to my toilet. "It's not a these. It's like…a this." Leah squints like she's trying to understand the entire manufacturing process for the potty handles.

Then she looks at my face. "Hun, you look like death. I think we should get you back in bed and I can bring some of these dumplins that MH sent."

"You went by Mary Helen's house?"

"Oh yeah—and I got cards from your darlins. Real cute, too. I'll grab my purse and get 'em out. It's in the den with him." She says "him" with arched brows. While she helps me back into the bed, Leah regales me with the tale of how she had forgotten Burke would be here, and she found him in the yard with Tink and Petey. "Girl, he didn't have a shirt on. It was masterful."

That makes me laugh. "You know his last name, right?"

"Nu-uh."

"Masterson."

"Well I understand. He is a masterpiece of sculpted man meat. I could lick that six pack. Might of even been an eight pack."

"Leah, this is outright disloyal. You and Shawn and MH." I told Leah and Mary Helen in particular—*before* the rodeo—to steer clear of the devil.

"Bug, maybe you were wrong about him."

At that moment, there's a knock on my door.

"Come in," I call. Then I flop back on my pillow. Better to make him think I'm half asleep. Maybe then he'll leave.

Leah turns fully away from me so she can smile at him. I can hear the smile in her voice. "Well hello there, Mr. Masterson."

Burke looks gorgeous, damn him all the way to Hades. He's got on a sort of snug gray T-shirt and those dark jeans and those black boots, but what's such a show stopper is his face with stubble on his jaw. There's a pair of aviator glasses hanging from his shirt collar, and his dark brown hair looks windblown.

"How's it going?" he asks softly, taking a few slow steps into my room. His eyes find mine. "How're you feeling, June?"

"Like she just got hit by a Mack truck," Leah supplies.

"I brought another one of these." He holds a pill up, and I let out a sigh.

"I don't really think I need it, honestly." I'm looking at the ceiling. Better there than at his devil blue eyes.

"You don't?" He steps closer to my bed, and I can feel him looking at me, even as I refuse to look at him.

"Nah."

"You sure?"

"I'll take some ibuprofen. Leah knows where it is."

As soon as I say that, I wish I could slap my own face. Now I'll be left here with him!

"I can show you," Leah coos.

The little hussy.

She walks toward the door, and when Burke doesn't follow, she's got tact enough to carry on by herself. Or I could choose to view it as her choosing to abandon me.

"Are you sure you don't want it?" he asks. "You don't have to take too many more of them, but right now, it's still a fresh break. Lots of pain the first day or so."

I nod. Swallow. I look up at him because I have to. I'm trapped in the damn bed.

I'm surprised and unnerved to find he looks...worried. Or something different than I've seen before. His face is nice, like a nice guy's face. Those blue devil eyes are gentle as he looks me over.

"I'm not sure if I believe you."

"Oh, how would you know?" I snap.

"Because your jaw is tight." He taps his own. "And you look tired, but also tense around your eyebrows." He rubs his finger over his brows.

"That's not how to tell."

"I've been watching you since last night."

"Oh, since last night." I shut my eyes and turn my face away from him.

"Yes, since last night. And I can tell you need this. Why don't you want to take it? Are you scared of taking pain pills?"

I look balefully up at him. "I'm scared of you. Being all up in my business. Trying to charm my family, win them over so they'll love you, and they won't know you're the devil. I don't need to take those hard drugs." I saw Mama take so many of them in her last days. I don't want to be all drugged out. "Not when I can get by on Tylenol and Advil."

I'm surprised when he sits on the edge of my bed. "Juney. Would the devil buy you toilet armrests?" He quirks a brow, and I hate him for being so attractive.

"He might."

"If he did, what would his evil motive be?"

"Maybe to have them malfunction so I would fall in."

He grins. It's a smile I've never seen before. It lights his face up so he's fifty times more hot than he is when he looks all scowly.

"What joy would the devil get from that?"

I shrug. "Delight in other people's misery."

His face falls. "You think I would delight in your misery?"

"This from the man who gave me two puppies that I didn't ask for?" I lift an accusing brow.

His eyes widen. "You want me to take them?"

"Well not *now*. The kids love those little fluff balls, and I'm partial to them, too. But it's still your fault."

He scrubs a hand over his face. "Yeah...I hate to say it, but you might have called it right."

I lift my brow again.

"I am an asshole. I know. I just...wasn't myself lately. Even when I am, sometimes I'm a dick." He looks so somber, almost uncomfortable with this confession.

I give him a smartass smirk. "The dark arts can be hard to give up." I flex my toes—a habit, I guess—and pain shoots up my hurt leg.

His eyes widen again, and again, he holds the pill out. He gives me a stern look.

"I'm tired of sleeping," I whine.

His face gentles. "Sleep is what you need, Gryff."

I yawn, and then laugh as he says, "See?"

"My brother's coming," I say with a warning look toward him as I reach for my water. "Leah says he's bringing kegs with him, which means he'll be trailed by his friends. His redneck, lunatic friends. If someone lights my yard on fire, I'm holding you responsible."

His dark brows rumple, and a crooked smile twists his lips. "Me?" He gestures to himself, and I nod solemnly.

"You're my proxy."

I swallow the pill and blink up at him. Burke looks down at me. Nobody breaks the gaze until Leah flounces into the room. Then he steps back, hands in pockets.

"You two need anything?" he asks.

"How are the dogs? Where are the kids?" My voice is hoarse. I swallow, and Leah leans in to press her palm against my cheek.

"Dogs are great," she supplies. "Your boy here has been walking them and all that good stuff. Pups and big ones. Kids are eating burgers at MH's before they all come over here."

"Sensible. Clearly I'm throwing a party."

"I'll host for you," Leah says with a wink.

A few minutes later, she and Burke leave the room together. It takes a minute for the knot that's in my chest to loosen up. Maybe it never does. I don't know. Sleep takes me.

CHAPTER 14

JUNE

Leah is a traitor. I need a shower. As my best friend, she should know that, but she's clearly got her mind on other things. When I wake up—still early enough that there's dim sunlight bleeding through my bedroom curtains—I lie quietly in bed and listen to the house.

I listen to the voices, ticking off attendees to my broken ankle party one by one, and then I wait for Leah. When she doesn't pop in—and no one else does, either—I shoot her a text.

Can u come in my room? I'm a beached June...

Fifteen minutes later, I hop out of bed onto my good foot and grab for a crutch. I've got it and am wobbling toward the other one—a little farther toward the bed's footboard—when the bedroom door opens and Burke steps inside.

"Whoa..."

He's over to me in an instant, wrapping an arm behind my back and leaning me against his big, warm body.

"Shit, are you okay?"

I've grabbed onto his forearm with one of my hands, and I realize my fingers are shaking. "Totally fine."

I look up at him, and he grins. "Your hair."

"Crazy?" I ask.

"A little."

I sigh. "I tried to summon Leah, but I guess she wasn't checking her texts."

"She's been grilling." I frown, because that's weird, and he explains, "Your brother burned his hand, and then he got caught up talking with a friend of his."

"Foster?"

"Yeah, the blond guy?"

I nod. He looks down at me, and I look up at him, and suddenly I'm too warm. "I just need to get these crutches under my arms, and I should be good to go."

"Where are you going?"

"Powder room."

"What is the powder room?" He looks genuinely puzzled.

"It's the lady's room, Burke."

His eyes light up, as if he finds that funny. "I can help you over there."

"No thanks."

"No?"

"You know. It's kind of personal."

"Even walking to the door?"

I sniff. "Just pass me that crutch there and leave my bedroom door open. Then skedaddle."

"Is your lair a women only space?" He's smirking.

"Just no snakes."

That brings forth his quiet chuckle as his big hand grips my waist and he helps me steady myself on the crutches.

"What do you think?" he asks. "Have you ever used crutches before?"

"Nope."

"Why don't we do a little practice? Oh, and—" He pulls something from his pocket.

I shake my head before he even opens his palm. "Not another one of those. I'm like a zombie already."

He smiles and shakes his head and then he pulls three Advil from his other pocket. "This more your speed right now?"

"Thank you." He holds my water glass for me, and I swallow the pills using the red straw. After that, his eyes are on me, and my freaking cheeks are burning. There's not enough air for both of us in this little room. "So I guess my family just abandoned me to the stranger."

HATE YOU NOT

"A handsome stranger," he says. "Charming, too. At least that's what I heard them say." He shrugs.

I roll my eyes. "Keep fishing like that and you might just fall in."

That makes him laugh again. "You Southern people and your phrases."

"Down here, we call them sayings."

"Do you now?" He does it again! Smiles at me until my cheeks are too hot.

"Okay, so what do I do? Just like this?" I swing my body in between the crutches, moving toward the bathroom. "Pretty easy."

"You're a natural."

A thought hits me like a lightning bolt. "Hot Rocket! What happened?" I try to whirl around so I can face him, and he's there to grab my arm so I don't bust my fool ass. When I'm steady, I see something like concern pass over his face. My stomach lurches so hard I feel sick.

"Oh, please—"

"He's okay."

I shut my eyes against the tears that burn behind my eyelids. "Okay." I swallow, and I can feel him stepping closer to me again.

"He's okay. He has a fracture, but it's an incomplete fracture. One of the small bones in the right front leg. It's just a crack, upper part of the leg. He's going to be okay."

I nod, but a tear drips down my temple. *It was my fault.*

"It wasn't your fault."

My gaze snaps to his. "Yes it was. I felt him struggle with his footing a few seconds before he fell, but I didn't adjust course."

"Define a 'few' seconds."

I swallow, shaking my head. I don't know. It might have been milliseconds, but it still counts.

He nods. "There wasn't enough time. It might have felt like seconds, but it wasn't. It was fractions of a second, more likely."

Another thought occurs to me. "Where is he now? Who has him?"

"He's at a vet in Albany."

"In Albany," I repeat slowly. The vet we usually use is over in Dawson.

"Your brother and I talked about it at the hospital. By phone. We've got it figured out."

I sigh, because I'm sure that means Shawn is, again, spending money on me that he doesn't have.

I'm surprised when Burke's hand skims my shoulder. "Don't worry about this stuff now. I mean it when I said he's going to be okay. Shawn can tell you more about him. If he slows up on the drinking." He grins.

"Oh, he won't. Especially not if Foster's here. Those two could drain the ocean."

He smiles like it's a novelty—my country brother and his dumb friend.

"Bunch of drunks around here."

"They're just having fun," Burke says.

"So much to celebrate."

His face softens. "Yeah...I'm sorry."

I hiss softly as I crutch my way toward the bathroom. He says, "I heard that." Then he adds, "Want me to wait outside?"

"No thanks."

"I'll leave your bedroom door open, and I'll be watching for you coming down the hall. I already pulled the runner up."

I should thank him for that—for all of this; he's doing one hell of a nice guy impression—but I can't seem to find the words. I shut the bathroom door behind me, feeling annoyed. I'm tired and confused, and evidently my brother has used the occasion of my injury to hold a kegger. I realize I asked Burke about Hot Rocket but not the kids, and I feel like a crummy guardian to boot.

I look at myself in the mirror, and I shed a few tears, feeling sorry for myself and feeling like I'm failing Sutton. Then I wash my face, spray dry shampoo into my hair, and balance my hip on the counter while I braid my hair, so I look less rumpled.

I go back into my room and open the drawer that holds my pajama pants, but quickly realize I can't fit them over my boot thing. I could wear shorts, maybe. One-size-too-big Nike running shorts and a cozy sweatshirt. I shut my door and check my phone again before endeavoring to dress myself.

Freaking Leah.

I heave a heavy sigh and use the armchair near the bed to dress myself, praying the whole time that Burke doesn't pop in. When I'm ready, I crutch my way into the hall and down the rugless floor, into the den, where Leah and the kids are playing Chinese checkers. The kids jump up and run to me, their faces rapt and their eyes wide as they check me out.

"Poor June!" Margot says. "But you look so beautiful."

That makes me laugh. "Do you think so?"

"I do," Leah says.

I shoot her a quick look and then focus on Oliver, who's tilting his head. "Why is your cast plastic, and it's black? When Margot broke her arm, she had a real cast. It was purple."

"Oh, I'm getting one of those soon. In a few days. Would you like it to be purple?"

He shakes his head. "I want it to be camo!"

He tugs at the ball cap on his head—a Dawgs cap. My family works fast to indoctrinate.

"Your sister bought them both hats." Leah looks around, and I hear Mary Helen laughing loudly in the kitchen.

"Mine is pink!" Margot runs and grabs it from the coffee table.

"I love it, honey."

"Go Dawgs!" Margot does a little jump, drawing my gaze to the dress she's wearing. It's denim and some kind of burlap, with a big bow tied in front. She's wearing little leather boots with it, and in her hair is a big, satin bow.

Leah smirks behind Margot's back, as if to say, *Yeah, I saw.*

In addition to the camo Dawgs cap, Oliver has on navy blue cargo pants, loafers, and a button-up, plaid shirt I've never seen. Like I said, they're fast workers.

At that moment, Mary Helen comes into the living room, holding a plate of cheese dip and Fritos. I spend the next five minutes being fussed over by her—right in front of Oliver and Margot. Like some kind of child.

She leans in when she's finished with her hen-pecking, and murmurs, "Took them shopping. What do you think?"

"You didn't have to do that. Thank you, though."

Head-sized bows and church attire for everyday wear is one of those Southern things that never really appealed to me. Mary Helen still won't let any of her kids pick their clothes. I'd like to let Oliver and Margot have some choices.

"You look exhausted," she says. "Let's get you down on the couch."

"Actually, I want to go outside."

It's still light out. From where I'm standing, it looks near sunset.

"I want to sit on the porch swing."

"And let your ankle hang down?" Mary Helen looks at me like I'm crazy.

"Fresh air might be good for her," Leah says, and I feel grateful.

"Let's play Frisbee outside!" Margot and Oliver race out onto the porch, and that makes me smile.

"They *are* thriving," Leah says with a grin.

"Unlike others of us," I hiss to her as Mary Helen heads back toward the kitchen. "Have you checked your texts?"

"Um...no. Did you send a message?"

"No, I'm just asking about your texts for shits and giggles."

"Someone's grumpy."

"I'm not grumpy."

The kids left the porch door cracked, and at that moment, I hear someone's laughter through it. My stomach does an actual flip, and Leah narrows her eyes.

"Something's got you thrown off." She steps closer to me, and her eyes spark with recognition. "Is it him?"

"Who, Shawn?"

She rolls her eyes so hard, I think they might fall to the floor. "C'mon. You might hate him, but you do have eyes."

"Not sure if you're aware, I broke my ankle last night." Now it's my turn to roll my eyes. "It's literally throwing me off my ability to walk in the bipedal fashion. Which can make one grumpy."

She makes a yeah-right face. "That's not it."

The front doorbell rings, and Leah gives me a look before dashing off. Classic. Ever since we were kids, Shawn has been known for throwing impromptu parties. Probably because he's a classic extrovert. Also possibly because he has a low-key drinking problem.

I don't even stick around to see who's at the front door, although I hear Ben Hollis, Leah's latest fuck friend, as I push the screen door partly open with my crutch.

Then I hear my own name. I peer through the screen as my brother, who is standing beside the porch swing, gestures with a red solo cup. I can't make out his words because Leah is guffawing loudly somewhere behind me, probably at something not funny that Ben said.

Then I hear that chuckle again. It makes my whole face heat up. Fucker.

I push the door further open and there he is. Not my brother, but the stranger among us. Burke opens the door, holding it wider than necessary as I hobble out onto the porch.

"The woman of the hour," Shawn says, grinning. "Were your ears burning?"

"What the hell does that mean?"

He wisely tries to change the subject. "How ya feeling, sis?"

"Just dandy."

"How do you feel, really?"

"I'm fine. Hate to interrupt your conversation about me."

He has the good grace to break eye contact and look embarrassed. "Oh, just talking a little shit."

I look at Burke. "What was he saying?"

"Don't put him on the spot, June," Shawn answers. "I was telling him about that time you tried to raise those chipmunks."

"What?" I fix Shawn with a go-to-hell look, because that particular story isn't funny.

"She was so cute," Shawn tells Burke. "Maybe seven or eight. Is that right, Buggie?"

"I was nine." I look to Burke. "It's not a funny story."

Shawn presses onward, just to be a dick I'm sure. "She found a mama chipmunk by this log in the yard. There were little babies in it, so she busted them out. Took them inside and tried to raise them. She didn't tell our mama, so it didn't work out real good, but June thought she was their new mama."

Fury throbs through my head and tightens in my throat as I realize how tone deaf this story is, now in particular. My fatally flawed maternal efforts should probably be shoved under the rug right now.

"Then there was the wild hare. Did Buggie mention him?"

I shoot Shawn a fury-filled look. *No, I didn't, dipshit. Because I barely know Burke, and I've spent approximately 89 percent of the time I have known him hating him.*

"One of our cousins—was it Carla, Bug?—she had this giant ass black hare. You know, like a big ole rabbit?" Shawn spreads his hands about a foot apart, to show how big the hare was. "That thing was a psycho." He chugs down more of his beer, and I notice a keg set up behind him on my porch rug.

"It could jump from the kitchen floor up on the counter in one leap, with those big ole feet. Kinda creepy."

Burke chuckles. When I catch his eye, his smile softens.

"She was always taking things in. Real maternal like that," Shawn continues. "Mama caught her trying to breastfeed a baby doll when she was, I don't know, maybe three?"

"Shawn!" I jerk my head around so I can glare right at him. "Would you like me to tell your bath bomb penis story?"

His lips press together, twitching at the corners. "Not particularly."

"That's what I thought." He holds a hand up, saunters toward the door that leads from porch to yard. "I gotta check the grill. Burke, you get her some beer and cool her down."

I shut my eyes. Because if I don't, I'll either blush so hot my head will explode, or I'll lose my shit and cuss my stupid, sexist brother out.

"You want to sit down?" Burke asks when it's just us on the porch.

I hobble to the swing, and he follows, grabbing my arm gently.

"Let me at least stop the thing from swinging."

As I'm sitting down, the door bursts open, and the kids—all five of them—rush onto the porch, trailed by Peach and Mario, the puppies. I don't have the energy to police that situation—what I really need is to get my foot up on the swing, too, or go to the couch—but Burke disappears behind them. A second later, Leah and Ben step out.

For a few minutes, the three of us chat. Ben's family owns a local landscaping business. His family is really nice, but he's never been the brightest bulb in our crowd. I carry the conversation even though I spent the last twelve hours drugged out of my gourd. Then Shawn and Foster call to Ben, and he's out the door, down the steps, and into the lawn, cast orangey with the sunset.

Leah drops into a chair beside the swing.

"You making that work?" she asks, running a fingertip over the swing's arm.

"Yes."

"You pissy with me?"

"No, Leah."

"Your britches are burning. It's not my fault I think he's a catch. Guy's worth more than the bank."

"I don't really think that's how banks work, L."

She shrugs. "You want me to give him the frosty shoulder?" I can tell from her tone that it's an actual offer.

I sigh. "No. It's okay."

"He seems like he's being nice to you."

"He is."

"So what's the trouble?"

I rub my forehead.

"I'm gonna read my crystal ball, how about that?" She waves her hands around in a vaguely circular motion and peers down at them. "You're fussy that you got stuck with him last night. Felt too intimate and personal for your introverted self. Then your dumbass brother decided to do a neighborhood cookout. For you, but we know how Shawn is. More of his crew will be over in a little bit. Someone's gonna end up passed out in the bushes." I widen my eyes at that tidbit, and Leah nods. "Heard them talking."

I sigh again.

"You know Shawn thinks he's doing it for you."

"Oh, he is doing it for me. I just don't want it."

"Mary Helen cooked enough to fill your kitchen. Did you go in there yet?"

"No." I roll my eyes.

"Fishing for the compliments," Leah says of Mary Helen, smirking.

"No doubt."

"What can I get for you, darlin'?"

The kids streak by us again—and again, they're trailed by the puppies. I wrap my arms around myself. "Maybe some water?"

"Sure thing."

Leah knows me well enough to know it's time to stop discussing Mr. Ritchy Ritch. I spend a few minutes alone in my thoughts, and then, like a ghost, there he is. I look over, and he's standing by the screen porch bookshelf, hands stuffed in his pockets, looking at me like a dog that's looking at a bumble bee, all puzzled.

"What can I do for you, Mr. Masterson?" My voice sounds much more casual than I feel.

He smiles, lips pressed lightly together. "What can I do for you, Ms. Lawler?"

"I'm just fine."

Some truck rolls up into the yard, and I'm pretty sure it's that ridiculous, gas-guzzling F-350 that belongs to Slim, another of Shawn's bros. Shawn calls for Burke—probably to drunkenly introduce him—and I shoo Burke toward the lawn. "Go on, Sly."

In the next half hour, two more of Shawn's friends pop up, followed by Latrice, a high school friend of mine who helps me run the farm as sort of a chief operating officer. Our families have worked together for two generations, so it's really pretty cool. She comes bearing a plate of my favorite fried chicken and a tub of okra, plus a hug I guess I kind of need, because when her arms go around my shoulders, tears burn at the corners of my eyelids.

"Aww. Poor Buggie. Are you worried about your partner in crime?" She means Hottie.

I nod, wiping my eyes. "Sorry. I think I'm just over-tired."

She nods, but she sees through me. Overtired means overwhelmed.

"Kids still look real good. How's that been going?"

"I don't know. Maybe okay? They had to stay with Mary Helen last night." I glance over at the lawn, where Shawn has set up three card tables and a variety of chairs, complete with checkered plastic tablecloths. Actually, I bet that bit was MH.

"It's okay for them to stay with her," she says. "They're loving those puppies, aren't they?"

"Yes."

"I'm surprised you got them, though. They from the Danson's place?"

"I didn't get them."

So begins a fifteen minute conversation about Burke—a conversation during which I try to keep my feelings hidden, but Latrice knows me too well for that.

"So he's sort of a bastard, but he's tall and...what is it? Tall, dark, and handsome?" She smirks, and I shrug. "Handsome to someone."

"I'm not really into white boys, but I know a fine ass when I see one."

"Oh, go eat a drumstick."

She grins. "I think I will."

In the end, Oliver, Margot, Latrice, Leah, and I eat dinner on the porch, while all the others—including Burke, who apparently is now a member of my family—eat out on the lawn, under the glow of tiki torches. The kids entertain us with handstands against the screen porch's plywood scaffolding, and Shawn's nine million friends tromp up the steps to refill at the keg and ask how I'm feeling.

Leah brings me Tylenol and Advil as the night wears on, and later, right around the time I start thinking the kids should go to bed, Shawn appears on the porch stairs and says, "We're gonna do a truck ride!"

"Right now?"

"Huntin' for dem snipes," he says in an exaggerated twang.

Margot and Oliver start to giggle, and Shawn pulls the porch door open. "Come on down, little lady and gent. It's time to hop up in the truck bed and go see some stars and see if you can catch some snipes."

Leah stands up, looking wide-eyed. "I'll drive!"

CHAPTER 15

BURKE

I watch through a living room window until the yard is empty and the truck bed teems with shadow figures, glowing faintly red from Shawn's brake lights. Oliver and Margot are surrounded by their cousins, sitting near Mary Helen, and if the truck's cab light is any indication, it looks like Leah got the driver job she wanted. For the best, since she's the only one of them who seems sober.

When I squint, I'm pretty sure that's Shawn by Mary Helen; he's laughing.

Everyone is ready to go except June.

I wait until the truck disappears down the driveway. Then I look around the kitchen, grab some kind of homemade cookie—oatmeal?—and a glass of water, plus her pain meds and the Tylenol and Advil, and, with my pockets stuffed full of pill bottles and the big dogs snuffing over the gate at the laundry room door, I step onto the porch.

June whirls around so quickly, I'm afraid she's going to tumble off the porch swing.

"Jesus Lord! You scared the bejeezus out of me!" Thankfully, she laughs then, her face lit up and her hand drawn to her chest. "What are you *doing* here?"

I grin and pull pill bottles from my pockets. "Brought you dessert."

"What?" She gives me a funny look, like she's not sure why I would bring her painkillers, but I know she needs them. Her face looks tired, a little tight around the brows and mouth.

"What will it be? Ibuprofen? This handy bottle of Acetaminophen? Or the big guns?" I jiggle the prescription bottle. "Often considered more necessary after the sun goes down." I gesture at the dark sky.

She snorts. "Why are you here, anyway?"

"I told you. To bring you your dessert."

She narrows her eyes. "Just know that I'm skeptical."

I open the prescription bottle, and she shakes her head. "I'll take Tylenol. And then I think I can have more Advil in—"

"An hour," I say with her.

She puts her hands over her face. "Now I'm really troubled. Who are you and where did you put the devil?"

I tap my chest and do my best to give her an evil look to match the evil voice I use when I say, "Don't worry, he's still in here."

"You are so weird."

I keep the strange expression on my face as I hand her the water, but I'm grinning as I watch her swallow the Tylenol.

"What do you think about me sitting by you?" I ask.

"Well if you mean swinging on that imaginary swing there"—she points a finger at nothing— "that would work. Because, I don't know if you can tell with demon vision, but I'm kinda occupying this one."

"Yeah. But you won't be if I do this." I lift her leg with care, sit down, and set her boot atop my thigh. I lean my head back and look at the porch's ceiling and the lazily turning fan.

"I love swings," I tell her with my eyes shut.

"Why are you being so nice to me?"

"This is my routine to get you comfortable so I can eat your soul. Don't question it."

She sighs. "This is so awk."

"Does that mean is aw-akened? Cousin to the hyper-trendy 'woke'?"

She widens her eyes, giving me a scolding type of look. "Burke, it means awkward."

"You want me to get up? That would work, too."

"I didn't say that. But this is a boyfriend thing to do."

I take that like a kick to the chest. But I don't want to make things even more *awk*, so I roll with it. "Well, I'm a boy. And I'm your friend. You don't strike me as girlfriend material, though."

When she gasps, I laugh and press on. "Not for me. I think you're looking for more of an angel type. Less on the two horns and pitchfork. At least that's what I'm hearing," I say in a therapist type manner.

"For sure. If I was looking at all. And I'm so not."

"No?"

"Oh no," she says, leaning her head against the swing's back. "This is definitely more communicating than I normally do with people who hiss, but yeah. I mean, there's nobody around here."

"Really, nobody?" I tap my fingers to my chin. "Does that mean there is literally no male your age in this corner of the state, or more like no one you *prefer*?"

She sighs. "I can't believe I'm telling you this. My sworn enemy."

"We're not enemies anymore. Remember? I surrendered."

"I think I remember something like that. And an apology? I was sort of out of it, though, so I may need to hear it again. Just to really enjoy it." She's trying to keep a straight face, but I can see the little smirk at one corner of her mouth. And then I see the dimple. She's so fucking pretty.

"I can do that for you," I say.

June blinks a few times quickly, which makes me laugh. She winces, and I look down at her boot on my leg.

"No more laughing," I pledge.

"Should be easy for you."

"So easy." She blinks again, and I can't help grinning. "Okay, so where was I? I was going to say...I'm sorry."

She nods, urging me on.

"I'm sorry I came to your house and was presumptive." That make her lips twitch. "I was condescending and dickish. I had a goal in mind, and I was going after it. But I was still a shit about it, and I'm sorry."

She moves her hand in a circle, urging me to continue.

"And now, I want to start things over. You're their aunt. You're keeping them here. I'm the uncle with the asshole tendencies and the fat wallet. You keep me updated on them, tell me what you need, and I can help—if that works." I rub my forehead, looking at the patterns on the porch rug as I confess, "That's really all I want." I bite down on the inside of my cheek and force myself to lift my gaze to hers. "I want to make my brother happy."

The confession makes my throat tight, so I shift my eyes toward the dark night framed by the screen porch's wood beam scaffolding.

ELLA JAMES

"I know," she whispers. "Because that's what I want, too. To make both of them proud."

I don't know if I can talk about this—not even with her. I run my fingertip along the outside of her plastic boot and blink out at the field that spreads out on the right side of her house until I feel more steady.

"How are you feeling?" I ask after a minute of silence.

She sighs. "Tired and grumpy. It's annoying, breaking an ankle. And I'm pissy about Hot Rocket."

"I really think he'll be okay."

"You're really a horse guy?"

"You might say that."

"You been riding since the preschool age bracket?"

I grin. "Have you?"

"Since I was two."

"Wow, really? Three in my case."

"I was a little green bean. Tall," she clarifies.

"Were you really?"

"No, I'm just making shit up." She smiles, and I squint as I try to picture her standing upright. Is she taller than I recall?

"I only grew to be five-foot-four," she clarifies. "I think that thing about the correlation between two year old height and adult height is baloney."

"Oh, you mean *bologna.*"

She snorts. "You are something else."

"Do you drop all your 'g's?"

She shoots me a warning look, like she thinks I might really start to make fun of her.

"You know we do. They're not really needed."

"I think I've come to agree with you. I think maybe they're better dropped." She's still giving me a skeptical look when I give her another I'm-your-friend smile. "I like your accent."

"If I hear it's cute or sweet or funny from another stranger, it'll make me puke."

"You get a lot of that?"

"Oh yeah. Mostly it's so *sweet.* That's not real aspirational for when you're in your later twenties." She shakes her head. "Margot and Oliver have got that Yankee accent."

I guffaw at that before I can stop myself. "Did you just say Yankee?"

134

She's glaring at me again. "What do you want me to say? Northern? It's the same thing."

"No it isn't. For one, California isn't really northern."

"Beg to differ. North of here."

"It's West Coast."

"Like Tupac?"

I grin, imaging her listening to Tupac. "It's more west than north."

She rolls her eyes. "Semantics. I'm not wrong, either. They were on the Union side in the War of Northern Aggression."

I think she's being serious until she throws her head back laughing.

"Oh, c'mon," she laughs. "Nobody's really calling it that with a straight face."

"I've seen no less than two Confederate flags since I got to Heat Springs."

"Some people are dumbasses."

"So you're going to call our niece and nephew little Yankees, and you're still pissed off that California helped the Union cause, but you think it's dumbass to fly the Confederate flag?"

She shakes her head. "It's complicated. But here's what it boils down to. I don't like the flag or what it means these days, and we can do without those statues. I'm siding with living, hurting humans over and above the legacy of some dead soldiers. We all know what went down. Nobody needs a statue to remind us. So no, I don't fly that flag because it's hurtful. And I only called them Yankees because that's what my mama used to say, and you say what you hear. And anyway, you're not getting upset."

"Oh, I'm totally offended. Is my accent the Yankee kind?"

"Well, *yeah.*" She blinks at me a few times.

"You think it sounds bad?"

"Nah. I like it just fine. I'm not making you my boyfriend. I can handle hard Gs sometimes. They ain't gon kill me."

I lean toward her, stretch my arm along the swing's back. "Is that how you really talk? Like if you're drunk, do you slip into Southern dialect?"

"You were in the ER with me, what do you think?"

"I think you do a little bit."

She grins and shakes her head, and I think maybe she's embarrassed. "Hard to change an accent. Or a 'dialect.'"

"I wouldn't want you to."

"I wouldn't care if you did, Sly." She regards me for a minute, and I can tell she's thinking something.

"What?" I prompt.

"What kind of ladies go for tall, dark, and Slytherin out there in San Francisco?"

That makes me laugh. "I'm not a Slytherin."

"What are you then?"

"You already guessed it one time."

"Oh, because of MIT. You're saying you're a Ravenclaw." She quirks a brow up. "Nah. You ain't no Ravenclaw."

"I am. I'm Ravenclaw."

She shakes her head. "You keep telling yourself that, darlin'. I know if you pull your britches up, you've got some green socks hidden underneath there."

I pull them up and show her my black socks, and she snorts. "Well black'll do, too—for the devil."

I rub a hand back through my hair, and she smiles. "You're a little funnier than I was thinking."

"So a half step up from total bastard?"

"Maybe like a quarter step." She sinks a hand into her own hair, which is flowing down around her shoulders.

For a moment, it's just the wind through the trees. Then she shifts her weight a little, and the swing creaks.

"Entertain me, Sly. Tell me things about you. I'm not taking another Percocet because I've gotta watch the kids tonight, but I would like a distraction."

"Oh, so what I'm hearing is you want a houseguest—me. Someone to put the kids to bed and sleep on the couch to help if they get up at night. Which works out well, because I'm leaving in the morning, and I want to see them more."

I try to soften my expression so I look like a nice guy. I'm rewarded by another of her googly-eyed skeptical looks.

"First you didn't do the truck ride. Now you want to spend the night. Is this the prologue of a murder mystery?"

I'm laughing my ass off, so much that she winces. "Shit. I'm sorry." She looks disgruntled.

"No, it's not a murder mystery. This is Burke the *friend*."

She throws her head back, and her long hair falls over her breasts. "Burke the friend. You should trademark that and make a figurine. What is it they say? That's rich. And you're *rich*, so see, it works."

She chortles, making me want to deny it. But to her, it must seem like I am. "All my money isn't really...money."

She gives me a look that says she thinks I'm completely full of shit, but I shake my head. "It's not like you think. It's tied up in investments." Almost all of it is powering the startup right now. It's so expansive and complex, it's going to take a fortune just to get a workable beta running. "It's not in my bank account," I assure her.

"Oh yeah, I'm sure none of it's in your account."

"Okay, some of it is," I admit.

She leans back a little, picking at one of her fingernails before flicking her gaze back up to mine. "You need to drink some more so I can ask you what it's like to have that much money, and you can tell me."

"I can tell you now, I guess."

She arches a brow—an expression that should be dubbed the June Sees Through You. "When you buy food," she says with a blink and a faint accusing edge, "do you ever think about the price of things?"

I swallow...press my lips together.

"Mmm-hmm, didn't think so. What about clothes shopping? Do you buy your own stuff?"

Well, shit. How do I tell her my assistant does it? She laughs. "Lord, who does it?"

I'm not saying "my assistant," so I say, "Someone in my office." I tug at my shirt, hoping for a little relatable levity. "In fact, she got my last round of shirts a size too small."

"That does explain why I'd need some Paraflexx to peel it off you."

I flash her a grin as I notice she said "I" when speaking about who might pull it off me, and it's her turn to look awkward. "Not *I*," she quickly clarifies. "Somebody who wants to do that."

I let out a whoop. "Ms. Lawler with the burn." She shakes her head and rolls her eyes.

"What is Paraflexx?" I ask.

"Next question." She sits up a little, her eyes brightening like she just remembered something. "Do you cook your own food?"

"No, but I—"

"Next question." I widen my eyes and fix them on her face, and she locks her gaze onto mine like this is a fourth-grade staring contest. "Do you have more than one car?" She puts emphasis on the end of the sentence, inflecting it less like a question and more like an accusation.

I feel guilty.

"I'm guessing that the forehead rumple is a 'yes ma'am.' Is that your official answer, Mr. Masterson?"

I bite my lip, and she shakes her head. "How many?"

I wince. "Do you really want to know?"

"I *really* want to know."

I swallow. Seven is the answer, but I'm going for Joe Average when I tell her, "Four."

It's not uncommon for people to have just two or three cars, right? Four is only one more than that.

Her eyes bulge like they're going to pop out of her head. "*Four* cars? And one of them's not a practical pickup for hauling stuff, is it?"

"One of them's an Escalade for Tahoe," I try in a hopeful tone.

She looks confused. "Oh, *Lake* Tahoe. Is that in California? I don't even know. Geography was never my thing."

"It is."

"Tell me what other ones." She nudges my ass with her unhurt foot, and I grit my teeth as my cock throbs. "I bet I won't know any of their fancy pants names, but it's worth a try."

I shrug. "Oh, they're just...sedans."

"Is sedan code for flashy sportscar?"

I rub my forehead, holding my leg out a little and rolling my ankle like I'm distracted by a pain there—although in actuality, I'm avoiding her accusing eyes. "Define flashy."

June cackles. "Spit it out, showboat."

"Well." I cut my eyes her way, and decide I'll just let her have it. "I've got a Rolls-Royce Wraith. But that's for picking up investors...you know, driving them around and shit."

She nods, her big-eyed, tight-lipped expression making it clear that she is definitely judging me.

"I also have a Cullinan."

"Bonus points because I've never even heard of that one."

"It's an SUV."

"Oh, I thought you only had a fleet of practical sedans."

"I've got a DBS SV. That one's a car." An Aston Martin convertible is *technically* still a car. "Anyway, cars are investments. People collect them."

"Oh, I know. One of my friends collects cars. Whole junkyard with all the parts in different sections." She smirks, and I feel wealth-shamed. Which I guess I probably deserve.

"I didn't really expect to be so successful." As soon as I say it, something in my stomach gives a quick twist, like I'm stepping out onto a wire.

She nods slowly. "Well, at least that much sounds honest."

"I don't know why things worked out the way they did with the first two. First two companies," I tack on, figuring she might not follow if I call them startups. "The third one—the one I'm working on right now—it's a lot different."

"How so?" She's leaned back against the arm of the swing now, her unhurt leg tucked under the one whose boot is resting on my leg. She tucks her flowing hair behind her ears and leans forward slightly, a rapt pupil.

"It's more a medical app. More complex, because it peripherally deals with other entities like the local and state governments. It's dynamic. And has multiple functions."

She asks me what exactly we're doing—what the app's primary function is. I answer in the most general terms. I don't want her tracing the app's functionality to my mother's situation. As far as I know, nothing about that is available for public consumption at this point. My father had all those records sealed, and if he hadn't, I would have.

CHAPTER 16

JUNE

His startup seems to have something to do with helping people call 9-1-1 via an app. But I don't know more than that because he didn't seem interested in expounding.

A beat of silence follows, and during that sliver of time where the only sound is the wind through the trees, I work up the nerve to ask him what I really want to ask: "Did you really think I took them in for the money?"

Even through my giant, plastic ankle boot, I feel his body tense. But I've gotta give him credit—the guy's poker face is flawless. He exhales, so I can tell he's thinking on his answer before giving it. Then his eyes pin mine and he says, "No."

He sighs. "I mean—I didn't know for sure. But no. I didn't really think that, or I wouldn't have if I had thought about it. I did the easy thing and believed what I wanted to believe. What suited me," he adds after a beat.

He swallows, and I can see his jaw tick. "I did that because I wanted them," he says, facing the porch screen wall in front of him. "I wanted them because"—he shakes his head, a single hard shake, like there's water in his ear—"I needed something external to direct my focus at." He says it quietly.

In the silence that swims between us after that, I find that I feel... grateful. There's a crest of gladness and relief, and then this gratitude that's almost overwhelming.

"That was generous answer," I say, surprise seeping into my voice.

He gives me a soft smirk. "I'm a generous guy." His lips twitch, and he shakes his head. "That's a lie. I'm a big dick." He pairs the words with a deadpan face that's actually hilarious. I'm laughing. Then we're grinning at each other like old friends.

"You're not so bad," I concede.

He lifts a brow, and I add, "For the devil."

Burke mutters something about being right back and disappears inside, and just a minute later, the truck pulls back up and everyone spills out of it with stories about snipes.

I don't see him again until the house has cleared out. I told everyone he was staying late to put the kids to sleep and tell them goodbye, and no one thought a thing about it—except Leah's dumb ass. She grinned like a fool when she told me goodnight.

Once it's just the four of us remaining, Burke says he'll clean up the yard and take the dogs out while I put the kids to bed—"so they can do their thing with you." He pops in when I'm turning off the light, and Oliver convinces him to tell a story.

I don't know where to go. If I go into my room and make it up onto the bed, I won't be getting down without a lot of trouble. So if the two of us chat at all, it'll be in my room. And if I have to use the powder room, I might need help. I don't think that's a smart idea.

I crutch my way into the kitchen, get myself a glass of tea and a cookie without busting my ass, and settle on the couch. There's still the armchair if he wants to come and join me.

Join me doing what?

I hear the kids screaming—I think in glee—and figure I've got a few minutes to figure this out. I spend them wondering why I agreed to let him spend the night, and then telling myself it's stupid to be nervous. We're nothing more than friendly acquaintances, at best, and even though he's beautiful, with the body of a god, he's still the devil. I'm not tempted by the devil.

Guy like him could never be my type. I bet his boots have still got the price tag stickers on the bottom. If I touched his hand, it would be softer than a baby's bottom. Lord knows I like calloused hands—and he's a city boy down to his wicked, devil core. I lick my lips. Probably better not to use "wicked" to describe him since it gets me thinking more about his body.

I wonder how much time he spends at the gym. One of those corporate gyms, I bet—the kind where you go up to the elliptical on the eighteenth floor after your chauffeur drops you off at work at 3:30 in the morning. Exercise, and then you have your black coffee and your orange and two point five egg whites. I bet his life is just like that.

And then—"*Whoa.*" I jerk as I spot him in the doorway between hall and living room. "You just sort of poofed there." I snap my fingers. "Apparated," I say, using Harry Potter language.

He pinches his T-shirt in between his fingers, pulling it away from his abs, and I realize there's blue stuff on it.

"What the what?"

He laughs. "I gave the kids a mint I had in my pocket, and Margot wanted to brush her teeth again. Got sparkle toothpaste all over my shirt."

"Well, hell."

He walks closer to me, so I can see how messy he is. "Looks like someone shot the tube off on you."

My cheeks blaze as those words spill from my lips.

Shot off? Really, June?

"Good smell," he remarks.

"Do you want another shirt?"

He starts to pull it off. "Yeah," he says from behind the fabric, as his abs peek out below the hemline. "I'll take one if that's okay."

Then the shirt is off. He's standing two feet from me in all his bulky, chiseled, smooth-skinned glory.

"They're in my room," I manage.

"Okay."

I nod and swallow. "I keep the T-shirts in that big drawer in the very middle of my dresser. Might be one your size in there if you look hard."

While he's gone to riffle through my stuff, I try to regain control of my vital signs. Holy hell, he's pure perfection. Even in my wildest dreams, I didn't know he'd look *that* good bare-chested.

A minute later, he strolls back into the living room holding a bright green T-shirt.

"Farmer's Market?" he says, holding out a shirt I won in a raffle there a few years back.

"Yeah, you can wear that one. What size is it?" I frown, because I thought it was a tighter one.

"Says large."

I nod. "That should work, then."

He turns toward the TV—I fumble with the remote, trying to pull up Netflix—while he pulls the shirt over his head. He gets one arm in and then starts laughing.

"Well, shit," I murmur.

He's stuck. He's got one arm in, and I don't think that he can get it out without ripping my shirt in half. I don't know how he misread the tag, but that is definitely not a size large.

"Step over here," I tell him.

He steps closer, his head partway inside the shirt. I tug on one corner, and he chuckles. Hell. That little V of muscle there above his waistband. I sink my teeth into my lower lip, wincing at the cuts I made when I broke my ankle, and I tug the shirt up. My fingers brush his hot skin, fingertips skating over his hard muscle.

"Whoa. You're pretty."

Did I just say that out loud?

He huffs out a laugh, and my face gets so hot, I swear I'm gonna cry like people eating hot sauce. I push the shirt up more. "Try to pull it off now."

"I'm trying." His voice is low and raspy. I lean up a little, wiggling my hand under the T-shirt and pushing my palm up his hard back so I can try to get the shirt around his thick arm, which is what it's really stuck on.

I feel a trail of chills under my fingers.

"Bend down more. Why don't you just kneel down beside me."

He does, his big fist gripping the couch cushion to steady himself since one of his arms is still stuck in my little bitty T-shirt.

"How is this a large?" he moans from inside the shirt.

"I don't know. It's been washed a bunch of times I guess. Oh wait!" I cackle. "It's a *youth* large! Should have thought of that."

"You think?"

I can't help laughing at him. He looks ridiculous stuck in the shirt, like some sort of trapped T-Rex. "Now you're down here beside me, I can maybe yank this thing off. If we have to rip it, so what? It's nothing special."

I move my hand along the shirt's seam, tracing around toward his right side, and I feel chills on his skin again.

I trace a line with my nail, and he groans.

"What the fuck?" His voice is muffled.

I do it again—because he's here beside me and his body's warm and hard and thick, and he's the devil. I do it because I can. Because his dark nature is rubbing off on me. I stroke my palm down his side, and he barks a groan.

"Jesus. *June*." My name's a protest.

I swallow as his ribcage expands on a big, desperate breath. "Is this your weak spot, Mr. Devil? You like a little back scratching?"

I trail my thumb along his side...down toward where his hip has got that sharp edge of carved muscle, and I can feel him inhale again.

I hear a rip as he tears the shirt off. Then his hungry eyes are locked on mine. His lips are slightly parted, and his chest is pumping. For a second, no one speaks. Then he rasps, "Don't do that again."

I don't know why I do what I do next. I don't like him. He's an asshole, and I've never been a girl who tolerates a lot of bullshit. Maybe it's pure animal attraction. All I know is that as I reach for his flawless six pack, I feel like a light that's been switched on.

My fingers brush his hot skin, and he hisses. His eyes shut. He grits his teeth, and I trace the taut ridge between muscles.

I stroke downward, and lust hits me like a lightning bolt.

He grits out, "Stop."

"Are you sure?" I nearly cream my panties when I see his bulge coming to life, pushing against his fly. "Because it doesn't look like you—"

His mouth clamps over mine so hard and fast that I gasp. When I do, his tongue glides inside. He kisses with what's gotta be some pent-up lust. His lips are hard and hungry—like my own. His hand, on my neck, pushes up into my hair as we taste one another. I grab his head and shoulder, pulling him in closer.

Then he's straddling my hips. I'm moaning into his mouth. He tastes hot and minty, and his hands are tugging my hair, holding my head as he ravishes my mouth, tightening their grasp on my poor tresses when I grab at his hip.

He pulls back. "June." Now it's a warning.

Then it's back to kissing—frantic. I lift my good leg so my knee rubs him between his legs. He rubs his dick against my hip, groaning loudly as his mouth devours mine.

"Damn you," he breathes as I wrench away to get a breath.

"Fuck you," I say before nipping at his chin.

"Oh God."

I unbutton his pants like I'm racing to some finish line, feeling warm and tight and heavy in between my own legs. When my hand delves into his underwear, he moans again. His hand cups my breast.

"Aunt June?"

OH.

HOLY.

SHIT.

He's off me so fast it makes me feel dizzy. Margot stands beside the TV, frowning at me first and then at him. He's on the couch's other side now, clutching a pillow and smiling in a way that looks a little scary.

"Hey, honey." My voice is shaky, and I bet my lips are red. They're throbbing. So are other places. "What's the matter?"

She reaches up to wipe some hair off her forehead. "Dream," she whispers.

"Oh, you had a bad dream?" I reach for my crutches. Then shirtless Burke snaps into motion, his back to Margot as he helps me up. My heart is pounding so fast, I'm barely tracking his hands on my arms, his palm against my back. And then he's sitting back down on the couch, holding a pillow in his lap to hide his hard-on.

I talk to Margot as we trudge back down the hall toward her room. She dreamed about her mother, sailing away on a ship with long white sails that looked like ghosts. Hearing her tell of this dream breaks my heart. It's such an awful dream to have—your mom sailing away—and yet it's no worse than her reality. Sutton is dead, the door forever closed. Okay, well, I don't know about *forever*, but it's firmly shut for a long time.

I spend a little while with Margot, perched on her bed's edge. I rub her hair until her eyelids are heavy, and then I hug her tight.

"I love you, sweetie."

"Love you too," she murmurs.

The kids' room smells of mint and toothpaste. I can taste that mint on my tongue as I make my way into the shadowed hall and down the bare hardwood. My throat is tight and thick with grief, and still, I want him. Maybe this is why I want him. I catch my sore lip between my teeth as I move toward the living room. I bite until it stings.

Burke is at the kitchen island, leaning on it with his elbows when I crutch my way into the room. When he sees me, he stands up like I caught him in some unforgivable act. He cups a beer bottle in his hands and looks at me, all somber eyes and bare chest.

"She okay?" His voice is husky.

I nod. "Dreamed about her mama."

He looks down, and I see his tongue move over his firm lower lip. He looks up and lets a breath out.

"Think I'm going to grab my stuff from that cabin I rented." He starts toward the screened porch door without pausing to look over at me. "I'll be back within the hour."

CHAPTER 17

BURKE

It's a problem. *She's* a problem. I shouldn't go back. I know I shouldn't, and those words fill up my mind until my head aches. Shouldn't go back, but I do because I'm weak. She nipped my lip so hard at one point that it's bleeding at the corner. Tastes bitter when I press my tongue against the spot.

The car over the road is rough and jarring, red dirt cracked open. Needs smoothing. The moon is bright tonight, no clouds. I see glowing eyes as I turn back into her driveway—something wild, maybe a coyote.

When I get inside the house, she isn't anywhere in sight. I took two hours—on purpose—so I'm not surprised. The laundry room is filled with dogs, the big ones sleeping on linoleum and the pups in their crate.

I eat some cornbread from a Tupperware container on her counter and pour myself some sweet tea. Shawn called it Southern table wine. Then I sit at her kitchen table and pull out my laptop. The table's a long, oak oval, with eight chairs and a fruit bowl in the center. It looks like it was hand-crafted. When I check out June's internet, I find a network called Platform934 that doesn't have a passcode. The Harry Potter-inspired name makes me smirk.

Little book nerd.

When midnight comes and goes, I tell myself I'm grateful that she hasn't returned. I've got enough work to last until morning, easy.

I think of going into the hall and setting up shop on the floor with my back against the wall, so I can hear if one of the kids wakes up again. I'm still mulling that over when I hear footsteps behind me.

I turn around, and there she is. She's wearing a deep blue robe, and she's balanced on her crutches.

"Hey," she whispers, sleepy-eyed.

Ah, shit. I stand up. "You need something?"

She shakes her head. The faintest smile plays over her lips. "What are you doing?" She smiles like we're co-conspirators.

"Working."

"At 2:50 in the morning?"

I shut the laptop. "Work from home work never ends."

"Do you work from home?"

"Not really."

She fiddles with the neck of her robe. I catch a peek of creamy skin over the gentle swell of her breasts. She yawns; clearly, she fell asleep before and is just waking up. "I brought some linens to the couch for you."

"Uh, thanks."

I want to fuck her. God, I'd love to take her to that couch and lay her out the way she was before and fuck her hard enough to wear myself out. I bet she'd be tight and hot. She'd be one of those that claws your back up. I grit my teeth.

"You should go to sleep," I tell her. "Did one of them wake up?" I open my laptop again and log in so I've got somewhere to put my eyes.

"Just me. I nodded off and came to check on you."

"I'm okay."

Silence spreads itself between us. It feels thick and heavy.

"Hope you get some sleep now," I say, tapping lightly at the keys.

"You too." Her voice is silken.

I let her turn around and head through the living room. I let her get almost all the way down the hall before I go after her.

I stop in the open space between the hall and living room, my heart pounding.

I can hear her breathing, although I can't see her for the hall wall.

"You better lock that door," I murmur.

I hear something that could be a laugh. Then her soft voice says, "Try it."

Don't do that. You can't do that. There are reasons why you can't.

When I move into her room, it's pitch black dark. I feel like a felon as I come to stand beside the bed.

That's when the heating system clicks on. The subtle current moving from a nearby vent tosses her curtains, casting moonlight over the bed. I can see her face—cool, tinted pearly blue. Her smug, small smile that says: *You wanted it. You wanted it so much you followed me into my room in the middle of the night.*

"June." My voice trembles on her name.

She blinks, her thick eyelashes casting pointy shadows over her smooth, creamy cheeks. "Yes, Burke?"

I feel my pulse drum just below my throat. I grit my teeth until it hurts and put my hand over my hard cock. And I whisper, "You win."

"We were playing a game?" Silky smooth. If I could wrap her voice around my cock, it would explode, and cum would drip between my fingers like one of her ice pops on a summer day.

You win, I say again. In my mind, the words are loud and firm. And then I drop my mental voice down to a whisper. *I would have you if you weren't her sister. If you weren't, I wouldn't care how much I damage you.*

Logical and restrained. I'm still on the shore.

With my real voice, I say, "Pull the covers down."

She does that.

I climb on the bed. I wade into the water.

"If you want my tongue inside you, pull your panties down."

She pushes them down to her thighs. Soft thighs. In the cool moonlight, they look thick and round and feel like satin. I trail my tongue over her warm skin, and she spreads her legs a little wider for me.

I lean down, hovering my mouth over her curls and breathing warmly on her. Then I spread her gently with my fingers. "Oh, June." I slip the tip of my tongue into her heat. Slick and tangy, fat and swollen, and her little bud is rising slightly from between her folds. I tongue it—just one lick—and swallow back a groan as she comes off the bed and yanks at my hair.

"Oh God." That's all she says, and I find I'm surprised. No wanton words or screams or grunted curses. Just this soft chant as her fingers tighten in my hair and I lap at her. Then I lift my mouth away and work my tongue into her. She yelps, and I clamp a palm over her mouth.

"Cover your face," I tell her.

She puts a pillow over her face, and I push my tongue back into her cunt. June thrusts herself against my face.

"Damn. Oh shit."

I know you wanna come. Her knees are pressed around my shoulders now. She's swinging her hips up toward me and moaning. I can feel her panting. I lift my head again and push two fingers inside where she's tight and slick.

"That's right. Soon you're gonna come on my hand."

For a while, I fuck her like that. I know she'll come apart the second that I touch her with my tongue again, and that will be the end of this. So I thrust my fingers in and drag them out, using my mouth to tease all around where she wants me till she's moaning and her good leg is thrown over my shoulders.

"What do you want, honey?" It's a whisper.

"Your dick in my mouth."

I'm so surprised by her throaty, dirty answer that my arms give way. I close my mouth over her heat and taste her sweet cream. I can feel her jerk, and then she gives a mighty groan, and she's lost.

I come in my pants like I'm in ninth grade, and my body trembles so hard afterward that I worry there's something wrong with me. When I do manage to make my body move, I bring her a hot cloth and tell her, "Thank you" in a voice that's way too rough. And then I leave her there.

It's so dark—the whole house dark, the wild yard dark and endless. The trees are whispering shadows.

I find a ladder in her shed and fix a bent spot on her gutter that I spotted while her brother walked me around the house, pointing out pecan trees. After that, I step into the kids' bedroom and dart my eyes over their bodies, two small bumps under the blankets.

My throat feels tight and the house is too small. I slip into the kitchen, quietly peel open the lid to the cornbread, and fill a Ziploc bag with the golden squares of manna. At first I empty the container, but then I think better of it and put one square back.

I could change my pants, but I don't. Not until I'm at the end of her dirt road. In the dim light of an orange sky, I take my pants off, then my boxer-briefs, and roll them up and stuff them in the bottom of my suit-case. I move the driver's seat away from the wheel and pull on clean clothes.

Then I point the Porsche back toward Atlanta, and I fly.

CHAPTER 18

JUNE

April - Two Months Later

My favorite Albany country music station is all about some Taylor Swift. I don't really get it, because she isn't "country" anymore. But I don't hate her songs or anything. They're pretty catchy. There's this one that Margot loves that comes on all the time, and it has a line that says "play stupid games you win stupid prizes."

Every time I hear it, I think of him. Stupid game, and I got the stupid prize of his ass running off with most of my remaining corn-bread, never even saying bye to me. Because he's him, and he's the devil.

He's talked to Margot and Oliver *once* since he left, and that was one time when Oliver called by accident when he was watching YouTube on my iPhone. I was in the shower, but the kids talked to him and were off before I stepped onto the bath mat.

"What did he say? Did he say tell me hey?"

Both kids just blinked at me.

"He asked about school," Oliver said, and I had to struggle not to roll my eyes.

Oh I just bet he did.

One way he has been communicating, I suppose, is by sending checks made out to me. I get them on the first of every month, right when SNAP benefits start over. I guess maybe he knows that, and he'd like me to stop claiming federal food benefits, but I'm not going to. I don't want to owe him anything. And anyway, when my new venture gets more steady on its legs, I'm going to make too much to qualify— even with three mouths to feed now.

I smile to myself as I peer into the newly built pen right behind the house. It's a school morning, a Tuesday, which means these babies are all mine.

I open the gate and smile down at my darling Nubian doelings: Rosa Parks, Amelia Earhart, P. Diddy, and Ellen. Leah's cousin Marco bought them from a milk goat breeder in Missouri, but turns out, Marco is really bad allergic to them. He had named them P. Diddy and the three bitches, illustrating just how terrifyingly unintelligent poor Marco is. Only girl goats make milk, but P. Diddy gets so excited when you call her by her insane name that so far, I can't bear to re-name her. We may have another Hot Rocket situation on our hands.

The kids and I named the "bitches" after our favorite women, to make up for Marco's shoddy treatment. And what that really means is, Margot did. And she's still campaigning to re-christen P. Diddy as Taylor Swift.

"P. Diddy..." I try it just to make myself laugh, and she rushes over to me and rubs her head against my thigh.

"That's right, sweetheart. What a good, good goatie you are."

I shift some hay off my back, where I had it wrapped up against me with an old paint sheet, and watch my four girls prance around. The puppies yip somewhere behind me, and I glance over my shoulder, but they're just playing by the back porch. My big dogs are warming to them, so this week I'll try another front lawn playdate with all four.

I love on the goats a bit, and then walk through another gate into another pen.

"And here are my sweet piggies!" I stretch my arms out, and Peppa and George run to me like the adorable oinkers they are.

I guess my family wants me to run a zoo, because my dad gave Margot and Oliver these cuties after he got home from a trip down to Mexico, about two weeks after Burke came and left. Dad's got a little bungalow in Tulum that he and Mom bought when she first got sick. He flew straight there from Sutton's funeral and was kind of off the grid until he showed up one day at the house with the pigs.

"What sweet little babies..."

They are babies. Right now, these Kunekune piggies are tiny—

smaller than the puppies. They're mottled black and pink, and oh-so huggable. I play with them for a while before going back inside, grabbing my yoga mat, and heading to the senior center.

The class I lead there is eighty minutes long—on the slightly longer side for yoga classes these days—but the retirees would rather take it slow, and so would I. After yoga, I stop by the Shake & Bake, a Zumba place and tanning salon where Leah's working, and we chat for a while. I'm home just in time to throw some chicken salad together for a late lunch and have a quick phone chat with Latrice, who's gone to Albany to sell one of the older tractors. The money we get from it should cover planting costs for the largest peanut crop we've endeavored yet.

I shower, change my clothes, and hop into the truck with two juice boxes and big, shiny apples for Margot and Oliver to eat when they hop in the truck after school. The dirt road's hazy when I reach the end of my driveway, so I figure Mrs. Manson just passed by with my mail.

I stop at the box and pull out a package. No return address. But it's from France.

"That's weird..." I use a key to slice it open. Inside, I find two tiny Eiffel Tower pencil sharpeners and three blue bottles of bubbles bearing a French brand sticker, along with three bags of Haribo Orangina Pik gummies. At the bottom, folded beneath a layer of tissue paper, is a soft, maroon Gryffindor T-shirt in my size and a paperback copy of *Harry Potter and the Philosopher's Stone.*

I grin at the cover. It's the original British edition. I thumb through it. Inside the cover, taped to the first page, is a pale green sticky note that says 1st Edition in familiar script.

Sure, enough, Bloomsbury is the publisher, and the publication date is 1997. I start laughing like a fool and hold the book to my chest.

"Oh my lands. Why did you do this, Burke?"

I set the paperback on the dashboard and tear through the box again. There's no note, though. I assume he put the sticky in the book so I didn't let Margot and Oliver run around playing with it. I assume it has some value.

A quick search on my phone's web browser reveals it could be worth...*four thousand dollars!*

There is no way.

Is there?

I flip through the book again. It does look slightly old; the pages are stiff and maybe just a little yellowed.

"Well hot dog."

I take off down the dirt road, tires spinning over stray pebbles, a dust cloud enveloping the truck as I speed toward the paved road.

He didn't do it. But I know he did. So ostentatious. It's his style. Didn't even leave a note in the box, but he spent around four thousand dollars. Dipshit.

I text him from the pickup line in front of Heat Springs Primary. *I'm sending this back to you.*

I'm in France.

One of your people can babysit it till you get home.

The little bubble showing someone's texting pops up and then disappears, as if he's not sure what to say. Finally he asks, *Are you anti vintage books?*

I don't want you spending money on me!

Someone gave it to me.

What? Really?!

Really, he says.

Are you sure?

I'm pretty sure.

Oh. Well...hmmm. I still don't like it.

You can keep it for Margot and Oliver if you want, he says. *I thought you would like it.*

Well now I feel like a jackass.

You're not a jackass.

For a heady second, I can't believe we're really texting one another. After two months of silence. Two months I spent wondering what he was thinking about me. Does he see me as some wanton woman, throwing myself at him? So confusing, because it didn't seem one-sided to me.

What are you doing in France?

Just had some meetings here.

I scan the school's front lawn, but it's still empty. I don't know if it's a bad idea to keep the conversation rolling, but I find I kind of can't stop. *U like it there?*

Yeah. I'm a fan of France.

What do you like about it? Lord knows I've never been. Probably never will.

He takes so long to answer that I wonder if he gave up on the text chat. *I don't know. I like the look of it, I think. Paris. That's where I am right now. I like the pace, the architecture. I don't know.*

What a thorough answer from the man who didn't want to stick around and say bye to me. *You don't know much, do you, Sly?*

Sorry, I'm kind of under the weather.

What kind of weather's got you down? I smirk to myself, even as my heart is going pitter-patter like jazz dance shoes.

Idk I think the flu.

Oh, dang. You have the flu?

Nah. Idk. I'm ok tho.

I think about his big body between my legs. The sturdy warmth of him. The way he groaned as his tongue painted me. And my whole body starts to buzz again.

Someone honks, and I realize I'm holding up the pickup line by two spots. Dammit.

I'm so sorry, I text after I pull up. *Are you at a hotel?*

I have a place I stay when I'm here. It's like an apartment.

What's the address?

Oh, it's okay. I'm leaving in a few days.

Still want it.

I see the bubble indicating he's typing, then deleting, then typing again.

C'mon, Sly. Don't overthink this. The kids just want to do a Google street view.

He sends the address.

His typing bubble comes back as the kids pour from the schoolhouse doors and spill onto the lawn.

How are they doing, he says.

Fancy you should ask. I know I shouldn't be snarky, but I can't help myself. *They're doing great.*

I figured that. They like to call me when you're in the shower.

Well, they did once, I say.

They do it almost every night.

What?! Are you serious?? I gape down at the phone's screen. How did I not know this?

Do you ever look at your call log?

Who does that!?

Look at it now.

I do—and I find...he's right. How...creepy. I had no idea the little beasts were calling him. Looks like four nights out of the last six.

How long have you been in Paris? Looks like they called the last four nights around 8 central time. Is that the middle of the night for you?

Ha, kind of, he says.

Wow. I'm really sorry. I guess it must wake you up.

No it's okay, I like to talk to them. I'm usually awake.

Not tonight. You need your beauty sleep.

Are you calling me pretty, Ms. Lawler?

I don't know who Ms. Lawler is, but *I* am absolutely not.

I swallow hard. I'm such a liar.

Get some rest, Sly. We'll talk to you later.

I turn my phone off until we get back to the house, where I dole out the pencil sharpeners and candy and bubbles. The kids rip into their candy, and after I snitch one of theirs, I open my own bag. It's citrusy and tart and sweet all at once, and I wonder at how the French seem to have all the tasty things.

Then the kids and I crowd around my little laptop and look at the Google street view. The building where he's staying is made of orange brick, and it's got cement-colored accents that are ornate, plus a lot of windows and a black roof with lots of small chimneys. I don't know enough about architecture to know the name of the style, but it's beautiful.

"I wanna go there," Margot murmurs.

"Maybe one day we can." The words roll right out of my mouth, but I find that I can't take them back. Sutton wouldn't mind if I used some of her money to take the kids to Paris, would she? I think she would love that.

I ruffle Margot's soft hair. "Uncle Burke isn't feeling so well today. I'm going to have some soup delivered to him."

"All the way to Paris?"

I smile. "Yep. I found a web site that can help me do it. Sort of like an app." I wink.

"He likes miso soup," Oliver offers.

"How do you know?"

He shrugs. "I don't know. I just remember."

I costs almost sixty dollars to have soup and tea delivered. I cringe at the total, but it's something that I want to do. It'll put us a little tight for the month, but that's okay.

The kids and I spend two hours outside playing with the pigs and goats, and then we head back in for dinner.

"Oooh, chicken salad!"

They sit at the table with the water bottles they use most of the time —stainless steel ones, the same brand Sutton has always bought for them—and I serve them chicken salad, crackers, and a big helping of grapes.

"My friend Mia says she has to eat spinach for dinner! Spinach salad," Margo says, scrunching her nose.

"I'll have to make a salad for you guys soon. What about a citrus salad, with almonds and some sesame dressing?"

"Eghh." Oliver shakes his head.

"You know I've never fed y'all something bad yet."

"Yes you have!" Margot sits up straighter, waving her hand in front of her face as if to clear a nasty memory. "You made us eat gizzards!"

"That wasn't me. That was your Grandpop."

"At least he gave us Peppa and George."

I nod. "At least there's that."

I say grace, hissing at Oliver to shut his eyes. The moment I say "amen," the phone rings. A FaceTime call—from Burke.

"Well, heck."

"Who is it?" both kids cry. I turn the phone around toward them, and Oliver grabs it and answers.

"Hellooooo." He makes a silly face, and Burke's voice fills the kitchen.

"Hey there, buddy."

"Aunt June said you're sick!" Margot says, leaning over the phone so close he's probably looking at the inside of her nostril.

"I got some soup from you guys. Thank you."

"Miso soup," Oliver says proudly.

"You remembered that's what I ordered."

Oliver sits up a little straighter.

"Thank you, dude. And you, dudette."

"I miss you," Margot says.

"Did you climb up the Eiffel Tower?" Oliver asks.

Burke laughs. "Not this time. Maybe we can come over sometime together. Would you like that?"

Oliver nods.

"Can I talk to Aunt June for a second?"

Oliver hands the phone to me, and there he is. He's so *Burke*, with messy, dark hair, stubble on his square jaw, and those piercing blue eyes. For a second, all my words are caught in my throat.

"Hi," he says.

I fake a smile. "Hey."

"I can't believe you did that." He smiles. "How'd you manage the French?"

"I'm fluent. Kidding. I ordered online with the help of a website. It only took about twenty minutes."

"That's a while." He rubs his hair then props his face in his palm. "You sound sick."

"I'm cool."

"You're *not* cool," I tease.

He snorts.

For a second, no one speaks. Then, in a low rasp, he says, "How are you?"

"Fine." It's a chirp. "I'm good," I tack on.

Totally appreciated the oral you gave me right before you fixed my gutter and then disappeared like a thief in the night.

"I have a working gutter that doesn't leak. So that's real nice."

Oh my God, I just said both "gutter" and "leak." I can feel my face burn.

"Good."

It's all he says. His lips twitch slightly, and his head tilts just a little. I feel like he's looking through me. So I do the most June thing imaginable. I step into the living room and whisper-hiss: "You were looking so hot. And you were such a jerk. And then you weren't...I mean, you weren't the whole time. But I had animosity. This was a pent-up animosity situation."

He laughs so loudly, I consider hanging up. He drops his phone, he's laughing so much. Then he has a coughing fit that sounds like it hurts.

When he picks the phone back up, his eyes are closed. The bastard is still grinning.

"Pent-up animosity—" He breaks out into another coughing fit. "I think the term you're looking for is *lust*." He grins once more, and it's a cocky grin. A grin with swagger.

I decide to own it, though. I shrug. "Maybe it was. I'm a living, breathing woman. And you have abs with a capital A."

He chuckles.

"It will never, ever happen again," I say softly.

"Oh yeah," he says with a nod. "Never."

"It's inappropriate, for one." I lean against the living room wall, smirking as if my heart's not pounding.

"Oh yeah."

"I mean, you're a douchey Slytherin, and I'm a noble Gryffindor. So that's a basic compatibility issue."

"Noble is the first thing that comes to mind when *I* look at you."

"I know," I say sharply, arching one eyebrow at my phone's camera. "Beautiful and noble. Like a unicorn."

"Oh yeah. Just like…a unicorn." He mutters something I can't hear, and I say, "Pervert."

"What?" he asks.

"You know what."

He rolls his eyes.

Awkwardness steamrolls over me. I try to fight it with more small talk. "What were you doing to get sick?"

"Um, what?"

"Like, were you out a lot or staying up late?"

He frowns. "I'm not sure I understand the question."

"Well, I have a regimen. It involves elderberry, vitamin C, vitamin B, and D. All sorts of stuff. I don't usually get sick unless there's something special going on—like I forget one of those things or do some kind of weird all-nighter, like to help birth a calf."

He shakes his head.

"You think I'm insane now?"

"Did already."

I sigh dramatically and walk back toward the kitchen. "Well anyway. This was nice to check in. Re-establish how you're a snake and I'm a magic unicorn."

"That's my takeaway," he says gamely.

"Oh, and get well. Don't forget you're still the understudy."

He lets out a hoot of laughter when he realizes what I mean.

I give him a bright smile.

"Thank you for the soup, June." Now he's smiling brightly back at me.

"Thank you for the candy, Burke Bug—I definitely did not already eat the whole bag—and the pencil sharpeners and bubbles and the T-shirt. Oh, and the bamillion dollar book."

He snorts.

I turn the phone toward the kids, still eating at the kitchen table. "Say goodnight and get well, Uncle Burke."

They chant it after me. I make a kiss face at the phone's screen and hang up.

CHAPTER 19

BURKE

Two pajama shirts, I text her from my office desk. *Ravenclaw for me, and the extra one is perfect since I only fuck Slytherins.*

Did I go too far with that? I rub a hand back through my hair, pushing the base of my hand against my throbbing forehead. *Shit,* I think that sounded dickish.

Those little dots are visible at the bottom of my screen—a sign she's typing. When nothing comes, I know she's typing and deleting as she struggles to decide how to reply.

That's her reply. She called me a pig—at least I think she did. I have to double check my iPhone symbols to confirm that it's a pig snout.

I can't help a laugh. *Well, we know how you feel about pigs.*

Pigs are a delightful barnyard animal. A definite asset for any small farm. 10/10 would recommend. BTW the kids would like a picture of you in your shirt.

I grin and text, *"The kids."*

I look around my office, like the walls are watching. Then I unzip my briefcase and pull the shirt out. It's navy blue and silky, with a faux Ravenclaw tie design going down the front, and a pocket with a pair of round-framed reading glasses printed on the fabric.

I inhale it again. It smells like her house. Which smells like cinnamon and flowers.

I push my office chair back and step over to the door, twist the doorknob lock, and unbutton my work shirt. Then I pull that off and drape it over my chair. I pull the silky shirt over my head, ruffle my hand back through my too-long hair, and take a selfie where I'm doing this weird crooked smile.

I frown down at the shot. And then I send it.

She replies a second later.

THAT'S THE WRONG SHIRT!

I type: *If the shirt fits...*

Snort.

I think the convo's over at that, but a few minutes later she sends another text. *So are you at work? Or are those stark white walls at your house?*

My place also has white walls. And isn't a house. But this is my office.

You can't really live in an apartment?

Google street view it & u'll see.

What?! Really? There was no apartment number when you gave me your address the other day!

That's because my building only has two penthouses, and they have different addresses.

Pfft, she sends. *I knew you lived in a mansion. I didn't Google it because I kind of didn't want to know.*

Why not? I frown down at the phone.

Why do you think?

I rub a hand over my face, rubbing my temples with my fingertips. *That's why I'm asking*, I say. *I don't know.*

I don't want to see the place where Margot and Oliver could live if I had let you take them with you. Duh.

There are more dots, as if she's saying more. They disappear and return a few times before the screen settles without them.

Do u know how long I was in Paris? I ask her.

Negatory.

I was gone almost two weeks. When I got back, there was a problem with a technical element of the app's development. I was at the office for three nights in a row, all night. Now I have pneumonia, not that I'm telling her that. I'm also going to be up here tonight again for sure. That startup life.

Next week, I'm going to Hong Kong to meet someone for three days. Then back here, and then I have to go to Manhattan.

Just to make her feel a little better, I add: *I live on the fourteenth floor. The floors above floor four are mandatory child-free. I don't even have a fish at my place. It's a hipster place, so even if I did sneak kids in, they would have to climb all the stairs.*

Again, with the dots appearing and disappearing. Is it weird that I like knowing she's taking her time with every text? Finally she says just: *Thank you.*

You're so welcome, Gryffy. I delete that and instead ask, *How are you guys? Things going ok?*

Yep. A few minutes later, she adds, *We have a nice routine now, I think.*

I toss my phone from one hand to the other, cough until my head feels like it's going to explode, and then rub my temples till they stop pounding. Then I man up and just ask her: *You gonna cash some of those checks, Gryff? Make things easier for you three?*

She doesn't reply for almost two hours. I'm stepping into the men's room after a meeting when the phone vibrates in my pocket. Her text is very June-like, therefore not surprising: *I don't need your money.*

I lean on the cool wall of the bathroom. *I'm not saying you do. I sent it because I want you to have it. No because you have to have it, but to make things easier. To me, it's not much—$3,000 a month. I can spare it without thinking twice.*

Dots and then no dots. Dots as she types and no dots as she deletes.

I know you know I'm poor, okay? That the farm's not making like a robust income right now. But it's going to. We're planting the biggest crop of peanuts we've ever had. I have goats now, and I'm going to make goat cheese. I'm also getting subsidies at times, which help things. We're fine. I know to you it probably seems terrible, but I promise they are fed and happy.

To *me*...it sounds terrible—is what she said. I blow my breath out, do my business, and wash my hands before replying. *I know, June.* I know the kids are fucking fed. That's not the problem.

What about you? It's what I want to text her. I think about the puppies, and I feel so damn bad. That was thoughtless. Dickish. She's gotta be run ragged, chasing after kids and dogs and pigs and goats. But she accepted the puppies with hardly any complaint.

I have a thirty minute teleconference about cell phone towers and dispatch centers, and then I check my texts again. She's sent nothing more...so I do.

U always been June who saves the day?

I see the dots just once before they're gone. And for a long time, there's no answer. I get lunch and lay my head down on my desk because my forehead's hot, and I'm so tired I can't see straight. When I check the phone again, she's said, *I'm not that.*

Something tightens in my chest. *Don't sell yourself short.*

U don't even know me, dude.

I know some things about you. When she doesn't reply to that, I add, *I know you left high school to help your mom.*

I took a break from school to help my mom die. And I didn't go back, as you already "know some things about."

I don't, not really.

Of course not, she says, her hackles up now.

I want to ask her more. And, also I don't. The idea of having a sick mother—of caring for a mother who was terminally ill, but who wanted to stay with you—makes my chest feel weird and sore and tight.

How is your ankle? I can't believe I haven't asked her before now. *Because you're a dick.*

Almost fully healed.

How is Hot Rocket? I know the answer since I'm paying his bills, but Shawn and I have made sure June doesn't know that.

He's doing well.

You don't like what I said about you saving the day, I observe.

Yes. Because it's not true.

Is it true your dad walked away from the farm?

I watch the bubbles that show her typing for the longest time—so long my eyelid starts twitching. *My dad met my mom when he was 12. And she was 13. He was dyslexic, and he couldn't read. My mother was book smart. She tutored him in reading.*

Immediately after I read the message, I can see she's writing more.

When Mama died, he didn't eat for four days. I don't remember, it may actually have been five. Mary Helen made him some eggs dyed green like in that book, and told her that the kids made them, and he ate them because he felt like he had to, to make his grandkids happy. But he stopped seeing his doctor, and to this day, he won't get checkups. And he doesn't take his blood pressure meds, we don't think.

I shut my eyes and keep them closed until the feeling in me passes. Then I blow a long, long breath out.

Maybe he's a hero too, for still being around at all.

I delete that sentimental shit as soon as I type it.

I didn't meet your dad. But I'm calling you the way I see you.

Better wear those glasses on your shirt, she fires back.

Then she sends: *Snake*.

JUNE

I shouldn't have sent him those pajama shirts. But if I was going to, I should have only sent the Slytherin one. Make it clear that it's a mean joke.

I think about him all night that night and half of the next day, even when he never texts me back, and so our conversation ends when I call him a snake.

Doesn't matter. I don't need to talk to his ass. Leah asks about him when we get lunch at the Mexican place, and I tell her I don't know.

"The kids like to call him when I'm in the shower," I say, dipping a tortilla chip in salsa.

Leah studies her nails, painted purple. "I know you're lying about that night, Buggie. I have known you since we were three."

I shrug. "Doesn't mean that you're a lie detector."

She rolls her eyes before popping a cheesy chip into her mouth. "Does so." She stuffs her face for just a bit before dabbing her lips with a napkin. "You know," she says from behind it, "since you won't tell me what happened, I've just gotta assume that you got down and dirty. Sixty-nine and all that kind of thing."

It's my eyes that betray me. When I try to make a neutral face, I tend to bug my eyes out just a little, and that's what happens at our booth right at that moment.

Leah shrieks, and in about one second, two waiters coming rushing around the corner to check on us.

"We're okay. We're fine," she assures them. When they walk away, she shrieks again.

"I *hate* you."

"You *didn't!*" She says it on a gasp, as if I just told her we ate George the pig.

"I *didn't.*" I poke at my food, feeling defensive.

"What *did* you do?" She laughs.

I sigh. "God. Nothing."

"Don't be a liar, Buggie."

I cover my face with my hands, letting out a big sigh. "Fine, okay? We *did*. We messed around."

"The night he stayed? After the kegger?"

"Yes." I peek out at her from in between my fingers.

"What happened? Did he take advantage of your compromised state?" She waggles her brows, and I cover my eyes again.

And then I tell her. "It was me...who went for him. It was pent-up rage and loathing."

Like Burke himself, Leah thinks that's just freaking hilarious.

"Don't laugh," I order. "This is a known thing. He was made *hotter* because he's such a dick."

"And his actual dick?" Her eyes are alight.

"Shut up, Leah."

"Oh, c'mon! You know you want to tell me."

"I just...felt it," I whisper. I hold a napkin over my red face and whisper, "As opposed to seeing it. But it was perfectly acceptable. In fact, I give it five stars."

"Five out of five, or five stars out of *ten?*"

"Out of five." I lower the napkin so she can see my eye roll. "You know, like on Amazon."

She nods, popping another cheese-slathered tortilla chip into her mouth. "So?"

"So?" I echo.

"Now I need the context, dumbass."

"What context?"

"Like...your feelings?" She rolls her eyes, as if she really does think I'm a moron.

"I don't *have* feelings. About him."

Her mouth blooms into a big grin. "You've got it worse than I knew."

"What would they be—these special feelings? I mean...he's just a guy I know. Like any guy."

"He's one of your babies' only accessible relatives on their daddy's side," she points out.

I smile at how she called them my babies.

"Do you think Sutt would mind?" I muse. Leah knows me so well that she understands the question.

"That you kind of think of them as yours now?" She smiles sadly, shaking her head. "She would love that more than anything, Bug. You know that."

Our food arrives. I can barely look at the waitress, as if she knows what we've been talking about.

"I know," I say after she goes. "It's so weird, the way it's sad and happy at the same time."

Leah nods, cutting a piece of enchilada with her fork. "I'm sure it must be so weird. But like...good weird?"

"Yeah." I blow my breath out. "I think that's why I find it so strange. Because my feelings about it are mostly good. And not sad. And isn't that...disloyal to her or something?"

"What, you mean like when you think of them growing up with you as their guardian, it makes you happy?"

I nod, and she grins. "That's nothing but amazing, chica. That's why she picked you. Because you've had a while to sit with it—a while to mom them—and it makes you happy. *Truly* happy. I know you would tell me if you weren't."

I nod. I would tell Leah. "I love having them at my house. I feel happier. I really do. They're fun, and so cute and smart. I think I just feel so sad that Sutton's missing out."

"Did you decide that she'd go early?"

I frown, not understanding what she means.

"Did you? Like, was her death your choice?"

"No," I say, aghast.

"Then *don't* feel sorry, June. If you start to feel guilty or sorry for her, just don't. Because that part was not your choice. What you're doing is honoring her legacy, and raising up her babies right. As your babies. Margot taking gymnastics and Oliver in karate...that would make her so damn happy. Driving them to Georgetown to take piano on Saturdays... we know that would make her happy."

"Yeah, well, they were taking lessons back at home."

"In San Francisco," she corrects. "You realize they will grow up with

Heat Springs as home. And they will be just fine for it. If they turn out to be little budding rocket scientists, we'll drive to Albany for school for them once they hit high school, or even middle school. All of us will help you do it. I don't care what Snobby Pants said, smart kids are smart kids. They will not be held back by a small town. Small towns are enriching. Their tribe is bigger here than it was there, can't you just feel it?"

I nod. It's true the town has taken Oliver and Margot under its wing. It's been good to see. The kids are thriving. That's my honest assessment.

"And don't forget Dr. Weber."

I nod. I've been driving the kids to talk with Dr. Weber on Thursday afternoons. She's our friend Madilyn's uncle's new-ish wife, and she works in Albany. I talked to her a few times after Mom passed, and now the kids are talking to her about their stuff.

"I think that's been helping them. She wants to drop it back in a few weeks to once a month unless I think they're having trouble."

"See?" She grins. "You're so amazing, Buggie. I knew you could do this. When you got the call, I started sending up my prayers, but I knew you could. You're made for stuff like this."

"For stuff like what?" I smile at my own drawl, which is pronounced because I've been up late the last two nights doing some planting logistics.

"For picking up the pieces. Gluing all the broken stuff together. You're real good at that. You know you are, too."

"I just try my best."

"Your best is always good."

I look down at my plate, pushing some rice onto my fork.

U always been June who saves the day?

I clench my jaw. He doesn't really know me, and he's never going to. He lives in San Francisco and I live here. And anyway, it's not like that between us. It's just pent-up...what did I say? Pent up loathing.

"I hope he'll stay away from here for a good, long while," I murmur.

Leah laughs. "What does that mean?"

Oh shit. I shake my head. Guess I voiced that thought out loud.

CHAPTER 20

JUNE

We fall into a routine. I'm a creature of habit, and I take my shower every night around seven o'clock, just after dinner and our reading time. As soon as I close the bathroom door, Oliver calls Burke, and I can hear the rise and fall of the kids' sweet little voices as they talk to him.

Once, I'm pretty sure I hear Margot talk about my bath robe—how it's silky. Another night, they tell him how I shut my fingers in the car door as we hauled the groceries in that afternoon. I don't know what he says. I tell myself I don't care. When he texts asking how my fingers are, I reply: *Just fine, thank you for asking.*

It takes a few minutes, but my Southern manners override my common sense.

I hope you're well yourself, I text.

Just fine. :)

I'm glad to see he's decided that he'll act appropriate. And so will I. We're the aunt and uncle—and not the couple kind.

About a week after that exchange, Margot falls from the jungle gym at school and has to get a little butterfly bandage on her forehead where she hit it on the bar. She wants to FaceTime Burke from the car when we get done with Dr. Keller, before we leave the parking lot.

I set the call up for her even though it's early afternoon by San Francisco time.

He answers on the third ring.

"Hey there, princess."

"Look!" Her eyes well as she points to the white tape. "I hurt my head."

"Oh no...what happened to it?"

She tells him the whole long saga, and I start to drive back toward the school, where we've still got to pick up Oliver at three. I'm zoned out, trying to focus on the road, where it's just started raining, when I hear her say, "my birthday."

Right. Both of Sutton's kids have birthdays in the month of May. Oliver's is May 4 and Margot's is May 29.

"Are you coming to our party?" she asks Burke.

"Well I don't know. When is it going to be?"

"We'll have it when you're coming. You can pick what day!"

And just like that...the gorgeous villain I don't trust myself to be around has plans to come back for a little visit.

ᴴᴴ

BURKE

"I'm sure." I nod, my scruff scratching the phone's screen. I tilt it away from my cheek. "Yeah." It comes out sounding gruffer than I meant, so I try to sound chipper as I add, "I liked the photos of the staging."

I lean against the column beside the rows of leather seats outside my airline terminal as the woman rambles, trying to change my mind about dropping by to see how she's transformed the house I'm selling. I shut my eyes and rub my forehead, wishing she somehow knew what she was asking. Even though I'm hella grateful that she doesn't.

"I'm sure it's great," I say again. "In any event, I'm flying out right now for something in Atlanta, so I'll have to trust you. The pictures don't lie. Your team did a nice job."

I rub my eyes more as she babbles. Some people just don't know when to end a conversation.

"Yes," I tell her. "The realtor—you and Becky know each other— She should get in touch with you today. And thank you again, Sally."

People start to get up from their seats and line up at the terminal. I end the call in time to join them.

I hate to leave the office with so much going on right now—the app is at a vital stage, where we've got to develop a few things in a small time window to move forward without spending too much—but I will, for Oliver and Margot. I can only be gone two days, so I'm flying out now—at six o'clock on a Friday—and will fly back on a red-eye Sunday night.

I'll work the whole flight, which should be easy enough in first class, and when I land, June's brother Shawn is picking me up. I didn't ask him to; he texted and offered. Told me I can borrow his Jeep when I'm in town. Nice dude. Seems like everyone in June's family is more friendly than her, but I think I'm starting to see through her prickly act.

One of my objectives while I'm there this time is to learn more about her. If her dad's not a fucking bastard, why does she distrust men so much? What happened to her?

I glance down at my rolling carry-on and then make one more quick call to confirm delivery of Oliver and Margot's birthday gift.

Then, as I walk onto the plane, I call June.

"Hey," she says, sounding surprised and hesitant. "You calling to talk to the little minions?"

"Actually, I called for you."

"Oh did you?"

"I did. I wanted to ask you about their birthday present." *Please say yes*. If she doesn't, I'll have to call the whole thing off and come up with something else.

"Let me guess, two penguins to stash in the bath tub? Just a little ice required," she says drolly.

I snort. "Nah. But you're warm with that answer."

"Oh Lord above, just tell me."

I smile. "Okay...so I want to buy an above-ground pool. I already did, and they're planning to set it up early tomorrow morning. *If* you approve."

"A *what*?"

Her incredulity makes me grin. "You know...an above-ground pool. The round ones with the ladder on the side? It would require some maintenance, but I hired someone from the company to come and clean it during summers. I'm told the Southern experience is mainly had inside a pool in summer time." I smile at the thought.

"Well, there's a creek on the farm," she says slowly.

I heft my rolling bag into a compartment above my seat and sink into the leather chair beside the window. "Well that's good. But this is a pool. I thought it could go beside the house."

"I've got the pens there now. For the goats and the pigs. They're right behind the house."

"What about out to the left, like in the front. On that side where we had the bounce castle thing, but back a little? Under that big tree?"

She sighs. "You're really giving them a big ole pool? Are they even good swimmers?"

"The best. C'mon. I'm sure you know they're both good swimmers."

"Well, we'd have to be real sure. It's different when you have something right beside the house."

"I've seen them swim. You're good."

She sighs again. "Okay. If you say so."

I smile. "Let's have it be from both of us."

"We're not their mom and dad." She says it like she's rolling her eyes.

"No, but we're their aunt and uncle. You're giving the biggest part of it—the yard to put it on, and all your time to watch them swimming in it."

"I'll be swimming in it, too."

"Get yourself a swimsuit, Juney."

"I've got seven. You better bring yours. Nobody's getting in wearing their boxer-briefs."

I smirk at that, but decide not to be a pig about it.

"Scout's honor. Got a suit in my bag."

"We'll see you and your suit later. Don't let my brother get you too drunk this weekend. I heard he's making hunch punch."

"Nah, I've gotta work."

There's a brief silence, during which people stream past my seat toward the back of the plane. "Have a good flight, Mr. Benefactor. Don't let all your altruism go to your big head."

"Don't tell the kids ahead of time if you can help it, okay? I want to come over in the morning and see them see it. If you don't mind, of course."

"We'll be seeing you."

I realize she hung up and shake my head at my phone.

"If that's not reaction to a woman—or a man—then I'm not sure what is."

I look up, blinking at the now-familiar face. "What are you doing here?"

***

Sabal Gurung, the hiking partner and hoped-for investing partner I was with when Asher and Sutton died, has decided that he wants to buy me out. I showed him our numbers and explained our plan when he and I spent time together at his mountain home. I told him all about the regulations, the municipality piece of things when we spoke during all that hiking.

I also confided in him about our AI challenges. AI is a vital piece of the app—without it, the app can't do its main job, which is assessing its user—but I don't have access to that...and he does. He seemed enthusiastic. Even said he thought the app could be important. "I'm an old man," he told me then. "I need a legacy."

It seemed like a sure thing, but then he didn't buy in. I wondered about it briefly, but I was pissed off that I'd been with him, unable to be reached by phone, when Asher passed. So at the time, I sort of didn't care.

Now he's popped up on my flight, and as it turns out, he's spent the last few months freeing up the capital to try to buy me out.

I listen quietly for most of the flight—as he tries to make a case that I'm spread too thin, "just one man," and at risk of burning through my money before the app is able to be monetized.

"Yes, you have a degree of wealth," he says, looking at me over the rim of his bifocals. "But I have so much more." He lifts his gray brows—partly teasing, I think—and I laugh.

It's true, and for a moment, I feel torn. It would be such a damn relief to pass the impossibly complex tangle that is Aes' development on to someone with deeper pockets and more resources than I have. And he's not wrong; there is some chance I could run through my money.

But...I don't know. I shake my head and finish my gin.

"I don't think I can." I grit my teeth and pull a slow breath in through my nose. It's too hard to explain to him.

He tilts his head to one side, giving me his thin-lipped smile. His brown eyes seem to see into me.

"Okay," he says simply. He taps the side of his head. "I know."

Whatever that means. The man is one of the wealthiest tech barons living right now. Who knows what he does know.

For the rest of the flight, we talk about baseball—one of his favorite topics.

Before the plane lands, I give him my apologies and let him know I'd love to have his bank account on board, even though I feel the need to steer the ship myself. He's a good sport about it, but by the time I climb into the cab of Shawn's truck at the airport, I'm fucking exhausted.

"Hey there, man!"

Shawn's as friendly as I remember, carrying the conversation for most of our drive to Heat Springs. After the first hour, I get out of my head and pull more of my weight. He asks about my brother—in a way that doesn't bother me—and I tell him how it's weird it feels to constantly re-remember Asher is gone and not just waiting around at his house for when I get a chance to stop by.

"That's exactly how I feel about Sutt, man. She was always way out there in California. I'll be thinking she's still there, doing her thing while I do mine. And then I remember..." He shakes his head. "She always was a shitty driver." He shakes his head, and I can't help laughing.

"I know, I'm so bad. She would expect it, though, believe me," he says. "She and I were the two oldest. It was us who shared the bunk beds and all that good shit. Mary Helen was sort of in the middle and then June a little younger than her and a whole lot younger than Sutton and me."

"What was that like?"

He starts talking, and I swear he keeps the conversation going solely on his own for at least twenty minutes.

"Am I boring you to sleep?" he asks with a guilty grin.

"No, I like to hear about it. Sounds like you guys grew up...in a really good place."

He nods. "Yeah, our mom was awesome. Like the kind of mom that did all this crazy craft shit. She had us making bread that rises on its own, like painting pottery and making clay beads. One time she had this kiln, you know, the real hot things that bake the clay and seal it up and make it shiny?" He shakes his head with a small smile. "She just really liked being a mom. Hell, I just remembered last time you said your mom passed away. We can just move on from moms if you want to, to my dad," he says, barely taking a breath. "That dude's crazy. Runs away from everything. He ain't like he used to be. Losing our mom made him skittish. You hang out with him one weekend, and then he's shutting himself off again."

I nod. "Yeah. I get that." I don't, of course. The last time I saw my father in person—intentionally, anyway—was the day Asher moved into his college dorm.

"Were you guys little kids and shit?" Shawn says. "Do you care if I ask?"

"We were younger, a lot like Oliver and Margot." For the first time, I realize how true that is. We were so damn young. I let a breath out. "We were on our own, too. Pretty much," I hear myself say. "He was better off if he was working."

"That sucks, man." His gaze flickers toward me. "You're the oldest, right?"

"Yeah."

"Always feel responsible for the younger ones, or I do anyway. June or Mary Helen needs help, I'm always trying to be there. Like June when she wanted to take the farm over…"

I find out more about June in the last half hour of the drive to Heat Springs than I did in all of Molly's reports.

"It wasn't so much that she couldn't let it go," he says, of the farm. "I think it was more like she just didn't want to give up. June is a stubborn ass. When she wants something to go her way, she's gonna make it go her way. Ever since she was a little thing with pigtails. Mama used to braid their pigtails every day…"

It's oddly comforting to hear about June's childhood. I was never sure if people had lives like the one Shawn is describing—at least outside of TV and fiction. But apparently they do. And June is one of them.

Shawn talks about their dad a little more, how everyone is sort of worried about him, but no one really knows what to do or say.

"He's never been the real emotional sort of person. He's a hunter and a golfer," Shawn explains, as if that settles things.

He talks about the farm again—"June should be planting and

harvesting more, I think. But I think she's scared of hiring more people. She wants to pay fair wages and gets scared about letting people down if things go bad." He snorts at that. "She's got her own way of doing things. And she's not running it into the red more than it has been. She's pulled some parts out of the black. June knows how to steer the ship. She'll get it figured out. She's got some good help there, too. Just takes time."

It probably takes time because no one has any money to invest on the front end. I want to say that. I almost tell him I've been sending her checks and she won't cash them. But I keep my mouth shut, because telling him won't make her happy. When we finally get to his place—a small, brick house—it's 2:00 AM local time, and I'm ready to crash.

"I've got a spare room. My girlfriends stay in there sometimes when we get in a fight." He flashes me a good ole boy grin and waves me over to a door just off the living room.

"It's kind of a girly room, see all these sunflowers?" He opens the door, revealing a bedspread covered in sunflowers. "My current girl-friend decorated in here. She's asleep in our room. Remember me telling you about her last time? Sandi? She was in Aruba when you came last time."

"Oh yeah," I say, even though I'm not sure I do.

"You'll love her. Real sweet. We'll see you in the morning? Oh, and there's a shower off your bedroom, too."

"I might go to June's house in the morning."

"What time?"

"Maybe seven."

"Oh, well here." He tosses me some keys. "That's to the Jeep. You said you're good at stick shifts, right?"

I nod.

"She'll be good to go. Got you some gas today."

"Thanks, man. I appreciate it."

"Anytime. You're sort of family now. Us uncles have to stick together."

I laugh, but when I shut the door to the bedroom and look around, I feel like my throat's closing up.

I don't belong here. Fuck. Why did I come for this party?

Margot and Oliver, I remind myself. And for Asher. He would be here if he could be. I'm his proxy.

I undress and step into the shower. Get out, put on boxer-briefs and sleep pants. I lie on the bed, blinking at the ceiling for the longest time. I see Sabal Gurung's wise eyes. I think of the last time I hugged Asher. I shut my eyes and try to clear my head. Instead I picture being hugged by June.

I sit up. Get out my laptop and my travel modem. I work until 6:30. Then I fire up Shawn's old Jeep and drive toward her house.

CHAPTER 21

JUNE

I wiggle out of my little black shorts and then kick them across the room.

"Ugh. This is stupid, June."

I march over to my T-shirt drawer, jerk out the first thing I see, and yank it over my head. It's a battered gray T-shirt with tiny holes along the collar and a tear at the top of its front pocket. Bonus points because it says Heat Springs High Band. What better than to remind him that I didn't finish high school?

I riffle through another drawer and come out with a pair of black Nike running shorts with mint green piping along the seams—the kind that come with built-in underwear that are somehow superior to all regular cotton underwear but also make you feel like the most basic bitch alive.

"That's me," I murmur.

I swipe my hair into a bun on the top of my head, smooth on some nude lip gloss, and slide my feet into my beloved Teva flip-flops.

"I don't even want to see his fancy ass," I mutter as I huff into the hallway.

It's early, and the kids are still asleep, but I know the pool people are here because I heard their giant truck pull up a few minutes ago. It backed into my yard, the brake lights glowing against the blue dawn hue. I can only assume Mr. Startup King of Silicon Valley will be rolling up next in his rented Maserati.

I stop in the kitchen for some coffee and reluctantly whip up a second cup. I sweeten it a little less than what I personally enjoy and leave it on the bookshelf in the screened porch. The dogs whine as I shut the living room door, but I'm not bringing their hyper little asses outside at 5:30 AM.

It's too early for anybody with good sense. I take a long, slow sip of my coffee and then head down the porch steps, into the dewy lawn, where a whole bunch of people are doing a bunch of different things. The damp grass blades stick to my flip-flops and the top of my feet as I walk over to the guy who's got a short-sleeved button-up shirt on and is holding a clipboard.

"Hey there…"

He smiles, phony as all get out. "Matt. I'll be your site manager this morning." He taps a name tag that I hadn't noticed. "I don't think we've talked, but we're here for the accelerated assembly for the most luxurious pool in our collection, which holds—"

I wave at him. "You don't need to tell me the specs, Matt. Thank you for that, though. I mean, we already bought the pool, right?"

He nods, looking chastised.

"I just want to know how long will it take?"

"It should take about two, two and a half hours."

"Whoa. So that's not real long."

"This pool has a frame that's—"

I hold my palm up again, and his face reddens.

"Sorry, I'm just not that good at mornings. Do you need me for anything?"

It turns out, they need me for a lot of things. I'm finally sitting on the porch swing about fifteen minutes later, having picked out the exact spot for where the pool will go, when I see headlights shining down the driveway.

It looks more like an SUV than— *Oh yeah*. Shawn the Traitor invited Burke to stay at his place. Loaned Burke Bug his old Jeep. Told me all about this…oh, about twenty-four hours ago. I wasn't even completely sure that Burke was coming. Afterward, I got his call about the pool.

I tuck some hair into my bun and keep sipping my coffee, trying not to look over there while he parks the Jeep and talks to Matt and pokes around the pool parts. My cup is empty by the time he climbs the porch stairs and peeks through the screen door.

"Here," I say from the swing, and his face bends into a smile as his eyes find me.

"Oh." He squints. "It's darker than I thought."

He steps into the porch, and I try not to stare. He's wearing dark shorts—navy?—and a gray T-shirt that sort of hugs his biceps but it's not tight like *tight*. It's got a pocket on the front like my shirt does, except his isn't ripped. His hair is longer than last time—a little curly, I think?—and he looks like he forgot to shave. My gaze wanders down his muscled calves to his shoes, which are Vans-type sneakers.

"Hello." It comes out sounding low and sort of hoot-y, like a cartoon owl.

He laughs, and when he does, his face transforms into a brilliant grin. "Hello to you, too, June."

His gaze holds onto me, making me feel like I can't pull air into my lungs. I swallow, sit up straighter, and try to use my wit and charm to play off this racing-heart sensation I've got going on. "What kind of greeting were you hoping for?"

His gaze falls to the floor for a second. Then he smiles, more guarded.

"Oh, I don't know." He brings his palms together, trying for a smirk, but it looks kind of tense, as if he's not so sure about me this go 'round.

Good.

I might have lost my mind over him last time, but this time, I'm playing it cool. No narcotics messing with my head. He's only here for two days, so says Shawn the Traitor. I can do it.

Have a little self respect, I coach myself. *He doesn't care about you. Observe how he left last time. He's just an ordinary man, and he'll act like they all do.*

I draw one leg up onto the swing and wrap my arm around my knee —because even when I'm trying to be icy toward him, I'm still awkward.

"Well, you made it here in one piece," I remark, and then I have to hide a cringe because comments like that remind me of my sister and Asher now—who didn't make it home.

"Yeah," he says, nodding. "Your brother's Jeep is kind of...eccentric."

"You mean it's a piece of shit?" I laugh. "Yeah, that thing's ready for the junkyard."

His eyes light up as I say that—as if he's just so thrilled to hear me talk or something. He bounces on his heels a little, folding his thick arms across his chest—which I happen to know firsthand is thick, too, with all that muscle.

"So how's it going?" he asks.

I lift a shoulder. "All right. I made two cups for myself but I'm stopping at one. If you want it." I point to the coffee on the bookshelf.

"Are you sure?"

Lord, he's so polite this go 'round. Clearly aliens stole the other one and left this clone behind instead.

"I'm sure." I push off the porch rug with the toe of my shoe, remembering last time he was here. I was sitting on this swing, and he sat down and put my leg on his lap. Just remembering that makes my face feel too hot.

He leans against the wall between the living room and the porch and sips the coffee, his eyes moving from the floor to the pool assembly before finally settling on me.

His mouth twitches at the corners as he squints, and I realize he's reading my shirt. "Band," he murmurs, smiling softly. His eyes meet mine. "You were a band geek?"

I nod. His smile widens. "Me too."

"You were?"

He nods. "Trombone."

"Really? Trombone?"

He quirks a brow up. "Can't envision it?"

"I don't think I can." I fold both my legs onto the swing and turn sideways, so we're facing. "I see you as more a...I don't know."

"What?" he prods.

"Maybe like the debate team."

He rubs a hand over his face, shielding himself from my eyes for just a second. "Yeah," he says from behind the hand. "I guess I can see why." He pulls his hand down, and I find that he looks abashed. "Sorry again about all that stuff last time," he says quickly. "The...*debating.*"

"Water under the bridge." I wave my hand dismissively—because apparently that's something I'm doing today, dismissing people with waves.

"You'll see," he says. "I'm not really like that."

"Mmmhmm." I nod once. I'm trying to be generous, but he laughs, clearly thinking I'm trying to be a dick about it.

"It's okay," I tell him. "For real. I mean, I'm not fully going to trust you, but I don't fully trust anybody." I say the end part with a faux mysterious flair and comically big eyes, so it doesn't sound so pitiful.

He sips his coffee. "Who betrayed your trust before?"

"Oh, just people being people."

"Did you date an asshole, June?"

I think we've established I like assholes. If not their glowing personalities, I like them for their hot, hard bodies. Assholes make me mad, and when I'm mad, I want to bite and scratch and screw. Because I'm stupid that way.

"I dated more than one," I say. "But now I'm single, and that's how I'm gonna stay."

"Really? You want to stay single?" He seems genuinely curious, which for some reason throws me off.

"I mean...for a long time. There's nobody here, and I've got kids now. I'm content with that. With them. I really love being their guardian," I confess. I immediately wonder why I did. It just sort of sneaked out of my mouth—maybe because I do love the little critters, and that love stuff always bubbles to the surface.

"That's good," he says, and he sounds sincere. "I'm sorry again. When I think about those few days, I feel like shit about it."

"Oh, you weren't such a villain. You were doing thoughtful stuff like fixing broken gutters." I grin as I say it, because I can't not.

He chuckles.

"June, June..." He shakes his head.

He wants me. It's there on his face, under the awkwardness and alongside that heat in his eyes. I want to tell him he should lock it down, but he steps closer to the swing instead.

"I *am* sorry," he says after a moment, looking thoughtful. "I was fucked up from my brother. But it's better now."

There's something about his face...about the look on it. It tugs at my heart. "That's good," I murmur.

"AUNT JUNE!" Oliver's voice precedes his body by about a half a second. Then he rockets out the living room door and onto the porch, trailed by Mario and Peach. He sees Burke first, and then his gaze snaps to the lawn.

His jaw drops. "Is that a *pool?*"

"A *pool!*" Margot bounds out, too, still in her nightgown.

Burke says, in a low voice, "Do you want a pool?"

The kids start screaming, jumping up and down. After their rejoicing, I send them back inside to put on real clothes.

"After they put it together," Burke says, "then we'll have to fill it up. They told me on the phone that even with this special model that has the foundation underneath it and all that, it'll probably be this afternoon before it's swimmable."

So we'll go to breakfast. The kids are too amped up to sit at home, and I don't want them running around while the workers try to do their thing.

"There's a place a few miles outside town...this little shack that serves homemade biscuits with bacon and pimento cheese. That might sound bizarre, but it's heaven."

"Sold," Burke says. "Do you guys want to take the Jeep?"

Of course, the kids want nothing more than to ride in the POS Jeep, so into the Jeep we go. I sit in front by Burke and try to maintain a polite neutral face and avoid looking at him for too long while he drives, and Margot and Oliver talk his ears off about everything from school to Hot Rocket to therapy with Dr. Weber.

Burke is quiet but friendly as we get the biscuits then drive to visit Hot Rocket at the vet—he's now recovering at our usual vet in Dawson —and then take the kids to the playground behind the local library. There's a porch swing by the playground, its chains bolted to the underside of a small party pavilion.

I sit down on it, and then Burke does. The swing creaks under his weight, and he makes an alarmed face. He rolls his shoulders like they're sore, and laughs at something Oliver calls out to him.

Then he pulls his phone out, looking down at it. He mumbles something about "the office."

"What's going on with your work?" I ask.

"Mm, just everyday things."

I study his face a second. "You look tired."

"A little," he says, giving me a crooked little smile.

We get up and cheer the kids on as they race across the monkey bars. Then the pool people call. The assembly—which apparently was some sort of super-fast, patented process—is finished, and they've started filling it up.

When we get back home, the kids check it out, and then race inside to put their swim suits on—even though their party doesn't start for three more hours.

Burke takes a work call out on the porch and then sits on the couch, his hand cupping his phone as he frowns down at it. I go into the kitchen to dig out some food that I can offer him, but when I poke my head back into the living room, I find him asleep, his head tipped back against the couch's spine.

His throat is thick and kissable. I can see the subtle swell of his Adam's apple. And that jawline. Most of the time when I look over at the couch, I see a tiny kid there. Seeing his big body makes my belly tighten.

Take a chill pill, June.

There's a throw blanket in a basket by the couch. I pull it out, shake it to be sure there are no bugs inside—this is southwest Georgia, after all—and drape it over his shoulders and chest, covering him down to his knees. He doesn't move. My eyes roam over him a few times, admiring how good-looking he is—even though I know I shouldn't.

I wonder what the deal is with his job. Why does he keep doing these startups? I get it, it's a "lifestyle," if the articles can be believed, but he's done three in a row. Last time I saw him, I didn't know him, but this time, I think he seems exhausted.

I tell myself that's not my problem. Well, maybe a little bit my problem. He's the kids' uncle, and they don't have a lot of people left, so he matters to *them*.

The kids do quiet time in their room for about an hour and a half. Then we sneak outside with all the dogs. Oliver and Margot steal into the animal pen to play with all our new pets—pardon me, *investments*—and I supervise the four-dog playdate.

I'm throwing a Frisbee for Tink when Burke saunters down the back steps, rubbing his face and looking sleepy as he walks over to me. He pulls his sunglasses on and murmurs, "Hi."

"Hey there, Sleepy."

He gives a shake of his head. "Sorry about that." He yawns, and I can't help smiling. I try to make it look more like a smirk.

"Yeah. I kind of suck at sleep." He runs a hand back through his hair, and then his eyes sweep over the pens. "Wow. You've got a lot of new… pets." His gaze fixes on Oliver and Margot, who are holding George and Peppa. "You're not gonna eat the little pink dudes, are you?"

I grin, wiggling my eyebrows. "What do you think?"

He looks aghast. I up the stakes by giving him an evil grin. "We do live on a farm, Burke."

"You'd really do that?" His mouth twists into a troubled frown. "Maybe could I buy them?"

I throw my head back, laughing my damn ass off. "Ohhh, Burkie Bug. Do you have a weakness for the 'little pink dudes?'"

"Pigs are smart," he says defensively.

"You ever had a conversation with one?"

He frowns. "No, for real—they really are. They're—"

I jab his side with my elbow. "Burke," I murmur, and his gaze rises to meet mine. "I'm just teasing." I smile. "Do you think I'd give the kids pigs just to show them how to make bacon?"

He recoils, and I laugh. "I'm just kidding. And we eat turkey bacon."

He shakes his head, rubbing at his forehead again.

"Heathens. Am I right?" I ask.

He blows a breath out, still massaging his temples. "You had me going for a second there."

I grin. "You're a pig enthusiast."

"I'm no different than the next guy."

"Who loves piggie wiggies."

He gives me an unamused look, and I grab his arm. "C'mon. I'll let you hold one of them."

"I don't have to—" The kids interrupt him, cheering as we walk into the pen. "Hold him first," Oliver says, thrusting George toward him, his little legs kicking in midair. Burke looks alarmed and scoops the little snorter right up.

"Don't hold them out like that, remember?" I remind Oliver. "We don't want to drop them."

"Sorry."

"That's okay."

We all watch as Burke grins down at George. It's maybe the softest smile I've ever seen on him.

"You're a cute guy, aren't ya?" he croons.

"Look, here's Peppa!" Margot moves to stand by Burke, rubbing Peppa's belly as she cradles her like a doll. "They're best buddies," she says.

Burke rubs Peppa's velvety little pig ear. "Look at you," he murmurs.

But I'm looking at him as I lean against the corner of the small wooden roof that covers a corner of the pig pen. He crouches down and plays with George, Peppa, and the kids for almost half an hour. Then the kids drag him back through the goat enclosure, and he makes his rounds with the goats, giving each one attention and stroking their necks and backs.

Finally, when the heat is frying my brain and I'm feeling red-cheeked and off-kilter, I check my phone's clock. "Let's go check the pool, and then you kids will have to start your movie. It's time for me to start the decorating. Leah's coming over to help."

Burke is quiet as we walk around the house. He rides the kids on his shoulders. I catch his gaze on me once as we move, but when I meet his eyes, he quickly looks away.

As it turns out, the pool is only halfway filled.

"They told me on the phone that we can get in when it's sixty-five percent filled," Burke tells us. "There's a line there on the inside."

"Are you going back to Shawn's place for a while?" I ask.

He nods. "He wants to go riding *dirt roads*," he says, using air quotes. His brows arch behind his sunglasses.

"Ahh. So, we don't really do helmets or anything with that. Be careful."

"Is riding dirt roads like...riding ATVs?"

"Yeah. We call them four wheelers around here, though."

He nods, biting on his lower lip, and I smile. "Really, do be careful. Sometimes people get bad hurt on those things, and Shawn is a nut."

He nods. "Will do." He walks around the pool, climbs one of the ladders to peek in, and then steps over to me with his hands in his pockets. "You good here?"

"Me? Oh yeah...I'm fine. Leah and I have totally got this. Some of our other friends are coming over, too. You'll see the whole crew when you and Shawn get here."

"What time will that be?"

"Oliver wanted burgers and hot dogs, so I think we'll kick off around 4:30. Shawn said he wants to man the grill." I roll my eyes.

"I'll help him."

CHAPTER 22

BURKE

I don't know why it matters, but I need her to see me as a good guy. Not some dude from *Forbes,* but like an actual nice guy who just does normal shit like ride an ATV and use a grill.

When we return to June's house for the party, first I find the kids—they're in the pool with their cousins, clinging to those colored noodle things—and tell them that I like the dinosaur balloons and décor tacked onto the front of the house.

They want me to referee a speed contest across the pool's diameter, so I do that from up on the ladder and proclaim Oliver the winner before heading toward the house. When we were riding the ATVs through the woods behind Shawn's house, he asked me if I'd fire the grill up once I got here. I want to get that done and then find June.

The problem is, the grill that's in her front yard, parked near the card tables between the pool and the porch, doesn't have a gas tank. There's a bag of charcoal by it, but I don't know what to do with the charcoal to get it going.

Shit.

Mary Helen and a red-haired woman I don't think I know walk past me with a bucket of wine coolers, and I nod, tipping the ball cap Shawn loaned me.

"Burke. So glad to see you again!" Mary Helen does the arm squeeze thing that's always awkward, but then flashes me a sincere-looking smile. "This is my friend Shelly."

I shoot the shit with them for just a second. Then I steal around by the side of the house and pull my phone out of my pocket. I Google "charcoal grill how to light" and jump about a mile as someone says, "Burke?"

Holy fuck!

"June."

She's wearing some kind of loose white...jumper thing with sandals and a ponytail, and she's got her hands shoved into her pockets.

"Hey." She gives me a look that's part expectant, part tense, and part friendly.

I slide my phone into my pocket. "Sorry, were you looking for me?"

"Nope. Just..." She tosses a pained glance over her shoulder, toward the backyard. "Needed to escape. Really, I need a drink, but that requires human interaction, so I settled for escaping. This is where I come to get away when there's a party. These bushes"—she nods behind us—"are a little prickly, but if you stand right in front of them, no one can really see you from the front of the house."

That makes me smile—the thought of June hiding at her own parties. "I thought that seemed to be the case."

She peers at my phone's screen. "You doing some work over here?"

I slide it into my pocket. "Something like that."

She laughs. "Oh, you look guilty. Are you a smoker?"

"Nah." But I can't admit it to her that I don't know how to start a charcoal grill. "Just listening to a quick voicemail. What about you?"

For half a second, she looks like she just bit into a lemon. Then she sighs and steps a little closer to me, cutting her eyes toward the back-yard again like she's worried someone there will overhear her. "I'll tell you. I've gotta tell someone. This is insane. I just saw my dad..." She drags air into her lungs, then exhales, covering her face with both hands. "My dad kissed Leah's mother. Mrs. Kensington."

Mrs.

Oh, hell.

"So she's married?"

"Leah's father passed away. Last year." She moves her hands down off her face. "Not even a whole year. It was last June." She heaves another sigh and then shakes her head. "They were in the laundry room. So all the puppies saw."

That makes me snicker. "You think it was traumatic for them?"

"Yes, I know it was. And you know the worst part of all this?"

I shake my head, and she squeezes her eyes shut, rubbing her brows. "Leah's mom was 'at the beach with her best friend' who doesn't live here in Heat Springs when my dad was in Mexico." She shakes her head again.

"Wait, your dad was in Mexico?"

"Yeah, remember? Last time you were here."

"Ohh, that's right. I do remember that."

She tilts her head back. "He was obviously with Mrs. Kensington. Leah will be crushed."

"Will she, though?"

"Yes, I'm sure. My dad...he's nothing like hers."

"Yeah?"

She nods. "Her dad was the chief of police here. Old reliable. He was older than her mom, and he had some health problems, but he worked every day, rain or shine. He was the extrovert in the relationship. Her mom is more reserved and aloof. Nothing like *my* mom," she says almost resentfully.

"For sure, yeah—that's some strange stuff."

"This is what happens when the population doesn't top four hundred. People lose their minds!"

She looks so matter of fact, so flustered and so pretty, that I can't help smiling.

"I think people lose their minds pretty much everywhere."

She sighs again. "Yeah." Then she narrows her eyes at me. "Why were you really over here? I saw you from the window. You were standing by the grill."

"I'm going to start the grill," I hedge. "But I think I need something to help the charcoal ignite."

"Oh, like lighter fluid. Yes, you do. There's some inside—*in the laundry room*," she says with exaggerated trepidation. "If I were you, I'd go through the front porch door. In fact, I will go with you that way. Better to avoid any hanky-panky," she whispers.

June starts walking and I follow, trying not to stare at her ass even though I can see her sweet curves underneath the cottony jumper thing she's wearing over her swimsuit.

She slows when she walks into the kitchen, which is filled with faces I don't know well, although some I think I've seen before.

"For those who haven't met him, this is Burke, the kids' uncle," she says.

I flash them a quick smile.

"C'mon." She beckons me. Before she steps into the laundry room, she peeks around the corner of the door. I hear her soft "whew."

"C'mon," she says again. "Nobody's in here."

"Hey, that's not true." I lean down to pet her older dogs, then crouch to rub the puppies' heads.

I look up to find her holding the lighter fluid. She grabs something else out of a cabinet—a long, thin candle lighter. "Use these things."

She gives me brief instructions for getting the charcoal started. My neck flushes. She smirks. "It's okay, Mr. Bigshot. I'm sure some hired help does the grilling where you're from."

I shake my head.

"You don't look like a rich boy today"—she gives my mud-crusted boots a pointed look—"but I know how much you're really worth." She says it with a little smile, like to her it's a joke.

Something tugs in my chest. "It's not a good expression."

"What's not?"

"How much someone's *worth*. Only in a capitalistic society would we even use that language."

She covers her face and turns her back to me. "When I turn back around, we're gonna pretend that you didn't just say that."

"Say what?"

"You're not bashing capitalism with a cool one hundred million whatever in your bank account."

"I told you—it's not in my account."

She snorts. "I don't want to hear that you're some kind of super liberal. Please don't tell me that."

"Oh, Christ. Are you some kind of super conservative?"

"First," she says, "don't take the Lord's name in vain. I'm no holly roller but it does offend my Southern sensibilities. Second, I'm a moderate. Almost all reasonable people are actually moderates— whether they know it or not. That's just a little theory I've got. I mean really, who wants to just do things all batshit crazy with the pendulum swinging way far in one direction—like okay, let's hike up taxes by *forty* percent across the board. Or way the *other* way, like okay nobody's paving roads or running ambulances anymore, y'all just take care of yourself. Be moderate, don't be an asshole. That's my campaign slogan."

It's so clever, so articulate...and her voice is such a soft, sweet drawl. I want to throw my head back laughing, but that's rude as hell, so when she turns to face me, I just let my mouth hang open a little. I laugh, reaching out to squeeze her shoulders.

"June Lawler—a noble Gryffindor and a damn good politician."

I'm being sincere—I love that she has such clever political opinions —but clearly, it doesn't translate. She gives my chest a hard shove and says, "Don't be lighting yourself on fire, *Sly*."

And, like a hot wind through the kudzu leaves, she's gone.

***

I feel like a stalker for it, but I watch June throughout the party. I'm mostly in the pool with the kids—the only adult not snarfing down the huge spread of food on three card tables.

I play the role of Evil Noodle, a monster that has three foam noodle arms and likes to whack kids (lightly) in the shoulders or the back of the head. When the kids steal all my noodle arms, I submerge myself, pinch at their ankles, and then snatch the noodles back. But between enacting my evil agenda, my eyes are glued to her.

I've never met a woman like June. Those fucking looks she gives me —sort of pissed off, a little flustered sometimes—are because she *does* think I'm attractive; I can tell. She's so...unexpected. Being with her is an open-ended question, always. And I'm not even really her friend. I don't know her well, and still, I feel drawn to her like a magnet.

Maybe it's because of how she feels about me. In the past, with other women, I felt...obligated. With June, I'm the puppy nipping at her heels, hoping for the time of day.

I'm pushing off the pool's floor as that thought runs through my mind. As I break through the surface and the noise of the party hits my ears again, I realize I must be crazy.

Other women? Like I'm with June?

I know I'm not with her. But I have opinions about her. She's a woman, after all, and I'm a man. Last time we were around each other...

Let's just say I can't help being attuned to what she's doing as she moves around the yard.

When it's time to do cake and presents, I help the kids out of the pool, wrap them in towels, and end up at the cake table with Margot sitting on my knee.

"You help me blow out the candles," she says. "I'm not very good at dragon breath."

I refrain from pointing out that dragons blow fire, not wind to put out fire. "I don't think you'll need my help. You're a big girl."

June is flitting all around, her loose jumper flowing around her tanned legs and her hair flowing around her shoulders.

"Need anything?" I ask when she steps by me.

"I can't find a lighter."

"I'll grab the one I used for the grill." I plunk Margot down in our seat and go get it.

By the time I'm back, everyone is gathered around the cake. Margot holds her arms out to me, like she did when she was little, so I pass the lighter to June and go to her.

"You said you would help me!"

"Yeah, for sure."

I do a quick head count as we sing Happy Birthday: nineteen people. There's a man who stepped out of the house in the last few minutes. I think he's June's dad, because he has her eyes and tanned skin. The woman beside him must be Leah's mom, because Leah is beside her.

Leah and June cut and serve the cake, and I help hand it out to people at the other two tables. I get a few glances—I'm still shirtless, with a towel draped around my neck—but none from June. She's in her own world, talking to everyone in that grateful, effusive manner that parents have when you're doing something kind for their kids. A few times I catch her tossing prideful, happy glances at Margot and Oliver—the way a mom would.

She reminds me of Sutton, which is pretty weird. And then I start thinking about Asher. He never said much about Sutton's family, and I wonder why. There's so much to say.

I'm talking to Mary Helen and her friend, tracking June as she stuffs wrapping paper into trash bags, when someone's hand covers my shoulder. Shawn.

"Come over here..." He waves me toward the porch, where I find all four dogs—and a guy with bleached blond hair.

"Remember him from last time?" Shawn asks me, jerking his thumb at the guy as we walk up to him. "Marcus?"

"Yeah," I lie. "Good to see you again, man."

Shawn dips inside the living room, but he's right back out. He's holding a glass pitcher filled with something I can smell when he's still three feet away.

His face lights up just as the door opens and his dad steps out onto the little porch behind him. At the exact same moment, they say, "Moonshine."

CHAPTER 23

JUNE

When I was still with Lambert, my high school boyfriend, who had moved up to Atlanta for college, Lambert brought a guy named Penn home for Thanksgiving break. Penn was from somewhere up north—I think maybe New Hampshire. He wore loafers, skinny jeans, and big sweaters. I remember I thought he was hot in that nerdy kind of way.

When they first rolled into town for the break, Shawn was watching movies at my house with me. I remember he took one look at Penn and told me he could turn Penn redneck in one weekend.

It turned out to be true. Penn was stuffing his face with dumplins and fried bacon and biscuits and guzzling down sweet tea like it was his last meal. At some point, Shawn and his friends brought moonshine to my house, where Penn and Lambert were camped out—Mama had just passed the year before—and Penn got so drunk, I thought we might have to take him to the ER. The next day, Shawn had him smoking cigars on the porch swing, drinking Dickel Barrel Select straight out of the bottle.

It's the same damn thing with Burke, or that's the look of it. Shawn has set his sights on Mr. Sly, and he's not giving up until Burke passes out cold on the porch swing or swears he'll live and die a Dawgs fan.

I can tell they're drinking moonshine because when I pass through with a swarm of kids, headed for the back porch via the kitchen so they can do a pinata I set up back there, Shawn and Burke hold their Solo cups behind their backs and sit up straighter on the swing, both smiling too big for the occasion. Also, No-Good Marcus is around. That guy's a drug dealer, I swear, but Shawn thinks he's just a nice dude from Albany.

It irks me that Burke is hanging out with them. Even though I guess I should be grateful. If Shawn hadn't taken such a shine to Sly, he might be staying with me here. And I don't know if I could keep my hands to myself then.

He does have the body of a god. It's not my fault he's ripped and lean and got those graceful, muscle-flexing movements like the Instagram models. Also, when he smiles, I feel like *I* just took a shot of moonshine. He's temptation on two legs, and I'm a girl who's got a broken vibrator and no extra money to spend on another one.

So it's better that Shawn gets Burke shitfaced and hauls him off. Makes my life a little easier. In fact, to ensure that very outcome, I take to avoiding Mr. Sly and that whole front porch region.

I take the kids to the pens behind the house, and we play with the critters. It's our own little petting zoo. Then we go inside and change into dry clothes, have popsicles in the kitchen, and everybody slowly starts to go home.

I stay inside while people wander in and out, "cleaning up the kitchen." When Shawn saunters inside, smelling like the inside of a bottle, I dart off to the bathroom, where I stay while I can hear Sly's voice coming from the den.

Leah's in there; she'll be here with me tonight, so we can catch up and use these collagen masks she ordered. I can hear her laughing at everything he says. And he sounds like he might be tipsy—voice a little lower, his low laugh a little richer.

Leah's liked my boyfriends since we were in first grade. My cheeks blaze bright red as I scrub my hands in the sink. Not like Burke is mine. That's crazy. It's so crazy I laugh, giving myself a look in the mirror.

Then I go into the den, and it's just Leah and the kids, all snug on the couch, and I forget about Burke. I'm sure he's partying it up at Shawn's. My brother throws big, stupid parties where everyone in the county shows up with a cooler full of beer. Super classy. That's the Lawlers.

Burke is used to a party bachelor lifestyle, no doubt. Maybe he'll fit right in.

The kids are so zonked, they go to bed early, leaving Leah and me in the den to shoot the shit and watch *You* on Netflix.

I'm not sure if I should tell her what I saw between my dad and her mom. I think I won't until she brings out some wine and sprawls out on the couch under my big, fuzzy throw blanket and tells me she's afraid her mom is dating Ryan, her fifteen-years-younger lawn landscaping guy.

"I thought Ryan was into Russell who runs that Conoco down near Albany, so that's just weird," she laments.

And I just blurt it out. "NoIsawyourmomandmydadkissinginthelaundryroominfrontofthepuppies."

Leah gasps and shoots up off the couch.

"My mom is such a hussy! And your dad! June, eww. I'm sorry, but your dad's moustache is not my favorite situation."

"Lord, Leah. That's not very nice. My dad is still a catch."

"This is so weird." She paces the floor. "I just can't!"

She's so scandalized, she says she doesn't want to do the collagen masks. Despite her upset, Leah tends to crash as hard as she works and plays. In half an hour, she's asleep, looking like a Disney princess with her pretty dyed hair flowing over my couch pillow.

I'm not tired at all, so I decide to take Mario and Peach out for a tinkle. That's how I come to be out in my front yard under the full moon, tapping my toes while the pups take care of business. I turn a few slow circles underneath the stars, hoping to feel something besides weary and a little annoyed—though at who, I'm not exactly sure.

I hear a coyote somewhere, sounding lonely and restless. *I hear that, sister.* I strain to listen for her howl again, over the song of crickets. And that's how I hear the splash.

At first, the only thing I can think of is an animal. Or snake. Snakes do love the water. Maybe it's a squirrel, fell in. My mind races as I take the puppies inside. I steal back onto the porch, lock the screen door as a safety measure, and spend a minute listening to the pattern of the splashes.

That's somebody. Gotta be. Somebody came and took a dip in my pool! Somebody or some animal. But what could get in? It's so high up off the ground.

I step back inside and use a stool to reach the cabinets over my refrigerator. There's a gun up there—a little .22 my mama used to carry if she ever had to drive somewhere at night. I check that it's loaded and take off the safety. Then I slip onto the porch and creep down the stairs.

It's a quiet enough night. I mean, the crickets are doing their thing, but it's not windy, and there's no other noise, like from someone driving by. I can't even hear the faint sound of county road traffic I can hear sometimes in winter, when some of the trees have lost their leaves.

When I was little, Mama used to watch those USA Network murder movies. I think about them as I creep toward the pool. There's that one big boulder in the front yard, and a few trees, but no good place to hide. Moonlight spills over the lawn in silvery swaths, fading into skinny pine tree shadows and seeping into wet spots in the grass around the pool.

I stop maybe fifteen feet away from it, and I'm sure it's a person. Someone big. Their movements aren't erratic, and it also doesn't sound like they're trying to be quiet.

I'm aware, as I move slowly toward the pool, of what I want it to be. *Who* I want it to be. I've read my share of Danielle Steel and Nora Roberts. I like those plots better than the Mary Higgins Clark. I like happily ever afters, and a little strangeness. Some surprise and pitter-patters of the heart, and that sweet roller coaster feeling.

I feel all of that and more as I climb up the ladder that leads over the pool's side, and I see it's him.

It's Burke in the pool, treading water on his back with his head tipped toward the moon, the contours of his gorgeous face outlined in pearly light. Each time he moves, the muscles of his chest flex, making white light and shadows sluice over him.

"Burke."

I don't mean to say it. His name rolls off my tongue like a marble. When he hears it, he paddles around to face me, and he smiles a little crooked smile.

"Hey there, June."

His voice is soft and slow, almost a drawl in this one moment. My chest gives a little kick, like meeting his gaze sent electric current into me. I have the sense that he's been waiting for me.

His eyes hold mine, and I'd bet the whole world that he has been.

He tilts his face toward the sky again, shuts his eyes.

"What're you doing?" It's a murmur.

"Nothing," I say. "Are you drunk in my pool?"

He opens his eyes again, gives me a smirk. "I didn't drink it."

"What do you mean?"

"Didn't have much of the mountain dew, as he called it. Your brother didn't notice."

"Why not?"

I think he shrugs. He sinks deeper into the water a little on one side, then paddles more to get himself back up. "Just had some work stuff to take care of."

"Where is Shawn?"

"He's at his house with some friends."

"Oh you mean the whole town and their lady friends?" I roll my eyes.

He grins, but he doesn't comment. "I wanted to unwind a little."

"So you came to my house."

His lips twitch into a smile—smug or abashed?

He strokes closer to me and looks up, dark hair falling over his temple. "Yes. I came to your house."

I hear myself rasp, "I guess my house is happy to have you. If not happy," I add, climbing over the pool's side and perching on the top rung, "at least accepting of your presence."

He chuckles. It's a nice, rich sound that finds its way into my bones and warms them up like whiskey.

"Is that right?"

I nod. "Nobody was in the pool, and I guess it *is* sort of yours."

He gives a shake of his head. "Nah. It's yours now."

"Mr. Moneybags." I roll my eyes, mostly to pry them off his bulky shoulders, where they're lingering.

He swims little closer still.

"Is that how you see me?"

I shrug. "Waddles like a duck, quacks like a duck, floats like a duck…"

That makes him snicker. "Ducks float better than me."

He shifts onto his back, and I watch him sink until all I see is his straight nose and edible lips.

"You have a low percentage of body fat. Others"—I gesture at myself like Vanna White—"float more easily."

He grabs one of the ladder's rungs and holds his hand out. "Come show me."

I'm still in my swimsuit. Never got in the pool at the party, never took my cover-up off. Now I have no excuse for why I can't get in with him. And I find I don't want one.

I sigh, so he doesn't think I'm overeager. No reason to reveal all my cards. Then I peel my jumper down. "Lest you judge me for bad guardian-ing, know that Leah's in the house with the kids."

"I know you're good to them, June."

I drape my cover-up over the pool's side. Then, aiming away from his shadowy form, I hop down off the ladder, cutting feet first into the water. It's warm—not bath warm, but like a bath you've sat in too long—and surprisingly deep. My pointed toes hit the smooth bottom, and I push up toward the surface, breaking through to find him grinning.

I tread water, staring at him and his almost-silly grin. "That was quite an entrance."

I swipe my hair out of my eyes. "Shut up."

"No, it really was graceful."

I want to make an offhanded comment. Something like, *There's a word not commonly used to describe me.* But I can't find my voice. I swim a circle around him, loving how my muscles feel. Like most Southern girls, I've always loved to swim.

"When I was in tenth grade," I manage, when I come to a stop near him, "we had cheer tryouts at school, to go from JV to varsity. I was already on the team. But we had judges come in from Atlanta. There were twelve varsity spots." I laugh, shaking my head. "Twelve girls tried out, right? I found out from our cheer coach—in private—that they only recommended eleven. They thought the squad would be better with eleven than a twelfth one—a *current* cheerleader. Me."

Even now, the memory strikes me as hilarious—maybe especially now that time has dulled my shame. I shift onto my back, kicking and spreading my arms as I belly laugh. When my giggle-fest loses steam, I stare up at the trees as swaths of moonlight beam down through pine needles. Then I shift so I can see him, and I find his eyes are trained on me.

I'm aware that how I'm floating makes my breasts jut up out of the water. For a second, I'm going to sink back under. Then something in his eyes sparks, and I feel pinned in place. I inhale, the air in my lungs causing me to float a little better.

"You're right," he says, grinning as he paddles closer. "You do float."

His eyes look dazed. His lips are parted slightly as he comes in close enough to kiss my cheek...close enough so I can feel the water moving with each smooth but forceful kick of his legs, stroke of his arms.

"What about you?" I manage in a hoarse whisper. "Are you a California water baby?"

"Grew up with a backyard pool."

He's so close I feel his breath against my jaw, can almost smell the minty scent that I remember last time he was here. To give myself some space, I kick a few times, sending myself toward the side of the pool, where there's a round flamingo float with a long, thick neck and two wings surrounding a flat spot in the middle. I drape my arm across its middle, and there's a *plop* as something falls into the pool.

"What the what?"

He's over to me in a second, so close that my pulse kicks up a notch. He grabs the dark thing bobbing in the water. "Wine cooler." He grins at it. "Your sister must have left them."

"Oh my gosh, she left a bunch of booze in a float at a kids' party?"

He chuckles and then reaches over me to grab another one from the flamingo's middle; there's a small indention where a few more are propped up.

"Peach," he says, reading the label. I sigh.

"Moonshine and wine coolers at a children's birthday party. Welcome to southwest Georgia." I let go of the flamingo as Burke twists the top off.

I watch as he swallows some, pauses, then gulps more. He brings the bottle down from his mouth and gives me a crooked grin. "It's kind of good."

"Yeah, I bet it's good like sugar cereal. I got the kids some Trix the other day. Did you know they literally threw it away? Bad dyes and too much sugar in the morning. Did you know morning is the worst time of the day to eat a lot of sugar?"

He's grinning. Just grinning. Saying nothing. And I'm rambling.

He holds the drink out to me, and I take it, sinking down into the water as one of my hands stops paddling to hold onto it. As I take a swallow, the crickets seem to buzz more loudly. His eyes look like molten silver in the moonlight. Chills sweep up my arms, and my heart-beat seems to stutter. I smack my lips to break the spell of the moment and shake my head.

"Better hot than cold, I think." Burke grabs the flamingo float, pulling it back toward me. "Hold onto this and you can hold your drink with your other hand."

I snort. "Classy." But I do it.

He's smiling like we're sharing some fun secret as he twists open another bottle.

I watch him drink it with one hand while treading water with his other. I can feel the water bend where his legs kick under the surface, but he doesn't look off-balance with just one arm treading.

"You must work out like a maniac."

He shrugs a shoulder. "Just average."

"Average for a millionaire." I'd wager nothing about Burke Masterson is "average."

He frowns deeply, shaking his head. "I wish you wouldn't say that."

"What?"

"I don't know." He shakes his head again and has another swallow of the drink. When he lowers it from his mouth, he looks angry...or maybe that's a contemplative face. The fact that I'm not sure just under-scores how little I know him. In this moment, I wish I knew him better.

"I guess it's not fair for me to have objections," he says, clearly thinking aloud. "Not with how I treated you."

How did he treat me? "You mean like...you put me in a box or something? And now you feel like I'm putting you in one?"

He presses his lips into a firm line, still looking troubled. "Yeah. I guess so."

Empathy wells in me, fierce and unexpected. "I've been making you pay for that ever since. I'm sorry." I take a swig of my drink, chewing on it. "I think part of it is that I like to pick on you, like back in kinder-garten. Tease you."

He gives me a small smile. Then he grabs hold of the flamingo. We're side by side, and so at first, we almost tip the float over. But Burke swims around so he's across from me and lays his big, muscular arm across the middle. He reaches his fingers out, as if he wants me to grab on, and I grab his hand.

Our legs brush beneath the water as he seems to look right through me. Heat blooms up my arm, and then my face is burning. I wait for him to let go of my hand. Instead, he threads his fingers through mine.

For the longest moment, we're just there together, our calves brushing again underwater, our hands clasped. He adjusts his grasp on my hand and glides his thumb over my knuckles. I stop kicking, just holding onto the float and letting my legs drift aimlessly.

"What were you like in kindergarten?" I whisper, trying desperately to ease the tension in my chest. "Tell me what baby Burke was like."

He smiles again, and it's this tentative smile—almost a shy smile. For a second, he looks like he's debating what to say. Then he says, "I didn't like school."

"Really? But you're a Ravenclaw."

That makes him grin. "I was a homebody," he says as our legs brush once more, and sparks of heat shoot through me. "My brother was still home then, when I was starting. As well as my mom," he says.

He swallows, and our eyes are locked over the flamingo's wings. I can barely drag air into my lungs.

"So you were sad to go?" I manage.

He props his chin on his thick arm, the one that's stretched across the float, and grips my fingers, giving them a little squeeze. "Yeah. I didn't like it."

"Aww. That's kinda sad."

"It was a good school," he says. "Good people. It worked out." His eyebrows arch. "What about you?"

"Well, I was at the slum school. Kidding." A breeze blows through the pine trees, and I let myself sink down into the water just a bit more. "I was here, and it was okay. I had wanted to go for years. Because of Shawn and Mary Helen and Sutt. I was a dramatic child." He smirks at that. "I thought it was hell to be left with my mama playing Play-Doh and watering the flowers and swimming in our pool all day."

He frowns. "Wait, so you didn't live in this house?"

"Oh, no. We had a different house. I mean, it's still there. Down the dirt road a little ways." I nod in that direction.

"Does your dad live there?"

I make a face then take a long swing of my drink, and he says, "You don't have to—"

"It's okay. He never came back to the house after Mama died. Like, not once. The ambulance took her away to the funeral home, and he got in his car and left. It was her place. Mama was a decorator, and she had it all done up just right. And then with what happened…" I try to swallow, find I can't. And then I do—I get a breath—and words are falling from my mouth like bricks into mud. "It was just the two of us that morning. She'd been doing good, and then she wasn't. It was so fast." I blow a breath out, and his fingers squeeze mine. "My daddy checked out, moved himself into town, so we cleaned out the important stuff and shut it up."

I glance up at his face, and my stomach does a slow roll. His features are stretched into what looks like horror. As soon as my eyes catch his, he shuts the look right down, but then he takes a long pull from his bottle.

Getting way too heavy. Running your mouth, I chastise myself.

I rub his hand.

"What about you?" I'm going for a palate cleanser. "Did you grow up living in the same house the way I would think? *If* I was putting you in a rich box, that is. Which of course I'm totally *not.*"

He gives me a quick smile. Then he's looking down, away from my face. I see him swallow, see his jaw tick. His head bows a little.

"I'm sorry." I don't know how I know to say it, but I feel it—something sad about him. And I know that it's because of what I said about my mom dying. Guess it got too close to something.

He looks up, and there's this lostness in his eyes.

I don't know why—there's no forethought involved. But I reach across the middle of the float and walk my free hand up his arm…and then lean forward so I can stroke his shoulder. He leans into my touch, leans his head down on my hand. I sift my fingers through his dark hair.

Poor baby.

I can feel his muscles tighten in the first few seconds. So it's easy to tell when he relaxes. He pulls back a deep breath, lets it out…and for a little while, I just play with his damp hair. We've been floating all around the small pool, both still kicking gently underneath the float, so there's a moment when his shoulder bumps the ladder.

He lifts his head, and our eyes lock, and I can't read his face. He grips the ladder behind him. Then he lets my hand go, and he starts to turn the float around, bringing my body to him—so his chest is right behind my back, my rear brushing his swimsuit. His arm comes around my hips, hugging me against him, and I swear I think I feel him tremble.

I feel his breath near my throat as he brings his mouth close to my skin. For a long moment, I think he's going to kiss me there. Then he grips my waist with both hands, turns me around to face him, and he seals his hot mouth over mine.

CHAPTER 24

JUNE

He tastes like peach and nighttime, like pool water and pain and just a pinch of starlight. He kisses me long and deep and hard, and I return his kisses—not by accident this time but because I want him.

I want the hot stroke of his tongue against mine and the way he holds me not just close but also up, so I don't sink into the water. I want his warm, sweet breath against my temple when we wrench apart to gulp the humid air. I want his gorgeous body, how he's hard where I'm soft, he's groaning when I'm sighing.

We lose hold of the ladder, end up paddling together for a second, laughing. Then he's kicking both of us toward the ladder as his hand supports my head.

"High school lifeguard," he whispers, as he leans me against the ladder. Then his mouth is crushing mine again.

Some men are smooth and careful. Burke is rough, demanding. I can feel the prickle of his shadow on my tender skin, and when he holds me to him, his strong arm is gripping just a fraction too hard. As if he wants me so much he forgot his manners.

But he didn't. When his fingers tease my nipple through my swimsuit top, he stops and looks at me with lust-drunk eyes and rasps, "Okay?"

I nod, and our foreheads press together. My fingers stroke back through his hair. I nip at his mouth and he laughs, and I feel it move from his chest into mine, and then we're at it again, going at each other until I have no more thoughts, only the need to rub myself against him and wrap my legs around his waist.

"Fuck, you taste so good." His gentle hands are on my forehead, pushing my wet hair back. His eyelids are heavy, but his mouth is smiling softly.

"I've been thinking about this." The words are rough; it's a confession. He looks dazed, with hair that's sticking up from my tugging hands.

"Oh, have you?" I plant a kiss on his hard shoulder, my lips finding chills on his skin. I bite down on the muscle there, and he groans.

"Yeah."

"Thinking about what?" I murmur.

"Touching you."

"When you thought about it...like a daydream...what would I do to *you*?" I trail my fingers down his bare chest, toward the waist of his swim trunks.

"Don't do that, June."

I kiss his throat, rubbing my palm over his six pack. Then his hand is cupping me through my bikini bottoms. His lips trail over my forehead.

"Don't try to distract me, Mr. Masterson."

He strokes my tender, swollen skin through the thin fabric of my suit. "What, like this?" He's grinning wickedly.

"You could do that..." My voice trembles with nerves and lust. "But if you did—" I lift the waistband of his swimsuit and reach inside, where my hand finds the thick head of his thick cock, and for a moment I still. "Then I might have to do this."

I give him a slow but firm stroke, trying not to gape as I feel how thick and long he really is. Then his fingers delve under my bathing suit. One rubs over my skin and another traces my slit.

I can't help a loud moan. My hand around him loosens, but I tighten it and stroke him again.

"June." His voice sounds desperate. Another stroke, and I can feel him swell and throb. "Oh *God*."

His fingertip dips into me, making me lift my hips. Then he pushes his finger inside, and my body starts to quiver.

"*Burke...*"

"Relax." His palm is spread between my shoulder blades. With his other hand, he adds another finger, making me groan. He rolls his thumb over my clit. My breathy cries rise up above the lapping water and the night's song.

"This is what I want to make you do. Come for me." He fucks me with his fingers till I'm crazy, clutching his shoulder and moaning as he fills me up and then drags out...then stuffs me full again and kisses my clit with a fingertip.

"Oh God..." I reach for him. "I wanna feel you."

He presses into my hand, and I grip the thick tip of him. Both of us are moaning, but he shifts his hips away. His eyes are half shut as he draws his fingers out of me, putting his hand behind my hips and lifting me out of the water.

"Please!" I gasp.

"Please what?" His smile is wicked.

"Fingers," I rasp.

I grip the ladder from a different angle, holding myself up, and I realize that must be what he wanted me to do, because he groans, a growl-like sound, and then he's feasting on me. He's holding my hips at the water's surface, licking me as he thrusts his fingers back in. It's perfect—*perfect*—and my back is arched, my legs are clamped around his shoulders, my legs sometimes kicking.

I feel it building as I grab at his hair. Then, with no warning, the bomb goes off. I yell out, and he groans with me.

Suddenly the water's cool, and I'm too warm. I'm drunk and dizzy, and I want to touch him. I want to make him make these sounds; I want to make him lose himself. I paddle upright, and then I reach down underwater for him. When my hand rubs his bulge through his trunks, he squeezes his eyes shut and grits his teeth as if it hurts.

"You're *so* hard."

"Can't help it," he says.

"I can help it." He's close. I can tell because his balls feel taut and swollen. I give his erection a few strokes, and his forehead comes to my shoulder.

"Fuck, June."

I drag my fingertips around the crown of his head, wrap my fingers partway around him, stroking. He lets out a harsh moan, and I love the sound.

Then he's thrusting his hips at me, pressing himself against me. I'm teasing his heavy sac and stroking back up his shaft.

I urge him into my arms, wanting him up against me, even though his torso's heavy and we're sinking in the water again. I'm focusing on his thick shaft, squeezing harder than before, and pumping faster. I feel him swell sharply. Then a burst of warmth fills my hand and his arm around me squeezes.

He lets out a tortured groan. I wrap him closer to me. I can feel how fast he's breathing. I think I can hear his heartbeat—or maybe that's mine.

I laugh. "That was so hot."

I feel him smile against my shoulder. "No girl's ever said that to me."

"No guy's ever been so hot. You're hung like a horse."

He chuckles, and I rub his abs. I feel heady, almost drunk—although I barely drank the wine cooler.

Burke lifts his head, kisses my lips. Then he hugs me up against him.

"Thank you," he says into to my hair as I hug him back.

"Ditto." I laugh. I stroke his scruffy cheek. "Hey, Burke baby?"

"Yeah?"

"You're beautiful. You know that?"

He lifts his head again so he can look at me. He gives me a strange smile, both sad-eyed and happy at the same time. "You're the one who's beautiful, June Lawler. I've been aching every time I'm near you. Wanting what I shouldn't have."

He kisses me again, and it's a deep, slow, lust-drunk kiss.

My hand moves between his legs—because I can't not touch him. I'm surprised to find him hard again. With my hand cupping his bulge, I say, "You got a girlfriend, Sly?"

He shakes his head.

"Too busy?"

"Yeah." He groans as I rub him. I cup his balls—so swollen and heavy, I can almost feel myself creaming for him again.

"I've never dated anyone for very long," he says.

"I don't since I got cheated on. The high school guy," I explain, working him with my fist. "He went to college and thought he'd have somebody there and me here, when he came to town." I rub my thumb under his rim and feel his hips tremble as he sucks a breath back. "That didn't work out too well." I find the spot there at the tip of his head—the little slit—and rub it with my fingertip. "His loss, don't you think?"

He groans in reply. I'm still sitting on the ladder with one leg hooked around a rung. He's still treading water, and I think he's getting tired, because he's shaking slightly. He wraps his arm around my waist, pressing his cheek against my shoulder.

Due to how he's floating, sort of horizontal, I can still I stroke him. I work him a few times firmly, and he groans, and I can feel his dick throb.

"That's right, darlin'. I think I could make you come again—what do you think?"

"I want inside you." Holy Lord, his voice is rough and ragged. His whole body trembles now, like he's on some drug. I know I'm clever with my hands. I'm good in bed, too. All it takes is paying attention to their sounds and how they move, and you can drive them crazy. I like making it good for the man. At least in theory. In my real life, I don't have a lot of practice. Less than four hundred people, remember?

"I've got some blankets in the tool box of my truck."

That's all the nudging he needs. He scoops me up and sort of tosses me over his shoulder. Then we're moving up the ladder like a caveman and his lady.

"Your friend up?" His words are grunts.

"I think she's sleeping."

He sets me on the ground and holds onto me as I slip into my sandals. Then he grabs his shirt, a pair of kicks I can't see in the low light, and my hand. We're heading to my truck, across the yard maybe two hundred feet, and he says, "Only if you want it too, June."

I laugh and tug his hand. "I always want you."

It's like jumping off a cliff—this fierce attraction, and admitting it. Off-limits, insensible and reckless. He's not mine...but I want to pretend, just for this one night. Call it an itch that needs scratching.

I open my truck's tool box, pull out two blankets, and he turns on his phone's light. We check the blankets and the bed of the truck. Everything is clean, though. I'm meticulous about my truck. He spreads the blankets out and sheds his wet trunks. My eyes lap at his flawless body. Then I'm sitting and he's kneeling by me. He starts to peel my swimsuit off.

"You sure?" His mouth curves into a smile; his pale eyes twinkle in the moonlight.

"Only if you make it good," I tease.

"Oh, you'll see." He lays me on my back and moves between my legs. "You're good with your hands. So am I."

But it's not his hands he really works me with. He licks at me until I'm brainless, till I'm thrusting at his face. I feel full and heavy at the same time, achy and empty and needy for him. I pull his hair and wrap my legs around his hips.

"I'm ready now," I murmur.

"June. Jesus, you're fucking beautiful." He rises up on his knees, his dick pressed against my leg before he leans over again to tease my nipples with his tongue and teeth.

I can't help a sharp cry.

He rubs his erection against my thigh. "I'm so hard it fucking *hurts*."

I trace the V at his hip with my fingertips. "So give it to me, big boy."

Burke is panting as he rises up above me again, positioning himself right there where I need him and then rubbing.

"Oh Burke...*please*."

He spreads me open with careful fingers and rubs his thick tip around again until I'm nearly screaming. Then he comes in with one smooth stroke, one heavy stroke—and then I've got him. I'm pinned under him and filled with him and shaking with him.

He's so big...more than I've taken. I can't get a word out, just these shaky cries and whimpers.

He groans, low and ragged. Then he shifts his hips and plunges deeper. I grunt, and I think I hear him chuckle. Then he's moving...and I'm moving. His hands grip my face, and I focus on his tightly closed eyes.

"Oh fuck. God. Oh June." I feel him swelling in me. He comes in a little harder with each swing of his hips. *"Fuck."*

"Come on." I lift my hips, rubbing my hot spot against him so it feels just right. "I'm ready," I manage.

He comes with a guttural groan, and when I'm filled with all the warmth of him, and his shuddering body is heavy over mine, I come undone just the same.

It's a crashing feeling, a hot flush and swell of pleasure that steamrolls me as my body trembles. Then he's out, he's on his side beside me. Burke is pulling me against his chest, wrapping his arms around me.

"You okay?"

"Yes." I laugh. "Better than okay."

I hear the smile in his voice as he says, "Same."

I can feel his heartbeat through his hard chest. His big, damp body feels so foreign, but it also doesn't.

"So much bigger than me," I murmur, curling up against him.

He makes a soft sound in his throat and tucks me up against him, bending his knees until they nest against mine. Then he inhales deeply, holds it for a second, exhales.

"That was...really fucking good," he whispers. "Thank you."

He looks into my eyes, and I give him a big grin. "Did it for myself."

He laughs at that.

"I'm just being honest, Sly."

His hand strokes my shoulder. "Got a lot of pent-up lust to spend since there's no dudes around here?"

"Yeah, and wanted to spend it on your fine ass."

He laughs, and when I peek up at him, he's grinning like he's overcome by my wit. I can't help a cheesy grin. "Just being honest," I say again.

"You're one of a kind, you know that?"

"I've been told." I kiss his chin. Then I yawn, suddenly sleepy, and he reaches over me to grab a corner of one of the blankets. His palm strokes my arm before he spreads the fleece over us. "You're cold."

"And tired."

I feel a brush of his lips over my hair. "Close your eyes for just a second."

CHAPTER 25

JUNE

Sleepy...comfy...warm. I'm being carried. I note these things from a vague distance, each step jostling me—but not enough to make me open my eyes. Then things shift, and I'm completely vertical.

"June?"

I feel the floor under my feet and strong arms around my waist. Something hard is right behind me. There's a gold light that's too bright, and a faint breeze. Pictures stream through my mind—memories. And then I know where I am.

"Hey, honey." Burke is standing behind me, his arms wrapped around me. His lips are near my ear, so I can hear him when he murmurs, "The sun's coming up. I should probably go back to your brother's place before they wake up."

I squint and blink around the screened porch, finding that the black of night has given way to deep pink with the rising sun, which hasn't quite spilled through the trees yet. I glare at the bright light of the porch lamp.

"Okay." I rub my tired eyes, and Burke turns me around to face him. He's smiling, which makes me smile and feel kind of shy. He leans down to kiss my cheek...and then my lips, and then we're kissing and I'm holding onto him. He's got me pressed against him. We can't let go. We kiss and break away and step back three times in a row—each time moving back into each other's arms. After the third time, he smooths his palm over the back of my hair and rasps, "Bye."

I look over my shoulder just in time to see the small smile on his lips before he turns toward the porch door.

ɥ͏ɥ

BURKE

I try to wait a little while to text her. In the end, I only wait an hour and a half before I send a picture of my hand around a fish. I had forgotten Shawn and I were going fishing in a pond behind his house this morning. We catch twelve small fish called crappies, and I manage not to fall asleep or say anything about June—although she's all I think about.

Two hours after we set off in a little motor boat, we return it to the muddy pond shore, and Shawn takes me by Hardees for a "good ole artery cloggin' biscuit," which tastes better than I expected. We shoot the shit about football, with some lulls of silence between conversation. I feel half asleep as he drives us back toward his place.

"Wild night," he says, shaking his head. "You fell asleep early. Or did you go do some work?"

"I didn't get enough sleep," I evade. "That's for damn sure."

Back at his place, I go to the room that's mine for now and stretch out on the bed. This feels surreal—everything about last night.

While she slept on my chest in the back of her truck, I never even closed my eyes. Just laid there thinking, looking at the stars. I replayed what she said about her mom, and my reaction to it. It surprises me how I reacted—and I know she noticed. Usually I've got that shit pushed so far back, it doesn't bubble to the surface. But things are different with her. I find that it doesn't bother me as much as it might.

Still, it's something I try not to think about, so having all that dust kicked up in my head makes me feel a little off.

I try to do some work, but I can't rip my mind away from her. Gabe calls once, then texts me—call back—but...I don't. I pace around the room, then shower, thinking about her hands and mouth and little throaty whispers. I feel different than I ever have before. It's just...this *rush*.

I wonder if she feels it, too. I check my phone; she hasn't replied. I pull on some clothes, and when I look again, there's a text.

Hey there. I was sleeping. You went fishing... ;)

Yeah. We caught 12.

She waits a few minutes to reply—and I can see her typing. When the message comes through, I feel it like an electric jolt: *When will I see you again?*

Rather than reply, I get in Shawn's Jeep and drive over. It's a bright, clear morning with a soft breeze and birds chirping and a hazy kind of sunlight that contributes to the feeling that I've stepped into a dream.

By the time I park in her yard, my hands are sweating, and my heart is pounding like I'm in eighth grade. I walk slowly to the porch and stand there for a long moment before pulling the screen door open.

••

JUNE

I wake up grinning, and I can't stop. The photo he texted is the first thing I see when I pick my phone up. I don't reply to him for half an hour because I just want to savor this.

Burke texted me when I was sleeping. I was with him last night. He ran his hand over my hair as he left here this morning—at dawn—and that was after we kissed goodbye three times.

It's wild and crazy stuff. Which means it's smarter not to think too much about it.

I debate my next move only for a moment. Then I send a text that asks when I'll see him again. If anybody knows how dangerous this is, it's me, but I can't seem to help myself.

I shower and throw some clothes on—my favorite soft white shirt and jean shorts—and pad out into the living room to hug the kids and thank Leah for letting me sleep in.

"Any time, babe. Auntie gotta get her Zs where she can."

Latrice bustles in the door a minute later, her dreads piled high on her head, carrying a bag of popcorn and a plastic bag of uncooked pasta. I give her a wonky, silly frown.

She tilts her head at me in reply.

"Did you bring us some carbohydrates?" I ask.

"Did you bring me some attitude?"

She turns and rolls her eyes at Leah, and then holds her arms out to the kids. "All Latrice's babies come and gather 'round."

I join the kids at her side, teasing, "I'm one of your babies."

"We don't want you here, with that side-eye look you got on. We've got food to feed the piggies and some crackers for the goats."

Turns out, pigs like popcorn and pasta. I put up a small fight—is she sure these foods are healthy for the animals?—but Latrice always wins. She shepherds the kids outside to feed Peppa, George, and P. Diddy and the newly re-named "bitches."

"We'll deal with the chickens and check on the horses next," she calls over her shoulder as they go out the back door of the laundry room. "I'm needing a break."

As they walk off, I notice that her boots are muddy. I told her not to worry with our broken disc plow until Monday when Burke had left and I could help, but I bet that stubborn hussy didn't listen.

I check my texts there in the privacy of the now-defiled laundry room, disappointed to find that Burke hasn't replied. I try to brace myself for if he doesn't, but the truth is, I can't imagine that he won't.

I step into the den, and Leah turns off Netflix and waves me toward the hall. "Come talk to me while I shower."

Leah is the danger zone. If I shut myself up in the bathroom with her, I'll spill all, and telling her will make things more real. But if I put up a fuss, she'll really know something's up—so I go with her.

Luckily for me, I hear—really, I *feel*—the screen door slam a minute after she turns on the shower.

"I'm going to check on that," I tell her as she steps in. "Just to be sure it isn't Shawn and Co."

"I know you'll be sooo disappointed if it's Shawn and Burke," she calls as I go.

Brat.

I find him standing in my kitchen. He's facing the refrigerator, which means my first glance of him is his broad back, covered by a white T-shirt. His neck is tanned—maybe sunburned—and his longish hair is curling just slightly above his collar.

I make an effort to sneak up behind him, but he feels me at the last second and turns partway around. When our eyes catch, a grin lights up his whole face.

I come in close enough to wrap my arms around his shoulders. Then I rub my palm over his scruff and run my fingers into his hair. I pull him down like I might kiss his mouth, but I don't. I rub my forehead against his rough jaw and kiss him on the throat.

Then I draw away and smile up at him. "Hey there, Burkie baby."

He laughs like he thinks I'm crazy, but when he smiles at me, it's real and warm and happy.

"You're sunburned." I stroke my thumb over his cheekbone, touch a little curl just over his ear. "And you look exhausted."

He seems almost shy as he looks down between us. "Sort of," he says gruffly.

I can't help wrapping my arms around his waist. I'm relieved when he folds me up against him and rests his cheek against the top of my head.

"You smell really good," he whispers.

I squeeze him. "You feel really good."

He sweeps me off my feet and spirits me into the laundry room, whose door is right beside the fridge and has never seen so much action before. I pull the door shut behind us, and he leans me against it. He cages me with his arms and nuzzles my shoulder, kissing my collarbone with his hot mouth, and then my throat.

"Damn," he murmurs.

I run my fingers into his hair, hugging him to me. He kisses further up, just under my ear, where at first his mouth gives me chills; then it leaves me panting.

I grab onto his shoulder as I try to catch my breath.

"Damn you, June. All morning...couldn't get a damn thing done for work."

I stroke my hand down his abs, covered by his cotton T-shirt. When my fingers brush his pants, my hand bumps into his bulge. "I know what needs to get done."

I think he tries to snicker, but he ends up grunting as I grab him. "Fuck." He breathes hard as I trace the rim of him, and his whole body shudders.

"That's right," I murmur. I rub his erection through his dark green shorts, and he kisses my throat again. Then his lips find mine. His tongue glides into my mouth, and the whole world seems to speed up as we go at each other, my hand rubbing him, his fingers crawling up into my shorts from the pants leg, lifting my underwear and stroking where I need to be touched.

ELLA JAMES

"Wait," I gasp. I pull away from him and double-check the lock on the door that leads onto the back porch. Then Burke lifts me up and sets me up on top of the dryer. I wrap my legs around him, and we make out till I'm desperate with the need to get off.

He slips a finger into me and teases my hot spot with another gentle fingertip. Then he kisses me dizzy. My senses short out, and I'm groaning into his mouth. I come in a rush that nearly levels me and want to lie down and curl up and sleep, but he's still straining at his pants.

I'll have to fix that.

"Sit on the floor with your back against that door," I order, pointing to the door that leads into the kitchen.

He gives me an amused grin but does it. I get on my knees in front of him, unbutton his shorts, and wrap my fingers around his long erection.

"God, you've got the perfect dick." I bend down and wrap my tongue around the tip of it, and give his shaft a few slow strokes, taking him a little deeper as my hand moves down and drawing him out as my fist moves up. I don't even have time to find a good rhythm before he groans as he comes, with a thrust and a tremble of his hips.

His hand is fisting my hair. He laughs as he lets me go, but he can't stop panting.

"Fuck, June, that was so good. I was ready."

I grin and brush a kiss over his lips. Then I ruffle his hair. I smile, and he smiles back, and there are actual butterflies in my belly, just like in the romance novels.

I kiss his cheek, and he looks down again, like he's not quite sure what to make of my attention. "I like you like this," I whisper.

"How?" he asks, the word a rumble.

"Cuddly and shy and un-Burke-like."

"I'm not cuddly." But he's grinning, and he still looks sleepy, like a bear emerging from some hibernation.

"You are, too." I stand up and hold a hand out, as if I can help him to his feet. "Come with me. And hurry."

He lets me pretend I'm pulling him up. Then I lead him through the kitchen and into the living room, past Leah, who—*oh, shit!*—is sitting on the couch eating an apple. Her whole face stretches in shock as I drag Burke past her down the quiet hall. He chuckles darkly as I pull him into my room.

"Lie on the bed, boy toy."

He looks around the room, as if he thinks someone might be hiding in a corner, but he does what I say, kicking his flip-flops off before hoisting himself up atop the duvet.

I walk over to the bedside, riffling around my nightstand drawer for...*this*. I hold up a white bottle, twist the top off, and shake a small pill out into my palm. I hold it up to his lips.

"Do you trust me?" I grin. "It's a chewable, so nothing crazy."

He laughs as if he thinks I've lost my mind—which I probably have.

When I move the pill toward his mouth, he opens for me. I set the small, white tablet on his tongue, holding his gaze as he closes his lips around my fingers. I pull them out one by one, suppressing a shiver.

"Let that dissolve." I put my hand on his chest, urging him to lie back on my pillows. Then I pull the covers over him and make a silly show of tucking them around his big, hard body.

"And now close your eyes."

He does as I ask, but he takes a deep breath, like it costs him something.

I smooth his hair back off his forehead and trace his thick brows with my fingertips. Then I reach over to my nightstand and turn on the little white noise machine beside my landline phone.

"Keep your eyes closed," I murmur. "And think about me sliding under the covers beside you. Put your hand here—" I take his big, thick hand and spread it over his heart— "and just feel yourself breathe."

I lean down and kiss his cheek. "I'll be back."

When I check on him in fifteen minutes, he's asleep.

CHAPTER 26

BURKE

I wake to the sensation of something heavy on my lap...and someone's hands in my hair. June. She smells so damn good. I smile as she rubs her cheek against mine. I can feel her smile back.

"I'm your stubble's biggest fan." She kisses my temple, and I lift my heavy eyelids.

Her brown eyes are soft on mine, her face more gentle than I've ever seen it. "How do you feel?" she murmurs.

I blink around her room. Still daylight. "Did I fall asleep?" My voice is hoarse. I clear my throat, looking around for a clock.

"Yeah, you slept a while. It's just a little after one." I watch as she reaches for the nightstand, grabs a Ball jar glass, and brings its straw to my lips. I close my eyes and take a swallow of what tastes like lemon water.

Now that my eyes are closed, it's hard to pry them open again. When I sleep, I tend to be too slow at waking. I feel June messing with my covers. Then I feel the mattress indent and the blankets lift off me as she slips into bed beside me.

She wraps both of her arms around me, rubs her face against my shoulder, and folds a leg over mine.

I feel a strange surge of longing—like some kind of want of *more* June...even as I'm wrapped in her arms in this moment.

"Did you dream?" she whispers against my neck.

"Yeah." I press my cheek against her fruity-smelling hair and let a breath out.

What are the odds—that she makes me feel this good, just curling up beside me?

"Was it nice?" she murmurs.

"I don't know." I give a little laugh, despite myself. "What was that stuff?"

"It's called GABA. It's like a relaxant. For exhausted, sexy workaholics."

She finds one of my hands, lacing her fingers through mine. My heart starts to beat a little faster.

"Where is everybody?" I say in a voice that sounds tight.

"I sent the kids with Leah."

"So she knows?"

"Yeah. I'm sorry. She won't tell Shawn, if that's your next question."

"No...don't be sorry." I turn to face her, end up kissing her, running my hands into her soft hair. God, I want her.

June reads my mind. She hops down off the bed and strips her clothes off piece by piece, twirling her panties around her finger before tossing them behind her with a laugh. And then she straddles my hips.

It's so fucking erotic, so damn sexy...I let myself get lost inside her, lost along with her, and I when I finally finish, I don't think I've ever come so hard. Afterward, we lie in her bed, and this time I hold her against me, tracing patterns on her back with careful fingers.

"You're so good it almost scares me," I say. The words roll out of my mouth before I can think to stop myself.

"Why?" she whispers, smiling slowly.

I can feel her eyes on my face, so I shut mine. "Like losing control."

"We both did."

I roll onto my side so we're more fully facing one another. I trace her jaw and chin with one finger. "You good?"

"Of course." She smiles. "Are you?"

"For sure."

She shuts her eyes and snuggles closer, and I inhale deeply. There's this moment where I feel things lift away—everything fades except her now-familiar face and her warm, soft body. *Peace.* Maybe that's what this feeling is.

I shut my eyes, and she says, "There's a place I want to take you. If you want to go. I thought we could ride the horses."

JUNE

We ride maybe half a mile to the old white chapel. Burke seems somber —more so than I've ever seen him, and I wonder what that means. I feel his eyes on me almost the whole time, as we make our plodding journey. When Tango, my ride, trips on a rock, Burke and Lulu are a stride ahead of us, so I can see him blanch as he looks over his shoulder.

He shakes his head and gives a quiet laugh.

"Scare you?" I laugh.

"Just a little."

"Let's get our blood pumping." I point down the dirt road. "Want to race to that catch pen down there—the one with the brown fencing?"

He lifts his brows, and for the first time since we set off, seems to loosen up a little. "You sure about that?" He smirks. "There are no barrels on this track, so you won't have the upper hand."

I give him a mocking laugh and nudge Tango with my heel. We race off, leaving Burke and and Lulu in the dust. Both horses are galloping about a third of a mile, but they can't recover from my dirty head start.

When we get to the chapel, he wipes a hand over his face and shakes his head. "You damn cheater."

I laugh wickedly. "I know. But I won. No barrels in sight."

He gets a good laugh at that as we guide the horses through the tall, green grass.

The chapel's been shut up for years; it's too expensive for me to restore—yet. Its pretty white facade has been overtaken by kudzu, but it's still got a certain beauty. I'm pleased that he seems to agree. I show him the cemetery in its backyard, and Mama's grave, and we get off our horses.

Burke kneels down and traces the stone-etched letters of her name. Somehow it's the perfect gesture.

He stands up with something knowing in his eyes, and for a moment, I think he's going to say something. But he just drapes an arm around my shoulders and pulls me against his side, and when I look up at his face, I find it kind and curious and gentle.

"How are you a nice guy?" I tease. "I so thought I had a read on you."

"Different layers," he says, teasing too, but I think he's right. Everybody wears so many different masks. Who we are is constantly in flux—so who you get from someone else at any given time is something special, if you think about it. Relating to another person in a real way—even if it's brief—is a rare gift.

"I like this layer," I say as I climb back onto Tango.

"I like you."

It's sweet and simple. For a shining moment, as we ride under the hot sun, glancing at each other with our fleeting, bashful smiles as birds chirp and the breeze caresses us, the whole world seems to be.

We stop at a little tin-roofed shack known as the "water cooler," where there's a food pantry and free gasoline for everyone who works here, and we talk about all that: the farm's employees, how they're treated.

"Southern farms have history, so I'm careful how I treat employees. I don't hire more if I can't promise a living wage. There's a college fund my Mama set up, too."

I can see the shock in his eyes. For some reason, in that moment, as we both rip open candy bars I climbed down off Tango to grab, his surprise makes me snicker.

"Mama never wanted me to not get finished," I explain, meaning high school. "It was my choice. And then I just...stayed. A lot of my employees go, though. In a weird way, it's less essential for me. I don't need college to tell me how to do a job my family's done for generations."

I see admiration in his eyes, and understanding.

"Also, by the way," I add, "my farm is going to last. I know it looks a little dicey on paper, but I've got a master plan."

"Shit, June." He shakes his head. "I'm so sorry that I ever said that."

I give him a bratty grin. "You know I like the sound of sorries. Just for that, I'll take you one more place before we go back."

We start down a red dirt road that's lined by mossy oaks and follow as it winds up a slight hill into thicker trees. And there's my parents' house. Really my great-great grandparents' house. I watch

230

Burke's face as we approach it, and I know he thinks it's beautiful. It really is.

It's not truly antebellum, but it looks the part. It's big and white, with stately columns and a fine front porch, my grandma's rocking chairs still on it, along with giant potted ferns that were my mama's. I still come here to water them—me or Latrice. I know it's weird, but I can't stand to see this porch without my mom's prized ferns.

"This place is mostly empty," I say. "Would you want to go in, take a look around a real old Southern home?"

"If you do. Yeah. I'd like to see it."

I show him a rusty metal post where people used to tie their horses, and he's fascinated. He's rapt as I lead him in through the big, pretty front door and then all through the first floor, with its vast, formal dining room, antique hardwoods, gold flocked wallpaper, and a wall-sized mirror with a curling scroll-style carving on top. There's a piano in one of the parlors, and he plays a few keys, then winces at their lack of tuning.

When we get to the winding staircase, his hand catches mine. He's quiet again until we step onto the balcony that hangs over the front porch. We stand side by side, a most unlikely couple—tech tycoon and farm queen, I think wryly—and I watch as he takes in the lush grass and stately trees around us.

"Beautiful."

I nod as my throat tightens. "It was an amazing place to grow up. I felt like a princess. Sutton used to say she was the queen, so I was the princess."

"Where was Mary Helen?" he asks, smiling.

"She was also the queen. Or also the princess. Depending on the mood of the day." I laugh. "And I mean Sutton's mood. She ran the show."

That makes him smile. We wander back inside, and I show him my old bedroom. It's empty but for an old oriental rug, since I moved all my stuff into the small house. I stretch out on my back on the dusty rug, and, to my surprise, he sprawls out beside me.

"Pretty," he says, stroking my jaw as he turns onto his side to face me.

"You are." I grin.

He shakes his head. "I'm dirty. Need a shower."

His hand tunnels into my hair, and we kiss, gently this time, until I have a sneezing fit. "It's the damn dust." I rub my watery eyes. "Even though I have somebody come clean sometimes."

Burke helps me to my feet, but I'm loath to leave. "All my memories are in this room. Feels like almost all of them, at least." I run my finger over the windowpane where, in high school, I kept a row of scented candles, and he makes a sympathetic sound.

My chest starts aching, and I know it's time to go. Lingering in this place only ever makes me want things I can't have. I lead him downstairs, detouring briefly so he can admire a mural in the library.

"So this is it," I say as we step back onto the wide front porch. "This is my mausoleum."

We clasp hands, and I walk him over to a porch swing. We sit side by side, my legs swinging while his shoes on the porch floor keep us moving. He traces my wrist with roving fingertips, and I smile as I realize I was wrong about this as well—his hands are rough.

"Don't be sad for me," I tell him.

He looks into my eyes, and I can tell my gut feeling was right. Seeing this old, empty house—and what it once was—makes him feel a little sorry for me.

"Everybody's story has a sad part. You have to get through them to get into the happy parts that happen at the end."

"The happily ever after?" He says it with a teasing smile, as if it's fool's talk.

"Yeah." I'm surprised to find I mean it in the moment. I believe it.

He scoots just a little closer to me. Then he drapes an arm over my shoulders and pulls me against his side. He doesn't offer any words, is silent on the subject of the happy ending.

I wish I knew why.

His eyes are sad on the ride back to the house.

After we return the horses to their stalls, I take him to my bed, and we enjoy each other's bodies again. His default is gentle, playful, but I make it so he's groaning and tied up in knots in no time. We both laugh when he finds a small piece of kudzu clinging to a lock of my hair.

After we both scratch the itch, I fall asleep in his arms. When I wake up, he's smiling like he's content.

"Can you stay?" I murmur.

"Mmm?" He widens his eyes, inquiring.

"Can you stay any longer this time?"

It's a while before he answers, but I feel the tension in him. It makes me think I was wrong for asking.

"You want me to stay here?"

"I would love it if you could."

He smirks. "What would you do with me?"

CHAPTER 27

BURKE

She kisses my chest and drapes her soft, tanned leg over my hard one. "Well, I would talk to you, for one."

"Talk to me?" I say it like that's absurd. "What about?"

"Your favorite everything. All the things about Burke—the devil is in the details." Her eyes shine as she sets an indulgent smile on me.

Despite the tightening feeling in my chest, I hear myself say, "Hit me with a question."

She sits up and pushes her hair back over her shoulders. Her face is thoughtful, like she knows she just has this one chance and wants to make it count. She screws her face up almost comically, as if she's thinking hard, then asks, "Do you feel smart because you went to MIT? The only way I really know it is from that movie *Good Will Hunting*."

"Good movie."

She thumps my chest. "That's not an answer."

I force myself to sit up, too. I lean back against her pillows, reaching out to trace her bare knee with my left hand. "No," I say after a second. "I would say it doesn't make me feel smart."

"But you know you are smart."

I shake my head. "There are lots of kinds of smart. I'm good at taking tests." I narrow my eyes at her. "I bet you are, too."

She shrugs.

I think it's meant to be dismissive, but instead she just looks sly, like she's keeping a secret.

"I'm right about that. You were, weren't you?" I grin as I picture June in some small, country schoolhouse sitting up straight like she does when she's eager for something. I can see her acing every test, being a little know-it-all.

"I was good in school," she drawls after a second. "Nobody said I wasn't."

"College doesn't matter. I'm so fucking sorry that I said that."

"Even if you hadn't said that, it *does* matter."

"We're just one meteor away from the world as we know it being completely different. And always just a second away from something way worse. Common sense matters. Business sense matters. Kindness matters. College, not so much."

"Good thing Mama taught me to be nice." June winks, and I shake my head.

"I'm not sure I'd use the word 'nice.'"

She jabs at my ribs, and I swat at her. After that, there's a weird silence in which she tilts her head at me as if she's thinking something. I have this strong sixth sense she wants to ask about my mom. She doesn't, though, and I'm grateful.

"Has anybody ever read your tarot?" she says abruptly. My eyes snap to her curves as she hops down off the bed. She's still fully naked, which makes my voice catch when I answer. "Um...not sure?"

She rolls her eyes as she opens her nightstand drawer. "Then you haven't. Trust me—you would know." I try not to ogle her as she climbs back on the bed, but damn she's gorgeous, with her hair falling over her shoulders, soft, curly ends brushing the pale globes of her breasts as she moves.

"I've just got a Rider-Waite deck," she says, sitting cross-legged by me unabashedly. "My fancy deck is in my car, and I'm not walking out there, so we're going old-school. We'll just do a three-card spread," she murmurs, shuffling the deck. "Let's do...opportunities, challenges, outcome."

She walks me through it step by step, and I try to be open to it, as she urges. I end up with the Magician, Death, and the Fool—a reading June goes crazy for. She's still shaking her head at it as we step into the shower in the kids' bathroom.

I watch her as she washes, especially when she can't tell I'm looking.

She's about as perfect as I can imagine any woman being, and I don't know when I'll see her like this again, or even if I ever will.

"Tell me something," she says as I scrub the mud and dust out of my hair. "Something about you, Sly."

That makes me smile. "Something about me?"

She nods, looking solemn in the shower's steam.

I don't know why, but I decide to give it to her: "I like making things."

"What do you mean?"

"I like making...furniture." It feels so strange to say it that I stop and cut my gaze downward, away from hers. "Sometimes tables and chairs and things like that. But there's something relaxing about working with wood." I shake my head. "I know. You can go ahead and laugh."

I look up at her, and she widens her eyes. Her face is serious; it's *interested*. "I'm not laughing. Do you really do that?"

"Not much yet," I confess. "But I have done some. I took a few classes, at a community college near my place. It was a table-making class and then a carving class. For stress relief when—" I shake my head.

"And you're good at it?"

I laugh at her face; she's practically got *confused; recalibrating* stamped on her forehead. "I'm pretty decent," I tell her. "But I'd like to do and learn more."

"Wow. That's pretty cool that you're techy and artistic, too. Will you send me pictures—like of something that you made in the class?"

"Sure."

After our shower, I change out lightbulbs in high places, fix a broken blade on her lawn mower, and am in the yard looking at a crack in her bird bath when I can't resist a look up at her. I find her smiling at me like she almost always is, and I blurt out, "Tell me something about you, June. You know...something special."

She does a little twirl, reminding me of the cheerleader she used to be. And she says, "Well, I make cakes. Really good ones. I could be a chef or something, but I like being a farmer better."

Unlike me, she doesn't mind sharing about herself, so she shows me some cakes on her phone.

"Damn, that unicorn one..."

She smirks. "Self portrait."

After that, we seem to drift toward the swing. When we sit down, she hooks her foot behind my leg, and I take her hand. Just one more time before I have to get moving.

She tells me about the peanuts—what her plan is for the year, in numbers. I give a few thoughts, based on the numbers.

Then a boxy, old white SUV is bumping down the driveaway. Which means the kids are back. When they get out, Leah won't stop grinning at us, and she won't leave soon enough. I'm not sure when I'm seeing June again, and I want a second to say my goodbyes in privacy. Just when I'm about to give up, Leah finally drives off.

June sets the kids up in front of the TV and steps onto the porch alone, with her hair twisted into curls at the ends, like it is when she's been twirling it nervously, and a cigar box in her hand. She holds it out to me and smiles as I open its top, revealing a Ziploc baggie of something that looks like hardened caramel.

"It's Southern candy," she says with a proud smile. "Homemade peanut brittle."

I bring the box to my chest. "Thank you."

"You're welcome, Burke babe." As she looks at me, her eyebrows pinch together and her mouth twists downward, like she's reading our future and doesn't like what she sees.

"What's the matter, Juney?"

She blinks fast, then shuts her eyes, and then she wipes them with force. "I'm sad you're leaving," she says thickly.

I'm frozen in place, struck to the core by that look on her face. Like something precious is within her sights, but she knows she can't grasp it.

She closes the distance in between us with two strides. Then her arms are locked around me. Her face is pressed against my chest, and she's urging me to lean down so my cheek is on her hair. She pulls me down lower still, and our foreheads touch.

"Burke," she whispers near my ear.

I kiss her temple. "Yeah?"

She just squeezes me more tightly. I wrap her in my arms and lift her off the porch. Then I kiss her cheek, her chin, her nose. She smiles, and it's like they say in songs and poems—it's like the fucking sun.

"You want me to send you mail?"

"If the mail's *you*." She sniffles.

"You want me to fly and see you Wednesday?"

Her mouth opens. Then she's laughing. *"What? You'd do that for me?"*

I hug her close, so she's cradled against my chest. Her softness feels incredible. She kisses my throat with her velvet mouth, and I'm surprised to hear a ragged groan pull from my chest. Something weird happens—I sort of shudder—and she hugs me tightly.

"Burke. I wish you didn't have to leave today."

"Me too." I wish I didn't have to leave her *ever*. Realizing that I feel this way—that somehow I've become addicted to June—makes my heart quicken with fear. But also fills it up with something bright and dense and…necessary. I have the sense that this feeling is vitally important.

I guide her to the swing, and we sit down together. Then I hold her so tightly, I'm worried I might hurt her. I can't seem to let her go. We're kissing—everywhere. Her lips are on my throat, my cheeks, my forehead. My fingers twine in her hair as our foreheads touch, and I try to look at her. We both go cross-eyed and then laugh.

"Don't forget about me. Promise," she whispers.

I laugh. "I'll call you from the airport." I hug her again, smelling the fruity smell of her hair. I kiss her lips again, and then we're at it. We can't stop. She pulls away first, breathing hard. "I could never forget about you. No one could. Trust me on that."

The kids burst onto the porch at that moment, yipping all around me like the puppies do, trying to say goodbye, chasing me down the porch stairs to give me one final hug.

They escort me to the Jeep, and I give June a big grin over their heads as I hug them.

She blows me a kiss. When she moves her palm off her lips, they're tilted at the corners in the sweetest little grin. It's all I think about as I drop the Jeep back at Shawn's and get into the car sent by the service I hired to take me to the airport.

I text June a picture of the view from my window—because I'm weak. I fucking need her. Maybe I should really ask the driver to turn around. It wouldn't hurt to miss a few days of work, would it?

I laugh, because the answer is "yes." I laugh because I find I don't care. When the phone rings, I answer with a grin because I know it's her.

"Hello?"

"Hello? Mr. Masterson? It's Sally Cadmus."

"Mm?" I frown.

"From Artful Staging?"

"Oh, yeah. Right."

"Yes…well. Do you have a minute?"

"Yeah." I lean forward in my seat, tugging at my seat belt as my heart pounds in prescience. "What's up?"

"I'm not sure how to approach this, so I'll just be blunt. Your real estate agent, Becky, is a friend of mine. I learned something about the house you've hired us both to work on. I had joined one of the neighborhood apps, of all things, hoping to see images of the interior of some of the other homes around the area. One of the neighbors had seen the for sale sign. There was a thread on…something delicate. I'm sure you understand. You know what you were…withholding."

My head spins as I sit back in my seat. I blink at the window. Let my vision blur, let everything go unfocused as the pine trees whip by out the window. "I told Becky. I felt it was only fair for her to know what she was getting into. No matter what measures you try to take, buyers will find out a house's history. Particularly if the owner is someone as well known in the Bay Area as you are, and your family has been. I do staging now, but I, too, have my real estate license and I can tell you for sure—"

I hang the phone up and return my gaze to the window. My fist clenches around the phone. My heart pounds so hard, I open my mouth to tell the driver to pull over.

I'm distracted by another ring of my phone. I silence it then see the name on the screen: June Bug.

My fingers fumble for the screen, but they're shaking too badly to answer. I put the phone between my knees. I put my head between my knees and try to breathe.

🐾

JUNE

I find out later that he left the Jeep at Shawn's and caught a ride share to the airport. Shawn was headed down to Destin, which Burke knew. Apparently, he had planned to do that—even though he had to

One morning after I take the kids to school in August, I drive myself to Mama's grave and sit down in the fluffy green grass.

"Tell me why I miss him so much, Mama. I'm so dumb and stupid. And I'm really tired of feeling lonely."

Tears are coming—I can feel the prickle and the tightness in my throat. Right at that moment, a black and orange butterfly perches right atop the letters of her name, right where his hand was that day. It just hangs out there and flaps its wings for a while. Then it flits to me and sits on my hand for the longest time; I think it has to be almost five minutes.

Tears fall down my cheeks and drip from my chin. When the butterfly goes, I do my best to wipe them.

Before I haul myself to my feet, I press my hand against my belly. It's so little right now, nobody can see. But I think my mama can.

CHAPTER 28

JUNE

My mom's birthday comes on August 19. I have my twelve week OB-GYN appointment that same day in Albany and sob my eyes out in the parking lot right after.

I don't know why. Maybe hormones. Maybe it's because I still feel very foolish. I just can't believe that I'm this girl. The one that lets stuff happen to her. After Lamb, I told myself I'd never be that girl again—the one he doesn't mind just up and leaving. The one who still wonders what she did wrong when she did nothing but right.

I was so damn happy settling in with Sutton's kids, and now they'll be confused...for lots of reasons. When the devil finds out—and he *will*, because I'm going to have to tell him in a few weeks—I'll be forced to take his devil money, because I can't even keep paying for obstetrician visits without it.

So far, I've kept myself from this black hole, but sitting there in my truck, I have a good cry. What was going on in his head that made me so disposable? I try my best to tell myself it wasn't personal—I mean, clearly, the multi-millionaire insomniac who runs hot as fire and cold as ice has got some issues—but it's hard not to feel like I messed up.

I go to the Steak 'n Shake, draping my hand into my purse over the glossy ultrasound paper as I order a chocolate shake. Then I sit by the window. I check my phone to be sure no one from the school has called —that's a reflex now, during the daytime—and I drain my cup until only a little bit of whipped cream and the cherry remain at the bottom.

I'm slurping at the whipped cream when my phone rings. I fumble for it. It's a California number, but I tell myself that's a coincidence.

I answer, and a woman says, "Are you June Lawler?"

"Yes." I draw it out, so it's at least two syllables. My heart starts pounding in the silence after.

"Burke Masterson had you listed as his emergency contact?"

Something sharp and cold pours through my body. For a second, I can't get my breath. "Is something wrong?"

And there's another awful silence.

"Mr. Masterson was in an accident," she says. "He's going into surgery this afternoon to repair one of his eyes."

"His eyes?" I spread my hand over my belly. "What happened to his *eyes?*"

"He was involved in a worksite accident. Sustained some damage to his vision. A surgeon here at UCSF will be working to repair his retina."

"Oh my God."

"He'll be admitted for about a day and a half after, for post surgical monitoring."

"I'm in Georgia," I say, standing up and grabbing my keys off the table. "But I can fly out today."

🐾

BURKE

For the first day and a half after surgery to fix my fucked-up eye, I have to lie in my hospital bed with my face parallel to the floor.

My back and shoulders ache from tensing every time the door to my room opens. I don't even remember giving them her name and number, but apparently I did—right after the fall.

For the first day after surgery, my hospital room door opens twenty-nine times, and none of the entrants turn out to be June. She's probably not coming, despite what she told the nurse who called her. Who could blame her?

I try to endure my miserable sentence without letting my mind spend too much time on her, but it's a losing proposition. I'm lying face down in a special bed that makes my bruised shoulder and chest hurt.

And my vision's fucked, so that means I can't look at screens to pass the time.

My stomach's churning, and my mind's foggy from the damn concussion. I can't see well out of my "good eye," and no one seems to really understand that. Most of them are blaming it on the concussion plus the damage to the injured eye. I don't get it, but I'm assured it will get better.

"When your next of kin arrives, we'll send you home," one of the nurses tells me, patting my hand.

And if she doesn't come? I'm not calling my father—that much I know. I don't want to call any of my old team from Aes, either. They're busy. And since I sold to Sabal Gurung, that's not my gig anymore. I have a few friends in the area, but if I call, I'll have to explain how I got hurt.

The sale of Aes has hit the news, along with the devastating and graphic write-up about my past by a local gossip rag, but no one knows I've been working construction sites to keep myself busy. If my friends found out, I don't know what they'd say. Scratch that. I do. They'd either believe I've lost my shirt or my mind.

Needless to say, I spend most of my face-down time thinking of June. I can't believe I told them to call her.

Around the thirty-six hour mark, when I'm hoping to be cleared to sit up, a nurse helps me get up off the bed and walk into the bathroom. I'm shocked to find that I can barely do it. My vision is still blurry as shit, and my legs are weirdly shaky.

"That will clear up as time passes," the dude nurse offers as he guides me back to bed.

I nod before I lie back down, moving carefully because my head is throbbing and my chest and shoulder ache. The nurse pulls the blankets back over my legs for me. I shut my eyes and bring my arm over my head a little. For some reason, right now, I feel like I might cry. I don't know if it's allowed—if it will fuck my damaged eye up more—but if I can't control it and the tears come, I don't want this random mother-fucker seeing.

The door opens again, and I grit my teeth. Lucky number thirty.

I can tell it's her in the first second. Maybe I can smell her or I recognize her gait. I don't know how, but even with my senses all fucked up, I know for sure it's June who comes through the door—and my heart slams into my ribs.

I'm holding my breath as the nurse says something to her, and she replies in soft tones from what sounds like over by the door. I can't hear over the whoosh of my blood in my ears.

Then I feel her by the bed. Her palm comes down on my back and then slowly rubs a circle, sending warmth all through me...making my throat tighten.

"B? Hey there." Her voice is so damn soft. It's like a fucking caress.

"He can get up," the nurse cuts in. "Mr. Masterson," he says crisply, "you've reached the thirty-six hour mark. I can help you sit up if you'd like."

But I don't want his help. I don't want June to step back. I grit my teeth and squeeze my eyes shut, forgetting about the hurt one and then panting from the pain I caused by tensing that part of my face.

"What do you think?" June says, her hand still on my back; her voice sounds right by my ear, so I'm pretty sure she's leaning down. "Do you think you want to sit up?"

I don't know. I look like shit, and I'm scared of what I'll see on her face. Her hand rubs my back again, and I let out a loud sigh. "Why the fuck not."

She moves away, and I feel like an invalid as the nurse helps me position to shift onto my back. Then I do—I turn over—and the pain almost makes me groan. I fell through a bad spot in some flooring down into the room below, which was filled with plywood scraps.

I don't remember the impact—it knocked me out—but I feel like I got trampled by a heard of buffalo. My ribs and shoulder seemed to take the brunt of it, along with my forehead—and this one eye—but I've got sore spots all over, and my joints all feel stiff and creaky.

I close my eyes as the nurse raises the bed's headboard. My hurt eye and my head start to throb from all the movement. Then the throbbing makes my stomach churn.

Oh, shit. I'm not gonna get sick.

I press my lips together till the sensation eases. Then I crack my eye open. My heart races when I realize June is right beside me. I look up at her, but I can't fucking see her. I blink twice, my brain unwilling to accept that I can't see her face—she's blurry—and when she doesn't become visible to me, my stomach lurches.

One of the machines hooked up to me starts a shrill beeping. "Maybe you should lie back down," the nurse says. He silences the alarm, then lowers the headboard without further conversation. "If you'd like to, we can elevate the bed again when I check on you next."

Did he leave? I can't even fucking see. My pulse surges. Lying on my stomach, I couldn't tell how fucking helpless I am. I'm like...*blind*. Or might as well be. I feel like I'm viewing things from underwater, and my "bad eye" is covered with a bandage, so it doesn't make sense.

I blink at June as both eyes and my throat start to sting. I can see her face a little better for a split second before my fucking eyes spill over.

I drag air into my lungs and cover my eyes with my hand, but it's too late. I feel her weight indent the mattress. She wraps an arm around me like we're lovers...or at least good friends. *Not like I disappeared on her without a word of explanation.*

She leans in so close that I can feel her soft breasts, smell her fruity shampoo smell. It makes my throat knot even tighter.

"Hey there, baby." Her fingers smooth my hair back off my forehead as she sits up a little more. Must have been a reflexive comment, because her body stiffens and she leans away like she's recoiling.

"It's okay," she whispers. Her hand trembles as it strokes into my hair, her fingers tickling under my ear, where I'm pretty sure there's bruising on my neck from how I landed—in that pile of two-by-fours.

I wince, and her fingers go.

"You've got a bad bruise." Her hand is back, tracing along my chin, where I'm swollen and sore.

I close my eyes and drag another breath in. Then I grit my teeth, and my head gives an awful throb. Maybe I wince, because she murmurs, "You're still sort of sitting up. Do you want to lie down more flat?"

Before I'm able to think of an answer, her cool palm covers my forehead. She pushes my hair back...and then does it again. A soft groan leaves my throat before I even know it's in there.

"Does that feel good?" her voice whispers.

I nod, and my head aches in protest of the motion.

She keeps doing it. The room is quiet except the sound of air moving through vents and the lull of hall noise. I don't open my eye, and she doesn't speak—just runs her fingers gently back through my hair over and over until my body's warm and heavy and my throat feels thick from holding back tears.

Finally, her hand leaves me. I hear her murmur to herself and feel her straighten my covers. Then she's sitting on the bed with me again. I crack my good eye open, bracing myself for blurriness, and find I'm pretty sure she's looking at me. I can't make out the expression on her face, but I can feel the warmth of her attention.

My throat cinches and my chest aches because I know I don't deserve it. I wait for some comment, for the accusations she should be launching at me.

I'm still waiting for her disappointment or upset when I feel June stretch out beside me. Her hand drifts over my chest, covered by a gown, before she shifts her hips slightly away, seeking to put distance between us even as she lies beside me.

She makes a sound—a sort of small sigh. I sink my teeth into the inside of my lip until I taste copper and put a hand up to my throbbing forehead, mostly to shield my face from her eyes.

"Are you hurting? I'll help you get medicine, okay?"

I feel her hands tucking blankets around me again. She rearranges wires and strokes my shoulder—maybe by accident. Her shampoo smell fills my nose and head, making my hands long to reach for her.

"We can't give the typical painkillers because of his concussion," I hear someone say some time later.

June's voice. Soft voice. Soft hands. Soft voice. Sometimes she's lying beside me. Once, I hear her say, "You're gonna be okay. Did you know that?"

When the surgeon stops by, uncovers my eye, and does something that makes pain shoot through my whole head, I feel June's hand on my leg and hear her soft voice saying, "I'm so sorry."

The eye hurts like hell, and my head throbs with each small movement. *You deserve it, don't you, though?*

"Little bitches have to toughen up."

I wake from the dream of my dad with a loud gasp, and I smell her again—June. Her palm smooths my hair back. "Just hang in there, okay?"

ᵘᵘ

JUNE

I'm not sure what I expected, but it wasn't this. From the moment I got the call, I imagined that when I got here, he would want to see me.

250

What I wanted was to be seen…to be wanted, if I'm being honest. Now I'm here, and he's not really even interacting with me.

When I first arrived, he barely even opened his eye—the one that's not bandaged. He seems so out of it, I just assumed he was on pain meds. But when I cornered his nurse in the hall to get more information, the guy told me that he can't take pain meds at all.

"He had a hard fall. Notes from the paramedics said it took them a little while to wake him up. The area where he hit his head is one that can knock some screws loose with your vision. Not forever," he says quickly. "But he's gonna be disoriented and sleepy for a few days. Might have some coordination trouble, memory trouble; that's all normal. We scanned him two times because the fall was more than fifteen feet, and it's not more than a concussion. He got lucky. Those construction workers, sometimes we see lots worse."

My stomach jerks into a knot when he says that. *Construction workers?* "So he was working at a…building?"

The nurse frowns like he thinks *I've* got a few screws loose, so I nod as if it makes sense to me.

If I was worried and upset before I got here, nighttime only makes me feel worse. Burke seems barely conscious, murmuring in his sleep and tossing and turning. I guess when he moves, it hurts his head or maybe his eye, because each time he shifts around, he groans.

I ended up standing right beside his bed for what feels like eternity—twice even climbing into bed beside him because he's having so many nightmares. When his good eye does blink open and he looks up at me, I'm not sure if he can see me. He whispers my name a few times, but doesn't hug me, grab for my hand, or address me in any other way.

It seems too soon when they say we can leave the next morning. He doesn't seem well at all.

"He'll be seen by the ophthalmologist in two days. We made the appointment." The day nurse gives me the details for it and warns me, "He can't go to work at a construction site—not for a few weeks."

I nearly laugh but manage to nod. "I'll be sure."

I step out of his room to get a snack, and when I get back, find him sitting on the hard recliner in the clothes I guess he must have had on when he fell—Carhart-type tan work pants and a black T-shirt, plus gray steel-toed boots. I notice the boots look somewhat new, and also that they aren't laced.

I feel relieved when I glance up to find his gaze on my face.

"You want me to tie them?" He looks down at his lap, and my heart falls. "I can."

I kneel in front of him and remind myself it's just basic kindness—this between us right now. It's strange tying such big shoes. It takes me a minute longer than it should because my hands are trembling just slightly. Finally, I'm finished. As I start to stand, his hand closes around my shoulder.

"June?"

I look at him. His face is a mess—pale and bruised in places, and partly covered by the gauze that's taped over his eye—and he looks thinner than he did when I last saw him last in Heat Springs. He just looks at me for a minute, his shoulders rising and falling a few times, like he's breathing maybe just a little quickly. His jaw tightens.

"You can leave," he whispers.

"You want me to go?" I have to swallow to draw more air into my lungs.

CHAPTER 29

JUNE

"I said you can," he rasps. "Not that you have to." He swallows then, wincing as if maybe his throat is sore.

"Do you *want* me to? Because if you do, I'll just..." I trail off because his gaze on me feels focused for the first time since I got here.

"I don't remember asking them to call you," he says, rubbing his forehead. He looks at me again. "They said I said it when I woke up."

"You fell through a building and then gave someone my phone number?"

"I don't know." His lips press together, and he looks down at his lap again. He seems so tired and hurt—even sitting in the chair, it's like he's drawn into himself in some way that's hard to describe.

"If you want me to stay, can you just tell me you do?" I don't mean to tear up, but my hormones and the stress have been wreaking havoc on my emotions.

I can see shock hit his face—shock, or maybe it's concern. "Don't cry, June." He wraps an arm around my shoulder, pulling me against his legs. "Whatever you do," he says roughly, "don't cry. Do you want to go home?"

I wipe my eyes, shake my head.

Burke's palm cups my head. I feel his fingers in my hair, and then he's standing. I take his hand, and together we walk to the nurses' station, where a wheelchair and someone to push it are just rolling up.

. . .

When we get in my rental car, he gives me an address to put into my GPS and then reclines his chair and shuts his eyes. He stays like that—quiet and still, seeming either tired or in pain—as I drive us to an area of San Francisco that's clean-looking, urban, and obviously monied.

There are big trees on every corner, fancy street lamps, sidewalks made of cement that look freshly poured, and houses in a lot of different styles of architecture. Some are more like townhouses, others small and angular and modern. All the yards are professionally land-scaped with lush green grass, and all the streets feel homey. But there are also wider boulevards lined with sleek office buildings, shopping centers with a bunch of fancy stores I've never heard of, and nice, wide bike lanes that run along the city bus routes.

Down toward the eastern end of some side streets, I catch glimpses of the Golden Gate Bridge, which makes me feel like I'm in a movie. Actually, a TV show: *Full House.*

After driving through the area for a while, turning here and there, moving toward the houses and away from commercial buildings, we come to a block of houses that are identical white two-stories, with porches on the side, big, grassy yards, and red, Spanish-style roofs. They remind me of beach houses.

I park in front of the one with a "For Sale" sign on the lawn, and Burke sits his seat up. He rolls his shoulder—the one I thought looked bruised and swollen through his gown—and glances out his window before staring down at his lap.

Can he see the house?

I nudge his elbow lightly. "This look like the place? I know you can maybe only see the—"

"Yes."

He glances at me and then shuts his eye again, and lets a breath out, like my talking was annoying. I take a deep breath and ask him, "Do you have a key?"

"There's a realtor passcode thing on the door," he says quietly.

"Okay. I'll come around, and we can walk up to the door together."

He nods, tight-jawed and angry-looking again.

I don't know what the deal is, but he definitely seems pissy as we walk the short path to the front door, my arm threaded through his. He tells me the passcode, and I punch it into a small box attached to the door handle; it swings open, revealing a key. As I unlock the door, I feel a shudder move through his big body.

"You okay?"

He nods once, his gaze on the ground—but I can see his jaw is ticking like he's gritting his teeth.

We step inside, into a spacious, beautiful foyer. His unpatched eye goes wide, and I can feel his breathing pick up. He gets a few deep breaths and then rasps, "Into living room...and down the hall. It's the first room on the right."

"Okay." Despite myself, I want to wrap an arm around him or say something soothing. I guess he really can't see much at all, and he's upset about it. I would be, too. Yeah, sure, it was shitty what he did—and I don't have a lot of patience for people who just disregard others the way he did me—but I'm going to need to move past that, given our current and pending situation.

Since I don't feel comfortable wrapping an arm around him, but I want to be sure that he doesn't trip or something, I put a hand on his lower back as we walk past a very formal dining room, beside a gleaming, curved staircase that leads upstairs.

Everything about this place is super nice, with fancy, new hardwood, fresh, smooth paint, elegant modern chandeliers, and furniture that looks like it was arranged by a decorator.

"This is your house?"

He doesn't answer.

Between the dining/foyer area and the kitchen, there's a little step-up, where the floor goes from hardwood to some kind of pale, slate-looing tile. I start to tell him, but he must be able to see it—or, more likely, this *is* his house, so he knows where it is—because he steps up at the right moment.

Then we're in the open living/kitchen area, a large square space dominated by a long, tan sectional couch and a fancy kitchen done up in stainless steel and pale green colors. Burke stops between living room and kitchen, his whole body tensing as he looks slowly around.

"Is this your house?" I feel compelled to ask again. He just...does not seem relaxed. Also, it looks like a showroom. "Maybe are you thinking about buying it?" I shake my head at that dumb question, and realize, "You must have bought it already, huh? I'm not firing on all cylinders today."

Burke keeps moving, past the living room's fireplace and down the sleek, hardwood hall. A few steps down it, he stops again and covers his eyes, breathing deeply. His eye must be hurting.

"I think I see the door you mentioned. Can you see it with your eye that's not hurt? Just a few more steps—like maybe ten or something—and we're there and you can sit down."

He moves slowly, stiffly, and I'm sure his whole body is sore. I take his hand as we reach the closed door. Something about him just says he needs it. When my fingers fold around his, I can feel his palm is sweaty.

"Let's go lie down." I push the door open, revealing a bedroom that's done in navy, beige, and royal blue. It's small—not the master—with a wall of bookshelves and a built-in desk, a wall of windows, and a queen-sized bed beside a deep wood armoire.

Burke goes straight for the bed, shoves some pillows aside, jerks the covers down, and climbs in on his side, facing the window. I can see his chest and shoulder heaving as he breathes hard, but from where I'm standing behind him, his posture looks unwelcoming and rigid.

Maybe he really *doesn't* want me here...or maybe he just feels like total crap.

"I'm sorry you're feeling so bad." I loosen his boot laces and slip them off, then lean against the mattress and pull the covers over him a little. "Are you hungry?" I ask. I inhale a new paint smell; I've always loved the smell of fresh paint. "I can order some delivery for us."

He shakes his head, then curls his long form into sort of a C shape. *Damn.*

After just a second feeling unsure, I climb into bed with him and lie on my back beside him. There's a little noise from him—maybe a groan—and my heart feels like somebody's squeezing it.

"June?" he rasps.

I scoot closer to him...wrap my arm over his back so that I'm sort of, kind of hugging him.

"Are you okay?" I whisper. "Is my arm okay here?"

Waiting on his answer seems to take forever. Then he murmurs, "I like it."

I rub my hand over his broad back, lightly tickling. "Is your back hurt bad anywhere?" He shakes his head, so I press gently into the ridges of muscle around his spine.

Burke lets out a little moan.

"I'm still mad at you, but I hate seeing you hurt," I confess.

A little shiver jerks through his hard body. "Sorry." It's half-groaned.

"We don't need to talk about that right now. We're good," I lie.

He covers his face, then shifts around a few times, seeming obviously uncomfortable.

"How about some Advil? I've got water in this purse, too."

He pushes up on one elbow, still facing the windows, with me at his back, and I drop two pills into his outstretched palm. He swallows water from the bottle I hand him, and I take it from him, twisting the cap back on.

Then I push my pride aside and snuggle up to him again. I shut my eyes and think about our baby, and I think about Burke falling through some warehouse ceiling, waking up confused and asking for me.

Poor darlin'. I'll be mad and demand answers just as soon as he feels better. It's not like I'm over it, but I can't not take care of him when he's like this. I wrap an arm around his shoulder, hold his back against my chest, and lightly stroke his dark hair. Like we're good friends. Like he's my little baby's daddy. Like he still has a piece of my heart.

He's asleep in minutes—so soundly that I order takeout food and get it from the door without so much as a twitch from him. I eat my sandwich, roll his bowl of soup and loaf of bread up in the paper bag, and lie back down, sending Leah a brief text so she won't worry before my eyes shut, and I start drifting toward dreamland myself.

Sometime seconds or hours later, Burke jerks up, breathing hard and murmuring about police.

His eyes are peeled wide, and he looks afraid, so I touch his arm. "Hey, babe. You're okay."

He wraps his arms around himself, looking pretty pitiful with that white bandage over his eye.

"I got some soup delivered. Nice and warm. You want some?"

🐾

BURKE

I don't know how, but when June spoons soup into my mouth, I manage to choke it down. I can't stomach much. When I'm finished, I lie back on my side, facing the window, where I focus on vague shapes of light through the curtains. Everything's still blurry. Less and less so all the time, but I hate being here when I can't see well. So it's best to focus on the window.

June lies on her back beside me at first. She does something on her phone, I think, and then clicks the light off. After a while of us just breathing in the quiet room, she lets a breath out and she curls herself behind me.

"Do you hate me?" I manage.

She leans her forehead against my nape. "I could never hate you, Burke."

I take a few deep breaths, trying to steady my voice. "I owe you an explanation, June. That's why I brought you here. But...I don't want to give it to you."

When she doesn't answer, I turn over so I'm facing her. I reach out and touch her face. "I have no right to..."

Her thumb traces my jaw. It's covered with two days of beard growth. She looks into my eyes—my *eye*—and I think I get a feel for her expression even though it's sort of blurry.

"When I'm with you, it doesn't matter...common sense doesn't, I mean. Do I hate that? Sort of." Her voice quakes a little on that word. "But that's just how some things are. I started thinking how some people just feel so *familiar*. When you meet them, it's like they're already yours. Happened when I first met Leah. Like we'd been best friends before, and there she was again; it was just natural. Sort of felt that way with you, too. As soon as I stopped wanting to slap you silly, I just...cared about you." She squeezes her eyes shut, inhales, and then covers her face with one curved hand. "Certain people bring out certain things. Sometimes you can't control it. Maybe it's our duty to endure that kind of feeling. Price of having bonds with people we love."

"Dammit. I'm so sorry." I squeeze my eyes shut—so hard that a bolt of pain strikes through the hurt one.

"You don't have to love me back, Burke."

She says that, and my heart starts to pound. I try to get my breath and calm myself down again, but... I can't. I sit up. Then I get out of the bed. I walk over to the wall, touch it with my hand. My head is buzzing like I'm going to pass out. It's like that day in the Floatin' Bean ice cream place, but about a hundred thousand times worse. I step into the closet and let myself sink down to the floor.

"You think you can hide in there?" He laughs, but it's not funny. It's a laugh that says he hates me.

"You leave him alone, Kirke!" Mom cries.

His footsteps recede from my closet door, heavy strides shaking the floor a little. "You shut the fuck up, you stupid twat! You think you can stop me from doing anything?"

"Burke?"

I blink, but it's dark and blurry. June's arms come around me.

"Mom, I just need vinegar! I told you last week, I need vinegar or it won't work! Ask Daddy to bring it when he comes home from work."

Her dull gaze flicks up at me from where she's lying on the couch. "He'll be home late, honey."

I start crying. "What about my baking soda vinegar train? It's due tomorrow for the science fair!"

"I'm doing my best, Burke." She sits up a little. "Asher, go play in the play-room, please." He runs off, and she grips my shoulder. "You know Mommy's tired, Burke. I'm so tired. After I nap, maybe we'll go down to the store and see if we can find the vinegar. How does that sound?"

Anger rises in me. "Dad made you this way! You're not acting like my Mom, and now you never do!"

I run off, to my closet, slam the door, and play with a train set I left in there. A while later, Asher comes in, and he plays with me.

"Burke, I'm hungry. Where is Mommy?"

"On the couch, where she makes her home." I roll my eyes.

He frowns. "She's not there..."

"Burke—you have to look at me. You're worrying me."

June's voice cuts through the thick fog. I tug air into my lungs, look at her and nod. I grip her arm, and she sighs.

"Okay. Burke?" Her hand is on my face, cupping my cheek.

I get up, even though my whole head throbs. "I want to get in the bed," I rasp. It's a different bed, and that whole room feels different. With June in there with me...

"Okay," she murmurs.

She helps me up into the bed, her hand on my back, which is sweaty.

I lie on my back this time. Fuck, I'm so damn dizzy. When she wraps her arms around me, my throat tightens up, and my eyes well.

I turn on my side and hug her hard—the way I've wanted to since she showed up in my hospital room. My lips press against her hair. "You smell good...like always."

"I *am* good." Her small body tenses in my arms, and I let out a long breath.

"You are. You're good, and I'm so fucking sorry." I brush my lips over her forehead. "I'm sorry." My body jerks as a little shiver moves through me. "I've never—" I bite my lip, not sure how to explain. I don't know what to tell her. How I've never let myself feel like this.

She strokes my hair. "We don't need to talk right now. You need to try to rest."

Tears fill my eyes. "Why do you make me this way?" I manage.

"Because you've got good taste, Sly. And because of what I said." I feel her let a breath out. "I know you're tired...and feeling bad. Just go to sleep. We can talk about how I'm a unicorn some other time."

I don't remember falling asleep. When I wake up sometime later, everything is dark and quiet and June's not by me.

A groan escapes me as I blink around the room. I think it mostly looks the same. My eyes are drawn to the desk that's built in between the bookshelves—where my school project sat that night. I can almost see the box of baking soda sitting there...the lightweight plastic train my mom had picked up at a local science store the week before.

I look at the closet, at the bedroom door—slightly ajar. The stupid shaking starts again.

I put my hand over my chest, the way June told me to that day I napped in her bed. I lie back and close my eyes and try to feel myself breathe.

I cover my eyes with my hands, rub my temples, roll over. June's careful as she climbs back into the bed. I can feel her hesitation before she wraps one of her arms carefully around me.

"Oh, Burke," she whispers, so quietly. "Where are we?" It's a question intended for a sleeping man.

I pull together the tiny bit of courage I have left and whisper, "This is my mausoleum."

She doesn't make a sound. But she holds me. It's what I need to stop the shaking. When I feel more steady, and I'm pretty sure she's still awake, I take a deep breath, letting June know I'm awake.

"B?" Her voice cuts like a light across the darkness in my heart. "This is your old house?"

"Yeah."

She nods, as if somehow she knows all the rest. "Was this room your room?"

"How did you know?"

She holds me a little tighter. "B? Why did you tell them I'm your person?"

"Because you're the one I want," I whisper.

"Why not your father?"

The shaking starts again. In its strange, awful way, it's so reliable—the things that trigger it, the places.

June holds me tighter.

"Burke...I tried to look you up. From my phone...when you were sleeping just now. I looked you up a while back...just to see. But there was nothing anywhere about your family. Just about Asher and Sutton." I hate the way my body trembles harder, knowing what she'll say next. "While you were sleeping tonight, I looked again. Google. I found this story from a few weeks back. It's from like...this gossip column."

I inhale, and she does, too.

"Did your— *Burke*. Did something happen here...that I don't know about?"

I want to laugh at how she's skirting it. I read the story, too—along with everyone in the Bay. Even the headline trumpeted the news: **Tech Titan Lived Through Family Tragedy**

I suck in a deep breath. Blow it slowly out. And turn around to fully face her. I can't see her clearly, but I feel her gaze on my face. I feel the warmth that's radiating from her, the concern.

I shut my eyes and just say it. "My mom died here."

"Did..." She hesitates, and I spare her the angst of asking what the gossip rag implied.

I shake my head. "There was always speculation...because they fought." Because he hit her, and me, and some of her friends knew that. "But he didn't kill her." Not with his hands. "He was gone that night. It was a school night," I choke out. "She was here, with me and Asher. I was ragging her about something...and she was on the couch."

I squeeze my eyes shut as tears trek down my cheeks. "It was me that set her off."

"You're not acting like my Mom, and now you never do!"

"She was depressed. I think she had been for a while. She wanted to leave him." I swallow to steady my voice; still, I can't seem to project above a whisper. "My uncle was a successful lawyer. Dead from cancer now," I add, just in case she wonders why she's never heard of him. "That was the irony. My mom thought she could never get away—not with custody of us. Because my father was vicious. And my uncle." I swallow a swell of grief, then do some breathing so I don't break down again. And still, my voice cracks when I say, "He died the next year. It would have worked, if she had stayed. She had to wait it out, but it would have worked, I think."

Instead... "She put a note under her bedroom door. I found it. It said 'call 9-1-1.' And—" my voice drops to a whisper rasp— "I love you boys."

June wraps herself around me. My whole body quivers with the weight of what's inside. I gulp deep breaths to keep it locked down.

"Burkie..." She squeezes me tighter. "I'm so sorry, sweetheart."

It's her voice that does it. Hearing June sound upset, syncing up the past and present while her arms are wrapped tight around me—it knocks down my last wall.

👣

JUNE

I hold him against me, and he sobs for what feels like an hour. He locks his arms around me and holds on so tightly, sometimes I can barely breathe, but I don't mind even a little.

"It's okay..." I say it like a litany. Because it's what I hope for. I realize, though, that it isn't. He's not okay, so I change my whispers to "I've got you."

I'm not even sure he hears me, nor that my words matter. His grief has been locked up for a long time. Pushed down, starved off, hidden. The stupid gossip column about Mrs. Masterson's suicide implied Burke had worked to ensure stories about her death that were in print newspapers and local magazines at the time didn't make it online and weren't searchable in any archives.

It makes sense now—everything that didn't. The article I found on my phone came out two days after we last saw each other—on a Tuesday.

"It makes sense," I murmur, when he's quiet, breathing heavy but no longer weeping. "Why you were so upset about Margot and Oliver, and how much you wanted them back." They're roughly the ages of Burke and his brother when they lost their mom. "You asked if I was dating anyone. Was your father..." I swallow.

"He was an abusive bastard. Just to her...and me a few times." His voice drops low on that, as if using a low volume makes it less relevant. "Asher was so little... And after she died, he stopped."

"You mean he stopped treating you bad?"

He nods. "He disengaged. It was like...we didn't have a family anymore." His voice wobbles on that, so he swallows and takes a second. "Before, it was a bad one," he rasps. "I watched Asher like a hawk...after. But Dad was done." He exhales. "He started a foundation in Mom's name—for a type of depression that's called PMDD. It's hormonal. Like...I think women get it at a certain time of the month. The thing is..." He huffs out a quiet sound almost like a laugh. "That condition is like...chemical. You can have it even if your husband treats you very well. So that was savvy. Helped imply that Mom was ill. And that was all."

But wasn't she?

"Maybe she was," he says, reading my mind, "but Dad beat the resilience out of her. I bet it went on for a lot longer than I even knew."

I tighten my arms around him. "Oh, Burke. I'm so sorry. And I'm sorry we came here."

"I wanted to," he says gruffly. "Like how you brought me in that day, to your old house. I had never been back. Dad moved us out but held onto it. The bastard gave it to me a few years ago. So I've been wanting to sell. All this furniture is staged, but..." I can feel—or maybe hear—him swallow. "That day I was leaving your place," he says in a voice that's barely above a whisper. "They called—the stager did—and she had found out. The house's history."

So that's what did it. Whoever that bitch was, she clearly told someone else what she'd found—because that local gossip rag published it just two days later.

"Was it..." I want to ask if the story was a big deal for him, but I'm not sure how. "Did you leave work?" I whisper, stroking his hair.

He inhales slowly and tucks his head against my chest, exhaling. "I decided to sell. I had been approached...and I decided I would. I just—"

He sighs, and I hold him closer. "Making apps is not a passion for me. It's more like a...challenge." I think I can feel him smile against my throat as he says, "I took the construction job...to learn more wood-work. Get the basics down. I don't think they had a clue about me till I fell. Then the foreman texted yesterday. I think he was worried I would sue or something. Anyway," he says softly, as he leans slightly away from me. "You can see I'm not really the man for you. Your family is..." He lifts his head, frowning. "We're not very similar," he manages through his gritted teeth.

Tears shine in his eye, and he winces, his hand going to his bandaged side.

I'm not sure I've ever seen someone in so much physical and emotional pain simultaneously.

I don't mean to, but I lose it and start crying. Burke is clearly horri-fied. He pulls me up against him and holds me between his legs, so I'm half on top him. He's leaning against the headboard. He strokes my hair and hugs me tight and whispers sorries until I can find the words to tell him, "You have nothing to be sorry for. Except disappearing. And not trusting me."

I look up and find he looks confused at that. "I wanted to know, Burke. I would have loved to know your story. Everything about you. But I didn't get the chance."

He shuts his eyes. "I know."

"You know what you don't know, though?" He looks down at me, his face strained.

"I'm not holding it against you." I reach up and stroke his scruffy, tired face. "I can forgive you."

"I'm sorry. June...the way I feel about you—" He shakes his head, looking miserable. "It scares me," he rasps.

I give him a teasing smile. "Say it again? The 's' word?" Before he can, I lean up, closing the small space between us, and I brush my mouth over his. "I'm just teasing."

I have the thought that maybe it's too soon to be kidding with him. As his hand moves down my side. I kiss him again, tasting salt and his soft tongue. And then his hand brushes my belly.

CHAPTER 30

JUNE

I try to lean back, but it's too late. His palm's cupping the tiny baby bump I'm sporting just above my pants waist. He rubs once, his mouth gaping. I watch as the realization transforms his face. His eye widens as his jaw drops fully, and his whole body freezes.

He blinks once, slowly. "You're *pregnant*."

"Yes."

He sits up straighter, looking absolutely stunned as he gapes at me. "I got you *pregnant*? That night?"

"Yeah, you did. I was on birth control, but something happened."

His mouth drops open wider. "Oh my—Fuck." He covers his mouth. "Fuck, June."

I laugh, slightly maniacal. "Maybe a little bit too much of that. Or maybe just enough, depending on your stance on babies. I like babies."

"Fucking shit. *June.*" His eye wells as his gaze moves up and down me. "I'm so sorry."

I grab his hand, squeezing so he doesn't lose his shit again. "No. There's nothing to be sorry for. I'm okay. I really am. But even if I wasn't, we did this together, you know? I was there. I wanted you, desperately."

He bows his head and closes a hand over his face. For a second, he starts breathing hard, like a football player who just took a hard hit and can't suck air in.

"It's okay." I rub his palm with my thumb. "We're okay and so is little baby."

He lifts his head. "You're pregnant." He blinks, still looking totally incredulous. "*Our* baby. I got you pregnant!"

I laugh. "Really, we both got me pregnant."

"Can I touch it?"

For some reason, that makes me laugh, and once I start, I can't stop. I flop onto my back, and he gets up on his knees and spreads his palm so carefully over my lower belly. "Holy shit." His face is still just total shock. "That's our baby in there." He's panting a little, and his poor hand on my stomach trembles at the shock of it.

"That's her or him." I hold my thumb and forefinger about four inches apart. "They're about like this now. Like a really small avocado, I think is this week's fruit mascot. I have an app."

He rubs a hand over his face and shakes his head, then winces like it hurts, and his eye fills with tears again.

"It's okay," I whisper. "Okay? Everything is A-okay, Sly."

"When were you going to tell me?" he says softly.

"Soon," I reassure him. "I was never gonna keep this from you. I just wasn't sure how to tell you, since you weren't talking to me."

A single tear drips down his cheek. I get a glimpse of his taut face before he's up and off the bed.

"I want to go." He rests his palm atop the mattress and looks up at me, still on the bed. "I don't want to be here for this." His voice catches.

"Okay, then. Let's go." I slide down off the bed, too, rubbing my hand down his arm till I catch his hand. "Let's go find a hotel. You can't wine but you can dine your baby mama."

He laughs so loudly, I think maybe he's finally cracked. Then he hugs me to him. "Jesus, June. You're really fucking something. Do you know that?"

"Something crazy. I know."

He falters in the bedroom's doorway. I can tell he's somewhere heavy in his head, because for just a second, his face is full of pain. His brows draw together, and his shoulders stiffen. But then his gaze comes back to me. He laughs, rubs his forehead.

"I knocked you up."

"You seem insistent on taking all the credit."

He scoops my hand up, threads his fingers through mine, and leads me to the front door like we've got hell hounds biting our heels. He doesn't look back as we walk down toward the car, our strides slow but steady. He keeps stealing glances at me, and I make silly faces when I catch him. Both of us are laughing by the time we reach the passenger's side door.

"Well fucking shit," he says.

"Well fucking shit, Sly."

Sometimes things work out different than expected—the good becomes real bad real quick, or a bad thing turns itself around.

We end up at the Cow Hollow Rollin' Motel, a two-star, two-story, weird ass stucco establishment that's got a skating rink attached because...why not a skating rink? We don't even make a go of that, Burke being temporarily half blind and me being in the family way.

Our room's on the first floor by the vending machines, and we make good use of that by loading up on Cheetos, cans of Dr. Pepper, and some mints, since Burke's obsessed with having fresh breath.

We lie on the lumpy bed with mildew-scented air blowing on us and a funny sort of watermelon smell tinging the air, and Burke pulls down my pants and leans his head down low so he can see the contour of my belly.

I wrap my hand around his arm and and bring his hand to me. "Might be better to feel it."

"Is he or she kicking yet?"

I smile. "Not quite. But maybe soon, like in the next few weeks."

"You're pregnant," he says with a crazed grin on his face.

"Knocked up with a pea in the pod. A bun in the oven." I cup my hand over his. "There's a little baby in there. I was feeling pretty nervous about telling you, but you don't seem like you're too upset."

"I'm not upset." His still-pale face is earnest.

"Are you sure you aren't? You're gonna have to come and visit in your private jet now."

He shuts his eyes—well, eye—and lets a breath out. Then he looks back at me. "I can do that. I'm not tied down like I was before."

"I'm surprised you did that. Just a little. But I'm happy if it's good for you."

"I think it was the weekend with you." He looks almost shy as he confesses that. "I told you about building the tables. After that, I couldn't stop thinking about it. I thought about doing the woodwork while working on the startup, but there's never any extra time. I get this weird thing—from my mom," he adds softly. "My mom was an ortho-pedic surgeon. How I knew what not to do for your ankle." He taps his head. "Anyway, her hands shook when she got tired. Notable trait for a surgeon. Well, mine do too."

"So you're saying you would be too tired from the long hours in the office to do woodworking effectively?"

He nods. "Working on a startup is consuming. Just the nature of the beast."

"You got tired of being consumed?" I give him a soft smile.

He looks down again before meeting my eyes. "I kept thinking about you. And how you were always going to be there, with Margot and Oliver. Just one plane ride away."

I snort. "Don't tell me you wanted to see me. We both know that's baloney."

He leans closer to me, so close I can see him swallow. "I think we're both fans of bologna." His lips brush mine gently. "I did want to see you. More than anything." He swallows hard and looks down. Then his eyes are on mine, and they're pooling. "I'm in love with you, Gryff. But the fact remains..." He gives a light shake of his head. "Look at what I came from. The kids were left to *you*. Asher didn't trust me. He thought I wouldn't be good for them." His voice thickens on the words.

"Oh, baby, that's not true. He just knew you worked a ton. And Sutton knew I loved kids and was living in the sticks with a bunch of rednecks on crotch rockets, so she thought I might never find somebody good."

His eye shuts, and I sit up, wrapping my arms around him. "News flash, Sly—people aren't their parents. Or their childhood, or their situ-ation." I rub my hand over his chest. "People are their heart and choices. That's all there is to it."

I'm surprised my eyes well up when I look up at him. I'm blaming Peanut. "I'm not gonna lie. It hurt when you Houdini'd. I was upset and confused. It sucked. If you let those things you're scared about define you, you'll be right. You won't be good for anybody. But Sly, what if you don't?"

He swallows hard, and something like fear flickers through his features. "Even if I don't, I might always be like this. I can promise I won't ghost on you again, but Gryff, I'm fucking skittish. I'm going to be so fucking scared of losing you. I already am," he admits.

"What?" I shake my head and pin him with a WTF look.

He blows a breath out. "Barrel racing isn't very safe. And don't some people die in childbirth?"

I blanch. "I hope not!"

"Sorry." He cringes.

"I don't think a lot of people die in childbirth, no." I change positions, moving so I can lie my head in his lap. He frames my face with his hands, and I yawn. "Look, I'm really tired, B. I get tired right after dinner now and need to go to sleep."

His fingers push their way back into my hair. "Shit. I'm sorry."

I sit up with a smile. "Just kidding. I am sort of sleepy, but I just wanted to put my head in your lap." I give him my best side eye. "So are we friends or something? What's the what? Suspense time's over."

"You mean everything to me," he rasps. "I want to be your friend— more than friends—" he laughs— "for a long time."

"How much more than friends?" I grin, and he wraps me up against him. "For however much you'll let me have. I'm telling you, I'm a little fucked up. Sometimes things..." He exhales. "Certain things kind of throw me off."

"You mean like PTSD?"

"Maybe. That day in the Bean place, with your friend who hugged me? She was wearing my mom's perfume." His voice goes ragged on the words, lips tugging downward. "I hadn't smelled it in a long time. It was weird because I didn't decide to leave, but I just...did."

I pull the covers back and motion to the white sheets. "Get in there, and you can tell me what else ails you. Sleeping is one, right?"

He lies back slowly, and I pull the covers fully back then tuck them over him. "I don't sleep well."

"You think you were working all the time to like...avoid the stuff?"

Using two fingers, he rubs at his forehead. He looks tired. "Maybe."

He holds his arm out, like he wants me to get under the covers with him.

I do just that, and he wraps me in his warm arms. "Can you really forgive me?" His lips brush over my hair, and I feel him draw a breath in. "It was unforgivable…the way I left you like that." Another deep breath, and his face is pressed against my hair. "After my mom died…" A little shudder ripples through his chest. I hug him tighter. "I was… scared that people would find out. What happened. It was me who… made her upset. I knew something was wrong. She would lie on the couch all the time and sleep. But I still got mad at her. It was because she didn't get me vinegar for a train powered by baking soda and vinegar. The worst part was she got the train." His voice breaks on the word. I rub my hand over his back. "It was this fucking cool train. Lightweight. After…" He swallows and inhales. "After she died, my dad threw it away."

"I'm so sorry, baby."

"She was a good mom. But it was me who wasn't grateful enough. You can say she was depressed, but…it was me, June. No one but me pushed her over the edge. My dad wasn't even there. It was just me. And I did that. So how can I be good for anybody?"

His whole body quivers so hard. Then I know he's crying. He's gulping air down like we're running out, and I feel something wet in my hair.

"My poor Burkie. I'm so, so, so sorry."

His shallow breaths come faster, and I try to get him to calm a bit. "Breathe in through your nose…and out your mouth." I can feel him trying. "It hurts really bad. Makes you feel so lost, right?"

I stroke his hair, holding his cheek to my chest. "It's okay. You are gonna be okay. At some point. It won't hurt as much."

"I didn't know. And I should have. I want to go back. So I can know, Juney. That was my app."

"What do you mean?"

"It's like…this dynamic depression screener," he says thickly. "It guides meditation…you tell it your moods. Like, let's say…you do the meditations for eleven minutes…usually. If you don't, if…for two days it's nine…and then six. If you click through in a certain pattern…certain speeds. The AI can identify depression. It can contact a doctor or call a help line. Monitor your browser history…if you ask it."

"Oh, sweetheart."

"It's really complicated. Who I sold it to—he's older. With a bigger team." He sighs. "I was tired."

"Of working frantically? I know you must have been. So is he going to do it like you wanted?"

He nods. "I've got some money in it. But I'm not in charge. I stopped developing...and left the team...for now."

"You were probably run down. You just need some time. Maybe you can support it with your money but let your day to day be something else."

He nods. I press a soft kiss against his damp cheek. "I forgive you, Burke babe. You just stick with Juney. We can figure out the way between us. We'll do it together. I'm strong and solid, and I think you're pretty damn strong, too. Together we're unbreakable."

He nods. I stroke his hair back off his damp forehead. "Kids lash out. You're gonna see that. It's a normal part of kids just being kids. When someone's...well...a parent with good mental health doesn't take that personally. You can dust yourself off. I'm so sorry for your mama."

He hugs me more tightly then and nods. "You wanna go by her resting place tomorrow? Take some pretty flowers?"

He shrugs, and I second-guess the suggestion. "Or we don't have to."

"I don't ever go. It's probably overgrown."

"They do maintenance. And your mama isn't in there anyway." I put a hand over his chest. "She's in here."

"I don't know if I can ever believe in a happy ending, June. You might need someone who can."

That breaks my heart. "You ought to know by now that I don't listen to what people tell me to do. Maybe you just need to see some happy things. Have yourself some happy endings."

I don't know why, but I kiss him on the mouth.

He wraps his hand around my head and kisses me more deeply.

"B—"

"I need it. I need this."

So he gives me oral on that basis—that he needs it. And I let him because I'm mega horny since he knocked me up. Also because I want him happy. And like I said, I like happy endings.

After that, I lay him down and take his dick and treat it like an ice cream cone. I think I do a nice job, because he starts pulling my hair, which just encourages me, and thrusting into my mouth, and then comes hard.

He squints at me after he takes a moment to recover. "Oh shit. Will that hurt the baby?"

"Oh yeah, jizz is a killer."

He blanches. I laugh.

"You're wicked, woman."

"I know."

We lie down together, wrapped up in each other's arms. His sweet face is in my hair. My leg is pushed between his.

"This is awfully comfy for a little slice of hell with Mr. Devil."

"Hey, now. You're the mom of my hellspawn."

"That I am." I snuggle closer.

CHAPTER 31

BURKE

She's asleep in what seems like a few seconds once we lie down in the bed together. I look at her face and throat and breasts and then her belly when she twists and pulls the covers off. She's fucking perfect. And she's got our child inside her.

There's a part of me that wants to stay awake and watch her sleeping, but I've been thinking—about the things about me that are the most incompatible with being a good partner to someone. To June Lawler. Getting sleep sometimes is probably important.

As I scoot closer to her, sleeping June wraps her arms around me.

Huggie buggie…

The words bob up from a well buried somewhere near the center of me. I can hear my mother's voice, can feel her arms around me as she murmurs the silly phrase, just something she used to say when she hugged us at bed time.

I don't know why, but remembering that makes my eyes fill with tears again. Once the faucet's going, it's so fucking hard to stop. I keep hearing all these other things my mom used to say…remembering some things she used to do. Like cutting shapes into our sandwiches with bread stamps and the way her white coat smelled when she would come home from the hospital with it on sometimes. I remember hearing her heartbeat through the stethoscope she always let us play with, and the specific little flower she would always draw when we'd hand her the sidewalk chalk.

The first night my dad ever hit me, she pulled me into the down-stairs bathroom and said, "Burke, honey. We'll get away. It just might take some time."

I wish it didn't, but it fucking kills me that we didn't get away. I know she had to be in so much pain to do what she did. (That makes more tears fall down toward my ears, to think about my mom being so sad and hurt). But...she left us. She left us with *him*.

Since I'm already crying, and it's dark and quiet, and June is wrapped around me, I just keep on going. I think of Margot and Oliver, and Asher, Sutton, and it's all so fucking sad, my chest feels like it's cracking open.

June stirs then and hugs me closer. I grit my teeth to hold back a groan that wants to come out.

Why does it have to be so *bad*?

Why does it have to be?

It makes me so mad that my mom's story ended pushing a note that said "call 9-1-1" under the door, and stepping off a stool in her closet. It makes me so goddamn fucking furious, I start shaking. My dad is a piece of shit, and he's alive and well—with a new, girlfriend younger than the one before. According to a local magazine, he just bought a small plane to fly down to Malibu on weekends.

I don't want it. That's the thesis of my life so far. I don't want things to be the way they are. When Asher died, I was so furious that for a second, it made me want to do a crazy thing, like crash my car, too. And then I met June, and we rode those horses to her family's home, and we were sitting on that swing, and she said that bullshit thing about the happily ever afters. And all I wanted—all I wanted in the universe, at that heartbeat in time—was to be able to believe it. Even just a little, just a sliver of belief.

As we rode the horses back to her barn, I realized I couldn't. And it made me feel so fucking...broken. Which just made me want her more. Like a fucked-up moth to a perfect, warm flame.

And as I lie there, letting my mind wander to the baby June has in her belly, I remember asking someone at the work site for her. The words just float into my head, along with a blurry picture of a plywood room—the room I fell into.

"Call June Lawler. Tell her I need her. I want June."

It's too much for one night. Too much to fit into my head. I push my face into the way-too-puffy pillow, and my eye hurts, and my head still aches some. I shift onto my side, and June shifts with me.

"Burke..." She murmurs something near my chest, her words a tickle.

I whisper "mmm," just so she won't be lonely in her dream.

I get up again and use a tube of motel toothpaste to brush my teeth with my finger. I look at myself in the mirror—I look pale and tired and fucked up—and I think about my mom and her pain. For years, I tried hard not to. Now it's like a jagged tooth that I keep pushing my tongue onto.

I look at myself—slightly blurry still, though not as much as even yesterday—and I feel like she's looking at me, too. I wonder what she'd say if she could, and somehow I just know she would be saying sorry.

I'm so sorry, sweetheart. It went so wrong, and I didn't want it to. I never wanted that for you, Burke.

I wipe my eyes with hotel tissue, but the faucet stays on for a while longer. I feel nauseated by the time I fall asleep in June's arms.

The next morning, I find I can see her face with almost perfect clarity. I can see Peanut better, too.

June straddles my hips and kisses my forehead when I tell her. "I'm so freaking happy. And I know you're relieved."

"You sure you can forgive me fucking up and ghosting?"

"I'm not mad if I can keep you." She smiles in that way she has, so I can see wheels turning in her head.

I see my mother smiling, so clearly it's almost like she's right there with us.

I nod twice before I find my voice. "Whatever you want," I rasp. "I'm yours already."

"You are mine." She leans down and kisses my lips, her hair falling over my neck and shoulders. It feels so good, I shut my eyes.

"What do you say we go out and you can show me all around to all the places I read about in magazines. We stay here for a few days, and then go back to the farm. Unless you want to live here? Do you want to live here?"

I laugh. "Do you?"

Her eyes widen. "I don't know." She takes a breath and lets it out and meets my eyes. "What if I spend time here and it turns out that I don't, Sly?"

I grin. "Then that's good. I don't know if I want to live here either." She gives me a questioning look, and I trace her forearm with my fingertip. "I want to be where you are, Gryff. I'd re-locate in a heartbeat if it means I get to be near you."

"You would, really?" Her lips twitch into a smile that turns into a big grin.

I smile back. "Really, really."

EPILOGUE

JUNE

"What do you think?"

I grin at Burke, and then reach out and run my fingertip over one of the crib's delicate spindles. "I don't have words." I throw my arms around his neck and sort of hit his six-pack with my basketball belly. "It's freakin' gorgeous. Peanut—a.k.a. Ashtyn Lawler-Masterson—is gonna love it."

I take Burke's hands, and we twirl in a circle over the pale pink rug in our baby girl's near-finished nursery. Margot and Oliver must hear me laughing, because they dash in and join the party. Somehow Margot ends up in the crib, and Oliver is hanging upside down from Ashtyn's rocker. Burke throws both of them over his shoulders and starts downstairs, roaring like the troll he sometimes pretends to be. His low voice echoes through the house's roomy corridors.

We moved into my childhood home a month ago, though we're not completely furnished with our renovations.

It took some thinking, but we ended up deciding to get rid of almost everything that had been in here and re-decorate a little bit, to make my family's home feel more like ours. And it *is* ours. Burke bought the house from my dad and then signed it over to me, so it's about as both of ours as anything could be. Daddy used the money to pay off his new house, where he's living happily with Mrs. Kensington—mustache and all.

As a "Baby Mama Token of Appreciation," B paid off the bank loan on the farm and even bought some acreage back from neighbors we had sold to in the last few years.

In the last couple of months, since he's been well and truly settled in here with the kids and me, he and Shawn started "S of a B Woodworking," which is quite a hit on Etsy and in a few showrooms up in Albany and Atlanta. When he and my brother get a few dozen more pieces—mostly beds and custom rocking chairs, although they plan to start doing some tables soon—Burke and I and the kids will spend some time in California, seeing how we like things there and letting Burke court showrooms in the Bay and L.A. areas.

I'm excited to spend time in California, soaking up the sun.

Now it's January, a little cloudy and a little chilly the way Georgia has a tendency to be in winter. But it doesn't seem dreary to me. I've got my hot tea and my Kindle and a bunch of plans I'm working on for when Ashtyn is born—which should be around February 21.

We didn't move out of the other house—just set up this one in addition to it—which has been good for Leah, who was looking for a new place. She's renting it for now. We moved our pig and goat babes to the field behind this house, and Latrice is checking in each morning with the chickens and the horses—including Hot Rocket, who's made a full recovery.

Ever since Christmas, I've been feeling merry and bright. I've started thinking all the butterflies aren't going to fly away. Burke and the kids go out to jump on our new trampoline, and I warm up some soup for myself. When my water breaks, at first I sort of think I somehow spilled some soup.

Then I start screaming my head off, and Burke comes running.

"What the—"

I shriek. "My water broke!"

"Oh shit. Shit! For real?"

I laugh. "Oh my gosh, go get a towel, Burkie!"

"What is going on?" Margot runs in, with Oliver and all four dogs on her heels. He stares at the puddle at my feet, mouth gaping.

"Aunt June! When the water breaks, that means baby's coming! Is the baby gonna be born *now*?"

"No!" Margot and I cry at the same time.

I've got everything packed, and within thirty minutes we're all loaded into the truck. We swing by to pick up Leah, and from the back seat, where she's sandwiched between Margot and Oliver, Leah calls my family one by one.

We make it to the hospital before everybody else does—and about ten minutes before Miss Ashtyn makes her grand appearance.

Afterward, I hold her in bed. Burke is beaming, and the kids are big-eyed as they tiptoe in to see her. My whole family gathers 'round, and they all coo at her but keep their distance because with wintertime and flu, Burke is worried that she'll die.

She has Burke's blue eyes and my pale hair, and I'm thrilled to find when you shift her around—like passing her from me to Burke—she makes the sweetest little squeaking sounds. Another little critter.

Everybody stays for a while. When they leave—Mary Helen takes our big kids with her—Burke climbs in the bed beside me. He beams down at Ashtyn.

"So that's ours, huh?"

I grin at him. "That thing's got a name. And yeah, she's ours. You gonna be able to handle being a daddy to a little darlin' that's this perfect?"

"I don't know." He kisses my cheek. "Her mom's pretty perfect, so I've had some practice with that."

I snort, and then yawn hugely. "You do know the right things to say, don't you?"

We lean on each other, and he touches her cheek with the back of his finger. "You know what this feels like?" he murmurs.

"Heaven?"

He smiles at me, and it's one of the brightest ones I've ever seen on his face. "It feels kind of like a happily ever after." He takes my hand and kisses my knuckles, sliding something on it. "Ms. Lawler...will you be my happy ever after?"

My hormones are already set on roller coaster mode. I cry so much, it takes me almost five minutes to say yes.

"I sure will." I hug him with the arm that isn't holding Ashtyn. "Will you be mine?"

"If you want me to be," he whispers. His face is solemn, his eyes locked on mine.

"I need you to be."

It's just in the nick of time for Ashtyn to start life a full-fledged

Masterson—just like her honorary older siblings. Within two months, we all are sporting the same surname.

We are the Mastersons of Heat Springs, Georgia, sometimes San Francisco, and really who knows where else we might try out.

We met through tragedy and started off as enemies. But then we won each other's hearts and made a precious peanut, married in a little white chapel on a sunny April Sunday.

We are the Mastersons, and we are going to have the finest happily ever after *ever*. That much I know.

ᴥᴥ

Turn the page for a sneak peek of *Covet*, A Sinful Secrets Romance.

SNEAK PEEK

COVET: A STANDALONE FORBIDDEN ROMANCE

One
April 2018

Declan

Smoke seeps from my lips, drifting out over the boat rail like a curl of fog. Tonight, the water's placid, an inky black with smears of pastel starlight. Out here in the middle of the Atlantic, the sky at night is more glitter than darkness. Hazy swaths of purple, peach, and green sky twinkle with diamond-bright stars, their reflection gleaming on the curve of wave that runs alongside the boat.

I curl my hand around my cigarette and bring it to my mouth again.

I'm standing atop the cargo ship's flat hull, hidden from most vantage points by the twenty-foot-tall boxy structure just behind me: the navigation post and captain's quarters. At this hour, both are likely empty. The crew is down below deck, playing poker. Still, I turn the cherry toward my palm.

Better to stay hidden.

That's been my game since I boarded *Miss Aquarius* back in Cape Town: wear my cap low, keep my mouth shut, and help out where I'm needed till I reach my destination.

I close my eyes on a long drag and lean against the railing. That'll be tomorrow. Fuck.

I finish off the smoke and light another one.

It's fucking cold out here. My T-shirt's not enough, even with jeans. South of the equator, we're headed into fall—in early April. Strange stuff. I swallow hard and look down at the deck under my feet. Then I cast my gaze up to the sky and fill my lungs with salty air.

When I feel something in my hand, I look down, finding a line of ash in my palm. I bring the Marlboro to my lips and take the last drag with shaking fingers before pinching the cherry out.

I should go below deck. Play some solitaire in my cabin. Instead I light a third smoke, and, with my free hand, rub my arms. Even after just a few months off, they're smaller than I'm used to, making me feel like someone else.

Laughter trills into the quiet, voices rising as footfall thuds inside the stairwell to my left. Before I can turn toward the sea, figures spill onto the deck. I whirl around, snuffing my smoke out against the rail. Then I turn the other way, aiming to sneak around the navigation post, but there's a loud "Hey, man."

I turn slowly. Half a dozen guys are lined up in some kind of formation, making a semi-circle between the stairwell they just came out of and me.

I nod, meeting the eyes of the one who spoke. Kevin is his name. I think. He's only an inch or two shorter than me, with blue eyes and close-cropped brown hair. He's one of the Americans on board.

I step toward the stairwell, but Kevin catches my arm. "Hang on a sec. We wanna talk to you."

I hear another say, "We barely know you," at the same time as a third—not an American, judging by his accent—is saying, "been six days."

I nod. Hold up a hand. "George," I say, as I step between two of them.

"That's the thing, though," he sneers. "We don't think it is."

"No?" I look behind me.

They're all grinning. "Hell no."

"We been watching."

"We've got an idea about you."

My stomach pitches as a hand claps my shoulder.

"You can tell us."

"We know you're not George."

One dude jerks a thumb at the captain. "You know Bo, don't you? He's the cap'n. No good lying to the captain."

Bo steps closer. He's older than most of the crew members, but still young. If I had to guess, I'd say no older than forty-five. He's wearing khaki-looking shorts and a stained Costa tee. "I know what your papers say. But take your hat off, mate, and help me win a wager."

I shake my head, stepping backward toward the stairwell. "Night, guys."

"I told you it's not him." Someone's in the stairwell, lighting a cigar. He grins around it.

At that same time, I lose my hat. I spin around and snatch it back, glaring at the fucker who took it. His eyes widen at the clear view of my face.

Gasps chorus around us.

"Holy shit."

"I fuckin' told you, Bo!"

The one in the stairwell spreads his arms, chuckling as he blocks me.

"That's some damn good camo, brother. I need something, though, before you get to pass."

He holds a slip of paper out, and the men gather around.

"Homer Carnegie on our boat, we're gonna need some autographs…"

I fake a grin and take the paper. Six thousand miles from Boston, and I'm fucking outed.

†††

Finley

I clutch the bottle to my chest and cross myself. Then I shut my eyes, bring my arm back, and throw it hard over the cliff's edge. With my eyes shut, I picture its trajectory as it plummets toward the ocean. I inhale, feeling dizzy as birds caw above my head, and far below me, waves break on the rocks.

Vloeiende Trane, these cliffs are called; it means "cascading tears" in Afrikaans. The highest peak is two hundred meters above the ocean's ragged waves. Midway between the cliff-top and the sea, water pours out of the rock in three long streams that look like tears from further out.

Standing atop Vloeiende Trane, the white caps look no bigger than a fingernail, the ocean's swirling cauldron just a gentle dappling of greens and blues.

Deceptive.

I wipe my eyes and fold my arms over my chest. *I won't throw another bottle*, I promise myself as I step toward the cliffs' edge. I search the waves for a flash of glass, for something that will give me satisfaction, but of course, I see nothing.

That's the point, though, isn't it? Throwing letter-stuffed bottles into the void. It's like a prayer. That's its magic. Still, it hurts to know no one will ever read my words. I wipe my face again and whisper, "Give me courage."

I lick my lips and stand with my eyes closed, thinking of Mum. It's something that I almost never do, because I can't bear it. Today, though, I can't seem to help myself.

When my eyes feel puffy and hot, I walk back across the stony plane that forms this small plateau and look down at the field below, its tall grass pressed flat by the wind. At the edge of the field, a cottage. Beyond that, the village valley—an expanse of lush, green grass framed by the cliffs that form the border of the island.

Three gravel roads stripe the valley where the village lies. Scattered along them are sixty-seven cottages, topped by roofs of thatch or brightly colored tin. My gaze runs over the island's few landmarks: the yellow roof of the café, the bare dirt of the baseball field, the green roof of the clinic near the village's east side.

The church's small, white steeple looks thin as a toothpick from here. I squint, but I can barely make out the blue tin roof of my dear friend Anna's house. I lift my hand to my eyes and stretch my thumb out sideways, and the village disappears—the whole world, gone.

Climbing down the plateau's steep side into the field behind Gammy's house takes half an hour. I move carefully without a harness, slow and steady in the warm glare of the sun, until my soles press into soft grass.

The wind-flattened field—Gammy's backyard—is big and round, hemmed in on one side by the dirt path that leads from the lower slopes of the volcano down to the village, and on the other by the rocky cliffs that overlook the ocean.

Before she passed, we built a table from wood scraps and set it near the field's center. I climb onto it and peer up at the sky. Early autumn now, its blue is almost violent. Today, for once, there are no clouds except some wispy tendrils behind me, wreathing the volcano's peak.

I watch the kingbirds fly, swooping off the cliffs and out of sight, and my heart aches for Gammy. She would have righted my course. Gammy would have told me to say "no" when I was asked. Probably "hell no," I admit. My stomach knots.

I shift my gaze to the cottage, to the stone kiln beside it and the blue sky spread above it, and the cliffs that rise out of the grass beside it. I inhale the salty air and tell myself *just stop*. Now is not the time for despair. Gammy would tell me to keep focused. There are options yet.

I swipe the hair out of my face and carefully re-braid it as my shoulders tingle from the sun's heat. When my damp shirt has dried in the breeze, I get up and walk to the kiln.

There's a small door on the front and two shelves in its slightly rounded belly, where I set my pieces. I haven't done enough of this lately. I'm not even sure I retrieved my last load. I open the door and find indeed I didn't. Two hunter green bowls and a thin, black vase with golden flecks wait inside. I gather them carefully into my arms and follow the stone path to the cottage's front door.

When I first moved in with Gammy, I called this the Hobbit cottage. She didn't know, of course—I wasn't speaking—but it reminded me of a Hobbit's house: the south side built into a hill; one small, round window punched into the grass; the rounded, dark wood door and beige stone facade in front; a thatched roof tilting low; chimes affixed to several spots; and a flower garden growing wild about the stoop.

The door opens with the old, familiar creak. I step into the tidy living area. I run my hand over the well-worn armchair and try to look at it through his eyes. The green and blue rug—woven by my great-grandmother—that's spread across the cement floor. The slouching navy love seat, with its tiny, beige polka dots. The boxy TV on a tiny cedar table in one corner. The wild banana plant dominating the other. Grandma's needlework adorns one wall. A fern hangs in a basket near the TV. The wall to my right, which divides the living room and kitchen, sports a horizontal bookcase.

It smells like rose and lemon here, and the lovely musk of aging paperbacks. I rip my eyes from the bookshelf and walk into the kitchen. Small and standard, I suppose, with a pale blue laminate countertop, a small, round table; some wall-mounted shelves; and a wooden cabinet/pantry in one corner. Wallpaper in a faded, fruit basket pattern adorns the walls.

I scrub my arms and hands with the same lemon pumice soap I use to get the clay grit off after I finish a new piece, and then unpack the bags of food I brought before my hike. I arrange apples, pears, and peaches in a small, wooden bowl and leave a shrink-wrapped loaf of friendship bread atop a matching wooden platter. I check the refrigerator again, as if the eggs, butter, chicken, duck, and various sauces I left there a few hours ago might have walked away. They didn't.

I line jam along the wall beside the sink, double-check the seal on three bags of homemade potato chips, and check the pantry for the pasta, canned goods, Pop-Tarts, and bags of popcorn I already know are there. I re-fold the towel on the oven—Home Sweet Home it says, in faded blue script—and drift back through the living room, picturing him walking down the short hall to the first door on the right, which I'll leave slightly ajar.

It was my mum's room, but when my parents passed, it became mine. It has one window, covered with a lace curtain and facing the ocean. When I was young, it held a full-sized bed, a bookcase, a dresser, and a rocking chair. Now I've moved the bookcase into Gammy's old room, where I store my pottery and package it for shipment on occasions when I sell a piece.

I step in front of the vertical, wall-mounted mirror by the dresser and peer at myself. Still no wrinkles, no more freckles than I've ever had. I don't look older than twenty despite my twenty-seven years. I pull my hair down from its tie and spread the long, rust-colored locks around my face. I blink my yellow-brown eyes, purse my lips, and study my cheekbones...the smooth skin of my throat and collarbones.

Will I look like an islander to him? Or just a woman?

I laugh. Does it matter? I suppose that shall depend on what I choose to do. The mere notion of that possibility brings about a need for smelling salts, so I move on from the mirror and my thoughts, stepping into the en suite washroom to pull open the curtains.

I look out at the vast, gray sea and smooth blue sky, and I try to imagine any other life for myself than the one I have. Could I have been happy here? *If Mum had lived.* The answer floats up from my bones, a truth too potent to quash.

The sea breeze slaps against the windowpanes and whistles through the thatched roof as I tidy up. Will our cottage be comfortable to him, or will this place appear pitifully lacking? The pristine American homes I've seen were all in magazines or movies, so I'm not sure they were the regular sort. Then again, neither is he. As my mum's stories alluded, he's more king than commoner.

I set my favorite eucalyptus bath crystals on the table by the claw-footed tub and arrange lavender fizzies in a wee bowl. These things were mine, once—but they haven't been for a while. Anyway, I don't mind sharing.

I stroll back into the bedroom, leaving a pack of Doublemint on the night table. I step over to the dresser and reach for the framed photo of Mum and me, twin flower halos on our twin red heads...but then I draw my hand away. I can't say precisely why, but it seems important that I leave it in its place, that I let her stay here—perhaps especially now.

Another spin through the house with the duster, and I call it ready. I linger in the living room, my chest aching and my head too light. On a whim, I turn back to the bedroom. I fetch a small bottle of rose water from the top drawer and spray the living area, tucking it into my pocket as I go.

⁂

Two

Declan

I press the power button on my phone and squint at the bright light. 2:49 AM.

I stuff the phone under my pillow, roll onto my side. A bolt of pain sears my right shoulder, sending me onto my back again. Dammit. I've gotta quit forgetting that. Left side it is. Except the left side has me facing the door to my matchbox-sized stateroom. There's a little window on it.

There's no paps here, asshat.

I made headlines in November, but nobody besides my team at Red

Sox headquarters and a bunch of folks in white coats know the worst of it. I've been out of the press since the TMZ video shit, in no small part because the Sox have taken care of me. I try to find some comfort in that. I think about my agent, Aarons; my publicist, Sherie. Even the Sox board was more than generous with me, more than forgiving.

Instead of making me feel better, remembering everyone's kindness makes my throat knot up. I run a hand back through my hair and tug until my eyes stop stinging. Nothing's fucking wrong. It's always this way, I remind myself. I fold my knees up toward my chest and cover my eyes. I just need to sleep. Even an hour or two would help. A nap before breakfast…

After my identity was revealed, the ship's cook demanded to know what I wanted for my last breakfast on board, and he's now planning to cook omelets starting at six. He wants me there while he cooks—"to make sure I get it just the way you like it." The chief navigator and the captain plan to join us in the kitchen. After that, more autographs. And pictures with the crew.

Fuck me.

I don't know what to tell them. "No" makes me sound like a dick, and "yes" means I'll end up trending on Twitter.

I sit up and rub the shoulder. Useless. Without my usual concoction keeping me numb, the fucker hurts every time I breathe. My Sox trainers pushed for surgery before this trip, but my med team pushed back. Of course they did.

I lie back down and shut my eyes and focus on my breathing. In and out…and in and out. Behind my eyelids, I see sunlight stretched in gold webs on the sand and on the underside of waves.

＂＂

My phone's alarm wakes me at 6:05 after one snooze. I throw some clothes on, climb the stairs on legs that shake, and step onto the deck, stopping as a soft breeze feathers my hair back. Fog settled sometime overnight, blanketing the ocean in a haze that's tinted sepia by the rising sun. It's so thick I can barely see beyond the deck's rail.

I know I should haul ass to the dining room, but we're close to the island now. I can't resist climbing up onto the deck atop the nav post. The damp stairs squeak under my shoes as I hasten my steps. The stair rail is cool under my palm. I step onto the upper deck, feeling my pulse quicken at the thought of being here again. At that moment, a breeze pushes the fog aside, revealing a sight that I haven't seen since I was six: Tristan da Cunha—a massive chunk of dark brown rock that rises to a cloud-swathed peak.

Of all the islands in the world, this one is the most remote—the most isolated patch of land where humans live. These thirty-eight square miles of land are 1,700 miles from South Africa and 2,000 miles from South America. With no airport and no safe harbor for large ships, no GPS or cell phone towers, people here live cut off from the world. Mail comes every two to three months, the birth of a baby is a rare occasion, and if someone has a medical emergency, it's flag down one of the fishing vessels or cargo ships that travel back and forth from Cape Town to Antarctica and back, and hope it's headed *back*.

My throat tightens as I squint at the island, searching the grassy valley at the foot of the volcano for cottages that I don't see from here. Somewhere, maybe on the other side, there's a little village. If the guidebooks are to be believed, there are just a dozen or so shy of three hundred people—fishermen and farmers, mostly descended from a handful of British.

I remember them packed in their church, their heads all bowed in prayer, some cheeks wet with tears. I can see the women clutching rosaries, the men pulling on jackets and stepping into boats. I remember the lights at night as boats arrived and departed. Each time they came back empty handed, more tears.

Despite the circumstances, Dad and I were welcomed right into the fold. I remember helping an old lady knead the dough for bread while my father went out in a boat and helped search. I remember all the misty rain. I shut my eyes, seeing Dad's face when he stepped back onto the dock for the last time. His eyes were closed, but hers were open. That's what I remember most. This little girl wrapped up in blankets, with a dirty, sunken face and ropes of tangled red hair. And weird eyes.

I remember how they stood out in her pale, grimy face. Unlike all the other eyes I saw, hers hadn't leaked with tears. They seemed as depthless as the sea itself, and hot, almost like brownish-yellow fire. I think they stuck with me because I couldn't pinpoint the emotion in them. Not for years.

A gull caws, bringing me back to the moment. I can hear the swish of waves against the boat, can feel the wet fog on my face.

I did it. I'm back here. I laugh. Genius or crazy?

I don't have time to decide before someone slaps my back. I turn around and give the captain a smile. For the next hour, I'm Homer Carnegie—household name. I tell myself to buck the fuck up, try to act like the record-breaking Red Sox pitcher they expect. I sign everything from baseballs to a woman's sports bra, telling jokes and answering a bunch of questions while the chef serves me two omelets I can't taste.

"Thanks, man. Real good."

I sign his apron, listen to someone's account of a record I broke last summer. When I can, I steal away to have a smoke and hide my shaking hands.

I close my eyes and try to feel the warm sun on my face, but all I feel is pressure in my throat and chest, behind my eyes.

"Hey, dawg." I look up and find one of the crew lighting his own smoke. I think his name is Chris. He's kind of short and wiry, with brown hair hidden beneath a gray beanie. He's another one of the American crew members. "Just want to tell you thanks. My kid loves the Sox. He's gonna be so happy when he sees that ball."

"Yeah—no problem, man."

"If you don't mind my asking...whatcha doing way out here, in the middle of the ocean?"

I smile tightly. "Here with the Carnegie Foundation. We're laying new phone lines. Maybe internet, too, if we can find a way to make it work."

He nods once. "Riding back to Cape Town with us?"

"Yeah."

"Damn, that's eleven weeks. I'm surprised you can be gone that long. Aren't things firing up?"

I guess this guy's an actual fan. I shrug. "I'll miss some, but it's a one-time thing."

He nods. "Yeah. It's cool you're doing what you're doing. It was nice to meet you." He holds his hand out. I shake it, squeezing harder than I have to so he can't feel my fingers shaking. "You're an idol to so many. Don't forget it."

I give him a small smile and a nod, and, thankfully, he turns and goes downstairs.

I spend the next half hour packing up and helping haul wooden crates—full of supplies provided by the foundation—to the boat's ledge. From there, they'll be lowered in an elevator type of apparatus that's hooked onto the boat's side, and eased into a boat from Tristan.

Since the island's coastline is mostly rocky cliffs, with just one tiny harbor, ships dock out about three hundred yards, and islanders come out in small boats to get visitors like myself.

Morning crawls toward noon. The fog burns off, and I can see the island more clearly. Is that a seal? Fuck, there's a bunch of seals or sea lions on the cliffs. I reach for my phone, snapping a few shots. I remember those guys.

Finally, I spot the smaller boat—a nickel-sized brown dot moving from the island toward *Miss Aquarius*. The crew shuffles around me. I step closer to the rail, stopped short by a hard lump in my throat.

Meanwhile, two crewmembers go overboard on rope ladders to attach the smaller boat from Tristan to the side of this one. After that, the crates are slowly lowered.

I fill out some departure forms, toss my pack over my shoulder, and move to the boat's edge, where my gaze falls down a rope ladder to the waiting boat. It's pretty small, maybe even smaller than a cabin cruiser—the smallest of all yachts—and looks like it's powered by a single motor on the back. I'm watching two guys strap down the crates when the captain's voice startles me.

"Pack off," he says. "We'll lower it. Just climb down and you'll be on your way."

Then I'm over the boat's side, clinging to the ladder as I inhale salt and brine and the scent of wet rope. I can feel the dim sun on my shoulders, the boat's slight rocking underneath my boots. One rung at a time, and I can see the sea shifting between my moving feet. Then I step into the boat and turn to greet my island escorts—two ordinary-looking, middle-aged men in ordinary, working-class clothes. One—in a pair of oil-smudged coveralls—reaches to shake my hand as the other tips his ball cap.

"Homer Carnegie," the hat-tipper says, as the hand-shaker says, "I'm Rob."

"Mark," the one with the cap says. "You got everything?" His face is creased with sun-lines, and his pale brown eyes are kind.

"Once you're here, you're here to stay," Rob chuckles.

I nod. "Good for it."

Rob nods to the wooden bench behind me. "Have a seat."

I sit, the motor rumbles, and we're off.

The sea looks like a sheet of black glass as we zip over it. A fine spray arches up on each side of the boat, dotting my arms and cheeks with cool water. The breeze lifts my hair off my head as we move along the island's rocky coast.

I look up at the grassy cliffs with eyes that sting. From down here on the surface of the water, I can't see the valley that covers most of one side of the island; Tristan da Cunha simply looks like grass-covered cliffs that stretch to an unseen plateau.

I'm wondering where the boat will land when its nose points slightly inland, toward the cliffs, and I see...yeah, that's penguins. A bunch of little dudes on a low-lying, flatter-looking rockface, hopping up and down and doing penguin shit. As we pass by, I swear one looks right at me. A cold sweat flushes my skin, but I shake my head and laugh and rub my hands together.

I'll feel better by the time I leave this place, if everything goes right. Until then, penguins.

We curve around the island's edge, and finally I see it—Edinburgh of the Seven Seas, the long name of the little village I remember.

From here, it looks like a smattering of brightly colored buildings in the shadow of a mountain. Fuck—it looks like almost nothing.

I wrap a hand around the top of my pack, take a deep breath. I rub my forehead. Christ.

We're headed toward the jagged shoreline, which has dipped down lower, rising only ten or fifteen above the crashing waves. I tighten my grip on my pack and try to look alive when Mark glances at me.

Soon the motor's noise softens, the boat slows slightly, its nose tipping up, and I see we're coming up on the strange dock—two lines of cement jutting outward from the shore like two arms forming an almost-circle. Waves crash into them, shooting toward the sky in a wall of frothy white. As we edge closer, spray slaps my cheeks. I push a hand back through my now-wet hair and smile as my escorts grin back at me.

As we idle into the gap between the arms of the dock, the waves beneath the boat smooth out some, so we're bobbing lightly. I can hear birds caw above us, smell the thick, salty air. A wave hits the dock behind us, and I see a flash of rainbow just ahead of the boat. I'm looking at it when I notice people standing at the shoreline—blurry figures through my wet eyelashes. They're clearly here to greet us. To greet me.

Fuck, I'm really here again. And suddenly I feel like I can breathe.

❦❦

**Download and keep reading *Covet* now:
bit.ly/EllaJamesCovet**

FOLLOW ME

Keep in touch!

Sign up for my Newsletter.
Keep in touch on Facebook.
Join my Facebook Group, Ella's Elite.
Follow me on Amazon.
Follow me on Bookbub.
Follow me on Twitter.
Find me on Instagram.
See my bookshelf on Goodreads.

ALSO BY ELLA JAMES

Contemporary Romance Standalone
Hate You Not

On My Knees Duet
Worship
Adore

Sinful Secrets Romance
Sloth
My Heart For Yours
Covet

Off-Limits Romance
The Boy Next Door
Fractured Love
The Plan

The Love Inc. Series
Selling Scarlett
Taming Cross
Unmaking Marchant

Young Adult Series

Stained Series
Stained
Stolen
Chosen
Exalted

Here Series
Here
Trapped